SHADOW'S DREAM

For Lynn Schuse

With Best Wishes

Madelyn Hallowell

Nov. 2004

SHADOW'S DREAM

Madelyne Hallowell

iUniverse, Inc.
New York Lincoln Shanghai

Shadow's Dream

iUniverse, Inc.

For information address:
iUniverse, Inc.
2021 Pine Lake Road, Suite 100
Lincoln, NE 68512
www.iuniverse.com

Also by Madelyne Hallowell
Ancestral Blood

Cover Design/Concept: Pandora Rose
PandoraRose@FilialunaDesign.com

ISBN: 0-595-33287-0 (pbk)
ISBN: 0-595-66820-8 (cloth)

Printed in the United States of America

For Shadow, Mesa and Cheyenne

Author's Foreword

In July of 2003, at a particularly low point in my life, I was introduced to my first wolf. Mesa was a member of the W.O.L.F. Sanctuary, located in LaPorte, Colorado. He and his companion, a wolf-hybrid named Sarah, literally changed my life.

I've never been one for animal stories. I have always carried a soft spot for all animals, imbuing them with human thoughts and characteristics. When I was a child my mother took me to see the movie Bambi. I was devastated when the fawn's mother was shot by hunters. I grew up avoiding movies with animals, not able to stomach when they were faced with perilous danger, injury or death. I have yet to see the movie Old Yeller—if it can make a grown man cry, it would surely be the end of me.

But when Pat Wendland and her volunteers at W.O.L.F. explained the plight of Mesa and Sarah, which included their abusive pasts, a part of me needed to learn more. I bought several books and searched the Internet for countless hours learning all I could about this misunderstood animal. Most of the information broke my heart, but I trudged through it, even watching documentaries and movies that showed, in living color, their past and current plight. In the past year, I have cried a lot.

My very good friend, and self-adopted sister, Marcie Cain, left Denver a few years back for the peace and quiet of Guffey, Colorado. Our main means of communication now is that fabulous invention known as email. As my quick notes to her detailed my growing fascination with all things wolf, she sent me a card with an intricate pencil drawing of a beautiful wolf. Inside the card was an invitation from her good friends Mark and Cheryl Johnson of the Rocky Mountain Wildlife Foundation, located a stone's throw (as the crow flies, not by car) from Marcie and her husband Jim's house, to come for a visit. In a driving rain and patches of dense fog, I forced my husband, Steve, out of the house at the crack of dawn one Saturday to make the three-hour trek to Guffey. I packed a bag of bones for the wolves and steaks for our human pals. By 10 a.m. Marcie, Steve, Mark and I were in an enclosure, soaking wet, getting kisses and licks from their 93 pound white, beige and gray wolf, Cheyenne.

Mark took us on a tour of the refuge, which eventually led to the rest of the wolves that were being sheltered there. Mark and Steve walked on ahead to the last enclosure that was separated from the other wolves by a blue tarp and more wire fence. While Cheryl was talking to Marcie and me about the other wolves, I heard the mournful cry of the beast that was sheltered in that last pen. I was drawn to the yowl of that animal and hurried toward the sound. I came upon the wolf hybrid who Mark called Shadow. The animal was sitting in the far corner of the pen, as far away from us as he could get. Mark explained that he wasn't fond of males, for the man who had owned him had used heavy chains to confine him between two trees where he was regularly beaten and incited to fight. When Mark acquired the large, black animal with white markings on his chest and face, the chains were imbedded in his skin and had to be surgically removed. As the refuge owner talked quietly about the animal, I crouched down to Shadow's level and he studied me with his large dark eyes. After a short while, he ceased to howl and just watched me as I watched him.

Covered in Cheyenne's shedding fur and soaking wet, Mark and Cheryl allowed me the rare opportunity to actually give the bones to the wolves. Cheyenne was given the biggest bone and she was proud of it, climbing on top of her little hut to keep her faithful companion, "Henry Wiggle Butt" from obtaining it for his own enjoyment. I traipsed back up the hill and threw bones to each of the other wolves, giving the last one to Shadow, who upon seeing me, retreated back to his corner, but did not cry.

Back at Cheyenne's enclosure, I chanced to look up the hill and there was Shadow, still watching me, with the bone clutched firmly between his jaws. The sight of Shadow looking at me with that bone in his mouth touched my very soul. Even today, his picture sits on the shelf beside me as I write. As time passed, an idea started forming in my head. If Shadow had been allowed to decide his own fate, what kind of life would he have chosen? The following pages were inspired by those ideas, the look in that animal's dark eyes and his doleful wail.

While this is a book of fiction, I have taken great strides to report events that have been told to me or I have read in books or on the Internet, by people who are passionate about wolves and know them. It is important to note, before we begin this tale, that wolves are wild animals and must be treated as such. Wolves do not make good pets. They need room to roam and they can be very jealous of other animals or people who vie for their master's attention. There are less than twenty wolf refuges that are trying desperately to protect and harbor unwanted hybrids and actual wolves. On a regular basis, they must fight government regulations and organizations that do not share their love of the wolf. If you wish to help, they appreciate and desperately need donations and volunteers.

Wolves are happiest and healthiest when they are left undisturbed, given the chance to live their lives with their packs in the wilderness, and are not hunted. A dead wolf does not feed the hungry, supply medicines for the sick or even make a high dollar fur coat. The wolf's preferred diet consists of moose, elk, caribou, bison, deer, rabbits and mice. Unlike the human hunter, who thrives on catching and killing the biggest and healthiest quarry he can find, the wolf—usually with the help of his pack—concentrates on the old, the young and the weakest members of its prey. Since the first settlers started ranching and eliminating the wolf's natural prey, they, themselves, have in turn provided another source of food—cattle and sheep. If hunters were not allowed access to decimate the wolves' primary prey and ranchers utilized the proper precautions to protect their herds, an alliance between wolf and man could be reached. There is no logical reason why wolves should be hunted and slaughtered as they have been for thousands of years. Man's desire to control them is no excuse.

If you find you are intrigued with these animals, I invite you to learn more about them. Please see the List of References/Further Reading page at the back of this book.

CHAPTER 1

Jesse was tired. She leaned back in her chair and pressed her fingers hard against her temples, resolved that nothing would make this pounding headache go away. She had taken the last of the remaining aspirin in her desk drawer early this morning and there was no one around who might have more. Those damned tears were on the verge of pouring out again. Upon hardhearted instruction from Brad Sterling, the sales manager and her immediate supervisor, she had fired the temp and fought the office supply company over an incorrect order, which had failed to deliver the supplies she desperately needed to complete the presentation packets for one hundred clients due tomorrow morning. After reconciling the books, she now had to restart the budget report, an hour overdue, because in her haste to solve an insignificant problem created by one of the salesmen, she had hit the escape button rather than the save button on her computer.

It was well past five o'clock, but because she was a salaried employee, each extra minute did not mean a little more, much deserved cash in overtime. She would work until her head split open and her fingers cramped, and receive nothing but another humiliating chastisement from Sterling regarding her ineptness. She sighed heavily, wishing she had a window to glance out of for a moment to remind her that there was a world outside this office, before getting back to work.

An hour and a half later—after hitting the save key at least one hundred times—she printed out the budget report and called it a day. She gathered her belongings, put the report on her boss's desk, spoke kindly to the cleaning crew and trudged down the empty corridor to the elevator. Her feet were killing her and she cursed herself for wearing a brand new pair of heels on a day she knew would not end quickly. She pried the shoes off her swollen feet painfully. The parking garage was cold and quiet and she did not disturb the ambiance as she walked to her car in her stocking feet. She did not care that she ruined a perfectly good pair of pantyhose on the rough concrete.

She was relieved to see her BMW M3 parked and waiting like a trusty steed at the end of the lot. The car beeped and flashed its welcome to her as she unlocked it with her keyless remote. She threw her purse and briefcase on the passenger seat and climbed into the driver's seat. In the rearview mirror she could see the dark circles under her golden hued eyes. She loosened the hairpins from her modified French twist and let her dark brown locks fall messily down around her shoulders. "Those thirty-seven years are starting to show," she commented into the mirror. "You, Jesse Harless, need a facial." She was not drop dead gorgeous, but she was attractive with a slim build and nice features. She carried herself well when her feet weren't killing her and she knew how to dress. She just wished she didn't look so worn-out. Perhaps it was time to buy a heavier make-up.

The key in the ignition revved the car to life and Jesse relaxed for a moment with her head against the headrest, grateful to be free from the confines of that office. She turned on the CD player. Wolfsheim picked up their song where they had left off. Buckled in, she sped off down the ramp and into the street.

She weaved through the traffic and headed for the shopping center rather than her residence. She had to stop at Office Depot and get those report covers—one more out-of-pocket expense. The lot was full, as usual. She crammed her swollen feet back into her high heels and cringed with each step toward the glass doors.

Inside the store, she feigned composure and searched the aisles for the supplies she needed. This time she was lucky. Everything was in stock. She was not surprised to find only one clerk at the checkout stand and several people already in line. A merchandise return took up several minutes and another person had been quite clever and chosen an item that had not been marked with a price. Jesse shifted from left foot to right and leaned heavily on her shopping cart. She wanted to scream in aggravation, but she knew it would only make the wait longer and the store manager would have likely kicked her out without her job-saving supplies.

Back inside the car, $149.58 poorer, she was finally ready to go where she wanted to go—home. She took the back streets to avoid the highway construction and another hour's delay. She didn't have the strength to deal with the road-ragers anyway. The downtown area, where she lived in a condominium loosely described as a loft, was hopping as usual. She paid no attention to the business people who were out for drinks and enjoying their evening. She had a box of macaroni and cheese in the cupboard and a bottle of wine in the wine rack. That meager repast and some much needed solitude would make *her* night complete.

She switched on the light just inside the door and smiled. Her home was as she had left it, warm and inviting. She considered taking a step out onto her balcony where she could toss the demented shoes down to the street below, but revised her consideration after leafing through her mail and seeing the credit card statement containing the extravagant purchase added to her never declining debt. She headed for the kitchen instead, prepared her food and settled down on her couch with her companion—the television.

When the phone rang an hour later, she felt no reason to answer it. It was her best friend and coworker, Eric Kressler, no doubt wondering why she was not at the club at her appointed hour. She liked to think of Eric as her voice of reason, the one person in the world who kept her from going insane. But lately his ideas weren't meshing with her mood. He refused to let her wallow in her depression. He didn't like her tears.

The call went to the answering machine and she was forced to listen to his voice. "Pick up, Jess!" he screamed into the phone over the din of the club. "Come on, I know you're home and I'll just keep calling back until you do! I found a new bar and you're gonna' love it! Get ready, it's getting late!" Jesse listened to the crowd noises while he paused for her to pick up the receiver. She took a gulp of her wine and sank deeper into her comfortable couch. He hung up.

She returned her attention to the television set and the program she had been halfheartedly watching—a lame comedy that gave her no reason to even crack a smile. It was better than the news, which only made her mad. Over the set, on the entertainment center, a photo of Eric gazed back at her. His short haircut, tousled with just the right amount of *product* framed his square-jawed face, which in this picture was free of the beard he had recently cultivated. His thin, well-toned body and long legs made anything he wore look good. Posed, leaning against Jesse's car with his hundred-dollar tie loosened and his designer suit coat tossed carelessly over his shoulder, he looked like a model. Those intense brown eyes that gave him that come hither (but not too close) stare always made her smile.

Eric was a modern day Renaissance man—hip, stylish, intelligent and rich—the quintessential *metro-sexual.* He was one of those rare males who appreciated the finer things in life and knew what it took get them. Because of his poise, fashion sense and confidence, he was often mistaken for being *gay*. No normal, red-blooded man could be that cool, according to regular guys. He was flattered by the comments—he loved the spotlight. Women knew what he was. He was sexy and they were drawn to him like moths to a flame. The lucky ones thrived on his attention. The not-so-lucky ones vied for it, waiting for *their* turn. Eventually, Jesse knew he'd probably get to each and every one of them.

True to his word the phone rang again. "Jesse! Don't make me come over there and get you, because you know I will!" Eric's voice was more persistent. "You'll regret the day you gave me that key!" There was another pause as he spoke unintelligibly to someone nearby. "Hey, kiddo, listen to the music. They're playing your fav…."

"Eric, damn it!" Jesse picked up the receiver and yelled into it. "I'm exhausted! I worked 'til 7:30, had to go to Office Depot and spend my own money on those damned report covers, and those damned Prada's you talked me into buying just killed my…"

"Hey, sweetie!" Eric's voice was dripping with charm, and as usual, he wouldn't listen to a word she said. "You're not going to believe this place! And it's right around the corner. You don't even have to drive. It's got all these different rooms, so whatever mood you're in, you'll be fine. I promise."

"Eric…"

"Okay, I know you don't like going to a new place alone. I'll come get ya," he resolved. "I'll be there in twenty minutes." He hung up and Jesse couldn't argue with a dial tone.

She dragged herself into the bedroom to change.

Eric plopped himself onto Jesse's bed and exclaimed, "Finally, a place worthy of our presence, Jess! It's a dream come true."

Jesse had just stepped out of the shower and jumped a foot when she heard his voice coming from the next room. She peeked around the door of the bathroom and looked at Eric incredulously. "Jesus! You scared the crap out of me!"

"Yeah, yeah," Eric noted, not apologetically. "It didn't take as long as I thought to get here, which is also good." He had found the half empty bottle of wine on the coffee table and helped himself.

"Don't spill a drop of wine on that bedspread!" Jesse hurried back to the sink to put her make up on. "Damn it, Eric! I am not in the mood for this!"

"That song is getting old, sweetheart," he stated, filling Jesse's glass with what was left of the wine. "I know Sterling's killing you. We hear his tirades, too, you know. You just can't let him get to you. You can't let him win."

"I'm tired," she sighed, trying not to look at the new wrinkles that had recently formed around her eyes. "No matter what I do, it's not enough." She blotted some extra makeup on to cover up the dark circles. She hoped this new place was dark.

"What you need is a new man to take your mind off things," Eric suggested. He got up off the bed and went over to Jesse's closet. "This place is full of 'em. And a few of them are almost as hot as I am!"

Jesse found the mascara and painted her lashes. She brushed her long, brown hair and put it in a ponytail to avoid any more fuss. Wrapping the towel tightly around her body, she ventured into the bedroom where Eric was inspecting one of her little black dresses.

"I've always liked this little number," he said authoritatively. "Where are those new Prada's?"

"Sticking out of your ass, if you mention them again," Jesse sneered. She snatched the dress from Eric and headed back into the bathroom.

"They looked sexy today," Eric commented with a wry smile. "But, I suppose the Gucci's will do for tonight." He returned to the closet and took out another pair of shoes. "What in the hell did you do to those pantyhose?" They were in a heap on the bed where Jesse had tossed them earlier.

"Just think Prada!" Jesse mimicked Eric's voice acidly as she came back out of the bathroom and found another pair of hose in her armoire. She slid them on under her dress and stepped into her more comfortable Gucci pumps.

"Nobody said fashion wasn't painful," Eric commented. He slipped up behind her and snapped a rhinestone barrette into Jesse's hair to dress it up a little more. He hated ponytails. "You know better than to wear new shoes for that many hours before you've broken them in."

"Tell that to Sterling! He's the one who expects me to be there 24-7."

"Here," Eric gave Jesse the rest of her wine. "It's time to lighten up."

Jesse finished the glass in one gulp. "It's getting harder everyday, Eric," she sighed. "Something's gotta' give."

"Well, let's give it to the dance floor," Eric smiled, giving her a peck on the cheek as he threw a jacket over her shoulders. "It's amazing what a little exercise, a little wine and a cute little blond will do for your rotten mood." He guided her out to the living room and grabbed her purse, not giving her a moment to reflect. He shoved her gently out the front door and locked it behind them with his own key. "I'll probably just crash here tonight," he continued. "You shouldn't be alone."

"With a friend like you, I'll never have to worry about that."

"Yeah, yeah," Eric cut her off, pushing her into the elevator. "You can thank me later for my invaluable friendship and the effort I expend to make you happy."

Seconds later, Jesse found herself out on the street with her best pal. The air was still hot and hovered heavily over the city streets. Spring had not been pleasant this year. It was hot and sticky, with no relief in sight. Jesse wished it would rain. They walked along the crowded sidewalk and turned the corner. In four more blocks they were at the new club. A line of people stood outside waiting to get in. The beat of the loud music filtered out the door and a plethora of voices and laughter rode above that. Jesse sighed as Eric, who had already chummed up to the bouncers, eased her past the line and into the front door. She showed her ID and Eric paid her cover.

Once inside, she was amidst the Denver nightlife in all its glory. *What a pity*, she thought to herself as she looked around at the innovative, expensively decorated interior. Just a few weeks ago, before this damned depression set in, she would have been thrilled to be a part of this new place. Now she just wanted to find a corner and cry.

Normally, with Eric by her side, the two of them were quite the socialites. They knew everyone in the scene; they were popular and well liked. Jesse was a good listener and club types loved that. They'd assail her for hours on their latest dilemma, who was dating whom, who left whom, their plans for the future that never quite materialized. She bought them drinks. She tipped the waiters well. She was always greeted with a smile and the latest gossip wherever she went. Unfortunately, tonight Jesse wasn't in the mood for their problems. She had enough of her own. This, she realized very quickly, was not where she wanted to be.

Eric escorted her through the throngs of partygoers with a firm grip on her hand. They reached the bar with fairly little effort. Eric was an expert at idle chatter, knowing exactly what to say to whom, sashaying in and out to keep them moving along. He ordered two drinks, with a wink and a smile, from the female bartender, who was a prominent member of Eric's fan club. After being served, Eric and Jesse settled against the expansive bar and took in the sights.

Jesse had to admit it was an impressive place. The main floor was two stories tall, filled with pulsating lights trained on the dance floor, showering the mob as they moved to the very loud beat. There was a walkway along the walls where the second story floor should have been, filled with people passing in and out of doors or leaning against the railing watching the crowd down below. The DJ was up there, too. His area was strategically placed along the back wall where he could look down upon his footloose charges and keep an eye on the pulse of the club. Metal gates prohibited people from venturing too close. An attractive young lady, in a very short dress, stood guard at the left gate and indifferently accepted requests.

"Those doors lead to other rooms upstairs," Eric filled Jesse in as she eyed the second floor with some interest. "There's a hookah room, a game room, a cigar bar and this blue room that has water fountains and huge couches. The New-Agers have claimed that one."

"Let's go see," Jesse suggested, beyond bored but trying not to show it.

"Actually, there's somebody over there dying to meet me, sweets," Eric answered slyly. "Why don't you go ahead and I'll catch up with you."

Jesse changed her gaze covertly and saw the blond in the low cut leather dress giving Eric an interested look. "Good God, man," she stated seriously. "She's not coming home with us!"

"Yes, mother," laughed Eric, requesting another drink before he embarked on his next conquest. "Conveniently, there are places for that, too. Just head downstairs."

Jesse rolled her eyes at her friend and turned away, venturing out on her own. Her small stature made it relatively easy to weave in and out of what seemed like hundreds of people to get to the stairs. She stayed to the right and climbed slowly with the rest of the mob. Her spiked heels didn't like the open weaved metal steps. At the top, she looked for a place to spy over the railing to see if it was possible to keep half an eye on her companion down below, but the railing was jammed packed. She pushed a fleeting thought of the whole walk-way collapsing out of her mind as quickly as it entered.

She ventured past the hookah room—all red and gold like a Middle Eastern drug den. She actually entered into the game room, filled with mahogany game tables and bookcases filled with books and games. That room reminded her of an English Gentlemen's club. There was a fireplace blazing, with high-backed leather chairs located cozily in front of it. Each room had its own bartender and bar. She bought another glass of wine in the game room and continued exploring, for while that room felt comfortable, especially with the big leather chairs and the many volumes of what looked to be very old books, it was still not quite the spot where Jesse wanted to be.

In the other rooms she found a Seventies Disco Club, a Cigar Room with Frank Sinatra crooning to the fat cats in their zoot suits, and a jazz club, complete with a live jazz ensemble playing the blues. On her way to the last room, she made a mental note to remember to ask Eric how much it cost to get into this place. It had to be a hefty price with all this entertainment.

The Blue Room loomed up ahead and the crowd was considerably thinner. She could tell it was the Blue Room by the soft blue light (neon no doubt) emanating out the door. Jesse chuckled to herself at her brilliant deduction. Upon entering, she was actually taken by surprise. It was quite lovely and extremely inviting. Eric was right, though. It was way too quiet for the other patrons in this club. There were a few people inside, but Jesse didn't notice them. She was attracted to the cloud painted ceiling and the walls that were patterned like a woodland forest. The couches were luxurious and there were beautiful fountains scattered throughout the room shimmering with alternating blue, green and purple lights. The bar in this room was constructed of glass blocks.

"Jesse! Is that you?" A voice came from nowhere, interrupting the quiet ambiance of the room.

Jesse turned sharply and saw who had spoken. She was an old friend, almost forgotten. "My God, Bianca! I can't believe *you're* here!" Jesse made her way around a couple of the fountains and walked over to the woman who was sitting in a corner.

Bianca Wheland, with a voluptuous body, mounds of flowing auburn hair and deep green eyes got up from her couch and welcomed Jesse with open arms. Jesse returned Bianca's warm, strong hug stiffly. "Sit down with me," Bianca offered, feeling Jesse's tension. "I haven't seen you for ages!"

Jesse sat down across from the woman rather than next to her as Bianca had proposed. It was good to see her, but they had not spoken for years. Jesse did not have the emotional strength to jump in and resume this practically forgotten friendship as though everything was the same as it was back then. "Life has obviously been good to you since you left the company," Jesse commented. "You look positively ravishing."

Bianca observed Jesse's body language—arms wrapped tightly across her chest with legs crossed. "You look tired," she surmised, reading her like a book.

Jesse laughed. "Well, hallelujah, somebody finally noticed!" Jesse leaned back against the soft couch. "If you see Eric, would you fill him in?"

"Eric is still around, eh?" Bianca smiled. "No wonder!"

A faint memory stirred in Jesse's brain. Bianca always seemed to know more about her than she knew herself and Jesse was not in the mood for that. She also didn't feel like dredging up the mutual dislike her best friend and her former friend held for each other. "Your business is doing well, I take it?" she asked, changing the subject.

"Very well, thank you," Bianca got the hint, but was not about to let up. "You should come by. I think it might do you some good." Bianca had left the corporate world to build her own business. She was a massage therapist now and a Reiki Master to boot. She and her partner, Joseph, ran a small but lucrative metaphysical shop in Littleton, Colorado.

"That would be great," Jesse said, her eyes now roaming the rest of the room instead of focusing on her one time friend. "If I could find the time."

"Sometimes you have to make the time," Bianca quipped. She took a long sip of her drink, still watching Jesse whose distress was plainly evident. This girl, even though she did not know it, was screaming for help. "Let's see," she started, keeping track of Jesse's eyes as they looked everywhere except to her. "You've still got the condo, so you can't see the pollution you've been breathing every day for ten years. Even though you're the most talented at your job, Sterling is still riding your ass. And he's never going to help you get a promotion because you still save *his* ass and his job constantly. Eric is still pulling you around by the nose. When is the last time you had a healthy relationship with somebody not of this crowd? Tell me, Jess, is this where you expected to be ten years ago?"

Jesse fidgeted in her seat. It was time to go. "I don't know where I was supposed to be." Those recently uncontrollable tears were welling up again in her eyes. She did not want to think about this topic, nor discuss it any more. Her head was throbbing.

Bianca got up with purpose and sat next to her friend on the couch. She placed an arm gently around her shoulders. Jesse's body started to quiver. "Hey," Bianca said soothingly, "let's start by getting rid of that headache, okay?" She didn't wait for Jesse to answer. She wrapped her soft hand around the side of Jesse's head. "Don't tense up!" she said with determination. "Just breathe for me, okay?"

Jesse, too tired to fight back, allowed her to continue. She closed her eyes in an effort to stop the tears. Bianca rubbed her forehead for a moment and then stopped, miraculously where the pain was the most intense. After a few moments Bianca murmured, "That's better. Just relax." Jesse did as she was told to do. The pain did seem to be subsiding, so she let Bianca continue.

"You've had this headache for some time now, haven't you? Don't say anything. I already know the answer. Just stay quiet."

Jesse breathed deeply. She did not know how many minutes sped by and she found it did not matter. The pain was dissipating. Bianca's cool hand felt good upon her head. Eventually, her friend removed her hand and rubbed Jesse's neck for a moment before taking it away. Jesse laid her head back against the couch and rested. When she opened her eyes, Bianca was still sitting next to her, smiling.

"That was amazing," Jesse finally uttered. "I do feel better."

"I know," Bianca agreed. "But you've got a ways to go." She handed Jesse her drink, which Jesse did not remember putting down.

Jesse took a sip. "I feel so lost. Nothing I've done seems worthwhile," she confessed.

Bianca shifted on the couch to face her. "It's time, Jess."

"Time for what?"

"There you are!" Eric's voice boomed in the quiet room. The few other patrons in the Blue Room gave him aggravated glances before returning to their quiet conversations.

Bianca smiled and got up. "I'll be in touch." She took Jesse's hand and helped her up before Eric got too close. "It's going to be all right, I promise."

"But…" Jesse did not want Bianca to go, but she did not have the strength to stop her.

"Well, well, well," Eric announced, "if it isn't Bianca Wheland. I thought you were dead!"

"Good to see you too, Eric," Bianca grimaced. "I'm so sorry I can't stay and chat." She leaned in close to Jesse's ear so Eric could not hear her. "Go home, Jess. You need some rest and you certainly don't need, nor want to be here."

"So, how's Witches R Us?" Eric continued, not happy to see Bianca talking with his best friend. Several years ago, Bianca and Jesse were quite close when he was hired as the attorney for the company where they worked. Bianca almost talked Jesse into leaving with her when she quit. It had taken Eric a long time to convince Jesse she had made the right decision to stay. Now that Eric and Jesse were devoted friends, he did not want her to experience those doubts again. "Are you making any kind of a living at it?" He stood in Bianca's way, blocking her egress.

"We get by," Bianca answered politely, giving him the once over before side stepping his blockade. "Still the fashion plate, I see." Jesse slipped in behind her, hoping to follow her out.

"I see you're still dressing like Stevie Nicks," Eric snapped. "How gauche." He grabbed Jesse's arm, preventing her from sneaking past him. "I knew this room was totally useless. I'll have to speak to the management and get it changed."

"Don't go to all that work on my account, Eric," Bianca stated flatly. "With the likes of you around, I won't be back." She hugged Jesse one more time, causing Eric to bristle. "Anyway, the purpose for my unlikely visit here is now clear to me. I'll be in touch, Jess."

Jesse hugged her back, which aided her in slipping from Eric's grasp. She quickly stepped around him and could have easily escaped his clutches. Instead, she stopped and placed her arm in the crook of his. "I look forward to it," she said, letting Bianca go. Bianca winked at her and disappeared quickly out the door. Jesse breathed a sigh of relief.

"What was that all about?" Eric was irritated. He let her lead him from the quiet room into the bustle of the club. "That was the last person I expected to ever see again, especially around here."

"Hey," Jesse answered, "let's get you another drink." Jesse was grateful to hear the noise level rise again so she wouldn't have to talk. She guided Eric into the disco room and bought him a shot. He downed it quickly and slammed the shot glass back on the bar. "That blond seems to be following you, no?" Jesse noted, catching sight of the woman he had chatted up earlier.

"Don't let Bianca fuck you up," Eric warned, his interest in Jesse's welfare waning as she had hoped. He winked at the blond, who blushed and started to dance. "That witch is nuts."

"Don't worry about it," Jesse sighed. "Like I've got time for Bianca Wheland. Just get out there and show Blondie your moves." Eric eyed her warily for a moment. Jesse laughed and pushed him into the crowd of dancers.

He glanced back at her one more time before he moved in on the blond girl. Jesse stood around for a while longer and watched her friend, the master, at work. With his focus elsewhere, Jesse stealthily exited the club and went home.

CHAPTER 2

"It's about time," Brad Sterling snapped. He leafed through one of the hundred brochures Jesse had completed and tossed it carelessly on the table. "I guess it will have to do, as they'll be here in an hour." He gave the conference room a cursory glance to make sure everything was in order. His disdainful smirk let Jesse know it was. "Make sure that coffee's hot and have everything set up. I don't need you skulking around after they've arrived." He surreptitiously snatched another brochure before he stormed out of the room.

Jesse waited until the door had closed behind him before she expelled a nervous sigh of relief. Of course it was done, she thought to herself. It always was. Usually, it would not have been down to the wire, but Sterling had made her redo the budget report because *he* had decided to change the layout at the last minute. Jesse cursed herself for not keeping the original report she had created a month ago, which he changed. When he threw the new one on her desk this morning, his multitude of red ink scratches indicated he was happier with the way she had prepared it the first time.

The first good night's sleep she had enjoyed in over a month was but a dream now. Her headache was back with a vengeance. She straightened the conference table again and went back to her desk. Eric, looking every bit the suave, confident attorney, was waiting there when she returned. A new stack of work, obviously from Sterling, was perched precariously on the seat of her chair.

"So you won't miss it," Eric offered his opinion on the stack, sipping his coffee. "That's probably more important than the crap on your desk. I'd venture to say he probably wants that stack completed today."

"Yeah," Jesse said. "Anything to keep me away from that meeting."

"You'll be pissed to know," Eric continued sarcastically, "that Hobbs is happy with your brochures. Sterling was taking credit for them when I passed his office."

"I'm sure he loved the new budget report, too." Jesse picked up the mound of papers, piled it on top of the rest of stuff on her desk and sat down. The company president, Jim Hobbs, was a great guy, but totally blind to Sterling's mendacity.

"So, where'd you hop off to last night?" Eric asked, oblivious to the work Jesse needed to get done. He wouldn't be needed at the meeting until later and because his workload was considerably lighter than Jesse's, his morning was blissfully clear with nothing better to do than chat with his best friend. "I couldn't find you."

"Since you weren't on the couch this morning, I assumed you didn't miss me," Jesse replied. Her coffee was cold and she didn't feel like getting up to get another cup.

"Of course I did," Eric smiled. "But I found a safe haven a little closer to the club. You know how treacherous the streets can be after two a.m."

"That explains why you're wearing the same suit." Jesse didn't really care to hear about his tryst, but she knew she'd be filled in on every detail sooner or later so she allowed him to go on. "Was she worth it?"

"I suppose so," Eric surmised. "No better, no worse than usual. She's got a nice place, though. I really need to move down here. I'm tired of the commute."

"Yeah, it must be a pain having to drive that Jaguar all over the place."

"I prefer your BMW. I think I'll get one of those next."

"Maybe with that bonus you get this year, you can have both."

"Maybe," Eric mused. "But have you seen the price of real estate down here lately? It's really high."

"I wouldn't know," Jesse half smiled. "When I bought my loft, nobody wanted to live down here. I was on my own and it was all I could afford."

"Yeah, and after enduring two muggings, along with the noise and inconvenience of a complete restoration of the downtown area, you're now sitting on quite a prized piece of property."

"Lucky me," Jesse sighed. "And the allergies from the smog are a special bonus."

"You wouldn't have that problem if you smoked."

"I've got enough bad habits, thank you," she snapped. She had to get to work and sparring with her best friend was not going to get it done any sooner.

The phone rang and Jesse picked it up quickly, thankful for the interruption. She took her time with the call. Eric, soon tired of waiting, roamed off to bother someone else.

The prospective clients arrived and the rest of Jesse's day was filled with keeping everybody happy and getting her other work done, too. It was four o'clock and she had forgotten about lunch. Loaded with work to drop off, she staggered to the candy machine and grabbed a Milky Way bar. The conference room doors opened and Eric was charming the clients with his charismatic personality and wit. He was cleverly herding them out the door to seal the deal over drinks and dinner. He winked at Jesse when they walked by and she shook her head in amazement. Even in yesterday's clothes he seemed as fresh and sure of himself as ever. In her own way she could win over clients, but she never could get that charisma thing down, even on her best day. The President and VP followed Eric like dogs at his heel, listening intently to his every word. They had long since given up trying to interject anything useful or clever. Jesse created the packages/promotions and Eric would sell them. That's the way it had been around here for years.

She went back to her desk, finished up the week's work and closed up shop. Two days to herself, she thought. She'd unplug that phone when she got home. She wanted absolutely no company *or* conversations.

"The secretary let me in," Bianca's voice filled her office as Jesse was turning off her computer. Jesse looked up and saw her standing in her doorway. "I hope you don't mind."

"Well, hi!" Jesse was surprised. "I was just closing up."

"I found myself in town again and I thought I might entice you to some dinner. There's a great little Italian restaurant right across the street from my shop." Bianca eyed her friend casually. She could tell Jesse's headache was back.

"Actually," Jesse sighed, thinking about Bianca's offer, "I was planning on going straight home to bed. My headache's back and I'm seeing double."

"Then I must insist," Bianca said quietly, grabbing Jesse's purse and handing it to her. "I've got something at the shop that will help with that."

"Whatever you did last night took care of it until this morning when I came back to work." Jesse stood up. She fondly remembered those few hours of blissful relief. Intrigued with the thought of feeling that way again, she followed Bianca out the door and to the elevator. It was silly to Jesse, but Bianca's presence just seemed to make her feel better.

"Joseph dropped me off, so I can show you the way if you feel like driving."

"That'll be perfect," Jesse responded. "My car is in the garage."

"So, tell me about the shop," Jesse asked as they drove south out of Denver. The traffic was not too heavy and the drive was actually pleasant for once. "Was it difficult to get started?"

"There were times," Bianca replied with a smile upon her lips, "when I thought it would never happen. Luckily, I'd built up a small client base so we had a little money to work with, and eventually it all came together. The shop's quite eclectic. There's a little of me, a lot of Joseph and everything else in between. Joseph calls it our *shop of horrors*. I think it's quite nice."

"It must be great being your own boss." Jesse followed Bianca's pointed finger to the left and turned at the next corner. "Nobody telling you what to do."

"I wish it was that simple," Bianca answered. "It comes with its own headaches. Suppliers and manufacturers can be a nightmare. Customers can make you want to pull your hair out. But, for the most part, it *is* great. And the *best* part is, it's work I love to do."

"I wouldn't know how to deal with that," Jesse sighed. "I've worked for someone else my whole life. I guess I'm used to being ordered around."

"I'd say *abused* is a better choice of words. Especially the way you've been treated by Sterling. How long has it been, Jess? How long have you worked there?"

"Just *celebrated* my fifteenth year last month," Jesse retorted. "Apparently, I'm 100 percent vested now."

"You are paid well, I take it." Bianca looked around the interior of the BMW. "That probably has a lot to do with why you've stayed."

"The company's done well, thanks to people like Eric and me. And despite Sterling, I do get the occasional raise. Eric will tell the President that I created the brochures for today's meeting. I'll probably end up with a small bonus or a day off or something for my work when Sterling isn't around." Jesse followed Bianca's next direction and made a left onto Santa Fe Drive.

"Just take this to Bowles and make a left," Bianca advised. "The shop is in downtown Littleton."

"Always a beautiful part of town," Jesse reminisced. "Do they still put up all those Christmas lights during the holidays?"

"Just like a Victorian village," Bianca smiled. "It's quite charming when it snows."

"I'll have to remember to try and come for a visit," Jesse mused. Thinking for a minute, Jesse started to chuckle.

"What's so funny? Bianca asked, perplexed.

"Where is Littleton—maybe thirty minutes from Denver?" Jesse laughed. "Here I'm talking like it's in another state. I guess I've been stuck in the city too long. After a while, you're scared to leave it. You're afraid you'll contract some disease if you experience fresh air."

Bianca laughed with her. "And, they've built this contraption called the Light Rail, just in case you don't feel like driving. You can come down for lunch."

"What a country!" Jesse pressed her foot a little harder on the gas pedal. She was growing anxious to see Bianca's world. The BMW hummed, speeding in, out and around the thinning traffic. They were in Littleton a short time later. They parked the car and Jesse took a deep breath. She coughed.

"We're not in the mountains!" Bianca remarked. "But the air's a little cleaner out here than under that damned brown cloud. "I'm surprised you're not asthmatic."

"Give it time," Jesse stated. "I've got just about everything else." She looked around at the different shops, which were located in historical houses along the main street. It was all very quaint. "Is that your place?" she called out pointing to a big house across the street as they walked toward the restaurant. It was a three story, gabled Victorian house brightly painted and trimmed. The windows were warm and inviting with glittering knick-knacks and soft glowing lights.

"That's it," Bianca announced, holding the door to the restaurant open for Jesse to enter. "The shop's on the first floor, my massage rooms and office take up the second, Joseph has his workshop and office on the third and we live in the attic." Bianca smiled when she looked at it. "It's just right for us."

"Can we skip dinner?" Jesse suggested as she entered the restaurant. "I'm anxious to see it."

"I think you need some food, first," Bianca gently ordered. "When was the last time you ate?"

"Aaaah," Jesse had to think, "sometime last night. I can't remember what it was, but I'm sure the dishes are still in the sink to prove that I ate something."

The waiter seated them at a table by the front window. Jesse could look over at Bianca's store while they ate.

After a fine dinner and continual conversation in which Bianca explained the history of the house, how they found it, and future plans for the store inside, Bianca paid the bill and they sauntered across the street. Jesse was positively brimming with excitement when they climbed the stairs and opened the door to go inside. In the foyer, they were greeted by the thundering paws of

Joseph's wolf dog, Max, who had clambered down the stairs from the third floor to meet Bianca when he heard the click of her key in the lock.

"I forgot to mention Max," Bianca declared joyfully as the dog pounced on her from the second step. "I hope you don't mind dogs!" Max covered Bianca with licks and kisses and a wagging tail that could have easily knocked knick-knacks off almost any shelf or table in the next room where the store was located.

After slobbering over his mistress for a moment or two, the dog turned his brown eyes toward Jesse. "I don't mind at all," she whispered. "He's beautiful!" She allowed him to smell her hand and Max immediately decided she was part of the family. Jesse put her purse down just as Max practically bowled her over with his paws. He covered her face with licks and Jesse submitted willingly to his amorous behavior.

"I'll just pick up your purse," Bianca mentioned as the dog and Jesse got to know each other. "We may never find it again if Max gets a hold of it." She walked on into the shop and put the purse, along with hers, behind the counter.

Eventually, Max quieted and allowed Jesse to get off her knees and back on her feet. She liked that the dog stayed right at her side. "Can he come in here?" she asked before entering the shop. His huge size made the shop look precariously delicate.

"He grew up here," Bianca said, turning on a few more lights. "He knows to behave."

Jesse stepped carefully over the threshold and ogled all the baubles, bottles and books. There were fairies and gargoyles, vampire bats and witches hats, wands and vessels, candles and intricate candleholders, jewelry and fabulous garments like capes and long flowing dresses. Bianca kept quiet and let Jesse meander to her heart's content. She also noticed how Jesse's hand never left Max's head. The dog followed alongside her, patiently waiting wherever she stopped. She scratched his head between his ears and after gazing intently at each table or shelf of wares, she turned her attention completely to the dog for a moment and scratched his neck and ruff. Max was quite pleased with Bianca's new friend.

"This is wonderful!" Jesse finally said, looking over at Bianca who was skimming the books. "Everything is so beautiful!"

"Thank you," Bianca smiled. "I thought you might enjoy it. There are some books over here that might interest you. *How to handle stress* are words that come to mind when I think of you lately."

Jesse laughed and walked over to the counter with Max still at her side. There she found beautiful necklaces, rings and bracelets. Her eyes grew ever wider as she studied each piece. "I've got to have that!" she mumbled, half to herself. "And that. God, that's beautiful! How does anyone make up their mind in here?"

"The first time is the toughest!" Bianca said, pleased with Jesse's reaction. "Let's go upstairs and see the rest of the place." Bianca led the way. "You should probably meet Joseph, too," she grimaced good-naturedly. "After all, he'll want to know who stole his dog!"

The massage center was warm and inviting with soft blue walls and gigantic Max Parrish prints adorning them. The massage tables were covered with beautiful blankets and soft satin pillows. There was a fountain that spanned one corner of the room, with lush green plants around it. The ceiling was painted with clouds and twinkling stars. There was a fireplace with two com-fortable chairs before it. Jesse's shoes sank deep into the plush, pale green car-pet. Incense filled Jesse's nostrils and permeated her senses. She was unable to form suitable words to express how beautiful it all was. Max kept her company again as she looked around.

"Perhaps we will stop back here before you leave," Bianca suggested. "We can give that headache another try."

"Okay," Jesse acquiesced with no reserve. She looked forward to it.

Following Bianca once again, she climbed the stairs to the third floor. It was a tight squeeze with Max climbing up beside her. On the landing she could hear the sound of a flute and the steady beat of a drum.

"This is Joseph's floor," Bianca announced. "It's a little different." She opened the door and let Jesse and Max step inside ahead of her. Jesse stood there, her mouth open in astonishment. The walls to her left and straight before her were hand painted like a forest. The trunks of trees covered the walls and branched out onto the ceiling. Some real tree branches were attached to the walls, which gave the trees a three-dimensional look. Located in the middle of the opposite wall of trees, a fireplace was bordered by a semi-circle of large throw pillows. Candles flickered on the hearth. There was a large drum in the center of the semi-circle. The floor was covered with large, hand loomed rugs made of dried sea grass. The music filled the room, but there was no sight of a stereo system. The corner of the room to her right and behind her was deco-rated from the floor to a point on the ceiling with yards of beige colored suede that resembled a teepee. Mountain scenery completed the walls and sur-rounded the teepee. A moon was painted over the mountain behind her. The ceiling was dark with billowy gray clouds. Stars twinkled in the candlelight that illuminated this indoor wilderness. In the center of the teepee stood a grand mahogany desk with oil lamps lighting up the polished surface. Joseph was sitting behind it, busily writing in a large, leather bound book. He looked up at Bianca and Jesse as they entered. His smile was guarded and slow to materialize.

"So, there's my dog," he said. Max had run into the room and plopped himself down on one of the pillows. When Jesse did not join him, he picked up one of the drum beaters with his mouth, carried it back to Jesse and dropped it at her feet. She was too busy at first, mesmerized by the room, to notice Max, who sat patiently down in front of her, waiting for her to find the stick. She just kept scratching him behind the ears, which he didn't mind at all. "Max, give the lady some room," Joseph commanded.

Her wits back, Jesse looked down and saw the present the dog had brought to her, but when she bent to pick it up, the dog snapped it up with his teeth and trotted back over to the pillows, where he sat down again.

"Jesse Harless, this is Joseph Stillwater, my partner," Bianca announced, going over to Joseph's desk and closing the book in front of him. "Joseph, this is my friend I was telling you about." She leaned over the desk and kissed him softly on his forehead. He squeezed her arm gently before she walked over to the sideboard to get a bottle of wine and three glasses.

"Max wants you to take a seat," Joseph stated. "It looks like he wants you to stay for awhile."

"It's a pleasure to meet you, Joseph," Jesse said, nervously taking a seat on the pillow next to Max. She wasn't sure if she should make herself so welcome, just because a dog had invited her to do so.

Joseph was an American Indian. His coal black, polished hair hung straight, like a satin sheet, halfway down his back. He was well built and muscular, his stature quite intimidating when he stood up. "My dog likes you," he said, coming around from his desk to join Jesse and Bianca. Bianca sat down on her pillow and opened the wine. "That means you must have a good heart," he said, still standing.

"Well, come sit down and find out for yourself," Bianca chided him, pouring the wine into the first glass. "No need to frighten her to death."

Jesse smiled weakly and accepted the glass of wine from Bianca. She drank a little too quickly, for she was oddly nervous at the sight of him looming over her. She had regretted not asking Bianca about Joseph. She had no idea what to say and he appeared to be a man of few words. Finally, he sat down cross-legged on the biggest pillow next to her.

Max had lain down close to Jesse and chewed a bit on the drum beater. His eyes watched Bianca to see if some of the wine might come his way. Jesse sunk her hand deeply into Max's fur. It was thick and comforting. The music from the mysterious source played on. It sounded soothing and beautiful to Jesse. She could not remember ever hearing such lovely tunes. The three sat silently for a few minutes and drank their wine.

"Bea says you live in the city," Joseph remarked, startling the young woman. "And you work there, too."

"Yes," Jesse stammered. "This trip has been quite a treat."

"If this is a trip, then you must not get out often."

Jesse regretted her words. She felt like a fool in this man's presence. He bewildered her. She hugged the dog closer to her side. "I rarely have time to leave the city," she explained. "I work most of the time."

"You do not enjoy your work," he said matter-of-factly. "Why do you do it?"

"Gotta' pay the bills." Jesse didn't know if she cared for his tone of voice. There was another awkward silence.

"Maybe you need a dog," he suggested. "You seem happy with Max."

"Maybe she doesn't need the third degree," claimed Bianca, feeling Jesse's discomfort. "It's not easy having a pet in the city. And, I don't think Jesse has the time to take care of one."

"Too bad," Joseph muttered. "The wolf dog's good for her. I'm sure you can see it, Bea. It might help."

"Well, let's start with a massage first, okay?" Bianca smiled. "She can spend time with Max when she comes for visits."

"This room is incredible," Jesse murmured, still entranced. "It feels like we're sitting in a forest by a campfire."

"It looks different during the day," Bianca said, pouring more wine. "The moon turns into...well, let me show you."

She got up off her pillow and walked over to the switch plate. She flicked on the overhead light and the room turned from night to day. The moon turned into the sun, the stars disappeared, the black sky ceiling turned to azure blue and the gray clouds turned bright and white.

"Whoa!" Jesse leaned back and looked around. "This is fabulous."

"It's like having the country in the city," Joseph observed, drinking a little more of his wine. "Bianca decorated it for me. She's very good." Joseph smiled up at Bianca before she turned the main light back off. "Maybe she could decorate your house. That might make you feel better."

Jesse smiled at the big man. He looked a little less daunting in the light, but she couldn't tell if he was a man of few words or if he just didn't like her. She relaxed a little—thanks to the wine and the dog beside her. "Maybe it would."

Joseph reached across Jesse and took the drum beater from Max's mouth. "How about a little drum playing? That might be good for you, too." He wiped the stick off on his jeans and handed it to Jesse.

"I don't..."

"Nonsense," Bianca laughed, joining the pair on the pillows again. She picked up a beater herself and one for Joseph. "It's easy. Just follow with the music." She started the ball rolling by hitting the drum herself. The sound reverberated through the room and Jesse was sure it must have traveled through the whole house. Joseph joined Bianca with his beater and they smiled at one another. Their beats grew stronger and louder as one.

Max nudged Jesse's hand that held her drum beater. She knew he didn't care whether or not she played. He wasn't tired of her attention, quite yet. She took the beater into her right hand and put her left back on the dog's ruff. Quietly, she joined in and was surprised she could keep the beat. It was uplifting, especially when Joseph started to chant. Her beats slowly got stronger and louder as her inhibitions dissolved. She actually started to have some fun, an event that had been missing from her life for a long time.

When the recorded music stopped, Jesse didn't notice. Bianca had taken up the chant while Joseph impressed them with his flute music. Max joined in at one point with a howl and Jesse thought, together, they made the most beautiful music she had ever heard. An hour sped by and whether it was the wine, the drumming, the chanting or the inevitable laughter and merriment that settled upon them, everyone had a very good time.

When their song was finally finished and they had all settled back comfortably on their pillows, Joseph declared, "Bianca is going to bring you to the powwow next weekend, so you can see, hear and feel the real power behind the drums." He glanced at Bianca, who was nodding in agreement. He followed her eyes to see what she was looking at. Max had fallen asleep with his head in Jesse's lap. Jesse's hand still rested on his neck. "This would be good for you, Harless. It will help you."

"I would like that," Jesse murmured. "And I am honored that you have invited me."

"Good," Joseph resounded. "You will be here for breakfast at eight in the morning. That isn't too early for a city person like yourself, is it?"

"I'll set my alarm!" Jesse laughed. "I wouldn't miss it for the world."

"Now," Bianca spoke out, getting up from her pillow. "Let's leave Joseph to his writing and try to work on that headache a bit before you head for home, all right?"

Max awoke with a start and lifted his head from Jesse's lap to see what was up. "You will stay with me," Joseph ordered the dog. He snapped his fingers. Max rose to his feet and trotted over to his master. "We'll see you next Saturday, Harless."

"See you then." Jesse got up and followed Bianca to the door. "Thank you," she said honestly. "It has been a pleasure to meet you."

"Don't be giving him a big head," Bianca warned, guiding Jesse out of the room. She turned and winked at Joseph before they left. "There will be no living with him if you keep that up."

"Tok'sa," Joseph called out as the women went down to the second floor.

"How about you taking a seat on the massage table over there," Bianca suggested as she turned on a little music and prepared some incense. "Just rest your head on that pillow and I'll see what I can do for you."

"I'm feeling much better," Jesse said, doing as she was told. "But I can still feel a twinge."

"There's more than a twinge going on in there," Bianca said calmly, preparing the room with a few more candles. She wheeled over a cabinet that contained some oils and lotions and took a seat at the end of the table where Jesse's head rested. "I'm sorry if Joseph frightened you at first. He can do that sometimes." She rubbed some exotic, scented oil into the palms of her hands with a few vigorous strokes.

"He's a kind man, isn't he?" Jesse asked, her eyes closing as she tried to relax.

"Yes," Bianca agreed, "but guarded." She placed her hands, with her palms down, gently on the sides of Jesse's face. "He studies people carefully and, as you can tell, uses very few words."

"The drum," Jesse whispered, inhaling the scent of the oil. "He can tell by the way people play it?"

"It's a test," Bianca talked softly, gently starting to massage Jesse's cheekbones. "I'd say you passed with flying colors. I bet you didn't know you were musically inclined." She moved her fingers slowly, but with purpose. "Now, just breathe deeply again, like you did last night. I'll take care of the rest."

Her hands were extraordinary—kneading their way to Jesse's sinuses, eyes, forehead and to her temples. Jesse relaxed fully and let Bianca do her work. It wasn't long before her headache was completely gone and she fell, without effort, to sleep.

Bianca worked her magic for another thirty minutes, letting her friend slumber under her touch.

"She needed that," Joseph murmured, standing at the doorway with Max at his side. "She's in a lot of pain."

"I think we can help if she'll let us," Bianca said quietly.

"She would not ask for it."

"I know." Bianca got up from her stool and placed a blanket over Jesse's body. "Her mind might not let her ask for it, but her body is screaming for help. I'm glad I found her before it manifested into some kind of illness." Bianca walked over to Joseph and put her arms around him. He kissed her gently and they hugged each other tight.

"Her soul pleads for peace," Joseph whispered into her ear. "It will be a long hard trail to follow, but she could figure out a way to do it, if she tries."

"Perhaps if we both helped," Bianca mentioned, her voice a little hesitant.

"You know that is not my way." Joseph's tone was serious.

"I know, but she was once my very good friend—so sure of herself and so full of life. *You* could help her find that road again."

"It is not my place. I will not teach a stranger."

"That makes me sad, but I understand, my love," Bianca sighed. "Let her rest, then. It's the best and only thing I can do for her right now." She nudged Joseph and Max out of the room to let Jesse sleep.

CHAPTER 3

Jesse was very embarrassed because she had fallen asleep, but Bianca laughed and convinced her it was a normal reaction to the massage. When she got back to her flat, she unplugged the phone, despite ten messages from Eric, and went to bed where she slept soundly through the night. She awoke refreshed with her headache gone and felt an enormous amount of energy. Her head was filled with new and confusing thoughts. She attempted to be her responsible self. She cleaned the loft, did the laundry and went out for groceries like she did every other Saturday morning, but she couldn't shake the feeling that she had experienced something magical the night before and she wanted more of it.

She called Eric and made excuses for her absence at the club. She was bored with the conversation immediately. She didn't care about how he closed the deal; how he got a couple of new job offers on the side, or how he ended up sleeping with one of their clients. She refused when he suggested they go to the mall and spend more money on more clothes that neither one of them needed. She did not lie when she remarked she wasn't feeling quite her old self and begged off going out that Saturday night. She cleverly talked him out of coming to her rescue by bringing her dinner and some movies that she didn't want to watch. She told him she needed to rest and would see him on Monday when everything in her life would be back to normal.

With the Eric situation handled, Jesse suddenly wished she had some of the music that Joseph had been listening to in his forest room. She longed for the incense and the oil that Bianca used when she massaged her head and neck. She missed Max. But, sadly, she did not want to be a pest and go traipsing back out to Littleton like an orphan hoping to be adopted by the nice couple living in the old Victorian house. She needed to take care of herself. She paced back and forth in her condo. She needed to find something to quench this new thirst.

So, Jesse got in her car and went to the bookstore. She searched and finally found a couple of the books that Bianca had suggested she should read. She then went to the CD section and found some American Indian Tribal music. She held on tightly to her cache of goodies as she stood in the long checkout line. She wondered why she was so driven to try something new. Eric would never understand, she thought. He would want answers to questions she could not answer. Where was the rock and roll, the gothic or the dance music she was always listening to? What was with the Indian stuff? What would be next? Turquoise? A cowboy hat? God forbid—chaps? Every fashion maven knew the western thing was so blasé. Turning western was like slapping Coco Chanel in the face. And what did she want those New Age self-help books for? Was she turning into Shirley MacLaine? She resolved to keep these purchases hidden, for Eric would certainly have her committed if he found them. She could see him in her mind's eye. This fabulous young man in his Hugo Boss suit with a troubled look upon his handsome face as he signed the commitment papers assuredly with his Watermark fountain pen. Of course, the nurse at the desk would fall hopelessly in love with him and not pay one lick of attention to Jesse as she was manhandled into a strait-jacket and thrown into a rubber room.

She drove home in silence, not daring to even try the CD out in the car. She waited until she was safely tucked away into her condo, with the deadbolt locked and half of a glass of wine down her throat before she turned on the CD player. She sat cross-legged on the floor in front of her stereo system and slowly turned up the volume. There were the drums, the flutes and finally the chanting. It was good. She settled down a bit.

After the music, she took a long hot bath and got into bed. There she perused the three books she had purchased. One dealt with reducing stress in life that Bianca had suggested; one was about animal totems, because it looked interesting; and one on the subject of wolves, because she was enamored with Max and had no idea what these animals were all about.

She started to read the book on stress first as that appeared to be her biggest problem at the moment and the most practical source to eliminate it. It was easy to read and was perfectly logical. There were rational methods to reduce the burdens resting upon her shoulders as long as she could play out the scenarios the way they were presented in the book. Perhaps, she considered, if she bought two more copies and placed one in Eric's apartment and one on Sterling's desk for *them* to read, this technique might work, for it appeared they had to drastically change their behavior before she could hope to change hers. It all made good, old-fashioned, American Board of Psychiatric Health common sense and she was proud of herself for buying it, yet her eyes kept wandering over to the two other books lying beside her on the bed. Despite her levelheadedness and prudence, those tomes seemed to be challenging her to take a chance and delve into mysteries she knew nothing about. She closed the book on stress and picked up the spirit guide to animal totems.

Hours later, her brain had devoured every word and was hungry for more. It was cast into a new world where all life was connected and had significance. She learned that besides the physical body, one must also consider the inclusion of the spirit and mind for total health, well-being and harmony. The health of that mind, body and spirit, tuned into the natural environment, helped to complete the proper balance in the relationship of all things. Finding that plants and animals, like humans, are part of the spirit world that exists along with the physical world, and realizing that she could use animal imagery and other totem images to learn about herself and her existence, gave her a great feeling of awakening. The book defined how to discover her animal totems and how to use them to grow and comprehend the world around her. She was surprised, when she got to *wolf*, to find a connection.

At dawn, she got out of bed and made some coffee. With her new music playing in the background, she sat at her kitchen table and explored the book on wolves. Her preconceived notions of the *big, bad wolf*, based on childhood stories like Little Red Riding Hood and the Three Little Pigs, was quickly shattered as she read the truth about these animals. Every page was a revelation to her. Wolves were friendly, social and highly intelligent creatures with a strong sense of loyalty to family and to each other. They were horrendously misunderstood for years by men who hunted them nearly to extinction, not just in America, but around the globe. Jesse cried when she read about the slaughter. She could not understand how it could happen. Clearly no animal, especially the wolf, whose existence was based on the kind of life most humans strove for, deserved that kind of treatment. She was beside herself with grief for their torture and near annihilation. Worst of all, she felt there was nothing she could do to stop it.

When the telephone rang, she hesitated to answer it. With no sleep and this new information, she was in no condition to hold a coherent conversation with any human at that particular time. But, for some reason, the answering machine failed to pick up and the phone kept ringing. Frustrated, she yanked the receiver off the hook and almost shouted an obscenity into the ear of the caller, except that her tears had choked her up and she was unable to speak.

"Harless?" a deep voice pervaded the line. "Are you there?"

Jesse sighed and attempted to gain her composure. "Joseph?" she sputtered. "Oh, my God!" she sniffed and tried to clear her throat.

"Bea said I should call you," the Native American stated loudly. "She thinks you should come over for a visit. Are you busy today?"

"I can't believe…" she uttered, a smile coming to her lips. Of all the people in the world, his voice was the one she needed to hear.

"Well, the dog would like a visit, too," Joseph interrupted. "He's been a little cranky since you left."

"I'll be there in an hour," Jesse said quickly. "I won't be a bother?"

"Better you be out here, than sitting home crying." The Indian's voice was gruff. "Bea is making lunch and she doesn't cook much. So, hurry! Any day I get food made by the hand of my woman is a good day. We're waiting."

Jesse laughed and hiccupped. "I'm on my way." Joseph hung up without saying good-bye. She did not need to hear it. She rushed to the shower and was in and out in five minutes. She pulled her hair back into a pony tail, barely bothered with makeup, threw on some jeans and a t-shirt and was ready to go a few minutes later. She grabbed her new books and her music and raced to her car. She was in Littleton in record time.

As she pulled the BMW into a parking place on Main Street, she smiled. There, sitting on the steps of the house, were Joseph and Max. When she got out of the car, Joseph raised his hand in greeting and Max ran to her with lightning speed. She stooped down and welcomed the dog's licks and kisses on her face. She hugged him close.

"Good time," Joseph noted when Jesse and Max came up the walk. "That car is fast."

"The driver has a lead foot," Jesse smiled at him and to Bianca who appeared at the screen door when they approached. "I can't thank…"

"There is no need for thanks," Joseph ordered, getting up from the steps. "Max and I are thanking you. We're getting lunch."

Jesse climbed the stairs and threw her arms around Bianca's neck. Bianca hugged her tightly back. Max rubbed up close to both of them. "I was…" Jesse started.

"Miserable," Bianca finished her sentence for her. "Joseph and I felt your pain." She ushered Jesse into the front door. Max pranced in with her. "You are always welcome here, Jess. Don't ever doubt that again, okay?"

"No one is in the way around here," Joseph commented on his way to the kitchen. "Pain is harder when faced alone." He snuck a piece of ham off the tray of lunchmeats Bianca had prepared for sandwiches. He ate half and gave the rest to Max who gobbled it down in one swallow.

"Hey, buddy!" Bianca snapped. "Carry that outside and don't touch another morsel until we're all at the table." Then, she said kindly to Jesse, "It's such a beautiful day, I decided we'd eat in the backyard. Grab that bread tray on the table and I'll bring the drinks."

"How did you know I was upset?" Jesse was compelled to ask while doing as she was told. "I couldn't believe it when I picked up the phone and it was Joseph."

"Some things are kind of hard to explain," Bianca offered. She held the back door open to let Jesse pass. "Suffice it to say, we figured you'd be a little con-fused. The massage can stir up certain feelings. People usually have a reaction of some sort after one of them. And Joseph has this strange intuition with cer-tain people."

"It's your medicine," Joseph stated, seated at the picnic table with Max beside him. "It is strong with you."

"That's what started it," Jesse retorted. "I got these books yesterday and I was reading all night." She sat down at the table across from Joseph and Bianca joined them. Bianca made up the sandwiches while Jesse talked. "The wolves, Joseph. The things they've done to them."

"It has not been easy for them," Joseph answered. "But they are survivors, like you." He smiled greedily at the sandwich Bianca gave him. "To understand them, you must relive their history." He took a giant bite. "I have more infor-mation to lend you when you leave tonight," he mumbled with a mouthful of food.

Bianca glanced at the books in Jesse's bag. "Did the one on stress help you?"

"I didn't read much of it," Jesse replied, eating as hungrily as Joseph. The food was delicious.

"The other one gave you more answers, I bet," Bianca suggested.

"But a lot more questions, too," commented Jesse.

"Learning means questions," Bianca smiled. "No one, ever, has all the answers."

Jesse nodded and they continued with their meal. The sun was hot, but the giant Elm tree in the backyard nicely shaded the area where they sat. Joseph ate three sandwiches and Jesse scarfed down two. Realizing she was most generous with her leftovers, Max joined her on her side of the table. Jesse was comforted by his close proximity to her. She petted him regularly and loved the way his fur felt to her touch.

The food disappeared quickly and Bianca kept the conversation upbeat and light. She knew that it was important to keep Jesse from getting more depressed. She talked about the store and life in Littleton. Jesse felt happy in their company. Joseph even made her laugh with a few stories about the neighbors. When Bianca felt Jesse had gained enough of her spirit back, she looked over at Joseph, who read her thoughts. Bianca had tenaciously continued her entreaty for his help, gently, for most of the weekend. He had persistently denied her request for thirty-six hours, but finally acquiesced. He would answer some of Jesse's questions, but that was all. He finished his drink and set the empty glass down on the table with a thud.

"Lunch was good, woman. It's time to walk Max," he said resolutely. "Harless, you will come too!"

"Great idea," Bianca agreed. "I've got to get a few things done around the store. It'll be good to have you out of my hair for a bit."

Jesse smiled at their gentle repartee. She could easily see how much Bianca and Joseph loved each other. She had never experienced a relationship like that. She got up with Max who was jumping with excitement at her heels. "Can I help with the dishes?" she offered as Bianca gave her another hug.

"That's women's work," Joseph shouted, heading for the back gate. "You will come with us."

"Good Lord, man. Just remember who the real chief is around here," Bianca rejoined, still smiling. "Especially, if you ever want to eat again." She gently pushed Jesse on her way. "Go with him," she murmured to her. "You need to talk." She also added, so Joseph would be sure to hear her, "And don't let him sit down too much. He needs more exercise than that dog!"

Max was busy running back and forth between Joseph and Jesse in his zealous appeal for her to catch up. Jesse ran a bit to do so and Max ran with her. At the gate, Joseph was waiting with Max's leash and collar, which he firmly attached before they went out. The dog and Jesse frowned at the constraint.

"The city doesn't like wolf dogs running loose on the streets," Joseph declared. "Max knows the rules." With the collar and leash firmly attached to the dog's neck, the trio took off for the street. Any thoughts of a leisurely walk was quickly abandoned as Max strained against his tether. Joseph held firmly onto the leash and walked briskly with large steps. Jesse had to canter alongside him to keep up. When they got to the other side of the railroad overpass,

Joseph reigned Max in and made him heel at his side. He handed the leash to Jesse. "Here," he said to her. "You can take him."

Jesse looked into Joseph's eyes. They were filled with dark mischief. "Okay," she said tentatively, taking the large rope from his hand. "But...whoa!" Max took off dragging Jesse behind him. Joseph roared with laughter before taking up the chase behind them. The wolf dog knew where he was going and loped around the corner toward the park, with Jesse holding on for dear life. "Good God, Joseph!" she yelled out at him as he lagged behind. "Are we at least going the right way?"

"Just another block!" Joseph bellowed back at her. "You're almost there!"

Stern's Park was a couple of hundred feet up on the left. Once Max's paws touched the grass he slowed down to a crawl, smelling every inch of turf. Jesse nearly ran over him, surprised at the sudden stop. She was panting like a dog herself, trying to catch her breath, when Joseph caught up with them.

"You did good," he noted, giving her a pat on the back. "Good exercise for everyone."

"Joseph," Jesse wheezed, "the wolves I was reading about this morning..." she drew another breath, "...it broke my heart to learn what happened to them in the past. That's why I was so upset when you called."

"It still happens, Harless," Joseph answered. "And I am sad for it, too." He offered to take the leash back, but Jesse held on to it. She wasn't ready to give it up quite yet. Max was busy marking territory and was in no particular hurry to do it, so their run had finally settled down to a meandering walk. "I am sorry that you found out that way," the Indian continued. "But you must learn everything in order to understand. The wolf has not had an easy road since the white man came into his life."

"The book said things are getting better. That we've realized our mistakes and we're bringing these animals back."

"Not everyone reads books," Joseph emphasized. "Not enough people know about wolves to truly help. In the meantime, wolves are still hunted and slaughtered for irrational reasons."

"But why are they so hated?" Jesse asked. "They kill only what they need for the pack. The animals they kill are usually old or sick or very young. The pack is just a family, actually more so than most *human* families. They protect their young and they mate for life. What is so wrong with that? Why can't man understand?"

"Man hates the wolf because the wolf represents what man was created to be. Wolf lives by the Creator's laws. Man does not always choose to do so. I think man feels guilt when he looks at the wolf. If they were gone from the earth, there would be no standard to remind man of what he has done wrong."

"Then there is no hope," Jesse murmured. "And I cannot believe there is a God. God would not create such a magnificent creature and allow it to endure such pain."

"The Creator did not intend this to happen. Unfortunately, he did not know his people would become so greedy. Man has many weaknesses, but the worst, I fear, is his demand for domination. Man has forgotten, with all his inventions and progress, that he did not make the earth and the creatures that inhabit it. The white man has gone so far as to put this control into his Bible, as though the Christian God would say, *I give you this earth to subdue it for your own purpose.* No *God* would utter those words and we must remember the Christian God did not write the Christians' Bible. It was written by men who wanted His blessing to do as they pleased. Man's desire to control and rule will bring his downfall one day if he does not learn to share and live in harmony with all life—human or otherwise."

"I want to shoot every hunter and every politician with their own guns," Jesse snarled, her body tense as she walked.

"Then you will be no better," Joseph commented. "You must lose your hate. Negative energy, when transformed into positive energy, can be the most powerful of sources. Positive energy can educate those people who can change things. That is the way it must be done. There are more good souls than bad ones. Win the good souls over to your side and you will have a mighty force behind you." Joseph touched Jesse's shoulder with his strong hand. The tension ebbed from her frame.

"I deal with so much negativity," Jesse sighed. "I wouldn't know where to begin." Max, with a stick in his mouth, pranced back to Jesse and laid it at her feet. She dropped to her knees and gave the wolf dog a hug. He licked her on her cheek.

"You are weak now. Learn what you need so that you can grow strong. You have suffered, not unlike the wolves, but you have the ability to make it better. The answers will come and they will be good for you as well as the souls you touch."

Max was insistent with his stick. Although he enjoyed getting hugs, now he wanted to play. Joseph leaned over and removed his collar. The wolf dog jumped into the air and landed on splayed paws, his face beaming with excitement. Jesse picked up the stick and threw it hard. Max bounded after it with his fur rippling in the wind. "Should I trust you know my future, Joseph?" Jesse asked with a smile upon her lips. She watched the dog, not him.

"Your future is yours to make," Joseph answered. "Trust yourself and you will find the way."

A few days later, Eric snapped, "Jesse, have you heard a word I've said?"

"Huh?" Jesse looked up from her book and saw the frustration on her friend's face. They had gone to their favorite restaurant for lunch and were enjoying the shaded patio. Jesse had been intolerably rude, she suddenly realized, paying more attention to one of the books Joseph had given her rather than to her friend of ten years sitting across the table. "I'm sorry, Eric. My mind was someplace else."

"It's been that way all week," Eric scoffed. "I wish you'd get it back. I knew Wheland was going to cause trouble the minute I saw her at the club."

"Eric," Jesse pacified, "it's not her fault. I'm just trying to get myself out of this slump."

"Then you should have been listening to me," Eric retorted. "I said, I talked to Hobbs and I think I've convinced him to give you that promotion. You're the best person qualified for the general manager position and he knows it."

"That's great," Jesse sighed. "It would really help if I could get out from under Sterling's hooks." Jesse glanced casually at her friend. She could tell he had made up his mind that Hobbs would give her the promotion; and he was proud it was due to his own conniving. Eric was a good man, she thought to herself, as he rattled on about his conversation with the president of their company. He cared what happened to her and he wanted her to succeed. He did not like it when she was upset and, in his own way, would do just about anything to make her happy. Here he was, trying to fix things once more.

Unfortunately, Jesse was questioning whether the promotion was what she was really looking for. Seeing Bianca and Joseph so happy, doing what they loved, made her stop and think about it. She wished she could discuss it with Eric, but the mere mention of Bianca's name careened him through the roof these past few days. She could see why they didn't get along. They were two different people with two completely different mindsets.

"And I told him he'd be a damn fool to pass you over again."

Jesse tried to concentrate on what Eric was saying, but her thoughts kept wandering. She was tired of talking about work, nightclubbing and the latest fashion trends; or how the new guy Eric had just met was sure to be her Prince Charming, come to save her at last. Every night this week she had begged off going out and rushed home to her books. She was fixated on wolves and American Indian music and anxious to be a part of the powwow with Bianca and Joseph.

"Now, I was thinking, after Hobbs offers you the job and you accept, we'll need to go out and celebrate. Serengeti or Enoteca? Of course, we could always do both. I think I can get Mark, that guy I was telling you about, to come along. I think you'll really like him."

"Have you ever noticed," Jesse inquired, "how the word *wolf* has such a bad connotation in our language?"

Eric looked at her in amazement. "What?"

"Well, you're good with the ladies, so that makes you a *wolf*. We eat like *wolves*. He's a *wolf* in sheep's clothing. The *wolf* is at the door. We cry *wolf*. Were you raised by *wolves*? It's so strange when you learn what they're really like." Eric watched Jesse intently as she rambled. "Even the Bible, which bugs the hell out of me at the moment, says, *I send you forth, as sheep in the midst of wolves* and *after my departing shall grievous wolves enter in among you, not sparing the flock*. That really pisses me off."

Eric sat back in his chair and sighed. "Jess," he asked gently, "are you okay?"

Jesse didn't hear him. "And almost every damn fairy tale we learn as a child does it too—the *big bad wolf* that eats kids and grandmothers and blows down houses. Do you know that a *lone wolf* is one of the saddest creatures on this earth? Not some stud or some guy who's crazy. It just doesn't make sense to me."

"I don't know what to tell you," Eric offered. "I never really thought about it."

"That's the problem," Jesse said. "I don't think anybody's ever thought about it. Just like those proverbial sheep, they just accept it and pass it on. Man, that's sad."

The waiter brought the bill and Eric paid it. "Yeah, I guess it is." He got up and Jesse threw her book into her bag and followed him blindly, still off in her own little world. Eric was starting to show some concern. "You're reading up on wolves quite a bit, eh?"

"Yeah. I can't seem to get enough of them."

"Well, that's good, I guess," he said, thinking that if she didn't want to discuss other things, maybe it was best to play along. They left the restaurant and walked slowly down the street. "You're learning a lot?"

"It's helping for some odd reason. I guess when you find something that's suffered more than you could ever imagine, your problems don't seem so big any more." Jesse put her hand in the crook of Eric's arm as they strolled down the street.

"I've noticed you don't seem quite as frustrated and tired as you used to be. So, maybe this is a good thing. And, when the promotion comes, it'll be even better."

"I'm not losing it, Eric," she smiled, sensing the anxiety in Eric's voice. "I just need to do this right now, okay?"

"But can we still go out and celebrate? Or is your new hang out going to be the library?"

"We'll celebrate," she laughed. "And, I suppose I'll have to go shopping. New job means new clothes, right?"

"Yeah," Eric said, pleased. "Maybe I should get that new Armani suit I've had my eyes on…in *Timber Wolf* gray."

"That would be fabulous!" Jesse agreed, seeing the smile returning to her friend's face. "We'll knock 'em dead at the board meeting on Monday morning."

Back at work, Jesse concentrated on the latest stack of work piled atop her desk and tried not to think how Hobbs' and Sterling's conversation was going behind the closed doors of Sterling's office. The president had been quite jovial with her before he went in and she truly started to believe that Eric might have pulled it off. She had to snicker at the thought of how Sterling was going to accept losing the best assistant he ever had. How would he fare, essentially having to do his own work? She looked forward to his first major blunder, which would happen quite soon without her help.

Eric passed by a couple of times, giving her an encouraging wink. Some of the other staff members came by, too, quietly congratulating her on her big break. When the door to Sterling's office opened and the two men finally came out, Jesse smiled broadly at both of them. She quickly assumed the new stack of work in Sterling's hands was his last ditch effort to get a couple of things done before she left. She tried to remain calm, waiting for Hobbs to pull her aside and give her the news. His conversation with Sterling never seemed to end. Eventually, they decided on an upcoming lunch date and Hobbs turned toward Jesse and walked up to her desk.

"Jesse," he said, "I wanted to thank you for getting everything prepared for last week's meeting. As I'm sure you know, it was a complete success."

"Thank you, Mr. Hobbs," Jesse replied. "I was glad to do it."

"You and Sterling make a good team," he smiled, turning and heading toward his office. "Keep up the good work!"

Jesse's puzzled gaze followed the president as he walked down the hall. He gave no indication whether she was getting the promotion or not.

"Harless," Sterling bellowed, slamming the files on top of the work she was already doing, "this stuff needed to get out yesterday. You'll probably need to work a little late, but it's absolutely got to be done by Monday morning."

Jesse's eyes turned back slowly toward her boss. He stepped into his office and grabbed his coat, obviously leaving early for the day. While Hobbs' words were a bit confusing, there was no doubt now she had the job. Sterling had probably just handed her every project on his desk in a last ditch effort to get everything finished while he could still order her around. Without another word, he slithered down the hall and out the door.

Despite the stacks of paper on her desk, Jesse felt pretty good. This, she considered, would be the last night she would ever have to work late because she was ordered to. Next week, she'd finally be her own boss. She dove into the papers fervently and with her expertise and organizational skills she was out the door, ready for her weekend, by eight o'clock. Confident that her life was back on track, she changed and grabbed a quick bite to eat before leaving her flat. She met Eric at the club at ten, where she danced, drank and hobnobbed until midnight. She was safe at home and tucked in for a good night's sleep by twelve-thirty.

CHAPTER 4

On Saturday morning, Max greeted Jesse at the door to the shop and guided her into the kitchen where she found Joseph energetically cooking up bacon, eggs and hash browns while Bianca read the newspaper aloud to him as he worked. The mood was warm and animated with an air of excitement. Jesse noticed Joseph's colorful clothing hanging near the back door, adorned with beads and feathers. Drums and flutes were packed carefully in a large box, along with Joseph's journal and some papers. They enjoyed a hearty breakfast and Jesse listened as the pair bantered about the day's upcoming events. Glad to be a part of their circle, Jesse cleared the table and washed the dishes so Bianca and Joseph could finish the last of the preparations. She laughed when Max brought her his leash.

"Okay, I'm out of here," Joseph finally announced, tossing his outfit over his shoulder and grabbing his car keys. "You know where you're going, right?"

"Of course," Bianca answered, holding the door for him. "Down I-25 to Colorado Springs and hang a left. First group of Indians we see on the right over the hill."

Jesse looked at Bianca, confused. She didn't understand why they weren't all going together.

"Her tracking skills would make any chief proud," Joseph quipped to Jesse, seeing the quizzical look upon her face. He kissed Bianca quickly and gave Jesse a wink. "And don't lose my dog!"

"Be gone already," Bianca shouted after him before shutting and locking the back door. She walked over to the kitchen counter, grabbed her purse and her own set of keys. "My SUV's out front, so we'll go this way."

Jesse followed silently, still wondering about the driving arrangements. She carried a small cooler that Bianca had packed with some sandwiches and bottled water, and, of course, Max's leash. The wolf dog jumped at her heels in excitement. With the front door locked, the SUV loaded and Max in the back seat they were finally ready to go.

"It's about an hour's drive from here," Bianca announced, pulling away from the curb. "I brought some music I thought you might like to listen to."

"Great," Jesse said. She reached her hand back and rubbed Max's head when he started nuzzling her neck and hair from the back seat. When they got out on the open road, the wolf dog sat back in the seat and stuck his head out the window, enjoying the fresh air. "Looks like it's going to be a great day. I'm really looking forward to this."

"I'm glad," Bianca smiled. "I think you'll have fun. Joseph thinks there'll be a big turnout today. The more people, the more music and dancing."

"May I ask why we didn't drive down with Joseph?" Jesse asked hesitantly a few minutes later. "We are going to the same place, right?"

Bianca thought a moment before she answered. She had hoped Jesse might not ask that question, yet she was not surprised she did. It was not going to be easy to explain. "We have to drive separately," Bianca replied calmly, keeping her eyes on the road. "We've always had to do it this way."

"Does he have to stay longer or something?" Jesse offered as an attempt to solve the riddle herself.

"I wish it were that simple," Bianca said quietly. She turned down the music so that it wouldn't interfere with their conversation. "You see, Joseph is an American Indian. I am not. He is considered an Elder in his tribe and, therefore, he has a tremendous amount of responsibility to his people."

Jesse nodded, listening carefully.

"And because there's no easy explanation," Bianca continued with a sigh, "I'm just going to tell you what I can. Joseph's tribe frowns upon interracial relationships. He is expected to only be with an American Indian woman. Not a white woman."

"No way!" Jesse spouted. "You're telling me..."

"I'm telling you," she went on quickly, "he does not acknowledge me at powwows or any Native American events. Other than a few very close personal friends, his people do not know that I exist."

"But, how long have you guys been together?" Jesse was stunned. She was having trouble believing what she was hearing.

"Ten years, give or take a month or two," Bianca declared. "And it's been that way ever since the day we met."

"I guess I should understand this," Jesse commented. "But I didn't think that sort of thing went on any more. I mean, people of different races are always getting together nowadays."

"It may look like that, but believe me, every interracial couple has their own issues to deal with. Ours involves at least two hundred years of mistrust."

"Seeing you two together at the house," Jesse noted, "you're so happy. You can't tell me that you shouldn't be together."

"And I never would," Bianca retorted. "It hasn't been easy, Jess. We had a very rocky start. If it wasn't his *I'm the man don't question me* masculinity getting in the way, it was my feminist *don't even think of controlling me* attitude that almost tore us apart on more than one occasion. There were lots of fights and lots of tears and one of us walked out in a huff every couple of nights. Neither one of us wanted to give in, but we just weren't right when we were apart.

"So, we had to compromise. We had to learn about each other. We had to recognize and accept those beliefs that are important in our individual cultures and to our own people. The Indian customs are steeped in tradition and I now understand why they don't wish to share it with outsiders. Our ancestors committed so many atrocities against the Indian Nations. They forced them from their lands, either killing them or leaving them to starve or freeze to death. And, it wasn't just Indian *men* who were killed, but thousands and thousands of women and children were also mutilated and destroyed in brutal, unspeakable ways. If they weren't killed in attacks on their reservations, most of them perished when they were forced to travel thousands of miles to new territories that were deemed appropriate for them by the new government; and how many were wiped out by the white man's diseases? Sometimes it makes me sick to hear the words *the home of the free*, for it surely wasn't that way for the rightful owners of this land."

"So, is it fair," Jesse interjected, "that you be punished for something our ancestors did?"

"Hell no, honey," Bianca snickered. "My ancestors didn't get here until the early 1900's. My people were fighting rotten potatoes and an oppressive church while these people were being slaughtered. But that doesn't make it any better for us. We didn't get the facts when we got here. We were told what the history books had recorded—written by white men covering their tracks—and we didn't bother to question whether they were telling the truth. Christ, we had our own problems, just like every other immigrant who came to this country, and God forbid we should mention the black man and slavery."

"I often wonder," Bianca mused after a few moments of reflection, "which ethnic group, who decided to call themselves Americans, allowed all this to happen? Was it the Brits? The French? The Spaniards? I really have no clue, and because of that, I have no one to blame."

"Maybe it wasn't one race so much as it was one desire," Jesse offered. "Doesn't all this carnage come down to one concept that is traditionally accepted by almost every race—greed?"

Bianca raised an eyebrow. "Hmmm," she murmured, considering this statement. "And, when you think about it, maybe there should be two—greed and the desire for control."

"Well," Jesse smirked, "that's a male thing for the most part. So, then we could blame all the men."

"Okay," Bianca laughed and Jesse joined her.

"I mean, if you think about it," Jesse went on, "...the Indians were removed from their land so the *new* Americans could sell it or mine it to make money. The black man was sold into slavery, which made more money. The French Kings prospered while *their* oppressively taxed subjects starved. In the last century, the Germans took what wealth they could from the Jews, and despite what they say about the subjugated people in the Middle East, isn't it all about oil?"

"And the wolves were killed for bounties and the elephants were decimated for their ivory tusks," Bianca added.

"The list goes on, doesn't it?" Jesse sighed. "And we'll only get madder if we think about it. So, tell me more about Joseph. What happens when we get to the powwow?"

"Oh, yeah," Bianca remembered. "We were talking about something else, weren't we?" She took a deep breath and continued. "As an Elder in his tribe, Joseph has to follow certain rules. He is expected to be a role model, and above all else, pass on the traditions of his tribe.

"When the Americans came, the Indian Nations asked only for their sacred land and the preservation of their beliefs and their way of life. The Indians loved and respected their land. Because they did not abuse it, they preserved the richness of the soil and minerals and were blessed with an abundance of wild game for food and clothing. The white man, upon seeing this, envied it and wanted it for himself. Therefore, he contrived to get it by branding the Indians as *savages* because they did not believe in the *Christian* God. That ideology gave the white man a clear conscience to break the treaties, steal their land and the riches it bestowed. But *good* Christians knew they could not just kill the Indians and be done with them, so they herded them off to reservations. If they starved or were killed on the way to those reservations, well that was God's will and the white man did not have to feel accountable for what happened. Conveniently, those Indians who fought them could now be killed because they were *fighting* God's people and the establishment of a free America.

"Unfortunately, not all the Indians died, so the American Government still had an Indian *problem* on their hands. To solve it, they killed the buffalo; made sure the reservations were located on useless land; and then left them to fend for themselves. The Indians were neglected and ignored. They were left penniless with no means of support. There was no industry; no jobs they were trained for; and the reservation land was often times useless for farming. The American Indian Nations looked on as the rest of the country grew rich and expanded. Their people, once proud and free, fell to alcoholism and depression—other gifts from the white man. Their children left the reservations to try to make a better life. Very few of them succeeded because the history books had been written and Indians were still looked upon as the enemy, or in later years as drunk and lazy good-for-nothings.

"Slowly, as the truth of their existence has been revealed and the world has taken an interest in their cultures and their ways of respecting the earth, the tribes are now gaining a strength of purpose once more. Joseph knows that the continuation of his people depends on his generation and those who follow. They must learn to honor and remember their past and to be proud of their heritage."

"And a proud Indian man should have an equally proud Indian woman at his side, right?" Jesse commented. Max pulled his head in from the open window for a scratch when Jesse reached over the seat to get some bottled water from the cooler. Max licked her face.

"That's the general idea," Bianca agreed, taking the bottle Jesse gave her.

"I understand, but it's still sad," Jesse lamented.

"And sometimes it's not too easy for me, either. I am a strong woman, Jess. It took me just as much chutzpah to get where I am today as it did Joseph. I had obstacles to overcome, too. I know what Joseph has to do and I respect him for it. It's his as well as his peoples' honor that he fights for. For a long time I wanted to be a part of it, not to atone for my forefathers sins, but because I am one of the few white people who recognizes their situation and truly wants to help. Now I understand it has to be this way."

"Will we be welcome at the powwow?" Jesse asked, concerned.

"Oh, yes!" Bianca replied. "Please don't think otherwise. It's just that Joseph cannot acknowledge me and I must not talk to him while he's working. He leads the gourd dance and emcees the processional. The people are wonderful and they are happy that we attend. After all, they have vendors and beautiful things to sell. We won't be outcasts, but we won't be the star attractions, either."

"What about Max? Won't he want to run up to Joseph when he sees him?"

"Max has his own friends to keep him company," Bianca smiled. "You'll see when we get there. We've been going to these powwows for several years now and I've slowly made a few friends of my own. Like I said earlier, it all comes down to a matter of trust." Jesse sat back and mulled Bianca's words over in her mind.

Bianca turned the music up a little louder and gave Jesse some time to think. A few miles later, Jesse seemed to come to terms with Bianca's situation.

"So, tell me about this promotion," Bianca finally said, determined to keep the rest of the conversation light.

Jesse had no clue where they were, but Max did when Bianca turned off the pavement onto the dirt road. The wolf dog yipped and talked to his fellow passengers, pacing back and forth on the back seat.

"Okay, boy," Bianca said, smiling. "Give me a second to pull off over here." She wheeled the SUV to the side of the road and let the car and the truck behind her pass. Max clawed at the back of the front seat and the door. "Do me a favor, Jess," she said to her companion, with her foot firmly planted on the brake. "Hop out and open the back door, will you?"

"For what reason?" Jesse asked, looking dumbfounded. Still, she did as she was asked to do. Max bounded out of the car and sniffed the ground excitedly.

"Okay," Bianca shouted. "Hurry up and get back in!"

"Are you crazy?" Jesse yelled, still following orders. She jumped back in the SUV and slammed the door shut. Bianca hit the gas and pulled back on the road. Max jumped straight up into the air and with his tongue wagging followed the car in hot pursuit. Jesse craned her neck to look out the back window. There was Max, looking positively ecstatic, running in the cloud of dust behind them.

"It's his favorite part of the day!" Bianca called out, making sure not to drive too fast down the dirt road, although she knew she had to hit at least 40 mph to keep ahead of him. At 30 mph, Max loped alongside her, egging her on. "Don't worry! He'll stay right with us. He loves the chase!"

Jesse shook her head, smiling. She stuck her head out the window and kept an eye on him.

"He's done it since he was a pup," Bianca called over the roar of the engine and open windows. "We were camping once and he refused to get back in the car. Joseph took off, Max ran after the car, and he's insisted on doing it ever since."

"Well, he obviously loves it!" Jesse yelled. "And I have to admit, with my head out the window, it does feel invigorating."

"You'll be washing dirt out of your hair for days!" Bianca laughed. She drove about a mile before they had to slow down. The parking lot was just ahead. She picked a spot just inside the lot, away from the other cars. "We can use a little exercise ourselves," she said, turning off the ignition and removing the key. "That saves a closer space for somebody who might need it."

Jesse got out of the car and Max stretched up and placed his forepaws on her shoulders. Swirls of gravel dust encircled them. Bianca jumped out and went to the back of the SUV to get their supplies. She locked up the SUV and came around to them. Max didn't look overly happy at the sight of the leash.

"I'm afraid so, buddy," Bianca sighed. "Here Jess, can you put it on him?" Bianca was weighed down with the cooler and their bags.

"Yeah, right," Jesse said disbelievingly. She took the collar and leash from the top of the cooler and looked at Max. "Come on, boy," she moaned. "Mother says you have to." Max crouched down and splayed his paws in front of himself. There was a devilish guise on his face. Jesse took a step toward him and he was off like a shot, stopping just out of her reach. "Max..." Jesse warned the dog, taking another step. "Be a good boy!"

Bianca watched the proceedings without saying a word. She leaned the cooler against the side of the vehicle for a little extra support.

Max ran again, defiantly teasing the woman. "Shouldn't he be tired after that run?" Jesse asked, a little worn out after the excitement of the trip herself. What she would have loved to do was stretch out the kinks from the car ride, not chase the dog back home.

"Maybe when he gets older," Bianca smiled. "Obviously, that's a few years off."

Jesse turned back to the dog and thought for a second. She was resolved to complete the task at hand. "All right, then," she said with a stern tone. Max sat a few paces away, panting and giving her that big dog grin. "I guess I'll just have to go without you." She turned from the wolf dog and started walking away. Bianca looked intrigued at her method. "You stay!" Jesse called out behind her. Max cocked his head to the side and watched her inquisitively. He hadn't expected that command. He stood up on all fours and took a step toward her. "No!" Jesse snapped. "You stay!" She headed off toward the other cars. Max looked at Bianca, who looked at him and shrugged her shoulders as though she could not help. Then she started after Jesse. Both women heard the little whimper that he let out, thinking he was going to be left behind. Jesse stopped and turned back toward him. "Oh, all right, then," she scowled. "Come on."

Max bounded over to her where she bent down and gave him a hug. With his tail wagging and tongue licking her face, he was quite surprised to suddenly find the collar around his neck, firmly attached. Jesse took hold of the leash with one hand and helped Bianca with the other, taking one of the handles of the cooler. Problem solved, the threesome strolled through the parking lot to the entrance gate.

Once inside the dilapidated fenced enclosure, Jesse saw a plethora of amazing sights. There were hundreds of people in beautiful costumes and just as many more in shorts, jeans and baseball caps. Along the main walkway, she found card tables and makeshift booths covered with Indian jewelry, Indian artwork and crafts of every sort. She heard voices speaking an unknown language, greeting each other and relating the latest gossip. She could tell that by the hugs, handshakes and soft-spoken tones directed toward an eagerly bent ear. Beautiful children with long black hair darted in and around the grownups. A woman, clad in beaded buckskin, played a wooden flute. Some faces beamed with laughter and gaiety, while other faces were stoic and cautiously observant. Through it all, she heard the steady beat of drums somewhere in the distance, beckoning to them, enticing them, and welcoming them to the powwow.

They walked toward the music, through the makeshift market, and up a gentle slope that was just steep enough to keep them from seeing what was on the other side. At the top of the hill, they stopped. Down below there was a beautiful sight. Throngs of Native American men, dressed in every color of the rainbow, stepped and danced in a myriad of interweaving circles. Their moccasin covered feet moved in tune with every beat. The smaller circles of dancers were bordered by a bevy of Native American women, who danced in a large circle around them. There were several men in different groups beating a wide array of ancient drums. Others played rattles, rainmakers and many other instruments that Jesse could not name. Some were chanting, others whooped and howled. All together they created a powerful song and Jesse was immediately entranced.

Bianca tugged gently on her side of the cooler to grab Jesse's attention. She indicated with a nod of her head as to where they were going. Stepping gently on the clumps of dirt and soft sand, they walked about halfway down the hill and made a sharp turn to the left. Bianca found a shady spot big enough for their belongings, where they put down the cooler and Bianca spread out a large blanket for them to sit on. Jesse poured some water into a bowl for Max. They settled in and watched the performance in silence. Max lay down next to Jesse. With his head placed on his outstretched front paws, he too watched the people—his master, Joseph, most keenly. Joseph stood tall above the dancers and musicians, announcing each group and their chief performers. He talked to the crowd, telling stories, jokes and explaining the events as they came up. Other times he joined one of the drum groups and beat on one of the larger lead drums (called mother drums by the Indians).

Jesse tried to see it all, but it was hard as there was so much to look at. She noticed a young man—his muscular, tanned arms and chest glistening with beads of sweat and his black hair shining in the sun—who left the dancers and walked slowly up the hill toward them. His eyes were locked onto Bianca. He said no words, but nodded to her as he passed by. She nodded back surreptitiously and smiled before returning her gaze back to Joseph.

Jesse could see that Bianca and Joseph looked at each other often, even though they were a distance apart. She thought about telling Bianca she was onto the small fib she had told her earlier regarding their mutual anonymity; for it was quite obvious from her viewpoint that Joseph acknowledged Bianca every time he cast his eyes in her direction. But Jesse decided not to, because she didn't want to break their spell. She enjoyed her furtive glimpse into their private world. Instead, she reached for a sandwich and another bottle of water. She leaned back against Max, sharing bits of her sandwich with the wolf dog, and let Bianca and Joseph take pleasure in their clandestine time together.

Max decided to take a nap after lunch. With her belly full, a soft breeze in the air and the steady rhythm of the drums, Jesse found it hard to keep her own eyes open. She had just started to give into her drowsiness when a strange voice came from somewhere behind them.

"White Fox, Dustu waits for you. He was afraid you did not come."

Jesse's eyes shot open to see Bianca look behind her and smile. "Now I told him I would be here, David. Have I ever broken a promise?" Bianca got up slowly and greeted the young man with a warm hug.

"So this is Waya, then?" David looked down at Jesse, who hurried to get up herself.

"This is Jesse, David," Bianca announced. "And Jesse, this is David. He and his father are two of the friends I know here."

"Hi!" Jesse said.

"Hello, Jesse," David smiled. Max was up, also greeting David. The young man bent down, took Max's head into his hands and rubbed his fur vigorously. "And here is our good boy!" Then he stood up and started back up the hill. "Come see father. He wants to meet Waya."

Perplexed, Jesse looked at Bianca, who gave her a wink and ushered her on ahead. They fell in behind the young man and walked briskly up the hill. At the top, sitting in a plastic lawn chair like a king on his thrown, sat David's father, Dustu. His face was weathered, but he watched them approach with clear, sharp eyes. His hair was gray and as long, if not longer than Joseph's. He wore jeans, cowboy boots and a western cut vest. Around his neck was a beaded elk horn necklace. Sitting next to him was a purebred, grown wolf.

The sight of the animal fascinated Jesse. Its golden eyes watched her as well. Max attempted to spring away from her to run on ahead. She almost lost hold of his leash. Bianca, right behind her, touched Jesse on the arm and said softly, "Let him go, it's all right."

Max bounded up the hill and ran smack dab into the wolf. Jesse groaned, fearing they might start to fight. But the wolf held his ground and let Max roll around him. The dog licked the wolf's face and crouched down in front of the animal in a submissive stance. The wolf, still keeping one eye on the people coming nearer, put a front paw down on Max's chest. Max whimpered and stretched his leg up, placing a paw on the wolf's face. Jesse started for them in an effort to stop a quarrel, but she stopped short when she realized they had actually begun to play.

"You are right, White Fox, you have found Waya," the old Indian said. "She has the wolf's eyes."

"Dustu!" Bianca called out, trudging to the top of the hill and over to the man to whom she gave a quick hug. He patted her arm with his hand. "Why didn't you call down to us? We were sitting right down there."

"I know," Dustu said. "I have been watching you...and the circle."

"Well, we would have come up and sat with you. I'm surprised Matsi didn't come say hi." She looked over at the animals, who were now playing in earnest. The wolf, Matsi, was much larger than Max and therefore had the upper hand. Jesse, attempting to pay attention to the human conversation, was obviously more interested in the animals' game.

"Matsi waited here, too," Dustu explained. "We *all* were watching."

"Oh," Bianca murmured, realizing what was up. She sat down in another lawn chair, provided by David. She followed Dustu's gaze and saw he was still watching Jesse. "So, what do you think?" she finally asked.

"I say yes," Dustu commented. "It will be a good match."

Jesse, who had been crouching near the animals, looked up and was startled to see Bianca, Dustu and David watching her. "What?" she asked dubiously. At that moment, Max rolled over and onto her. He tugged on her jeans and tried to pull her into the fracas.

Dustu waved his hand and summoned her closer. "Waya, come here! We will talk." Suddenly recognizing that it was she he was addressing when he said *Waya*, Jesse looked a bit disappointed. She wanted to spend more time with the wolf. "There will be time for that," the Indian said, noticing her quandary. "Come here now." Jesse got up and sat on the ground between Dustu and Bianca. Her golden eyes fixed on his coal black ones. "You feel for these animals," he continued. "They call to your spirit."

"Yes," Jesse murmured quietly. She felt a bit intimidated by the older man. Like Joseph, he was not quick to smile.

"Matsi is pure wolf," the man explained. A soft breeze came up and ruffled his hair. "He does not frighten you?"

"Oh, no!" She exclaimed. "I think I make him nervous and I am sorry for that."

"He is wary, that is all."

"And that I understand."

"You have learned about the wolf?"

"I'm reading books about them," she stated. "These animals are truly amazing."

"Yes," the Indian agreed. "They are the Creator's finest work." He took Jesse's hands into his own and held them firmly, palms up. He looked at them closely and then looked back into Jesse's questioning eyes. "If you want this, and it appears you do, go to Matsi. Touch your first wolf."

Jesse's eyes grew wide and she hesitated momentarily. Then, she got up slowly, walked over to the wolf and sat down again on her knees with her arms open. The wolf stepped up to her, sniffed a couple of times and then simply started to lick her face. Her heart racing with joy, Jesse smiled and let the wolf continue. She carefully placed her hands on the ruff of his neck and kneaded her fingers into his fur. The wolf came closer and she was able to hug him and feel his fur upon her face. Max crouched down beside them, waiting for his turn. After introductions were complete, Jesse petted Max, too.

"All right," Dustu called out after a while. He rose slowly from his chair and beckoned Jesse to join him with another wave of his hand. "There is one more to meet." Jesse got up and was thrilled when the wolf and Max followed her. They walked over to Dustu, who was now standing by a card table. A sheet was draped over the table and covered it to the ground. Dustu indicated for Jesse to get down on her knees again in front of the table. When she was settled, he raised a corner of the sheet so Jesse could see what was underneath. There, huddled in the back corner, was a solid black wolf pup.

Jesse's breath caught in her chest when she saw the quivering bundle of fur. The wolf pup tried to inch back further into the sheet. "Oh, my God!" Jesse whispered, afraid of startling it further. "It's a baby!"

"His parents were killed by poachers," said David, who had joined them. "This one's the last of a litter of five. We raised them, with the help of Matsi, and found safe places for all of them except this one. He's a little skittish, especially since his brothers and sisters are gone."

"Can I hold him?" Jesse asked, wanting desperately to get closer. She moved cautiously just under the table.

"You can try," David offered. "He's pretty scared." He pulled a dog biscuit out of his jeans pocket. Both Matsi and Max sniffed the air with interest. "Here, try this; sometimes he'll eat it."

"If it's okay," Jesse suggested quietly, taking the biscuit, "could you guys all step back? I just want to sit here with him for a minute. Maybe there's too much action with everybody around."

David took hold of Max and Matsi, and Dustu followed them to rejoin Bianca, a few yards away, where they all sat down to watch.

Jesse crawled under the table, curled herself up and tried to appear as small as possible. She then pulled the sheet back down, so that she was alone with the pup. "There's a good boy," she murmured in a soothing voice. "Your den is safe." She lay on her side, still trying to appear small. She stayed close to the ground, so the pup could see her eye to eye. "It's okay," she muttered softly. "I'm a friend." The little black pup, hearing her calm breathing, lay down cautiously on all fours and watched her carefully. His shivers faded, as he grew used to the sound of her voice.

She slowly loosened the grip on the dog biscuit and showed it to him, still whispering in an encouraging voice. The pup inched closer, sliding his belly across the ground. His eyes moved from the biscuit in her hand up to her eyes and back several times before he got close enough to take it. He didn't grab it from her, but ate it right from her hand. He licked her palm clean when he had finished.

Still lying down, Jesse moved her hand and scratched his tiny head with her fingers. He inched a little closer so she could scratch his back. Soon after, the pup was up and sniffing her. Eventually, he snuggled in close against her chest and she let him chew on her fingers. She breathed down on his head and held him close against her chest so he could feel her heartbeat. Within a few minutes, he was playing, as any puppy would, pawing at her and nipping at her arms when she hid her face; wrestling with strands of her hair; jumping on her and giving her plenty of licks. When she gently rolled a little way out from under the table, the puppy stopped and whimpered. But when she patted her legs and called to him encouragingly, he cautiously stepped out, still half covered by the sheet. She scooped him up in her arms and gave him a kiss on the snout. He reciprocated with lick after lick upon her face. She held him close and he nuzzled in her long brown hair, biting the fine strands when he got wrapped up in them.

Slowly Jesse rose to her feet, still holding the little wolf. He weighed about fifteen pounds. He sank into her arms and hid his face under her armpit at first, but as she walked carefully back to Bianca and the others, his little head popped up and he peeped over Jesse's arm warily. The safer he felt, the bolder he became. His little neck was stretched up high and within seconds he was observing everything around him.

"See how he grows, father," David said, smiling as Jesse approached with her prize. "His blue eyes are looking greener."

Bianca got up from her chair and joined Jesse where she stood. She offered her hand for the puppy to smell and then scratched his little head. "He's got to be the most precious thing I've ever seen," she cooed.

Jesse smiled and held the pup a little closer. "The *most* precious," she agreed.

"Waya," Dustu summoned Jesse to his side, "you make a good mother. My wife was like that. She was good at befriending the little ones." Jesse got down on her knees again when she got to Dustu's chair. He petted the wolf gently. "He has no future here, Waya. Matsi has not watched over him like he did over the other pups. The little one has bonded with you like no other. I give him to you so he may live to see many more years than he would if he stayed here. Do you accept?"

"Oh," Jesse stammered, taken aback. "I..." She lived in the city with a job that didn't give her much time to spend at home. There was no place for him to run. Eric would have a stroke. Her life would have to change radically. But, holding the puppy in her arms with his eyes so full of wonder when he looked up at her, she made up her mind quickly. She'd figure out a way. There was no other place for him, except in her arms. Other city folk had dogs. There was no reason she could not have one, too. "Of course I accept. This is a great honor."

"This is good," Dustu smiled. "David, bring to Waya the pup's things."

"What do I feed him?" she asked, suddenly realizing she needed information about the care and feeding of this animal.

"He's eight weeks old and we've started him on puppy chow and raw meat," David offered, bringing over a box. "There's a book in here that will explain that and the other joys of owning a wolf. And I'm sure White Fox can help too. She's done a good job with Max."

Jesse sighed, a little relieved.

"His blanket is in here and there's a toy he plays with."

"And keep anything you don't want destroyed well out of his reach," Bianca added, coming up behind her. "He'll be a pistol to train, I'm sure."

"Good God," Jesse murmured under her breath. She had expected to buy a trinket or two while she was at the powwow, but she had never imagined something like this. Her head was swimming with good as well as terrified thoughts.

"So you found someone to take the pup," Joseph's voice startled everyone, especially Bianca and Jesse. He walked up to Jesse and the little wolf, while an entourage of musicians and dancers stopped and waited for his return. He took it from Jesse's arms for a moment and held it in the air, perusing it carefully. "Fine animal. He'll probably top Matsi in size," he commented after giving the animal the once over. The Indian gave the puppy back to Jesse. It immediately climbed onto Jesse's shoulder and clung fast, hiding his face in her hair. "What name will you give it?"

Jesse thought for a second before she replied, "Shadow. 'Cos that's what he looked like against that white sheet when I first saw him under the table."

"Welcome Shadow," Joseph said kindly. "You are a lucky pup." He turned abruptly and rejoined his group. They disappeared into the crowd as quietly as they had suddenly appeared. Jesse could see that Bianca was baffled by the encounter.

The women stayed with Dustu for the rest of the afternoon. David and Bianca retrieved her cooler and blanket. They ate the rest of the sandwiches and drank plenty of water. Dustu and Bianca conversed while Jesse fed all three of the animals morsels of her food. Matsi and Max behaved themselves with the pup, who growled at them at first from the safety of Jesse's lap. After their meal, when the older wolves were off exploring the grounds, Shadow crawled timidly from the safety of Jesse's arms and found a place to relieve himself.

"Good boy!" Jesse called out, which brought the puppy tumbling back to her. In her lap once more, he settled down and took a nap.

When the sun started to set, after David and Dustu had helped the girls carry their possessions to Bianca's SUV, Bianca and Jesse headed for home. Everybody was tired. Max passed out from exhaustion in the back seat and Shadow slept soundly in Jesse's protective clutches. The girls chatted a bit about the day and the surprises they had encountered, such as Jesse's first sight of Shadow under the table and the fact that Joseph had actually spent a moment with them when he checked the pup out. But soon the conversation faded and they spent the rest of the trip enjoying the music while watching the twilight sky turn to night.

In Littleton, Bianca loaded Jesse's car with a baby crib, more food, a collar, leash and other items that had kept her from going insane when Max was a pup, before letting Jesse drive back to Denver. It was rather hectic, but after several trips up the elevator and a final walk with Shadow around the block, Jesse and her new puppy were finally settled in the condo. It wasn't long before Jesse realized her life was going to change whether she liked it or not. Looking down at the sleeping wolf pup in the crib next to her bed, she had to admit—at that point—she liked the idea a lot.

CHAPTER 5

"Oh, Jess," Eric sighed as Shadow crawled all over him on the couch. It was plainly evident that the young man found the little bundle of fur to be quite intolerable, especially as it nibbled and slobbered on his designer jeans and shirt. Unfortunately, this wasn't evident to the wolf pup, who was enjoying this new human. "I can't believe you did this!"

"Isn't he just the cutest thing?" Jesse called out from the bedroom. At the sound of her voice, Shadow stopped in mid-play and pricked his ears toward the other room. "And he's such a good boy. He slept right through the night once I put his blanket in the crib with him. David said it reminds him of his mother. It must be the scent or something."

"Adorable," Eric said sarcastically. "I'm sure every guy in Denver will be vying for your attention with this little attraction next to your bed."

"Eric," Jesse smirked, coming into the living room. Shadow jumped off the couch, fell on his hind end and scrambled across the wood floor to her, claws clicking and scratching into the polished wood finish. "I'm really not looking for a new *man* in my life. How many times do I have to tell you that?"

"I get the message now," he stated. "And I suppose shopping for a new outfit is out, unless they've started carrying Chanel at Petsmart."

"I hope you don't mind," Jesse apologized. "It's going to be hard enough leaving him all day tomorrow while I'm at work." She scooped the wolf pup off the floor and into her arms. Shadow covered her face with licks and Eric crinkled his nose, grimacing as he got up from the couch. "Why don't you go to the park with us?" she asked.

"Oh, yeah. I want to do that." Eric walked over to the table and grabbed his car keys. "How about I go shopping and if I find you something fabulous, I'll just pick it up for you. That way you can go pick up dog shit; and I can pretend you've got a cold and need to rest, and our life will be back the way it was, tomorrow."

"Don't be doing that. I've got plenty of stuff to wear," Jesse laughed. "And everything *is* normal. There's just a new addition to the family. Be happy for me, okay? 'Cos, for the first time in a long time, I'm feeling pretty good."

"I can see that," Eric admitted, giving her a quick kiss on the forehead. Shadow licked his face when he leaned in close to her. "Damn," Eric growled. "Does it have to be so friendly?" He found it difficult to ignore the little devil as it looked eagerly into his eyes. He relented and scratched its head before heading for the door.

"Think of it this way," Jesse smiled, "the next time you want to pick up a gorgeous little Goth chick, she'll just melt into your arms when you tell her you've got a real live wolf."

Eric raised an eyebrow, considering the new ploy. "Hey, maybe we could sneak him into the Church tonight."

"Why don't you just throw a party at your place instead," Jesse countered.

"It's *your* decor that attracts *that* crowd." He gave her one of his gloriously wicked glares. "That damn dog isn't going to destroy my place. It's bad enough that he'll probably trash yours." Eric let himself out.

Shadow whimpered quietly when Eric disappeared. "It's okay, puddin'," Jesse cooed, giving the wolf a squeeze. "He'll be back." She put him down on the floor and went to the kitchen. Shadow bounced alongside her, nipping at her shoes as she walked. "Let's get you some food and then we'll go out. I've got to get a ton of newspapers, 'cos Uncle Eric's right. You're probably going to make a mess when I'm gone."

Shadow gulped down a can of puppy food and Jesse munched on a piece of toast before they headed out for their third walk that morning. It was just a couple of blocks down to North Platte where there was a stream and some grass for Shadow to explore. Not being the athletic type, Jesse had never ventured to this part of town, so it took a while before both she and the puppy got used to the bike riders and runners who were traversing the asphalt bike path. She was surprised at all the people, especially girls, who stopped to visit with the wolf pup. She had to remember to inform Eric of her new discovery. She figured she'd have a pet sitter in no time when he realized what a chick-magnet her little wolf was.

Shadow took to the car easily. He liked sitting in Jesse's lap and looking out the window as she drove. They went over to Petsmart and picked up a cartload of food, some chew bones and any toy that Shadow showed interest in. The wolf got plenty of attention at the store, too. All the clerks spent a little time with him and asked Jesse all sorts of questions. Shadow loved the fuss and was presented with a handful of free dog biscuits at the checkout counter. After another potty-break, Jesse drove down to Washington Park and they walked around the lake. Shadow strained at his leash, engrossed with all the geese and ducks. At fifteen pounds, Jesse found him a handful. She would definitely have to get him trained before he got much bigger, she thought. He was a little wary of the other dogs in the park, for some of them barked at him. But for the most part, everybody got along. Jesse could tell how badly Shadow wanted out of his leash and collar, so she piled him back in the car and drove to Littleton.

Bianca, Joseph and Max were at home and welcomed them gladly. Bianca made lunch while Joseph, Jesse and Max played with the wolf pup in the backyard.

"You see how the pup rolls on his back when he plays with Max?" Joseph queried as Bianca came out with a tray of sandwiches. "He's being submissive to the bigger dog."

"Yes," Jesse said, smiling at Bianca while taking one of the sandwiches from the tray. "I have read about that."

"Some day," Joseph continued, "it'll be Max who will be submissive to the pup. It is difficult to explain the hierarchical structure within a wolf clan. Much depends on their personality."

"How many times have *we* gone for a walk so far?" asked Bianca, sitting down at the picnic table. Joseph grabbed another sandwich and took a seat.

"Three times before we went to the pet store," Jesse sighed. "He's got quite a bladder."

"How happy are you in your condo?" Joseph asked between bites. "Perhaps you might think about a house with a backyard."

"Already doing that," Jesse answered, joining them at the table. "I love my condo, but it's not very wolf friendly. Shadow's not going to like being shut up in there all day long and I'm not going to be too thrilled cleaning up the mess he makes."

"You bought that place over ten years ago, right?" Bianca queried. "Right about the time I left the firm, as I recall."

"Yeah, I got it for a great price. With the market as it is I could probably triple what I paid for it."

"Well, you could keep it as a rental, in case you ever want it back," Bianca suggested. "There are lots of cute little houses out here."

"We'll see what kind of raise I get with the new promotion," Jesse said. "Then I'll have a better idea of what I can afford."

"When do you hear about the promotion?" Bianca asked, looking slightly concerned.

"Hopefully, tomorrow," Jesse answered. "Staff meetings are on Monday mornings." She took another bite of her sandwich. "With the new job, things will be a lot easier. I'm not sure if the stress will be any less, but at least I'll be away from Sterling. I'll finally have normal hours with very little overtime and I can start living a normal life." She looked over at Shadow, who was chewing on Max's ear, and smiled. "…If you can call having a wolf puppy normal. You know, I don't think I would have taken him if this opportunity hadn't come up. I couldn't have given him the attention he's going to need."

"I hope it all works out for you." Bianca cast a glance at Joseph.

"After lunch we will go to the park," Joseph stated, changing the subject. "It's never too early to start training."

Jesse wasn't extraordinarily upset to find out the staff meeting had been postponed for a week when she arrived at work the next morning. Hobbs had taken an early morning flight to New York to follow up on another new client and best of all for Jesse, he had taken Sterling with him.

She took advantage of her boss's absence. With no one peering over her shoulder or throwing more work at her, she was finally able to get caught up and clear her desk. She went home for lunch and took Shadow for a nice long walk. She left at five on the dot and was pleased to find that the wolf had made very little in the way of a mess. She changed the newspapers in the bathroom where she had put him for the day, fed him and they took another walk. That evening, with Shadow curled up in her lap, she read more and studied what her wolf was all about.

The next two days were uneventful, which lulled Jesse into a false sense of confidence that everything was going to work out. But on Thursday it all began to fall apart. Sterling returned with a vengeance, giving her more work than he'd ever given her before. Suddenly, there were new projects she had no idea how to complete with time constraints that were totally out of line. She did her best to keep up, trying to focus on the fact that soon this nightmare would be behind her and she would be out of Sterling's clutches. But the stress was horrible, and by Friday night, she was at her wits' end.

Unable to get home for lunch and stuck at the office until seven, Jesse was afraid of what she would find when she got home. When she got there, there was a message taped to the front door from the condominium manager complaining about the noise. Visibly shaking, she had trouble getting the key into the lock and when she finally opened the door, she could have cried. Shadow had wreaked havoc in the condo. Somehow he had opened the bathroom door and done his best to tear the place apart. Jesse wanted to scream at the pup when she found him in the bedroom chewing on one of her designer shoes, but when he looked up and his blue eyes met hers, she couldn't utter a word. The little wolf was very upset and quite scared. He cowered in the corner and whimpered; his huge paws grasping at the shoe like it was a security blanket.

"Oh, my poor baby!" Jesse sighed, carefully walking over to him. She fell to her knees and started to panic when he tried to get away. She scooped Shadow up into her arms and held him close. He was shaking like he did when she first saw him under the table at the powwow. "It's all right," she soothed. "I'm so sorry, Shadow. Mama's home now. Everything's going to be okay." She rubbed her head against his and rocked him gently in her arms. It was a good ten minutes before he finally calmed down and cautiously licked her face.

That night, when they finally lay down, Jesse let Shadow sleep with her on the bed. She was scared of what she'd gotten herself into. She was even more afraid, because she had almost screamed at the puppy and destroyed whatever trust she had instilled in him. She did not sleep well that night, but she made sure that Shadow did.

That weekend, Jesse did not go into the office to finish her work. She did not talk to Eric or Bianca. She spent every minute with the wolf and showered him with attention. She made a promise to herself and to the wolf that he would never again be affected by the stress in her life. She dreaded Monday morning and the week ahead. She did not know what she was going to do, but whatever she did, she wanted to keep her wolf. She had to count on that promotion. Everything would fall into place once the new job was set.

Early Monday morning, Bianca Wheland seemed groggy when she answered her door, but not totally surprised to see Jesse with Shadow in her arms. Bianca took the puppy, happy to baby-sit, and sent Jesse off to work with a hot cup of coffee and a homemade blueberry muffin.

At the office, Eric greeted Jesse with whispers of encouragement and a promise that the new position was going to be announced at the staff meeting. Sterling jumped on her case for not finishing the reports he wanted and made sure everyone in the office knew he was displeased with her performance. Jesse let him rant and rave, knowing it was a last ditch effort to save his own job. He would be singing another tune soon enough, once Hobbs realized it was she who had been doing all of Sterling's work.

Eric had saved her the seat beside him in the boardroom. He also cut Sterling off when the man came in bent on telling the other board members about Jesse's incompetence. Hobbs entered a few minutes later, apparently oblivious to Sterling's tirade, and called the meeting to order.

For two hours, Jesse fidgeted and tried to appear interested in what was being discussed. They talked about the New York clients they were schmoozing and the new business Eric had helped to bring in two weeks ago. The budget was picked over and there was a good forty-five minutes spent on the possibility of expanding the offices to make more space. Jesse joined in where she could and it seemed Hobbs was pleased with her remarks. She scribbled on her pad of paper and took notes on the items that she would be responsible for in the future. Finally, the discussion turned to office reorganization and the creation of Jesse's new position.

She was made for it. The job description fit her to a tee. She smiled at Eric when he gently squeezed her knee as Hobbs rambled on about all the aspects he carefully considered before making his final decision as to who was the right person for the job. She was positively beaming while Hobbs described the person who was to be his choice—always makes deadlines, takes on more than their share of work. It came down to the name and Jesse held her breath. No more late nights. No more Sterling. Her hard work was finally paying off. She was getting the promotion she deserved.

When Hobbs said the name, Jesse was about to correct him; for her name was Harless, not Harold. Luckily, she stopped herself at the last second when she looked up and saw Brian Harold getting up from his seat and shaking Hobbs' hand. She looked at Eric and saw that he was not smiling. Actually, she had *never* seen that particular look upon his handsome face. It took a minute for the reality of the situation to sink in. But it hit her like a bullet when she saw the sardonic grin appear on Sterling's austere face.

With a flurry of congratulations and kudos to Harold, the meeting was over and the boardroom emptied out. It appeared the boss was taking Brian to lunch. Eric slammed his laptop shut and stormed out of the room after Hobbs. Sterling threw a file down at Jesse, but she did not hear what he said. She looked at the file and then she looked at him. Still smiling, he turned his back to her and walked out with the president.

As though in a dream, Jesse walked back to her office. She heard snippets of comments coming from her fellow workers as she passed by. Stuff like, *I'm sorry* and *that was your job, we all knew it.* Somebody was saying that Sterling was the one who convinced Hobbs that Harold should get the job. Somebody else said, *that fucking bastard.*

Oddly enough, Jesse didn't care what they were muttering. She went into her office, shut the door behind her and sat down at her desk. She leaned back in her chair and started to cry. Not for the job or the promotion, but for the fact that she was going to lose her wolf. She couldn't make him live in a condo. She couldn't let him grow up in a city. She couldn't come home to him tired and stressed out. He deserved a better life than that. A life she could not give him if things stayed the way they were.

She called Human Resources and told the secretary she was going home sick. She picked up her purse and walked out of the office. She got into her car and sped off. Soon she was in Littleton, holding her wolf and crying as Bianca held her.

CHAPTER 6

"I can't tell you what to do," Bianca said, giving Jesse a cup of tea. "I under-stand that not getting that job is a setback, but I don't think it's so bad you can't keep him. People with jobs have pets, Jesse."

"Not wolves," Jesse hiccupped, drying her tears. "I've only had Shadow a lit-tle over a week, but I can tell he's not going to be happy sitting home waiting for me all day. And he'll never get the exercise he needs with a walk around the block."

"He's just a puppy," Bianca offered. "He'll understand in time."

"A wolf puppy," Jesse corrected her. "And he won't. Shit. The manager is already complaining about the noise he makes. I can't let him run loose in the park. He's getting bigger every day and soon the condo is even going to be cramped."

"Then get a house with a yard like we have."

"Can I build a fence tall enough to keep him inside the yard? Or deep enough so he can't dig under it?" Jesse sighed, exasperated. "I've been reading everything I can get my hands on, Bianca. He'll never be a dog. He's a wolf. And wolves don't belong in the city."

"Then bring him here like you did this morning. We don't mind and Max loves his company." Bianca looked nervously out the window. She was praying for Joseph to get home so he could help talk some sense into the girl. "He's got the yard to run around in and Joseph can take him for his walks."

"Then he'll become your wolf. He'll end up resenting me for taking him back to the city every night." Jesse was distraught. Shadow bumbled up to where she sat, tripping over his paws. He presented her with a chew toy, hoping she would play. She smiled sadly at him and picked up the toy. It squeaked and

Shadow tried to crawl up her leg and onto her lap to get it. She tossed it gently into the hallway and Shadow bounded happily after it. "Oh, Bianca," she sighed, the tears welling up again in her eyes. "I don't want to lose him, but I just can't see a way out."

"Let's just calm down," Bianca suggested, "and get through the rest of the week. We'll take him during the day and then this weekend we'll look at the alternatives. I could start looking at some houses for you while you're at work. I agree—it's time you both got out of the city."

"That's easy for you to say," Jesse retorted. "You've already got a house and you've got a man to take care of it. All I know is how to type. I don't know what to do with a house. You've got your dream job and can be calm and relaxed. I hate my job. I'm absolutely miserable. Now, add an hour's worth of traffic to the picture every morning and every night and I'll shoot myself within a month." She was mad that Bianca kept looking at the bright side of all this. She had no skills to start her own business. She had no idea what in the hell she wanted to do. Nobody was going to be able to help her. She had to fix this herself.

She got up and took Shadow's leash off the table. "I know what I have to do," Jesse finally declared. The tears, welling up again, blurred her vision. "Some of the books I've been reading have talked about wolf refuges. I think this weekend I'll be taking him there. There's one just outside of Black Mountain."

"Jesse, please," Bianca begged, "just wait until Joseph gets home. I know we can come up with a better solution." She followed Jesse into the hall. "Joseph will know what's best."

Jesse picked Shadow up and he snuggled against her, licking the tears off her face. "Thanks for letting me keep him here during the day. It'll just be 'til the end of the week." She walked out the door and hurried to her car. She pretended not to hear Bianca calling after her. With Shadow safely in the front seat, Jesse headed home.

"I told that bastard just what I thought about his asinine decision in front of everybody right there at lunch," Eric fumed, pacing back and forth in Jesse's living room. "Sterling was pissed as hell, but I didn't let up." Jesse sat on the couch, stroking Shadow's fur as he slept contentedly in her lap. She was exhausted and didn't give a damn what Eric was saying, but she kept up a brave face and allowed him to continue.

She had ignored the anxious messages he had left on her recorder that afternoon after she had left the office. Unfortunately, she had not thought about the fact that he had a key and would come over, anyway. For an hour he had regaled her with the story of how he stood up for her and would not rest until she got the promotion she deserved.

"It was Sterling who talked him out of it," Eric continued, taking a swig of the bourbon he had helped himself to when he got there. "He told Hobbs you didn't want the job and that you preferred working with him. Hobbs feels really bad about it. I'm telling you it's going to work out."

"That's not fair to Brian," Jesse said quietly. "He probably deserves it more than I do."

"Damn it, Jess!" Eric snapped. "Get out of this funk. You've got to stand up for yourself and take control of this situation. You've got to decide what you want and don't give up until you get it."

"What I want is to keep Shadow," Jesse murmured. "But I can't do that. Without him, I don't give a damn what they do to me at that fucking job."

"I think you've made the best choice," he tried to pacify her. "Shadow will be with his own kind at this refuge place you told me about. And he'll be happier there. It's best for everybody in the long run."

"Then why do I feel sick to my stomach?" she moaned. "I feel like I'm letting everybody down."

"That guy should never have given him to you," Eric added. "He was the one that screwed things up." Eric took another drink. "Get this job thing straightened out, Jess. Then, maybe later, when you've got more time and money, you can get a dog or a cat."

Jesse looked at Eric with glassy eyes. He truly believed he was helping her out. It seemed like everybody knew what was best for her, without ever asking her what was in her heart.

"You'll see this weekend," he went on. "Shadow will love it up there and you'll be able to concentrate on what's really important—like your job and the rest of your life."

Eric smiled at her and gave the wolf pup a pat on the head. "I'm here for you, babe. Trust me, I've got your best interests at heart."

"I'm scared to death, Joseph," Bianca said early the next morning as they waited for Jesse to drop off Shadow. "What if she won't talk to you?"

"She'll listen to me, that's what's important," Joseph stated calmly, glancing out the window. Bianca had kept him up most of the night again, worried about her friend, and Joseph was getting tired of losing sleep.

"She was so determined when she left," Bianca rattled off. "I just can't believe that she's going to give him up."

"What time did she drop him off yesterday?" Joseph asked, keeping the fact that he was disappointed with Jesse to himself. He berated himself for trusting her and thinking she cared about anything other than herself.

"It was six-thirty, remember? We almost didn't hear the doorbell." Bianca fidgeted with some knick-knacks on a table in the shop. She was very nervous.

"Well, it's after seven now," Joseph observed, looking at his watch. "You're sure she was bringing him here?"

"She said she'd bring him over for the rest of the week," Bianca remembered. "I know she said she was taking him to the refuge this weekend. Then she just walked out. She wouldn't listen. She was so horribly depressed. I couldn't say anything to calm her down."

"Well, we'll give her another half hour," Joseph suggested, "and then I want you to call her at work. Maybe she went home, had a good cry and worked it out herself."

"God," Bianca sobbed, "that idea scares me to death!"

Jesse hadn't thought to call Bianca after she had called in sick again the next morning. Her thoughts were centered on the phone call she had made to the wolf refuge the previous night after Eric had left. She had spoken to a woman named Nancy Middlesex who hadn't seemed overly happy at the prospect of taking in another wolf, but had invited them to the refuge just the same. Jesse spent a restless night wondering if she had made the right decision, but when the sun came up, she had put Shadow and his things in the BMW and headed south to Black Mountain at six a.m.

It was raining in Colorado Springs and the lull of the windshield wipers and the Indian flute music playing on the CD player had finally put Shadow to sleep. He rested his head on Jesse's thigh as she drove, perfectly happy. Jesse fought the threat of tears that formed when she thought of the drive back, and life without him. She headed the car west into the foothills.

It was a three and a half hour trek into the southern mountains from Denver. There were several intermittent storms and a dense fog that lasted for more than a couple of miles as they drove up the steeper and steeper hills and down through glistening green valleys. When they reached the clean air of the higher elevations, the wolf's senses were piqued with smells he did not recognize. Wide awake now, with his paws on the armrest of the door and his rump placed firmly on Jesse's lap, he stuck his head out the open window. Like any red blooded American dog, Shadow reveled in the wind as it coursed across his muzzle and fur. Jesse kept watch over him from the corner of her eye.

The road to the refuge was not well marked, but after a few minor wrong turns, Jesse wheeled her BMW around the correct corner and drove carefully down a rutted road. She held her breath as she maneuvered the sports car along what seemed to be more of an old carriage road rather than a driveway. Finally, she pulled up to a muddy clearing that was already filled with dirty trucks, a rundown tractor and a beat up old station wagon. She parked her car next to them. A few hundred feet away stood a dilapidated shack, which was in desperate need of a new coat of paint. In the doorway appeared a woman. She had gray hair tied back in a ponytail and was wearing filthy overalls, a well-worn jacket and wading boots. She held a coffee cup in her left hand and beckoned Jesse to join her with a wave of her right.

Shadow jumped out of Jesse's arms when she opened the car door and into the mud. Jesse, struggling to keep up with him, immediately wished she'd dressed more appropriately for the mountains. Her expensive boots and jeans were covered with muddy dirt in seconds and as Shadow loped ahead of her, he kicked up more mud onto her jacket.

"Now, isn't that a happy pup!" Nancy Middlesex smiled, crouching down and welcoming Shadow when he ran up to her. "You must be Jesse Harless and this must be Shadow."

"Yes," Jesse panted trying to keep Shadow from jumping up on the woman. "I'm sorry we're late."

"It's all right. Nobody gets it right the first time they come up here." Nancy didn't mind Shadow's exuberance. She let him smell her hand and then gave him a healthy hug when he leapt up against her, covering her face with licks. Nancy took the leash from Jesse and surreptitiously checked the pup out. "I should have warned you that it's been raining up here. Your clothes will probably be ruined by the time you leave."

"It's okay," Jesse said. "That's not important, really." She tried to brush the mud off her jacket, but the action only smeared it deeper into the fabric.

"Come inside, then," Nancy offered, holding tight to Shadow's leash and leading the way. "It's a little cold this morning. The wolves love it; humans usually need something warm to drink."

Jesse followed the woman into the shack and stopped at the door. The place was cramped and messy. Bundles of papers were stacked high on a table. There was stuff on every piece of furniture in the house.

"Clear off one of those chairs and have a seat," Nancy suggested as if she had read Jesse's thoughts. Jesse wasn't about to move a thing for fear of making more of a mess. "It's pretty cluttered up here. As you can see, we don't have a lot of space." She poured Jesse a cup of black coffee and handed it to her, careful not to run into Shadow, who was darting back and forth in the small room inspecting every nook and cranny. She did not offer any cream or sugar. "We can't afford anything extravagant. What money we get goes mostly for the care and feeding of the wolves."

"How long have you been taking care of them?" Jesse asked. The hot cup of coffee felt good between her cold hands. She hadn't considered that she might need gloves. After all, the weather forecaster had predicted 80 degrees for the day in the city.

"Nine years." Nancy picked up a stack of newsletters from a couple of the chairs and piled them on top of some other magazines that were precariously heaped on the table. The chair creaked when she sat down on it. Jesse carefully sat on the other one when Nancy offered it to her. "It's been one hell of a battle, but worth every minute of it. You'll see what I mean when you see them."

"It's got to be better for them up here," Jesse put forward. "At least up here they're free."

"Free?" Nancy retorted. She reached behind her and grabbed the pot of coffee from the battered stove.

"Not penned up in an apartment or house," Jesse answered. "I can't take Shadow anywhere without a leash, especially the park. The tenants in my building can't stand the howling. At least here, they can run and hunt and do the things wolves were meant to do."

"Oh, child," Nancy laughed. She was an older woman, or at least her gray hair made her appear that way. When Jesse finally garnered the courage to look at her face, she realized they were probably close to the same age. There was a simple beauty to the woman's face and her eyes were clear and sparkling. "I wish it was that simple."

"But you're in the mountains. There's nobody for miles around."

"They're close enough," Nancy sighed. "Honey, we have 100 acres here, but the county has seen to it that only 5 percent of our land can be used for our wolves. They may have a little more space, but they certainly aren't free to roam. The folks 'round here would shoot 'em at first site if they left our property."

"But, how…" Jesse started.

"Come on, girl," Nancy interrupted. "Let's go out." She gulped the next cup of her scalding coffee and got up. Jesse followed her. Shadow was at the door in a shot. "I'm sorry, boy." Nancy grabbed Shadow's leash. "I'm gonna' have to tie you up." They stepped outside into the brisk air and the woman tied the leash to a post outside. Shadow was not very happy to be attached to the other end of it. Jesse's heart wrenched at the sounds Shadow made as they walked away. The pup strained at the leash, whining to go with them. "It's better we go have a look for ourselves. New wolves tend to rile the pack."

They made their way through more mud and brush. Jesse's feet were cold in minutes and Shadow's cries only seemed to get louder the farther they went. Just down the hill from the shack, Jesse was shocked at what she saw. Chain link fences, row after row, made up several large pens. Inside each one there were wolves of various sizes pacing back and forth, looking their way.

"We're one of the lucky ones," Nancy offered, seeing the look on Jesse's face. "Their pens are each a thousand square feet. They have plenty of room. And they get to come out pretty regularly."

"But, I thought…"

"They have to be contained," Nancy went on. "Like I said, if they get off the property, they're dead."

"The fences are high enough?" Jesse asked as they neared the cages.

"Have to be. They'd be over them in a second if they were any lower."

"When do they get to come out?"

"When there's enough volunteers to keep an eye on them." Nancy walked over to a gate that opened into one of the larger fenced-off areas. "We've got some good people, but most of them have regular jobs in the city. Weekends are the best time around here." She unlocked it and went inside. The wolves were anxious and paced from one side of their pens to the other side, all the while with a wary eye on the newcomer. "Come on in," she said, indicating for Jesse to watch her step. Jesse stepped over the threshold and stood close to Nancy as they walked inside the enclosure. All of the pens had shelters, water, and contained a natural habitat of trees and shrubs. "They're a little skittish 'cos they don't know you, but everything's all right."

"I just don't understand," Jesse sighed. "For some reason I thought they'd be wandering all over up here. Free to go where they please."

"And there'd be one big happy pack," Nancy stated quietly. "You've been reading Crisler and Dutcher, right? Most of our animals are wolf dogs and all of them come from abusive backgrounds. Believe me, they're quite happy here. They get medical care and the best food we can get, sometimes better than what we eat. They're expensive to keep and donations are not plentiful. They have a roof over their head and they are not mistreated. Trust me, they're much better off than where they came from."

"I'm so sorry," Jesse whispered. "I didn't know."

"Don't be sorry," Nancy smiled. "Things are looking up. Here..." she pointed to a gray wolf that was guardedly heading their way. "This is one of our ambassador wolves. Her name is Shenandoah. Hi, girl!" she said, stooping down. "We have a visitor." Nancy gave Jesse the once-over before the wolf got too close. "I'd take your watch off—and your necklace. Shenandoah loves shiny things and she has no problem taking what she wants." Jesse quickly removed her jewelry and slipped it into her pocket. "Now, just stand to the right of me, over there. We'll see what our girl thinks of you." Jesse did as she was told. The wolf trotted over to Nancy first and the woman gave her a big hug.

"Come on over," Nancy said. "She'd like to meet you." Jesse stepped carefully over to Nancy's side. The huge wolf sniffed at her for a moment and then took a step toward her. "She weighs 100 pounds, so be prepared. If she likes you and you're not ready, she can knock you down."

Jesse stood still and let the animal study her. "Can I pet her?" she asked as the wolf pressed up against her.

"Of course," Nancy approved. "She's just a big baby, at heart."

Jesse reached down and stroked Shenandoah's fur. It was wet and the animal's guard hairs stuck to her hand and quickly adhered to her wet clothes. Shenandoah decided she liked the woman and came close. Jesse was thrilled and bent down, giving the wolf a hug.

"We have started taking her to programs that explain about wolves," Nancy noted. "We've been getting some good responses and people are loving the chance to get up close and personal with her." Nancy smiled, watching Shenandoah and Jesse become friends. Shenandoah was all over the woman and Jesse loved it. "People need to learn about wolves, Jesse. They've got to understand they're wild animals, not dogs. They behave differently. They've got their own rules. They can be jealous if they don't get the attention they crave and they can cause a lot of damage and serious injuries if they're left to their own devices. You can't just swat them on the nose and tell them *no* if they've done something you don't approve of. Dominance comes into play and they'll even challenge their owners when they come of age."

When the wolf stepped away for a second, Jesse, still crouched down, rested her hands behind herself on the ground. Her right hand landed on what she thought was the root of a tree. When it rolled under her weight, she looked down. It was the femur of a deer, complete with fur and hoof. "Oh, my!" Jesse cried. "I suppose that's quite common here."

Nancy laughed. "It's a staple part of their diet. There's no meat there, so they play with it like a bone. It bothers you?"

"No, no!" Jesse burst out. "I just didn't expect it." She laughed at her own naïveté.

"Deer meat is a treat around here," Nancy continued. "It costs over $200,000 a year to keep these animals alive and well cared for. "We rely heavily on donations of dog food and horsemeat. Vet bills are high, of course, and many of the wolves come to us abused and sick, so doctors are a necessity. We do the best we can, but it's hard work and that work is never finished. We are constantly working to make this place better."

"So, tell me Nancy, are all the refuges like this?"

"Some are worse, but some are better. There is a beautiful place up north, called W.O.L.F. Sanctuary. They're accredited and their babies live in a mountain area with plenty of trees and wooded areas to call home. They've got the best volunteers in the state and they have some wonderful ambassador wolves. Unfortunately, they're at their limit right now, or I'd send you to them. As long as breeders are out there selling them to folks who will buy them, we're never gonna' go out of business. It's really sad. But it becomes a labor of *love* when you get to know them."

"You live here with them?" Jesse asked as Shenandoah returned to her, nearly knocking her off her feet.

"Yes," Nancy retorted. "Our needs are minimal as I'm sure you've noticed. The animals always come first." Nancy looked back up toward the house where Shadow strained on his leash, still yelping for Jesse. "Your pup is healthy. I can see that. You've done a good job with him, so far." Jesse turned her head, suddenly hearing her puppy's cries. "We can take him if that's what you want," Nancy offered.

Jesse got up off the ground and wiped her hands on her jeans. She was covered with Shenandoah's white guard hairs. "He was pretty shy when I first got him, but he's coming around. I'm sure he'll take to the other wolves quickly," the young woman commented.

"Not at first," Nancy warned. "He'll be isolated until we have the time to let him interact with the other wolves." Nancy saw the look on Jesse's face. "Wolves are very family oriented, Jesse. I'm sure one of the packs will take him in, eventually."

Jesse gazed down the long line of enclosures and smiled when Shenandoah rubbed against her again. She scratched the wolf between her ears before following Nancy back out of the pen. "There are so many," Jesse sighed. "Where do they all come from?"

"We don't have that many," Nancy answered as they walked. "We're one of the lucky ones. We only have fourteen to take care of. Other refuges have a lot more and the expenses are phenomenal. Most of us have gone non-profit, but the state and federal governments do all they can to make it as difficult and costly as possible. We have to count on ordinary people with ordinary jobs who, lots of times, don't have an extra penny, but somehow they find a way to give us a donation. A lot of them say it's the wolves that touch them and some of them give 'til it hurts. Sometimes the bigger corporations, like pet food companies or grocery chains, will help; but a lot of times they don't. It's politically incorrect to get involved in such a hot topic. For as many people there are who want to save the wolves, there are just as many, if not more, who want them destroyed.

"Someone once said, '*sometimes someone touches our heart and stays there forever*'," Nancy continued. "I believe when it comes to visiting with a wolf, no truer statement has ever been made. The infirm, as well as healthy people, carry locks of their fur and guard hairs for protection. Everybody feels better when they've spent actual time with a wolf."

"So why are so many of them abused and abandoned?"

"Because people think they can handle them. They don't realize they are quite a bit different from dogs. They don't think of them as wild animals, which is what they are. They'll chew up a house; I mean couches, chairs, rugs, doors, you name it. They can destroy a back yard with the holes they dig and get under the fences or over and out. They may kill smaller pets like cats and rabbits and they can get jealous if their owners don't give them enough attention. Once they've accepted a human as a primary member of their pack, the wolf could very well die of loneliness or a broken heart if that person disappears. Wolves are special animals. Their emotions and behavior are very close to their human counterparts. I think that's why man has often tried to eradicate them. Their race is actually better than ours. They socialize rather than kill each other, for the most part. Of course they protect their territory, and occasionally, some members are ostracized from the pack. But they take care of their young and believe in, and uphold, the family unit. They work cooperatively and kill only what they need to survive."

They walked slowly past the other wolves and Nancy filled Jesse in on some of the wolves' backgrounds. Some of the animals came right up to the fence and Jesse could touch their snouts poking through the holes. Others shied away from them, running for their enclosures as Jesse passed by. Most of the wolves had proven to be too much for the people who had bought them when they were no bigger than Shadow. Some had been horribly beaten or used in illegal fights. Jesse was heartbroken when she heard their stories.

A soft, cold rain began to fall and the two women headed back up the hill to Nancy's shack. Shadow jumped and pulled at his leash. His barks and whimpers grew incessant the closer they got to him.

"There's a good boy," Jesse's voice was soothing as she loosened Shadow's leash. "Mama's here." Shadow jumped up into her arms and nuzzled against her neck.

"Has he had his shots?" Nancy asked, noting how much Jesse loved her wolf.

"Yes," Jesse answered absentmindedly, "he has the best of care. And, he's quite spoiled."

"I've noticed," Nancy smiled, opening the door to her home. "You can bring him in."

Jesse, still holding Shadow, looked back at the other wolves for a while before she entered the small building. The wolves were now pacing in their enclosures with each pair of eyes staring back at her. All the books she had read said nothing about places like this. The one refuge she read about was in the mountains of Utah. Those wolves had no cages. She knew of the dangers; how modern man disliked them, just as much as his ancestors had done. In her heart and in this situation she knew this was the best place for these animals, although it hurt to think of them penned up here for the rest of their lives. The rain came down harder and Jesse was soon soaked to the bone.

Shenandoah, watching Jesse with her pup, suddenly raised her head and howled. Jesse was enchanted by the beautiful sound the wolf made. Shadow, who had been trying to get down, turned and looked in Shenandoah's direction. He stretched his neck out and tried to howl back. Jesse had never heard her pup howl. It surprised and thrilled her to no end.

She looked around at the landscape and remembered the book Nancy had mentioned. She had read about Lois Crisler and her husband who had raised wolves in Alaska. They had their share of problems, but never gave up. And Jesse did not want to give up either.

Dustu gave her Shadow for a reason. He would have never shown him to her if he hadn't thought she could take care of him. She had accepted the responsibility that the Native American had given her and she wasn't going to let him or Shadow down. She didn't want Nancy Middlesex telling visitors about the poor wolf pup that was left on her doorstep by a young woman who was too engrossed in her stupid city life to accept the task of raising him and giving him a good, safe home.

Suddenly, the young woman came to a decision. She walked into the small house, put Shadow down and grabbed her purse. Nancy, covertly watching her, poured some more coffee. Jesse removed her checkbook and sat down at the well-used table. With determination she wrote out a check for two thousand dollars. "I want to thank you for letting us visit you, today," she said to Nancy, accepting the cup of coffee she handed her. "I know this isn't much, but I am sure you can use it." She handed her the check.

"It will go into Shadow's upkeep fund," Nancy announced, her eyes widening when she saw the amount.

"No," Jesse countered. "That won't be necessary." Jesse gulped the coffee down and put the cup back on the table. "I'm going to keep Shadow with me."

"The city's no place for that animal," Nancy warned. "By the size of those paws, he's going to be a big boy, much bigger than Shenandoah."

"I realize that," Jesse said, getting up and shaking Nancy's hand. "And I know what I have to do." Shadow was dancing at her feet. She hung her purse strap over her shoulder and picked him up. "He'll be well taken care of, I promise."

"I truly hope so," Nancy said. "But I'm a bit concerned for the both of you." She walked quickly over to a stack of books that were piled haphazardly on the floor. She pulled a couple out of the middle of the stack. Miraculously, the stack did not tumble over. "Here," she offered. "Take these. Maybe they'll help you a little, or at least help you to understand what you've taken on. She looked seriously at the wolf. "He will be welcome here if you can't manage him."

"That's comforting to know," Jesse said, heading to the door. "Thank you again, Nancy, and do you mind if I keep in touch?"

"You're welcome any time," Nancy ran over to the table and uncovered a business card. "Here's our email address and phone number. If you have any questions, please don't hesitate to call. He's already a big boy. He's gonna' be a handful."

Jesse and Nancy walked quickly out into the now pouring rain. Jesse opened the car door and Shadow jumped onto his seat. He eyed the books Nancy placed on the floorboard in the car, no doubt considering their nutritional value. The lady shivered in the cold.

"Get back to the house. You'll catch your death out here and those animals need you," Jesse demanded after shaking her hand one more time. "Thanks for all your help!" Jesse ran around the car and got into the driver's seat.

Nancy stopped on the porch and leaned against the doorjamb, the check tucked safely into her shirt. Shaking her head in puzzlement, she waved good-bye as Jesse and Shadow drove away. The wolf pup stood on the seat and shook the rain from his fur. Jesse didn't mind at all. She turned on the music and welcomed Shadow onto her lap, smiling broadly.

Bianca was right after all. All she needed to do was clear her head. The mountain air and the abused wolves seemed to help her out. She wasn't stupid and she certainly wasn't helpless. She could find another job; maybe one she actually liked. There was nothing stopping her from starting down a new path, other than her own fears. She had money if she wanted it. All she had to do was sell the condo. Her resolve was going to shake things up in her dull, restricted world, but she was ready for the challenge. She was more than ready for a change and her little wolf was going to make her do it.

That night, following their walk and a dinner comprised of puppy chow, more ground beef, and a bowl of hot soup for Jesse, Shadow jumped up on the bed and cuddled next to her. Jesse smiled to herself, not paying particular attention to her latest book, because a familiar saying kept flowing through her head. She had heard and seen it through the course of most her life, but until now it never meant much to her. *Tomorrow is the first day of the rest of your life.* It sure meant something now, and she couldn't wait to get started with the rest of her own.

CHAPTER 7

"Where the hell have you been?" Bianca literally screamed out the front door when Jesse reached into the car to get Shadow and his things the next morning. "Didn't you get my messages? Where the hell is your cell phone?"

"Shhhh!" Jesse sounded with a finger pressed to her lips. She hurried up the walk and into the house so the whole neighborhood would not have to hear their conversation. Bianca stepped back and let her cross the threshold. "I'm really sorry, Bianca," Jesse apologized. "The cell phone must have been out of range at the refuge."

"The refuge?" Bianca asked, surprised. "You went to the refuge? What happened?" Max was jumping up between them, excited by his mistress's voice and seeing Jesse with her pup.

Shadow was doing his best to wiggle out of Jesse's arms. She put him down and he immediately jumped onto his big brother. There was a flurry of fur on the floor as the two romped and played in the hallway. "Nothing," Jesse continued. She saw Joseph at the top of the stairs and noticed that he did not look particularly happy to see her. "We had a great day and Shadow loved the road trip." It was getting late and Jesse had no time to chitchat, but she knew Bianca and Joseph deserved an explanation, however cryptic this one was going to be. "Can I have you baby-sit today and tomorrow?" she asked. "I've got to settle things at work. It shouldn't take any longer than that."

"What are you talking about?" Bianca was perplexed. "What has to be settled? Joseph, where the hell are *you*?" Bianca called out, not knowing he was already on the stairs. "Jesse's here, we've got to talk."

"Look," Jesse pleaded, stepping back to the door. "I really don't have the time right now, but I'll explain everything when I come back to pick up

Shadow tonight. Just trust me, okay?" She darted out the door and down the stairs of the porch. "Everything's fine and I'm keeping Shadow. I've got the situation under control!"

Joseph and Bianca reached the door at the same time. "You'll be eating here tonight, young lady!" Bianca warned her friend. "You're going to have a lot of explaining to do!"

Jesse waved from the car and merged into the rush hour traffic.

At the office, Eric was waiting with his arms crossed over his chest and his foot tapping impatiently against the carpeted floor. "Where the hell were you yesterday?" he sneered when she walked in. Do you know I had to resort to calling Wheland? We were about to call the police if you didn't show this morning."

"I can tell," Jesse said, putting her stuff down and looking at all the new stacks of work on her desk. "You're both asking the same question." She smiled at her friend. "I'm sorry, Eric. I had to do a little thinking on my own to work this mess out." Jesse cast a quick glance out the door and was glad to see that Sterling wasn't in yet. "How about lunch?" she continued. "I'll explain it all then, okay?"

"Well, Hobbs wants to talk to you. I think I've got this promotion thing back on track."

"Eric," Jesse sighed, "it really doesn't matter, okay? This is my battle and I'll take care of it myself."

"You're a wreck," Eric stated firmly. "You can't take care of anything right now."

"Believe me," Jesse answered, "I'm right on track." She gently shoved Eric out the door as Sterling started to come in, pushing them both inside her office.

"Harless, I've got to talk to you about a new report that's due on Monday. I can't believe you called in sick with everything that's on your plate." Sterling's voice was cold and menacing.

"I'll have to get back to you, Brad, after I get a cup of coffee," Jesse retorted, turning her back to both men. "Has anybody made any yet?" Eric and Brad looked at each other with puzzled expressions upon their faces. Jesse stepped around them and took the short walk to the cafeteria, leaving them gaping after her. When she returned with her hot coffee, both men were gone. She smiled to herself and walked into her office. She shut the door and locked it. Jesse sat down at her desk, turned on her computer and wrote a short letter of resignation. She signed it, stuffed it into her purse and then got out the phone book. She made one call and then completed a little bit of work.

About an hour later, Sterling called her into his office. She brought the reports she had finished and threw them on his desk.

"Look," he said, aware of the change in her demeanor, "I know you're pissed off that you didn't get that job, but I just couldn't recommend you for it. Take heart, though, because if you make me look good with this project I've been given for Monday, I'll finally get that vice presidency position I've been eyeing and we'll both win. I'll get what I want. You'll get a new boss and finally be rid of me."

"Oh, really?" Jesse snickered. "That's all it will take, eh?" She took the project he handed her. It was a lengthy budget analysis and future growth prospectus that would obviously be more than a monumental task for one person to undertake. "Tell me, Brad, who's going to do all your work when you're Vice President?" She knew what was going to happen. He'd try out a new girl, probably some bimbo who looked good in a short skirt but wouldn't be able to type. He'd have an affair with her and find some way to make Jesse clean up his mess. She'd have double the workload and get fired for not keeping up.

"That's not information you need to know. I'll take care of that myself."

"Yeah," Jesse laughed, walking out of his office. "I bet." She did not return to her office, but made a left turn and went into the Human Resources office instead. She met with the personnel manager behind closed doors for over an hour. When she walked back out, she had a huge grin on her face when she grabbed Eric from his office. "Let's go to lunch!"

"So, tell me what's going on," her friend asked when they finally got seated at the restaurant. "Did you get rid of Shadow yesterday? Is that why you took off?"

"Eric," Jesse started, "let's order a drink." She motioned for the waiter and ordered a glass of wine for herself and a bourbon on the rocks for Eric. They also ordered lunch.

"That's not like you to have a drink at lunch," Eric observed after the waiter had gone. "Do you think it's a good idea when you're meeting Hobbs this afternoon?"

"It's the best idea I've had today," Jesse answered. "And I'll probably have another one before we go back." She sat back in her chair and relaxed. She was glad they had decided to sit outside on the patio. The sun was out and the air was warm and comfortable. "I'm putting my condo on the market. Do you think three hundred grand is a fair price?"

"It's a steal, and what the hell are you doing that for? Have you totally lost your mind?" Eric looked at her, stupefied.

"Well, what should I ask for it, then?"

"Hell, I'd give you five hundred thousand today."

"Really?"

"You know how I love that place. I've always wanted it," Eric said. "But you're not going to sell it because that would be stupid. Where in the hell do you think you're going?" He furrowed his brow. "You're not moving to Little-ton, are you?"

Jesse laughed. "Of course not. And I'm not *going to hell* either." She leaned in closer to Eric and gently touched his hand. "I'm keeping Shadow, bud. I'm ready for a change. I don't know, at this actual moment, where I'm going to go, but it's going to happen." The drinks came and Eric ordered another one before slamming the first one down. "I called a realtor this morning. He's com-ing by tomorrow night."

"Don't bother," Eric said. "If you're sure about selling it, it's going to be mine."

"See," Jesse smiled. "How easy was that? Do I still need the realtor?"

"I'm a lawyer, sweetie," Eric gently chided her. "I'll draw up the papers myself. You said three hundred?"

"I'll take five, Mr. Lawyer. You're right, it's at least worth that."

"You're crazy. And how nuts is this? Now, *you'll* be staying at *my* place when *you're* too drunk to drive home." He smiled. "Shit, I can't believe you're giving that place up, but what's even harder to believe is that I'm going to get it. Cool."

"It'll be a regular bachelor pad."

"Don't let that animal scratch up *my* wood floors!"

"Yeah, yeah," Jesse laughed. She felt very good, crossing the first hurdle of her plan. There was no need to fill Eric in on any more of her decisions at the moment, for he'd find out soon enough. The food came and Eric ordered more drinks.

The meeting with Hobbs was short and sweet. He apologized for not giving her the promotion and prattled on about some other opportunities that were in the works. Jesse pretended to care about what he was saying, but in actuality she was counting her soon to be garnered monetary funds. The personnel manager had supplied her with a printout of the cash she would receive taking an early retirement. After fifteen years, she'd accrued a nice little nest egg and, depending on what kind of house she bought, she was pleased to think she would not have to work for quite a while. She was looking forward to the break.

She thanked the president and walked back to her office. She spent the rest of the day working on a couple of things, just to look busy. At five minutes to five o'clock she stopped by Human Resources and gave them the resignation letter before she left for the day. She told them she'd be back in the morning to clear out her desk and collect her check.

Jesse walked into Bianca and Joseph's around six o'clock. The traffic had been very heavy. Shadow and Max greeted her at the door and she found Bianca and Joseph in the kitchen preparing dinner.

"So, here's our wayward woman," Bianca announced when she heard her come in the kitchen. "I can't wait to hear the juicy details of the past two days."

Joseph handed her a glass of wine and it was obvious to Jesse they had had at least one glass apiece before she got there. "Where do you want me to start?" she asked, sitting down at the table. Joseph sat down too.

"How about the beginning?" Bianca suggested, wiping her hands on a dish-cloth and joining them at the table. "Let's talk about what happened after you left."

"Well, I went home and Eric gave me his two cents worth, pointing out that getting rid of Shadow would be for the best. The best for whom, I'm still not quite sure. So, instead of waiting for the weekend, I drove up to Black Mountain yesterday morning, spent some time with a woman named Nancy Middle-sex and her abused wolves. It started to rain. Shadow and I got filthy. I decided that no wolf of mine is going to live a life like that, drove back home and had a great night's sleep. I dropped Shadow off here this morning and went to work. I sold my condo to Eric at lunch for five hundred grand and handed in my resignation, effective today. I'll pick up my final check in the morning for another two hundred thousand and some change. Then I came out here to pet my wolf, eat a great dinner, and enjoy your company. I've never felt better or more relieved in my whole life."

Both Bianca and Joseph stared at Jesse in disbelief. "Jesse..." Bianca spoke slowly.

But Jesse cut her off. "Now, I was thinking on the way out here that I don't want to move into the suburbs. There's too much traffic and way too many people. Maybe I'd like to move to another state. Joseph, where's a place a woman can go and live happily ever after with a wolf?"

"Are you joking?" Joseph asked incredulously. "All this has happened and you're thinking of moving to another state?"

"I've got to find a place with a lot of property, don't I? If I'm going to take care of him properly, Shadow will need all the room I can get."

"You're not going to give him up?"

"That's out of the question. He's my wolf. He's my responsibility."

Joseph looked at Bianca out of the corner of his eye. "*Someone* said you were giving him up and that you would not change your mind."

"That someone," Jesse stated sweetly, "whom I love very dearly, made a mistake."

"I am very glad to hear it," Joseph declared. He poured himself a glass of wine and refilled Jesse's.

"Oh, and I've decided that I won't need you to baby-sit Shadow tomorrow. I think I'll take him with me to the office."

"Jesse, now you're talking crazy," Bianca said. "This is all pretty serious stuff."

"Yeah, Eric said the same thing," Jesse giggled. "I don't know what he's going to do when he finds out I quit. But I've been thinking about what all of you have told me and it does make sense. There is no reason I have to be miserable for the rest of my life just because I'm afraid to change it."

"I think it's good," Joseph offered. "I am happy to see you're taking charge of your life. And Bianca and I *both* know you can do it."

"Well, *Mr. Take Charge*," Bianca snapped. "Just where is this city girl supposed to go?"

Joseph smiled at Bianca. "I happen to know a place where she'd be pretty safe and have everything she needs to give Shadow a good life."

"Right here, perhaps," Bianca suggested. "Since we got her into this, I think we better let her move in."

"No," Jesse said. "That's not what I want. The more I think about it, the more I want to get to the country—the real country that is. Someplace like Utah or at least up in the mountains."

"I have a cabin up in Montana," Joseph announced. "It's close to the Blackfeet Reservation, not far from Dupuyer."

"You never told me about this," Bianca declared, looking at him intensely.

"You never asked," Joseph replied, still smiling. "Anyway, when I came here I never intended on settling down, but this woman came along and now I don't know if I'll ever get back. It's not a castle, but it's got indoor plumbing and electricity, and best of all, it's situated on plenty of land."

"Oh, that's too much," said Jesse. "You guys have already done so much for me."

"Well, my woman's right," noted Joseph. "We did get you into this. And Bea, what's good about it is I have an uncle who lives pretty close by and he could keep an eye on her for us. That way we don't have to worry about finding her and her wolf frozen to death on a rock somewhere after the spring thaw."

"What uncle?" Bianca asked warily. "I thought your family was here in Colorado."

"Not all of them," Joseph stated. "Charlie is an extended family member."

"Not blood, then?" Bianca was not happy with this new information. She wanted to talk to Joseph alone, but realized that wasn't going to be feasible until much later. However, she was afraid that would be too late.

"All Indians have the same blood, Bianca. Charlie took care of me for awhile."

"What would you sell it for?" Jesse broke in, hoping to stop an altercation. She could hear the tension rising in both their voices. "How many acres are we talking?"

Bianca held her tongue and looked at Joseph, waiting for his reply. "It's 640 acres and parts of it are even fit to farm. There's a cattle rancher who lives nearby. His name's Phillips and he's the Town Marshal, or at least used to be when I was there. He moved up there from California at least twenty years ago, probably longer than that. He's pretty cool."

"He'll be cool until Shadow goes after one of his calves or something," Bianca butted in. "Good God, Joseph. This is ridiculous!"

"How much?" Jesse asked again. "I am interested."

"How about I let you rent it for a while," Joseph answered. "That way, you will have time to decide if that's the kind of place you want." He poured Bianca and Jesse another glass of wine. "It's rough up there, Harless. The winters are like nothing you've ever experienced before. That BMW won't cut through the snow or do well on the dirt roads. There are no shopping malls or restaurants or supermarkets. There's a bank, a post office, a general store and a bar in the nearest town, and that's twenty miles away. You'll have to learn to take care of yourself." Joseph considered the matter a little more before he spoke again. "Bianca might be right. It might be too much for you. So, you better think about this very carefully. It's the country—if that's what you want—but be careful what you wish for."

"If you can help me prepare for it, I'll try it," said Jesse. She looked over at Bianca and smiled. "And if it doesn't work out, I'll take you up on your offer. Just until I can find a place of my own, alright?"

"We're going up there with her," Bianca insisted. "I'm not letting her do this alone."

"I'll be okay," Jesse placated her friend. "I'm a big girl and it is my decision to make. I think this is better than moving someplace where I don't know anybody. With Joseph's uncle there, I won't be alone. And I'm not a total idiot. I think I can figure this out. It's time I grew up a little, anyway."

"You can do it," Joseph added. "I wouldn't offer my place if I didn't feel that you could."

"We're still coming with you." Bianca was adamant. She got up from the table, not looking at Joseph, and prepared the plates for dinner. "I won't sleep a wink until I know you're safe."

Jesse got up from the table and went over to help her. "How about you giving me a chance to try it, first. Give me some time to get settled and then you can come up." Bianca was very roughly plopping mashed potatoes onto the dishes. Jesse touched her hand and made her stop. "I have to do this," she whispered to her friend. "If I want to keep Shadow, this is the best option I could get."

"I feel responsible for all of this," Bianca commented sadly. "I never expected…"

"To wake me up?" Jesse interjected. "Somebody had to do it, Bianca. I'm just glad it was you who did." She hugged Bianca, surprising her. "Relax and be glad for me! I've never been happier and I have you to thank for that."

"Well, we'd better eat, then," said Bianca after they shared their long hug. "Because you've got a lot to learn from Joseph before I let you go."

The next morning, Jesse walked out of Human Resources with a check and a smile on her face. She returned to her desk and placed the last of her personal effects in a box.

"You can't be serious!" Eric bellowed, surprising her as he rounded the corner. "What the hell is going on?"

"I am quite serious," Jesse answered quietly, turning off her computer for the last time. "So, why don't you pick up that box over there and help me get this stuff out to my car?"

Sterling was too flabbergasted by all the paperwork Jesse had thrown back onto his desk to notice the pair when they walked by. Jesse chuckled. Eric kept watching her with a puzzled look upon his face until they reached the elevator, stepped in and the doors finally closed, giving them some privacy.

"So, you just quit?" Eric burst, shifting the box in his hands. "Are you out of your mind? What did Sterling say? You didn't do that report for him, did you? He had to be so pissed. Shit, the rest of the staff is in for it now!"

Smiling, Jesse leaned back against the wall of the elevator and let him rant. He wasn't giving her a chance to answer him, anyway.

"Here you are all depressed one day. The next, you've lost your mind. I've half a mind to lock you up, but maybe you just need a stiff drink. God knows Sterling needed to be put in his place, but Jesus, you didn't have to quit. Tell me you've at least got another job. What are you going to do?" Eric finished, stopping to take a breath.

"That drink sounds like a good start," Jesse suggested, still smiling. The elevator doors opened and they stepped into the parking garage. Shadow was braced on his forepaws, gazing through the window of the BMW. Wagging his tail eagerly, he yipped as they approached the car and Jesse opened the trunk. Eric sighed, seeing that the wolf pup was still a part of their lives.

Jesse set her box into the trunk and held the lid open for Eric, who threw the other box in and slammed the trunk lid shut. Jesse got into the driver's seat and Shadow promptly landed on her lap, licking her face. Eric slid cautiously into the passenger seat, hoping to avoid the furry beast's *loving* licks. "Hey, boy," Eric grimaced, giving Shadow a cursory pat on the head when the wolf leaned over to sniff him. "I guess the refuge didn't work out," he murmured to Jesse.

"Nope," Jesse started the car and pulled out of the parking spot. She wheeled around the other parked cars and into the street. "Let's go to Monro's, where we can sit outside."

"Are you going to tell me anything?" Eric pleaded. "I'm dying here."

"It's okay, Eric," Jesse pacified the young man. "I haven't lost my mind. Actually, I think I've finally found it." The car maneuvered expertly as she drove the couple of blocks to the restaurant with Shadow sitting on her lap. "Sterling was furious when I came in this morning. Apparently, Hobbs wasn't happy that I quit, either. I thought Sterling's head would explode when I told him I hadn't bothered to write his report. It was priceless. You should have seen it!" She pulled into a parking space close to the restaurant. They had at least an hour before the lunch rush hit.

"But what about money?" Eric asked. "How are you going to feed that animal? Let alone yourself."

"I made out all right," Jesse answered. "With my vacation, sick pay, retirement and fifteen years of faithful service all totaled, we'll be able to get by for a couple of years."

"Get by for a couple of years doing what?"

"Hand me Shadow's leash, will ya?" she requested, not answering his question right away.

"This guy's getting bigger every day," Eric grunted when Shadow pounced on him for the leash. "You're going to buy a house with a yard, right?"

"That's kind of the plan," Jesse smiled, getting out of the car. She walked around and opened Eric's door, grabbing the leash from him as Shadow bounced out onto the sidewalk. "I'm famished."

"How can you think of food when you've just quit your job?" Eric asked, quickening his steps to keep up with Jesse and Shadow. The usual stares ogled them as they walked the short distance to the restaurant's patio.

"People quit their jobs all the time," Jesse remarked, keeping Shadow close by her side. "It feels pretty good. You ought to try it."

"Oh, yeah," Eric retorted. "That'll be rather difficult when I'm supporting you two in a couple of months after you've exhausted the job market trying to get another job."

"Don't worry about us," Jesse laughed. "I promise we won't darken your doorway." She smiled at the waiter, who opened the wrought iron gate for them, so they could enter the patio.

"Hey, Shadow!" the waiter called when the wolf entered. Shadow nuzzled the man, who had been kind to him and given him treats whenever the wolf and Jesse passed by on their nightly walks. "Jesse, has he put on another few pounds?"

"They're adding on by the hour, Jimmy," Jesse answered, taking the seat he offered her. Eric sat down across from her. "Could we get a couple of scotches?"

"Got the day off, eh?" Jimmy asked, handing them the menus. "We don't usually see you two during the week."

"It won't be a problem, will it, Jimmy?" Jesse inquired, looking up at him.

"It's early, Jess," Jimmy said. "The usual crowd won't get here for another hour."

"We'll be out of your hair by then," Jesse said. "And how about a couple of your fabulous hamburgers, one medium rare and one tar-tar." She handed the menu back without looking at it.

"Good choice," Jimmy recommended, taking out his order pad. "And for you, sir?"

"Day off," Eric was muttering to himself, scanning the menu. "Yeah, give me one too, but load it up and cook it." The waiter took the order and disappeared. "All right," Eric demanded while Jesse relaxed against the back of her chair, running her fingers through her long, brown hair. Shadow lay down at her feet, watching the action on the street. "You've got to fess up and do it now. And don't think about leaving anything out like you apparently did yesterday. We're not leaving here until I'm satisfied with your answers."

"Oh, Eric," Jesse sighed. "It's nothing, really." She laughed at the look of disbelief that crossed Eric's face. "Okay, let me be honest. I couldn't leave Shadow at that refuge. He deserves better than that. So, I sat down and worked it out. I'm getting him out of here. He needs some space."

"We're talking Shadow, right?" Eric asked incredulously. "You're doing this for a wolf?"

"Eric," Jesse sighed, "Shadow is really a very small part of this, even though I know it doesn't look that way at the moment." She straightened up, placed her hands on the table and met her friend's gaze. "We've been friends for a long time, haven't we?"

"Yeah, at least ten years," Eric noted, perplexed.

"How was I when you met me? Happy? Content?"

"Well, yeah," Eric answered. "I wouldn't have hung out with you if you weren't."

"When did that change, Eric?" Jesse asked. "Did you notice?"

"You've been down in the dumps for a while. But it happens to all of us. C'est la vie."

"What's *a while*, Eric?"

"I don't know, maybe a couple of months?"

"That's one of the things I love about you," Jesse smiled. "You're clueless when it comes to time."

"Hey, I finally bought that watch," he said, looking down at his wrist and his very expensive Rado watch.

"Eric," Jesse continued, "I've been depressed for more than a couple of months. It's been more like a couple of years."

"You're fine when we're not at work. You've had fun at the club and stuff, right?"

"Not for a long time," Jesse said. "I just didn't want to bring it up and ruin your nights. I've been hard enough on you at work."

"It's a slump, you'll get over it."

"You're right, I will," Jesse smiled. "Actually, it started a couple of weeks back when I acquired this wolf."

"Now, don't go there," stated Eric. "This last week's been the pits and that's *after* you got Shadow." Jimmy brought over the drinks and set them on the table.

"That's because I had to sink as low as I could go before I could start to see what put me in this depression in the first place. Shadow helped, but the real revelation came to me at the wolf refuge."

"The refuge?" Eric was confused. "But that's where all of this should have been straightened out. No more wolf—one relieved and happy friend." Eric gulped his drink. "I smell Bianca. She's the one who should be blamed for this. I told you not to get involved with her again. She's the one who got you that wolf. Damned crazy bitch if you ask me."

"She just opened some doors, Eric," Jesse said calmly. "I was the one who chose to walk through them."

"But the refuge would have been a good place for Shadow and you know it."

"You should see those animals. I mean, they're loved and cared for, but they shouldn't have to be penned up." Jesse glanced down at Shadow and scratched his head. They can't run like they're supposed to. They can't live the way they were meant to live. They're beautiful animals, Eric. And they're damned close to perfect when you see how they live in the wild.

"And while I was up there looking at those wolves, it dawned on me. Here I was, penned up myself with a job I hate, living in a condo in the city where the taxes keep going up and the rules keep getting harder to follow, allergy ridden and just plain cornered. I was brought up to abide by those rules and live like everybody else. The more money you make, the better off you are. It's like they put blinders on you. You have to be responsible. You make money so you can spend it, but then you have to pay your bills. The more you spend, the less you save and while you keep on buying stuff, you're just never quite happy with what you have. So you spend more, thinking this trinket or that car or that dress will do it for you, but it doesn't. People might be impressed for a second, but they don't really care, because they want you to notice their own newest toy or acquisition in return."

"So, are you saying what we have here is wrong?" Eric asked. "Was I the one keeping you penned up?"

"Oh, for Heaven's sake," Jesse laughed. "You are amazing, my friend. I put myself in this pen. I made it myself—link by link. I almost did the same for Shadow, but I saved him instead. Now maybe he can save me."

"So, you're selling your condo and God knows what else, to save yourself and a wolf," Eric reasoned. "Excuse me if I don't see the sense in that."

"I'm not asking you to," Jesse replied. "It's my life I'm trying to save, not yours."

"Well, I hope you know what you're doing."

"I'll be out of the condo by the end of the month. If you don't want the furniture, I'll give it away. I'm keeping what I need and I'm moving to Montana."

"Jesus! Montana?" Eric was astounded. "What the hell are you going to do in that God forsaken country?"

"I didn't say Mongolia, dumb ass. Montana is another state, just like Colorado," Jesse laughed again. "They have gas, electricity and phones. Last I heard they even have a computer or two."

"Don't be crass," Eric snapped. "I'm just trying to understand all this."

"I'm sorry," Jesse apologized.

"Why Montana? Can't you save yourself here in Colorado?"

Jesse took another sip of her scotch and continued. "I'm renting a place from a friend who doesn't need it right now." She felt it was safer not to mention who the friend was. Eric was mad enough at Bianca. "It's a cabin on a section of land. If it works out, maybe some day I can buy it from him, but if it doesn't, then I can come back. I'm not sure what I'm getting into, Eric. I just know I've got to make a drastic change. Something in my heart and mind tells me all of this is right. That it's meant to be. I was going to look for land around here, but this opportunity came up and my heart told me to grab it. The cabin has electricity and plumbing. I don't know how many other places can boast that without a thorough search and probably a lot more money."

"It's fucking cold up there," Eric noted. "You hate the cold and snow, remember?"

"I'll buy some warmer clothes," Jesse answered. "I don't want to keep doing what I've been doing. I don't want to keep going to clubs, or shopping, or working at a job I hate. I've got to get away where I can think. It sounds like this might be the perfect place to do just that. I'm dying here, Eric. I need a place where I can breathe."

"Oh, this is almost too much," sighed Eric, taking another drink. "I guess I should ask if there's anything I can do to help."

"Well, now that you mention it," Jesse smiled at him, "I want to trade the BMW for a truck."

"God, no!" Eric screeched. "I will not do it! You love that car! You worked so hard to get it! *I* love that car! We've picked up some great dates in that thing!"

"I know," Jesse replied soothingly. "I just can't get all of the stuff I need into it and, like you said, the winters are pretty tough. I'm going to need a four wheel drive vehicle with a bit more power."

Eric frowned, thinking hard. He finished his drink as the waiter arrived with the food, and ordered another. "Let's do it this way," he finally suggested. "I'll find you a truck—they don't cost that much—keep the car here, and once you're settled, I'll bring it up to you. I won't let you part with it."

"Eric," Jesse stated firmly, "I'll need the money." She took the raw hamburger and gave it to Shadow, who gobbled it up quickly and looked up at Jesse for more. "I don't think there will be much call for administrative assistants where I'm going. I don't know if I'll have the time to take a job, let alone find one." She took a bite of her own burger. "Of course, if you really want it, I could probably be coerced into selling it to you, too."

"That damn wolf is going to put me in the poor house," Eric grumbled. "All right. I'll get you a damn truck."

"Do you think…" Jesse asked, taking another bite of her hamburger and swallowing hard, "…that you could take the rest of the day off and we could start looking today? I might lose my nerve if I wait any longer."

"Then I should say I can't," Eric said, between bites of his own food, but there was a twinkle in his eye as he thought about it for a brief second. "Yeah, why not. Maybe I can finagle a raise out of this if they think I might be thinking about quitting, too. Get Jimmy over here. I'm going to need another drink."

CHAPTER 8

"...So, he writes the guy a check for $30,000 and says, *'let's call it even, bud'*," Jesse told Bianca and Joseph in their living room. "*'I'll keep the depreciating BMW and the lady gets her truck.'*" She glanced over at Eric, who was also in the room, and smiled. "And that my friends, is how I got my new Dodge Ram 2500 in midnight blue."

"That's incredible," Bianca said, watching Eric also. He was obviously uncomfortable, standing stiffly to one side of the group, in his charcoal gray designer suit. His eyes were distrustful as he suspiciously examined everything around him. "You're quite the salesman, Eric," she offered in an attempt to pull him into the conversation.

"The guy was a dick," Eric said smartly. "Jesse's car is worth twice the price of what that salesman was going to give her, and the truck isn't that fancy." Jesse had coerced Eric into coming to Littleton with her. He was out of his element and it showed in his behavior. "I made out on the deal. Got a sixty-thousand dollar car for half the price."

"The truck will work better for you up there," Joseph said to Jesse. "The car is not too practical for where you're going."

Eric's attention turned sharply to the Indian when he spoke. He was intimidated by the big man, which surprised both Jesse and Bianca, but he was doing his best not to show it. "So, you've been there, then," queried Eric, tersely.

"It's my cabin." Joseph was not particularly pleased with the lawyer, either. His eyes met Eric's callously. The young man in his fancy suit, expensive shoes and slick haircut represented all the things Joseph hated about the white man; power driven and greedy. "The winters are tough."

"And you think a woman like Jesse can handle it?" Eric's voice was sharp.

"She is strong enough," Joseph snapped back. "As her friend, you should know that."

"Okay," Bianca interrupted quickly. "Why don't we all sit down and have a drink."

"Sounds like a great idea to me," Jesse agreed, grabbing the sleeve of Eric's jacket while directing him to one of the chairs. "Maybe we could order a pizza or something. I'm famished."

"Don't you think we should be going?" Eric asked Jesse with tight lips.

"There is too much to discuss," Joseph cut in, seated comfortably on the couch. "I can see that Harless wants and needs all our help."

"Of course she does," Eric said. "That's why I'm here."

"Then you are a good friend," Joseph conceded. "So let us come to a truce here and work together. The women can take care of the food and drinks. Maybe we should talk."

"Whatever Jesse wants," murmured Eric.

"Ladies," Joseph suggested, ushering the girls away with a wave of his hand, "I like my pizza with lots of pepperoni. And for you, Mr. Kressler?"

"I like my drink stiff with no ice. Eric sat down in the chair, placed his hands firmly on the armrests and crossed one leg over the other. "I suppose a cigarette is out of the question in this place?"

"By all means, smoke if you wish," Joseph said calmly. "If you have an extra one, I would be most pleased to join you."

Bianca curled her lip in disdain, but grabbed an old metal ashtray from the sideboard and tossed it onto the table before escorting Jesse out of the room. Eric, pleasantly surprised, brought out his pack, gave Joseph a cigarette and provided a light for both of them.

Both men inhaled long drags of smoke from their cigarettes and avoided each other's eyes for a few minutes. Max, with Shadow in tow, ran into the room after Bianca had let them in from the backyard. Upon seeing Eric, Max stopped short just inside the door and eyed the stranger. Shadow tripped through the door, stumbling over his huge paws, and ran to Eric. He stretched his forepaws up Eric's leg and wagged his tail. Eric acknowledged the wolf pup and brought him up to his lap where Shadow quickly settled. His hand covered most of the puppy's head when he rubbed it.

"Shadow likes you, I see," Joseph noted, finally breaking the ice.

"You could say we've bonded over the past couple of days," Eric said, holding the wolf protectively. "He's a pretty good boy."

"What answers are you after, Mr. Kressler?" Joseph asked. "If the wolf is your friend, I must assume you deserve to know."

"Where is this place Jesse is going to?" Eric jumped in. "Why this sudden change? Why can't she raise Shadow here in Colorado? I have to think Bianca has put all this moving stuff into her head and I'm not very happy about it. I know Jesse's strong, but she's a city girl. This doesn't make sense. Up until a week ago, she wouldn't be caught dead in a pair of cowboy boots, and now all of a sudden she's talking cabins and life on the open range."

"For the record, it doesn't make much sense to Bianca, either," Joseph offered. "She's about as happy with this whole situation as you are."

"Then whose idea was this?" Eric demanded. "What the hell is going on?"

"She loves that animal you hold in your arms," Joseph stated firmly. "It has awakened the wolf spirit within her and she needs to answer its call."

"She doesn't know the first thing about living in the country, or wilderness, or anywhere outside a five mile radius of this city. In my honest opinion, I don't see how this can possibly work."

"That is why I've suggested she live in *my* cabin," said Joseph. "There are people there; my relatives, who can keep an eye on her until she's ready to come home."

"So, you believe she will come home?" Eric asked, hopefully. "Do you think she'll come back to her senses?"

"I cannot answer that," Joseph replied, "because I don't know if she has lost them. This decision surprised me as much as the rest of you." He took another drag off the cigarette and studied the face of the lawyer earnestly. "I thought she would give the wolf up. I never thought she would follow this path. It will be very hard for our *city girl*, I agree, but she seems determined to do it. I do not think it is our place to stop her, because in the long run, I believe it will be good for her. The life she just ended was killing her. I think she has a better chance in this new one."

"Slim one," Eric muttered. "She can't even cook."

"I think she will surprise all of us. We must wait and see." Joseph took one more slow drag off the cigarette and put the stub out in the ashtray. "I don't smoke these things normally. But sometimes, one just hits the spot."

"These relatives," Eric wondered aloud, "do you trust them?"

"With my life and Jesse's," Joseph declared. "They will let me know everything that happens. If we have to, we can be there in fifteen hours, it's about 900 miles to the northwest from here and we don't have to cross the mountains." Joseph got up off the couch and grabbed a bottle of bourbon from inside the sideboard. He poured two shots and gave one to Eric, who had no problem accepting it. "We'll let the women serve the wine with dinner," he said, toasting the young man with a clink of his shot glass against Eric's. "Let this be our appetizer."

"So, what do we do in the meantime?" Eric questioned, downing his drink in one gulp. "I'm just about tapped out of ready cash."

"Our job is to teach Harless everything we can before she leaves," Joseph ordered, filling up their glasses again. "Bianca can teach her to cook and I can show her how to plant a garden and store food. I spent quite a few years there, so I can help the most. As for you, you must take care of this condo she is selling and warn her about where to keep her money safe. She needs to know the law of the land and her rights as a *landowner*, so to speak."

"I'm not up on the latest trespassing laws," Eric mentioned, this time sipping his bourbon rather than guzzling it down.

Joseph set the bottle of bourbon down on the coffee table and returned to his seat. "You must find out. There are hunters up there and the cattlemen might try to run her off. We must be brothers—not enemies—in this endeavor, and it pleases me that we may be beyond that, already."

"Whatever it takes to get her back in one piece," Eric stated, raising his glass to Joseph as a sign of acceptance of his proposition.

Jesse was amazed with everything she accomplished in the next couple of weeks—with the assiduous help of her friends, of course. She got a nervous feeling in her stomach when she considered the fact that soon their support would be 900 miles away and she would have to rely on herself to get things done. She realized, somewhere in the middle of all this, that she had a great family of friends pulling for her, who wanted to see her succeed as much as she did.

Eric threw himself into the *father* role and completed miraculous feats of legal mitigation in record time. He had set up bank accounts and IRA's and educated her in the best ways to handle her money. He prepared her will. He bought the condo and helped her sell or donate the furniture and fixtures they did not want. He managed the *yard sale* of the rest of the stuff—shoes, clothes, knickknacks and the like—netting her another $2,500.00. He wasn't overly pleased with that amount; he was with Jesse when she bought most of that stuff at a significantly higher cost. But Jesse was pleased because it was more than she would have ever dared asked for, being used to the easy way of just giving things away, as was her nature. He helped her pick out a laptop with the money.

Once the condo was cleaned out and everything Jesse wanted to keep was safely tucked away in Joseph's garage, Jesse settled in Littleton for lack of any place better to go. Bianca and Joseph took over where Eric left off.

Bianca was like a mother to her, doting and providing little things like survival/first aid kits, cookbooks, home-repair books, a toolbox filled with tools, some down blankets, flannel sheets and a sewing machine. Jesse laughed at most of the stuff and scolded her for worrying so much. But she had to admit that everything Bianca had given her would probably come in handy some time in her future. Bianca gave her crash courses in cooking, canning, the repair of small leaks and how to clean a furnace filter.

She had taken Jesse and Eric clothes shopping to stores neither Eric nor Jesse had ever set foot in. Despite Eric's whines and callous remarks about the fleece and down jackets, the heavy woolen socks, the stocking caps and the horrendous looking boots, they had a good day and enjoyed each other's company. Bianca laughed to the point of tears at Eric's reaction when Jesse pulled on her first pair of cowboy boots. When Eric disappeared to do some shopping on his own for a little while, the girls took the opportunity to pick up Jesse's long johns and underwear. When he returned, he had three fancily wrapped packages. He ordered Jesse to keep them that way until she was settled in Montana.

Joseph, her teacher, instructed her on what to do if attacked by a mountain lion or a bear. He took her to a gun shop and helped her buy a rifle and a Smith and Wesson revolver. They went to a shooting range, where he gave her lessons on how to shoot the guns and how to clean them. He bought her a supply of bullets.

He gave her the quick low down on his family in Montana, his uncle's phone number, and a carefully drawn map that showed Jesse how to get to the cabin as well as other points along the way. He supplied her with road maps, a snow shovel, a boom box complete with radio, CD and tape player and a deck of cards.

They talked about what herbs to plant and why, winter gardens versus spring gardens and how to can vegetables and fruit. He told her how to look for changes in the weather and how to be prepared if she was caught off guard. He gave her a book on Native American history and filled in some of the gaps with his own stories. She filled a three ring binder with notes. Jesse's favorite gift from Joseph was a handmade wooden flute. Apparently, according to Joseph, she would have plenty of long nights to learn how to play it.

In the middle of this planning and teaching, Jesse made one more trip down to Black Mountain and talked extensively with Nancy Middlesex about wolves. Nancy gave her more books and a list of wolf refuge websites across the country so Jesse could see how each one operated. She spent time with the wolves and watched their behavior. Nancy showed her how to recognize certain medical conditions and what she could do to take care of them.

Shadow played a little with the wolves at the refuge, but seemed to enjoy human company more. Nancy noted how the pup interacted with the wolves as well as people and asked Jesse if she might reconsider giving him to the refuge, citing he would be a great ambassador. She pointed out, as part of her argument, that Shadow would probably be safer at the refuge where he could be kept in an enclosure and not be tempted by the freedom of the wilderness.

Jesse said *no* without even thinking about it. She and Shadow would take the chance at freedom, come what may. As they prepared to leave, Nancy gave Jesse a medicine bag filled with wolf fur and guard hairs from all the members of her packs.

"To protect you," Nancy said, shutting the door of Jesse's truck between them, "and bring you good fortune—as well as Shadow. Our hearts will be with you on your journey."

"Thank you," Jesse murmured, touching her hand through the open window. "I hope I can pay you back for your help and advice one day."

When the dust settled and the preparations were complete, Jesse decided it was time to go. She returned to Denver for one more evening of partying with Eric. They had dinner and buzzed a couple of clubs. The best friends refused to say good-bye, knowing it would be too difficult and distressing to do. They would talk soon and Eric would visit in the summer. That was the best way to leave it for now.

On her last night in Colorado, after dinner together, Bianca, Joseph and Jesse settled into Joseph's room for a quiet night of final questions and advice. Bianca gave her a beautifully framed picture of Bianca, Joseph, Eric and Max. It was to sit on Jesse's new mantelpiece to remind her of the folks back home, where she and Shadow would always be welcome. Jesse cried.

Long after Bianca and Joseph had gone to bed, Jesse picked Shadow up and put him on the futon next to Max who was already settled down for the night.

She pulled down the covers, slipped in beside the wolves and finally lay down. She hoped she could get some sleep before she and Shadow began the long trip to Montana in the morning.

Jesse could hear the soft breathing of the animals snuggled against her. The city outside her window was relatively quiet, save for the passing cars and the sound of the occasional train. The travel clock next to her bed ticked away the minutes toward dawn. She dozed a little, but never really fell into a deep sleep. When the alarm rang at 4 a.m., she lumbered out of the futon and headed for the shower. The wolves stirred, but weren't quite ready to get up.

By the time she was up and dressed and had the last of her belongings packed, Shadow and Max were stretching and ready to go out. She tried to keep everybody quiet as they headed down from the attic to the kitchen, but the thundering paws on the creaking wooden stairs gave away their presence. Jesse's efforts were all for naught. Joseph and Bianca were already awake and down in the kitchen when she and the animals arrived.

"Did you get any sleep?" Bianca asked, busy at the stove cooking breakfast.

"Enough," Jesse sighed, taking a big breath. The nervousness was creeping into her stomach again. She didn't know if she'd be able to eat.

"The truck's packed and ready to go," Joseph said, letting the wolves out the back door. "I fastened down a tarp over it. It should travel pretty well."

"I keep thinking we're forgetting something," Bianca said, flipping the eggs in the frying pan. "I just can't imagine what it could be."

"You've done way too much already," Jesse commented. "I don't know how to pay you all back."

"Just be happy," Bianca insisted. "And come back if it doesn't work out."

"I'm wondering if we should send Max with you," Joseph suggested, joining Jesse at the table. "He is a better watch dog than Shadow right now. We could pick him up when we come to visit."

"You're coming to Montana?" Jesse asked, smiling broadly. "When?"

"We decided to let you get settled and come up sometime at the end of July or beginning of August," Bianca said. "That is if you don't mind, of course,"

"Oh, no!" Jesse cried. "That would be perfect!"

"I had to suggest it," Joseph declared. "I don't think she would have let you go if I didn't."

Jesse smiled at her friends, her stomach settling a bit. It was early June. August was just a couple of months away. She could handle being alone for two months, knowing they were coming.

"And we can bring anything you think of that we've forgotten. Start making a list when you get there." Bianca put the food on the plates. "Maybe it would be good to send Max," she added to Joseph, handing him his plate. "He's very protective."

"But what if something happened to him?" Jesse was worried. "I wouldn't be able to live with myself. I don't know what to expect up there. I don't know if it's fair to put Max through all that."

"Max is a big boy," Joseph said calmly. "He can take care of himself."

"And *you*," Bianca added to Jesse, "which is most important."

"I'd have to load up more food," Joseph said, still thinking about it. "He eats like a horse."

"I don't know if I could handle both of them," Jesse said, taking the plate of food from Bianca and placing it down in front of her. She was not looking forward to taking a bite, even though it looked delicious. "Max is pretty strong, even on his leash."

"Eat what you can," Bianca encouraged, sensing Jesse's nervousness. "I've packed some sandwiches and snacks for later." She sat down across from Jesse with her own plate. "I don't know, either. Joseph, can she control him?"

"He would keep strangers from getting too close," Joseph said between bites. "He barks at the first sign of trouble."

"How about if we let Max decide?" Jesse offered. "If he gets in the truck with us, we'll take him. If he stays put, we'll know he doesn't want to go." She ate a piece of bacon quickly before her stomach refused it.

"That's fair," Bianca answered. "God, I just hope we haven't forgotten something major."

They ate their breakfast quickly with little conversation. Jesse, unable to finish hers, picked up her plate and headed for the sink. Bianca stopped her as she came around the table.

"Don't do that," she smiled weakly. "I'll have to have something to do to take my mind off all of this after you're gone."

"I'll just put it by the sink," Jesse murmured, placing a reassuring hand on her shoulder as she passed by.

"Everything is going to be all right," Joseph acknowledged, aware of their anxieties.

Another hour passed before Jesse was finally ready to go. Joseph checked the weather on the Internet for a tenth time before he was finally satisfied that the conditions were favorable. Jesse stood outside by the truck and let Shadow run for a little while before she had to shut him up in the cab of the truck. Joseph busied himself in the back of the truck making sure everything was tied down securely.

"Now, Charlie will be waiting for you when you get there," he went on, giving her last minute instructions. "You call us every time you stop, so we can let him know when you're close. You've got the cell phone charged, right?"

"It's plugged into the lighter," Jesse checked to make sure it was still there.

"I filled up the tank this morning," Joseph continued. "You shouldn't have to stop until you're out of Colorado. Just make sure you keep in touch."

"Yes, sir," Jesse sighed, smiling at his insistence. "I won't forget."

Bianca came out of the house with another box. "Good Lord, woman," Joseph snapped. "What else have you got?"

"Just some candles and a few things from the shop," Bianca snapped back. "I just can't think of what we've forgotten."

"She's not going to the outback, woman," Joseph persisted. "There's electricity and a propane tank for heat. There's running water and Charlie said they even got cable up there a couple of years ago. So, stop imagining she's moving to the desert."

"But that cell phone probably won't work!" Bianca walked determinedly to her lover and handed him the box.

"Let's just wait and see, okay?" he elected to keep the peace. "Good God woman, you'll drive me to drink."

Jesse laughed at their bickering and called Shadow with a quick whistle. The puppy bounded out of the bushes to her side. She scooped him up and put him in the truck. "He's heavier today than he was yesterday," she commented. Max, following behind Shadow, came up to the truck and looked inside. "Do you want to go with us, buddy?" Jesse asked while Joseph and Bianca looked on with baited breath. The wolf dog placed his front paws on the running board and sniffed the inside of the cab. Shadow looked down at him from where he sat on the passenger seat. For one moment it looked like the animal was going to climb in, but he retreated instead. Jesse knelt down on one knee and gave him a big hug. Max licked her face and ran off to join Joseph.

"That's good," Jesse announced, standing back up and shutting the passenger side door of the truck. "He can come up with you guys in August."

Bianca walked quickly to Jesse and gave her a long, heartfelt embrace. "You come back to us if it's not what you want, okay?" She whispered into Jesse's ear. "You don't have to do this, you know."

"We'll be okay," Jesse soothed into Bianca's ear. "Pretend like we're going on an extended vacation. We're just going to rough it for a little while, just like camp."

"Eric said you hated camp," Bianca murmured back.

"Well," Jesse giggled quietly, "I had to say something drastic to get you two talking again, didn't I?"

"Be safe," Bianca warned. "I'm not going to sleep a wink until I know you're in the cabin."

"I probably won't either," Jesse conceded. "We'll be fine." She hugged Bianca again. "We better get going before the traffic starts."

Joseph and Max had walked to the driver's side door, which Joseph held open for her. "Thanks for everything, Joseph," she offered to shake his hand. Joseph grabbed her and gave her a big bear hug. She gladly hugged him back.

"You take care, Harless," he said. "We'll see you soon."

"You bet," she answered. "We'll make you proud." She gave Max one more pat on the head.

"Make yourself proud. That's all that counts."

Jesse climbed into the cabin of the truck and Joseph shut the door behind her. Shadow jumped onto her lap and peered out the open window, wagging his tail. Joseph reached in and rubbed the wolf's head. Bianca joined Joseph, holding onto Max's collar.

"Take care of your mother, little one," he said to the puppy. "You are the luckiest wolf in the world."

Jesse started up the pickup and put it into drive. She looked at her friends once more. "I don't say good-bye very well, so I'll just talk to you in a couple hours, okay?"

"We'll be right here waiting," Bianca called out over the roar of the hemi engine.

"Get going now," Joseph added, tapping the side of the truck. "You'll never get there as long as you're hanging out here."

Jesse eased the truck onto the street and drove away slowly. She watched Bianca and Joseph in her rearview mirror until they disappeared from sight. She wiped a tear from her eye and concentrated on her driving. "Well, boy," she said to Shadow, who was still perched on her lap, "here's that first day of the rest of our lives. I guess we better stop wasting time and get out of here." Shadow licked Jesse's face. "That makes it all worth while, buddy. Thank you." She turned on the CD player and they hit the road, heading north for Montana.

CHAPTER 9

The sun was up, the pavement was dry and Jesse beat the traffic out of town. Driving north on I-25, she and Shadow were in Cheyenne, Wyoming, in an hour and a half. With a few stops for gas and potty breaks for the pup, they were through Wyoming and into Montana in another five and a half hours. The I-90 expressway travels through the Crow Indian Reservation, and Jesse considered pulling off the road to check out the Little Bighorn Battlefield, but decided against it. They were traveling well. Shadow slept most of the time. When he was awake, he chewed playfully on Jesse's sweater and arm as she drove or he just contented himself with looking out the window from her lap. He had his food and water on the floorboard of the passenger side of the truck and his favorite Prada shoe to chew on when Jesse was otherwise occupied.

The wolf was a hit at the rest stops. Children and adults were intrigued with the pup and they all wanted to pet him. Jesse was pleasant and answered their questions, but kept Shadow on a tight leash. She would have to leave him in the truck and go to the restroom first before she could take him for his little walk. Most of the time, no matter how quick she tried to be, people who were captivated by the little wolf's mournful howls were surrounding the truck by the time she got back to it. She found, as the trip continued, that she was most happy with the rest stops that were devoid of fellow travelers.

She phoned Joseph and Bianca regularly, but ended up having to use a payphone for most of the calls. The farther north she got, the less coverage there was for her cell phone. Joseph had warned her, so she wasn't too surprised. She tried the cell phone every once in a while and if it worked, the couple got an unexpected call. Bianca was amazed at the progress they'd made. Jesse and

Shadow had left Littleton at 5:30 a.m. Twelve hours later, Jesse was just outside of Great Falls, Montana, and almost to her new home.

Joseph suggested she stay at a hotel there overnight. He warned her that she was going to be out of expressways soon and the roads to the cabin were gravel and dirt. Jesse agreed with him over the phone, but after she and Shadow shared a quick dinner of hamburgers and fries, she decided to travel on. She sped north on I-15 and got to Conrad, Montana, by 7:30 p.m.

Her body was stiff and she ached all over. She was beyond exhausted when she stopped and filled up the gas tank one more time. The gas station attendant gave her a few more directions and after a long walk with Shadow, in the very quiet town, she drove on to Dupuyer. An hour later, she parked in front of a general store and was thrilled to see it was still open. She turned off the ignition and quietly slipped out of the truck. Shadow was fast asleep on the seat beside her and thankfully did not feel like getting up.

She set foot in the store and blinked her tired eyes. They were road weary and unaccustomed to the bright lights. A woman, about her age, was sitting behind the counter tallying the day's receipts. She looked up when Jesse came in, and smiled.

"You're early," she said, totally surprising Jesse. "Didn't expect you 'til morning."

"Excuse me?" Jesse asked incredulously.

"You're Jesse Harless," the woman continued. "Charlie told us you were coming."

"How did you know it was me?" Jesse limped a bit as she walked over to the counter. The bones in her knees and hips were most uncooperative and fighting her forward progress.

"We don't get a lot of strange women in here," she smiled. "Especially at this time of night. I was just about to close up." She stood up and offered her hand. Jesse shook it. "I'm Arleen Stewart. Welcome to Montana, Jesse Harless."

"I'm so glad to be here," Jesse responded, her voice crackling from disuse. "I'm a little tired."

"How long have you been on the road?" Arleen put the receipts in the cash register and shut the drawer.

"Since 5:30 this morning. I'm not sure how long that is at this moment."

Arleen laughed. "That would make it about fifteen and a half hours, sweetie. It's going on nine o'clock."

"It feels like fifteen days to me," Jesse stretched her arms back behind herself and looked around the store. "I'm going to have to lie down pretty soon."

"Well, you've got about another twenty miles to go, but those will be the roughest. It probably would have been better if you'd gotten here before sunset."

Jesse sighed deeply. "But I'm so damn close." She rubbed her eyes, removing any last vestiges of makeup.

"Is there anything you need?" Arleen offered. "Some coffee or something to eat?"

"The coffee sounds great," Jesse said. "And probably some bread, butter and milk." She saw a refrigerated cooler with glass doors and started for it, not wanting to take up any more of Arleen's time than she had to. Unfortunately, her knees buckled and she stumbled, just missing a rack of potato chips.

Arleen quickly came from around the counter. It was obvious the young woman was dead on her feet. "Well, let me help you get that stuff," she suggested. "And then I've got an idea. If you can wait 'til I ring out, you can follow me. I don't live too far from you."

Jesse's eyes brightened. "You mean it?" she exhaled. "I would really appreciate that. I'm not sure if I can see in the dark."

"I don't think you'll be able to, either," Arleen agreed. "Let's get you packed up and out of here, okay?"

"Okay!" Jesse shook the sleepiness away and concentrated on the shopping.

A short time later, Arleen placed the groceries on the backseat of the pickup. Shadow raised his head and looked at her with sleepy eyes.

"Now that's the cutest thing I've seen in ages," Arleen noted, seeing the ball of fur curled up on the front seat. "Climb in, girl," she commandeered Jesse, quietly closing the passenger side door. "Let's get you guys home."

The shopkeeper's truck was much older and very well used. She pulled out onto US 89 and headed north with Jesse doing her best to keep up behind her. They turned west after a stint on US 89 and the road was just like Joseph had warned her—dirt and gravel. Jesse kept her eyes on Arleen's taillights. Several miles down the road she knew for a fact that she would never have made it without those lights serving as beacons.

Arleen's red taillights and Jesse's headlights were the only illumination piercing the pitch-black night. There were no streetlights and no other cars, just dark shadows on either side of the two-lane road. The new moon showed only a sliver of white low on the horizon and there were millions of twinkling stars carpeting the night sky. Jesse leaned over the steering wheel and looked up through the windshield. She was fascinated with the beauty of the starry sky.

Some miles further, Arleen pulled her truck to the side of the road, stopped and turned on her left blinker. Jesse pulled up beside her and rolled down the passenger side window.

"That's your gate," Arleen shouted over the engines. "Do you have a key for the lock?"

"Yes, yes I do," stammered Jesse, grabbing for her purse. She threw the truck into park and got out quickly on rubbery legs. She found the padlock and slipped the key in the keyhole. The lock released and Jesse opened the gate.

Arleen had backed her truck up and lit up the area with her headlights. When Jesse had the gates opened wide, she walked to Arleen's truck. "You've got about half a mile to go, but at least you're on your property," Arleen said with a smile. "Welcome to your new home."

"I really need to thank you," Jesse called out. "What can I do to…"

"It's just nice to have another female around. Come see me at the store once in a while," Arleen laughed. "What is it you guys say in the city—we'll do lunch!"

"You've got it!" Jesse yelled. Arleen pulled her truck around and with a wave, headed back where they'd come from. Jesse ran and jumped into her own vehicle.

"We're home, Shadow!" she said excitedly, rubbing her hands vigorously in the wolf pup's fur. Fully awake now, he hopped up on her lap and peered out the glass into the darkness. "I kind of wish you were driving," Jesse sighed. "I bet you can see a lot better out there than I can right now."

She drove to the other side and parked. After locking the gates, she could still see a speck of red as Arleen's ride barreled down the dusty road. It took a second, but Jesse realized that Arleen obviously wasn't on her way home when she let Jesse follow her. Jesse wondered how far the woman had driven out of her way to help her.

Walking back to the truck, Jesse became aware of the stark darkness surrounding her. She had never seen so many stars, nor had she ever seen them so clearly. They blanketed the night sky from one horizon to the other, but without the moon's light, they did very little to illuminate her way. The dark shapes looming in the distance around her appeared to be trees—hundreds and hundreds of them. She recognized the tops of fir trees with their black spires pointing upwards. She honestly could not pick out any other familiar shapes. Was it a mountain or just more trees? The beams of the headlights skirted over some greenery, tall brush and bushes. There were other trees just a few yards to either side of what appeared to be a rutted road that wound on ahead.

The outline of Shadow's little dark head was in the window and Jesse could hear his whimpers. She got back into the truck and scratched his neck briskly. "We can do this, boy," she smiled. "We're almost there!" Shadow leapt back onto her lap as she threw the truck into gear and started slowly along the rough road. Jesse eased the vehicle over holes and puddles. Sometimes the branches of the trees closed in around them and rubbed against the sides of the pickup as they passed by. Everything looked green and lush. She could feel the humidity in the air as if it had rained not too long ago.

"Damn," she uttered, as they lumbered on for longer than she'd hoped they would have to. "I should have looked at the odometer, boy. I have no idea how far we've traveled." She looked hard out all the windows of the cab, almost desperately searching for anything that looked like some kind of shelter. The trees receded from the road and all she could see was prairie-like land in front of them. No dark shapes of a cabin; nothing that resembled a structure of any kind. Nothing but stars, even on the ground just a few hundred yards in front of the truck. She blinked several times and tried to focus. The stars kept getting closer and everything else was getting darker and blacker. Something wasn't quite right.

Suddenly, Jesse slammed on the brakes. The cargo in the bed of the pickup shifted forward. Shadow slid off the seat. He yelped at her and scooted under her legs. Jesse had racked her brain trying to figure out why the stars could be where they were. As tired as she was, it took a few minutes of concentrated thought to come to the conclusion that the stars on the ground were a reflection of the stars in the sky. Only one thing reflected like that—water. The wheels of the truck came to a screeching halt at the edge of a large lake.

"Shit!" Jesse cursed, taking a deep breath. "I'm sorry, boy. I didn't see it coming." She threw the transmission into reverse and backed slowly away from the water's edge. Once she felt somewhat safe, she shifted to park and turned off the ignition. She helped Shadow back up onto her lap and sighed heavily. She was shaking and quite terrified of what she almost did. With the headlights off, her eyes eventually adjusted to the lack of light. There, before her, was a very large, black mirror full of stars.

She held Shadow close to her and rubbed her face against his fur. He licked her and snuggled close to her neck. "I'm sorry, baby," she whispered. "I almost killed us both. "Maybe Joseph was right. Maybe we should have stayed in Great Falls overnight."

After a while, Jesse summoned her courage to step out of the truck. She put Shadow on his leash because she knew she'd lose him in the blink of an eye if she didn't. The air was cold and wet. Jesse grabbed her suede jacket out of the back seat and put it on. She was happy to see that there were two bottles of water and some food left.

What she was not happy to find, when she and Shadow got to the back of the pickup, was the certainty that she did not have a source of light to see where Joseph had put everything. If she hadn't been to the point of exhaustion, she might have laughed because now she remembered what Bianca did not. They had not thought to pack a flashlight and now the woman and her wolf were stuck somewhere in the wilderness on a cold, black night with no way of locating the few things they could use to make their evening a little more pleasant.

Jesse reached her hand under the tarp to see if anything felt familiar. She immediately found the box that Bianca had brought out just before she left. She finagled it out from under the cover and placed it on the ground beside her. Shadow sat next to her, sniffing the air and twitching his ears every which way. His gaze followed the direction of his ears and he intently studied the darkness around them.

Jesse rummaged a bit more and sighed with relief when she felt the rolled up sleeping bag. She had to tug at it for a while before she could work it free from the other items that Joseph had packed so carefully. Once she got it out from underneath the tarp, she held it close to her chest for a moment, silently thanking any entity that might be watching over them from above. At least they wouldn't freeze to death.

At that instant, Shadows ears pricked up again and he cocked his head to the side. Jesse didn't hear the call, but the wolf pup obviously did. He raised his head and howled into the night sky.

"What is it, Shadow?" Jesse asked the pup. "Did you hear something?" She listened as hard as she could, but the night was completely silent all around her. Shadow listened too and then answered with another howl.

"Okay," Jesse said. "You're hearing something I can't and I don't mind telling you it's making me a little nervous." She put the sleeping bag on top of the box and picked them both up in her arms, towing Shadow alongside her. The pup strained a bit on the leash but followed. They went back to the cab of the truck where Jesse set the box on the seat and looked at the contents under the dome light. There were candles of all sorts and a couple of lighters. She didn't want to take the chance of running the battery down in the truck, so she picked out the seven-day candles (set in glass) and lit them quickly. She did not have the slightest idea how to start a campfire, and to be honest with herself, she was deathly afraid of setting her new land on fire. She would make do with the candles and learn about campfires tomorrow.

She took the candles and put them on the ground near the cab of the truck, untied the sleeping bag and spread it out beside them, then went and got the sandwiches and Shadow's dog food. She poured some of her bottled water into Shadow's dish and saved the rest for herself. After she unzipped the sleeping bag, she crawled in and Shadow joined her. They ate their dinner in front of the lit candles, which, surprisingly, gave off quite a bit of heat. Jesse sat there wondering if the cabin had a fireplace. If it did, she vowed to herself they'd have a fire as soon as they got unpacked.

After dinner, she left Shadow in the sleeping bag and stored the remaining food in the truck. She hoped to God they wouldn't be attacked by a bear or some other creature who might smell it. Just to be safe, she pulled the revolver out from the glove box and placed it within reach before she crawled back in the sleeping bag and lay down with Shadow.

The pup howled a couple more times, and once Jesse thought she might have heard a distant howl answering back. She lay down on her back, resting the back of her head on her clasped hands and looked up at the carpet of bright stars blinking down at her. Shadow, covered by the sleeping bag, burrowed up against her and placed his head on his paws, still looking vigilantly into the night.

Jesse was too tired to cry or worry about what might happen next. It was too late to worry whether she had made the right decision to come all this way without stopping someplace for the night. If they were alive in the morning, she'd consider her actions then. An owl hooted from somewhere in the trees. She also heard some rustling in the underbrush. She mulled over the situation she was in and laughed quietly at the absurdity of it all. Eric would have been very upset to learn she was lying on the cold ground in the open air. She had never camped out or had any interest in the activity, but here she was, just like the cowboys in the Old West. And she might as well have been in the Old West, for there were no sounds to tell her that civilization existed. No cars, no sirens, no planes; not even a train could be heard in the distance. All she could hear was the wind rustling the leaves in the trees.

A little while later, with the soft, warm breath of Shadow against her neck, she finally closed her eyes and fell asleep—too exhausted to stay awake a moment longer.

CHAPTER 10

❀

Jesse burrowed deeper into the sleeping bag. She was dreaming and in her dream she was cold, lost and alone. She rolled over and her stiff fingers groped for more blankets. In this position she sensed the beginnings of a warm, white light. She stirred slowly to consciousness. Something was telling her to wake up. She could not feel Shadow's breath or his fur nestled against her. The situation was not right.

She opened her eyes and blinked furiously. The white light was the rising sun and it was so bright it momentarily blinded her. She propped herself up on her elbow and rubbed her eyes. She called out quietly, "Shadow?" The leash around her wrist was taut and tugged at her gently. "Thank God," she thought. Hopefully, it was still attached to the wolf. As her eyes adjusted to the light, she looked to her left and saw Shadow, with ears alert, sitting up and studying the terrain. "There you are, baby boy," the woman smiled. "What did I miss?"

Shadow scampered back and jumped on top of her, pawing at the sleeping bag and licking her face. She laughed and covered her head with the blanket, but Shadow was not having it that way. He yipped at her. It was time to get up.

Jesse sat up and stretched, stiff bones cracking into place as she forced her body into motion and shook off the cold that had settled into them. Afterwards, she took stock of their location. She drew in a sharp, clean breath of fresh air. The scenery surrounding them was breathtaking.

The water was there. It was a much larger lake than Jesse had imagined the night before. The water was crisp and blue and lapping onto the shore just a few hundred yards from where she had parked the truck. On the other side of the lake there were trees and rolling hills as far as the eye could see. Firs and pines and cottonwood trees reached high into the cloudless blue sky. A hawk was circling above them. The owl she had heard the night before clattered as he jumped from one branch up to the next before settling back down to watch the spectacle below.

Jesse turned and looked behind her. More trees and black mountains rose in the distance. Shadow jumped off her lap and ran until the leash stopped him. A bunny had chosen a path precariously close. It scampered quickly into the underbrush, eluding capture. Shadow strained at the leash and whimpered. It was all so beautiful, Jesse thought, and so wild. There was no sign of a cabin or a shed, or any kind of shelter. She did not even see the tracks she had followed to get her to this point last night.

Holding tight to the leash, Jesse got up on her knees and forced herself to stand up. She felt like she'd been hit by a truck. She kneaded her fingers into the small of her back. It seemed impossible to stand up straight. She also realized, disconcertedly, that she needed to pee. "Oh, Lord," she sighed, wondering what to do next. She turned to locate the nearest tree and was startled to see a man coming toward her. She froze in place. Shadow growled.

"There you are," the man announced, aware of her trepidation. "You gave us quite a fright." The man slowed down his pace, now that he had found her. He was older with long, silver-gray, braided hair. He wore jeans, cowboy boots and a vest over a dark shirt. He was Indian.

Jesse opened her mouth to speak, but nothing came out. The Indian kept coming closer. She took a step back toward the truck.

"I'm Charlie White Feather Stillwater," he added quickly. "Joe's uncle. You're on his land, Jesse Harless."

"Oh!" Jesse finally found her voice. "I didn't..."

"It's okay," Charlie said, approaching her. "I'm sorry. I scared you."

"I'm lost!" Jesse smiled, thankful now for the Indian's presence. "I don't know where I am."

"Arleen called last night and said you were here," Charlie continued. "When you weren't at the cabin this morning, I started to look." He approached the young woman, who eagerly shook his outstretched hand with both of hers. "You took the path to the right instead of to the left."

"Pardon me?" Jesse looked confused.

"There's a fork about a half mile back," Charlie offered. "During the day you can see the cabin up to the left." He sized the woman up with one glance. He knelt down on one knee and greeted the wolf pup. Shadow sniffed the hand he offered and then welcomed the pat on the head.

"I almost hit the water," Jesse rambled on, happy for the company. "I suppose I shouldn't have tried to do it all in one day."

"Well, you made it," Charlie smiled, glancing at the sleeping bag and candles. "That's what's important."

"I didn't want to chance a fire," she said, embarrassed. "I didn't know how dry it was up here."

"Mmmm," Charlie nodded, looking again at the city girl. "We'll teach you how to make a campfire soon enough." He walked over and picked up the sleeping bag. "Let's get you to the cabin and settled in."

Jesse quickly picked up the candles and headed for the truck. Charlie found the gun. "You do know how to fire this, right?" he asked, handing it over to her. "You could have needed it last night."

Jesse, even more embarrassed, took the revolver and put it on the floorboard of the truck. "Thank God I didn't. I still need to practice." She tossed the keys to Charlie, who was somewhat surprised to get them, but caught them just the same. "I'm going to let you drive." She walked to the passenger side, picked up Shadow and climbed in. "I don't need to run into any more lakes."

Charlie climbed in and started the engine. "Nice truck," he commented, throwing it into gear. "It will be good in the snow." He wheeled the vehicle around and started back through the field. Jesse really had to pee now, and the bumps in the makeshift road didn't help to ease the pain. Shadow was all over the front seat, checking out Charlie's lap for a second and then heading back for Jesse's. Jesse cringed each time his paws pressed on her bladder.

"Here's the spot," Charlie finally stated, making a sharp right turn. The road before them now was a little more defined. Jesse could not believe that she had missed it. "There are other roads around here, too. You'll figure it out once you get used to the place."

Ahead, Jesse could see the cabin. It wasn't very big, but it looked like a palace to her as it came into view. It was a two-story building with a large covered porch, which spanned the entire front face. It was a log cabin with a green tin roof and it reminded Jesse of the Lincoln logs she played with as a child. There was a chimney on the right side of the house and two windows up on the second floor, which were set into the roof. There was a swing, two rocking chairs and a small wooden table on the porch.

Charlie pulled up in front of the structure and killed the engine. "You're home, Jesse Harless," he said quietly. "I hope it's what you expected."

"It looks perfect at the moment," she sighed, handing Shadow's leash to Charlie and slipping out of the truck. "I'm afraid I really need to go…"

"Door's open," Charlie realized her dilemma. "Just past the kitchen to the left."

"Thanks!" Jesse called out, disappearing into the cabin in the blink of an eye.

Charlie White Feather Stillwater looked down into the wolf pup's eyes and shook his head. Jesse Harless seemed like a nice enough girl, but he didn't think she was very bright. "City folk just don't fit up here in the country," he said to no one in particular, but Shadow appeared to be listening. "I give her a couple of weeks before she turns tail and heads back."

Her bladder finally relieved, Jesse looked around the bathroom of her new house. The fixtures were old, but the toilet flushed and the sink worked. The shower was mildewed and needed a good scrubbing. And, while there was room for one, there was no tub. She imagined what it needed: a claw foot tub with room to soak. She zipped up her jeans and left the bathroom, taking a cursory look around her new digs. There was a staircase up the back wall just to her left that led to the second floor, a huge fireplace straight ahead of her on the opposite wall with a couch and some chairs in front of it, and a table by one of the two front windows with a telephone perched on top. The main floor was an L-shape with the kitchen to the right. There was a refrigerator, stove and sink and a bigger table with four chairs set in the middle of the room. The front door was just outside the kitchen area. She had left the heavy main door wide open and she could see, through the screen door, Charlie unloading the truck with Shadow jumping on his leash beside him.

She opened the screen door. The coils stretched with a long squeak and sprung the door back shut when she stepped out onto the porch. The cabin had been built on a hill and she looked out onto a vast green, grassy field. She could see the lake in the distance to the left through a forest of cottonwoods and firs. The sky was big and a beautiful shade of blue. White clouds were starting to billow up on the horizon. A soft breeze crossed over Jesse's face.

"So, what do you think?" Charlie asked, bringing a load of Jesse's belongings to the porch. "Is it what you expected?" He handed her Shadow's leash and the wolf pup jumped up into Jesse's arms.

"It's beautiful," Jesse commented, "and so very quiet." She knelt down and put Shadow down on the floor. "Well, buddy, I guess we're home." She unfastened the wolf's collar and freed him from his tether. "You don't have to have this on anymore," she said, rubbing his neck. Where it had fit comfortably a few days ago, the collar was now tight. "That wasn't a second too soon." Shadow wasn't sure what to do. He looked up at Jesse and put a paw on her knee. "We better get you fed." Jesse got up and headed to the truck. She grabbed more stuff while Shadow nipped at her heels.

"That's a fine animal," Charlie noted, putting another load down on the floor just inside the cabin and passing Jesse and the pup as they went in. "He's gonna' be a big one."

"He's getting bigger every day." Jesse had found the box of puppy food and took it into the kitchen. She dug out his bowl, filled it up and set it on the floor. The wolf attacked the food and ate voraciously. Jesse filled another bowl with water and put it down next to the animal. Shadow let out a little low growl when she got close. "Hey, bad wolf!" she snapped. "Nobody's going to take it away from you." Shadow settled in, with his tail wagging happily as he ate.

"We haven't seen a wolf in these parts for some time," Charlie continued, bringing in more boxes. "Although, we can hear 'em once in a while." Jesse handed the Indian a glass of water, which he accepted after brushing his hands off on his jeans. "We've got plenty of bears and some big cats, though." He drank the water in a couple of gulps. Jesse took the glass back and refilled it for him, before drinking her own. "I'm surprised you didn't run into any of them last night."

"I'm grateful we didn't," Jesse sighed. "Don't know what I would have done."

"You would have shot 'em," Charlie said, downing the second glass as quickly as the first. "That's what you do up here."

"Aren't they protected?" the young woman asked, following the Indian back outside to the truck.

"Yeah, they're protected. But when they're charging you, you better protect yourself."

"I'm going to have to get used to all this," Jesse murmured.

"They stay away from populated areas unless they're really hungry," Charlie quipped, handing Jesse a couple more boxes while grabbing the last of them himself. "Just keep the food packed up and put away. Joe packed this stuff pretty good. That's probably why they didn't bother you last night."

"Remind me to thank him," Jesse remarked, holding the door for Charlie to pass through into the cabin. Shadow was lapping up the water from his bowl and making his usual mess.

"Speaking of that," Charlie suggested, "let's give him a call right now, okay? They hooked up the phone yesterday and I want to make sure it works."

Jesse went over to the table and sat down heavily. She was still pretty tired. She picked up the receiver and dialed the number to Colorado. Joseph picked up the phone on the first ring. "Hey, it's me," she said.

"We were pretty worried when you didn't call earlier," Joseph broadcasted. "Where are you at?"

"I'm in my cabin and Charlie just brought in the last of the stuff from the truck."

"How did you get there already?" Joseph's voice betrayed his concern. "Is everything all right?"

"As soon as I get a shower and some food, everything will be just fine," Jesse calmed her friend. "Everything went without a hitch." She winked at Charlie, hoping he would not betray her little white lie. "I met a nice woman at the general store. She let me follow her the rest of the way last night."

"Okay," Joseph said slowly, not sure if he should believe her. "You say Charlie's there? Let me speak to him."

With a sheepish grin, Jesse handed the receiver to the Indian. "I don't think he trusts me," she volunteered.

"Hey, kid," Charlie spoke into the receiver. "What's new?" He let Joseph rattle off for a while before he spoke again. He smiled at Jesse, who wondered what Joseph was saying, and gave her a wink. "Nah, she's fine. Had no trouble at all. I woke her up this morning and we just got everything off the truck. Good packing, by the way." He was silent for a little while longer while Joseph kept on talking. "Well, she did and that's that. It probably was easier to come straight here. What hotel in their right mind is gonna' take in a wolf?" More silence. "Well, look. She'll call ya' back later after we finish breakfast. She's a darn good cook!"

Jesse winced, shaking her head. Joseph knew she wasn't.

"Well, nobody can screw up bacon and eggs now, can they?" Charlie tried to make the save. "Okay, okay. She'll call ya' back. Look I gotta' go. Bye." Charlie hung up the phone while Joseph was still talking. "You'd better call him later. I didn't give him the phone number so he can't call you back yet."

"Thanks," Jesse sighed, getting up. "I owe you one." She started for the kitchen. "How about that breakfast?"

"That's okay," Charlie stated quickly. Jesse surmised Joseph must have filled him in on her culinary abilities. "I gotta' get home and give you some space. My wife, Winona, wants you to come for dinner if you're up for it. Can I come get you around five tonight?"

"Sure," Jesse said with no hesitation. "I'd love to meet her."

"Okay," Charlie said, letting himself out. "Our number is next to the phone if you need anything. I think the most important thing for you to do right now is get some rest."

"Hey," Jesse called out after him. "Where's your truck?" she realized there were no other vehicles parked around the cabin.

"It's just a few miles by foot," Charlie answered back. "I'll show you the way later. It's quicker to walk."

Jesse furrowed her brow, watching as he disappeared across the field and into the trees. She could never have imagined walking rather than driving. One drove every place in Colorado, even the couple of blocks to the store. She sighed and turned her attention to the boxes. Surprisingly enough, she had a lot of stuff to unpack.

She dealt with the food first. Bianca had loaded her up with all the staples such as flower, sugar and salt. At the bottom of that box, she found the cookbooks Bianca had slipped in. She put a case of Coke in the refrigerator to chill next to the milk, butter and eggs she had purchased the night before. She had jelly and peanut butter, tuna and cans of soup. There were boxes of macaroni and cheese, Tuna Helper and noodles. She also found bologna, ground beef, a couple of steaks, cheese, a head of lettuce and some tomatoes in another cooler Bianca had provided.

Jesse unpacked some dishes, silverware and some pots and pans and put them in the empty cupboards. There were also rolls of paper towels, napkins, a tablecloth and toilet paper tucked neatly into another box. She found the packets of seeds for the garden and put them aside, along with a pair of garden shears and some garden gloves.

"I can't think of anything we're missing so far, Shadow," Jesse said, taking a little break. "Except for that damn flashlight." Shadow had done a little searching of his own and found his favorite Prada shoe. He lay down in front of the screen door and was contentedly chewing on the strap, while his eyes warily watched the world outside. He looked up when Jesse spoke and thumped his tail on the wood floor. "Geez," she continued, regarding all the boxes still left to unpack. "How'd Joseph get all this stuff into that truck?" She sat down on the floor next to Shadow and played with him for a minute. He rolled onto her lap and chewed on her fingers while she tried to pet him. He also tried to grab the silver chain Jesse wore around her neck.

She gazed around the room and took stock of their new home. There was a closet under the staircase and another door next to the bathroom door. She got up with a groan and started to explore. The other door led to a storage room of sorts. There was a water heater and furnace in the corner and a washtub with running water. "I wonder where the laundry-mat is, boy," Jesse thought out loud. Shadow was sniffing everything he could reach, checking out every corner. "Come on," Jesse coaxed the wolf, "let's see what's upstairs."

They climbed up the rather steep staircase and Jesse noticed Shadow was big enough to traverse the stairs with ease. Once on the landing, Jesse sensed she was in a very large room, but the only light switch she could find did not appear to work. In the shadows, she saw a beat up bed to her left, a tattered floor rug and a broken rocking chair. She could see a window in the apex of the roof that looked south, half covered with a very heavy looking curtain. It was so heavy, the rod was bent almost in two and the curtain hung precariously on the edge of it. Other than that, the room was just too dark. She had forgotten about the other windows in the front of the house. There was another fireplace behind her, directly over the one downstairs. Shadow sniffed around a bit, but then sneezed, dislodging a little cloud of dust. "Let's check this floor out later," his mistress said quietly, feeling awkwardly nervous. "That couch downstairs looked pretty comfy. We can sleep on that tonight."

They clamored back downstairs and Jesse was surprised to find some heavy men's jackets, two flannel shirts, a broom and an ironing board in the cupboard under the staircase. There was a door at the foot of the stairs that she assumed was another closet, and located next to that was the back door to the cabin. Instead of investigating, she turned back to the living room and unpacked a few more boxes. She put the toiletries and towels in the bathroom and stacked some books onto a bookcase. She then set the candles out on the kitchen table and put the cleaning supplies neatly under the sink. When she found a clock, packed in with Joseph's survival kit, she was shocked to see it was one o'clock in the afternoon. She put the clock on the mantelpiece and threw the extra batteries into a kitchen drawer before deciding to give up and take a break. She grabbed some bologna, a piece of cheese and a Coke out of the refrigerator and headed out to the porch with her wolf. She sat down laboriously on the steps and watched Shadow timidly check out their new surroundings.

A plethora of birds sang their unique songs in harmony, as if to counter the caws from the huge black crows nearby. Other creatures scurried in the tall grasses. Shadow, busy sniffing the ground, paid little attention to them this time out. It was warm and the sun shown brightly overhead. Fluffy white clouds were stark in contrast to the azure sky. Again, Jesse looked up to see a hawk still circling high above them. She wondered if it was the same one she had seen that morning. There was another rustling in the trees not far off. Jesse looked over to see a deer, suddenly quite still, staring at her.

She watched the gentle creature, who was mesmerized for a few moments by the wolf. Seeing enough, the deer scampered back into the woods for safety. Jesse considered lying down where she sat on the porch, the sun lulling her into an exhausted stupor. But Shadow finished his rounds, scuttled back up the steps and nudged her with his now very dirty nose. Jesse knew there was no time for a nap.

Back in the house, she took the rest of the boxes and suitcases filled with clothes and stacked them in front of the closet door. Her suitcase carried the essentials. She pulled out some clean underwear, socks, a new pair of jeans and a shirt. Her comfy sweater was also tucked neatly inside, so she pulled that out as well. Shadow was back at his dinner bowl when she went into the bathroom, dropped her dirty clothes and took a long shower. The pressure was surprisingly good and the water nice and hot. Shadow, exploring again, came into the bathroom and stuck his head in the shower. He yipped when the hot water hit his face. After he shook off the water, he lay down and watched Jesse from a spot under the sink.

Jesse wrapped her freshly washed hair in a towel and brushed her teeth. She felt better after she put on a little makeup and dressed in some clean clothes. She and Shadow moved back into the living room where Jesse found the boom box/CD player. She put it on the table by the phone and plugged it in. It took some maneuvering of the dial, but finally she found a radio station that was broadcasting the news. She didn't really care what the newscaster had to say. She was just happy to hear a human's voice.

Dialing the phone, she called Colorado. She was in the middle of a yawn when Joseph picked up.

"Damn it, woman," Joseph snapped. "Why did you hang up?"

"Charlie hung up," Jesse offered apologetically. "I couldn't stop him."

"Are you all right?" Bianca had picked up the extension and butted in on the conversation.

"Just tired," Jesse sighed. "It's been a long two days."

"So you didn't have any problems on the road?" Joseph asked. "Everything got there all right?"

"Everything is fine and I'm almost unpacked," Jesse lied. "Charlie is taking me to their house tonight for dinner, so I guess you could say I already have a date." Jesse laughed into the receiver.

"What time did you get there?" Joseph asked, still concerned. "You said you found Arleen Stewart, right? She's the woman who runs the general store."

"Yeah," Jesse answered. "She was really nice. I never would have found the place without her."

"Not last night," Joseph agreed. "Once the sun goes down, it gets pretty dark. It's not the city, you know."

"Yeah, I found that out," Jesse snickered. "But we made it and we're settling in. I don't think Shadow has figured it out yet. There are animals all over the place, yet he sticks close to me."

"That'll change soon enough," Joseph said. "Enjoy him while you can."

"Now, Joseph," Bianca reprimanded him. She did not want the man to upset Jesse so soon after her arrival. "Jess, did you find the cooler with the food in it?"

"Yes," Jesse smiled. "And thanks for all the stuff. By the way, I did figure out the one thing we missed."

"Good God, tell me," Bianca asked fervently. "It kept me up most of the night."

"A flashlight," Jesse said. "I could have used it when I got in."

"Damn!" Bianca cursed. "I knew it was important."

"It's all good, though," Jesse reassured her. "The electricity is on and the water's nice and hot. The bulbs are burnt out upstairs, but I'll get some new ones when I go into town."

"Have Charlie show you how the furnace works. There's a propane tank out back of the cabin that will need to be filled once every three months."

"Yes, sir," Jesse responded obediently. "He gave me their phone number in case I need them."

"Speaking of phone numbers," Joseph retorted. "What's yours?

Jesse saw a list of numbers next to the phone on the table. Hers at the cabin was listed first, followed by the Stillwater's number and Arleen Stewart's at the store. "406," she said, reading the number for the first time herself, "555-6576."

"Now, you've probably noticed the temperature drops at night," Joseph continued with his instructions. Jesse smirked, remembering her adventure near the lake. "Make sure you wear a coat if you're going to be out after dark. And take your revolver with you! There are wild animals out there and you don't want to get caught defenseless. And keep the garbage in the metal garbage cans that lock down. There should be one in the storage room. There's a dump just outside of town. Get to know it."

"Anything else, Dad?" Jesse smiled into the phone. "Do I have a curfew that I need to know about?"

"I'm serious, Harless," Joseph scolded. "You're not in Denver anymore."

"Now, Joseph," Bianca tried to calm him over the extension. "Jesse's a big girl. I think she can handle it."

"Yeah," Joseph snarled. "Don't blame me if we get up there and all that's left are some bleached bones on the porch. Then you'll wish I'd told her a lot more."

"Okay, you guys," Jesse interrupted, not wanting them to argue. "I've got to get ready for dinner. Charlie said he'd be here at four o'clock." She stretched the truth a bit, but hoped they wouldn't mind. "Make a list of what I need to know, Joseph. I'll call you in a couple of days and you can tell me the rest. I appreciate it. Really, I do."

"But you don't mind if we call you once in a while, right?" Bianca asked pleadingly.

"By all means!" Jesse answered quickly. "It's great to hear your voices. Things are pretty quiet up here, you know."

"And listen to the news reports on the radio," Joseph added quickly. "They'll give you weather updates and stuff like that."

"I just plugged it in," Jesse said. "I noticed there wasn't a T.V."

"Talk to Charlie about that," Joseph suggested. "They've probably got satellite dishes up there somewhere."

"Take care, you two," Jesse murmured. "I miss you both, terribly."

"We'll see you soon," Bianca announced boldly, prohibiting Joseph from going on. "Probably sooner than you think."

"The door will be open," Jesse laughed. "You're welcome anytime."

"And lock that door at night!" Joseph was yelling into the phone when Jesse hung up. She did miss them already. She also missed Eric. But she was too tired to make another call.

Jesse finished dressing and refilled Shadow's food dish. He had emptied it a while ago. The young woman looked at the remaining boxes, but couldn't lift another lid. She moved everything else off the couch and lay down on it. After munching some more of his puppy chow, Shadow jumped up on the couch and joined her. They both took a little nap.

CHAPTER 11

Jesse was doing her best to avoid some very big bears in her dream when Charlie's knock on the screen door woke her up with a start. She bolted straight up. Shadow was off the couch and at the door in seconds.

"How ya doin' in there?" the Indian's voice was music to Jesse's ears. "Are ya ready for some good, old fashioned home cooking?"

"Come in, Charlie," Jesse called out, clearing her head with a shake. "I'm starving!"

The screen door screeched open and slammed shut behind him. "Hey, the place is starting to take shape," he said, looking around.

"If you like that *just moved in* look," Jesse said, getting up. "I've still got a lot to put away."

"You've got plenty of time, I figure," Charlie smiled, petting Shadow on the back of his head. "There's not much else to do around here, other than to fix things up."

Jesse picked up her jacket and went to grab her purse. She realized, suddenly, that she didn't really need it and just picked up her keys to the house instead. "I hope there's a little more to do than that. Bianca packed a lot of seeds and stuff. She thinks I should learn how to garden while I'm here."

"Who's Bianca?" Charlie asked innocently. He held the door open for Jesse and Shadow bounced out ahead of her. "It's okay," he added, misinterpreting the perplexed look on Jesse's face. "Shadow's invited, too."

Jesse, of course, wasn't thinking about the wolf at all. She was cursing herself for saying Bianca's name. Too late, she remembered her friend saying that no one in Joseph's family would ever know about his white lover. "Oh, thank you," she stammered. "I didn't really want to leave him at home our first night here." She walked past the Native American and let him shut the cabin door. "Bianca's another friend of mine back in Denver. I'll probably talk about Eric too." She put the key in the latch and locked the door shut.

"Boyfriend, eh?" Charlie surmised, walking down the porch steps.

"Oh, heavens no," Jesse laughed. "Just a very good friend."

"You young people are sure different," observed Charlie, heading north in the direction he had traveled earlier that day. "Nobody gets married anymore. I don't think Joe will ever find a girl. I finally just got my oldest boy married off, and he's forty-three."

"Hmmm," Jesse muttered, "it just takes time to find the right person, I guess."

"I guess."

"So, you've got a son?" Jesse asked, eager to steer the conversation away from Joseph.

"Two," Charlie answered. "Still got one at home. Don't think he'll ever settle down, though. Too mean!"

"Mean?" Jesse was curious. She followed Charlie's footsteps on the path that led away from the cabin into the trees. Shadow romped along beside them, happy to be without his leash.

"The wife says he's got *issues*, whatever that means, and he'll grow out of it. At forty years old, I don't think so. I say he's just ornery. But, he's too big and too old to be whipped. He'd probably whip me back."

Jesse smiled inwardly. It appeared Native American families dealt with the same kinds of problems every other race had to endure.

"Now, this path is pretty clear," noted Charlie. "But I don't want you walking it alone until you get used to it, okay?"

"Okay." Jesse had no problem acquiescing to that request. The further they walked into the trees, the darker it got. The hues were rich and green and the soil was dark like the tree trunks. Shortly, when she glanced behind her, the cabin had disappeared. She stuck close behind the Indian, who was surefooted. Jesse tripped on a root or a branch or just over her clumsy feet many times in the first ten minutes of the trip. "What happens when it snows?"

"We'll keep in touch by phone," Charlie called out good-naturedly. Jesse sort of grinned, but her eyes divulged her nervousness. "My horse is pretty good at finding its way around, when the truck can't cut it," he added, in case she didn't catch his joke. "Is that wolf keeping up with us?"

"He's right behind me," Jesse stated, watching him out of the corner of her eye. He followed right at Jesse's heels when the path turned narrow.

"Good boy," Charlie declared. "Never known one to do that."

"Have you ever spent time with wolves, Charlie?" Jesse asked, scratching Shadow on the snout while they walked.

"Can't say that I have, missy," he responded. "There were a lot more around when I was younger, but the ranchers killed most of those who were brave enough to come around." He jumped over a little stream and waited to make sure Jesse and her wolf made it too. Shadow stopped and investigated the running water for a moment. He took a drink before scurrying to catch up.

"I'm sorry to hear that," Jesse commented. "I was hoping..."

"Oh," Charlie added quickly, "they're protected now, those that are left. But it's just better to keep him away from any cattle that might be roaming around."

"I take it there are ranches around here, then."

"Quite a few spreads all around us. Our Town Marshal's land butts up to yours."

"Damn," Jesse sighed. "That could be a problem."

"Just keep him close to home," the Indian warned. "It'll be for the best." They walked for a little while in silence before Charlie quipped, "Of course, the ranchers like to blame *us* for missing cattle, too. Indians and wolves have been the bad guys for two hundred years around here."

"When I was studying the map I saw that we're real close to the Blackfeet Reservation," Jesse ventured.

"So close, you'll be on it before you know it."

"Really?"

"Yeah," Charlie volunteered. "I've lived on the reservation my whole life. Joe spent a few years here, until he decided he'd rather live in Colorado." Charlie lifted a low hanging branch and ushered the young woman and her wolf under it. "I guess he's done pretty well down there for himself. That's not something that happens too often around here."

"He has done well," Jesse affirmed. "He's got a great house in Littleton."

"He was one of the lucky ones," Charlie remarked. "He made up his mind to use the white man's school to get an education instead of bucking it like most of the others. The Marshal helped him get his first job."

Jesse was a little embarrassed to realize she had no clue what Joseph did for a living. He was always at the house and it had never occurred to her to ask.

"It was tough at first," Charlie went on, "but he stuck with it and I guess he's become a pretty good cop."

"One of the best," Jesse figured, attempting to appear knowledgeable on the subject. The shadow of the mountains loomed over them from the west. Through the trees, Jesse caught glimpses of them rising so high in the sky, she could not see the peaks. Birds were singing and flying through the tall branches; fluttering by the strangers in their forest. It was difficult for Jesse to see it all; trying also to keep up with the Indian who walked swiftly along the path ahead of them.

"But he's never forgotten his roots," Charlie continued as they trudged along. "We are proud of him for that."

"Yes," Jesse was happy to be able to contribute to the conversation. "We were at one of Joseph's powwows when I got Shadow. He's an Elder, you know."

"Yes, I do," Charlie smiled.

"He was Grand Master of the festivities. It was exciting to watch and listen to him. I learned a lot about the dances and music. He's a good drummer too!"

"Takes after his grandfather," her companion related. "He's a good man."

Jesse saw a clearing up ahead. She focused on the sunshine over Charlie's shoulder and watched it brighten the closer they got. The tree line stopped abruptly and they were now in a rolling field of green grasses and wild flowers. When the trees stopped, the mountains to the left of them came into view. They jutted out of the earth majestically, dark blue with shards of white snow caught in their crevasses and valleys. The velvet green of the trees snaked up the hills to greet the big, blue sky.

"Okay," Charlie announced, after pausing a moment to catch his breath. That's the Blackfeet Reservation on the other side of that jack fence. You'll be eating fry bread, corn and chicken before you know it."

Shadow stepped apprehensively from the forest, sniffing the air. Jesse looked around, too. She knelt down on one knee and hugged the wolf around the neck. "It sure is beautiful out here, Charlie," she expressed.

"Come on, you two," the Native American hollered, walking on ahead of them. "I can smell dinner cooking!"

"Let's go, boy," Jesse urged the wolf, getting up and trotting after her guide. The wolf looked at her a moment with his head cocked to the side. He had never seen his mother run before. He dug his forepaws in the ground and leapt after her. Jesse ran a little harder to stay ahead of him for a hundred or so yards and Shadow's tongue lolled out of his open, *grinning* mouth as he chased her. Jesse felt invigorated. She could not remember the last time she had actually ran instead of walked. The Indian laughed, watching them cavort. The wolf pup caught up easily to his mistress and nipped at her legs playfully. They tumbled into the grass and Jesse rolled on her back. Shadow pounced on her, licking her face. "Guess I shouldn't have done that!" she exclaimed, struggling to get up. "Now, I'm a mess!" She joined Charlie a few moments later, brushing the dust off her pants.

"No trouble," Charlie smiled, showing her how to get over the fence. "We're not fancy around here." They carried on to the Stillwater house.

"There you are!" Winona Stillwater yelled from the door. "I was beginning to think you got a better offer."

Charlie, Jesse and Shadow thundered across the threshold, revitalized from the three-mile trek. "Woman, you should see this animal run! And Jesse's not so bad herself!" Charlie declared.

Winona wiped her hands on her apron before welcoming Jesse with a handshake. "Welcome, Jesse," she grinned. "I'm Winona."

"It's wonderful to meet you," Jesse smiled back. "Thank you for having us."

Shadow sniffed the woman and accepted the pat she gave him on the head. "This is a fine wolf, now isn't he?" Charlie's wife added, giving the animal the once over.

"Look at those paws," the Indian suggested to his wife. "He's going to be 150 pounds, easy."

"Good Lord," Winona muttered, "you're probably right." She turned her cheek to accept Charlie's kiss. "Now, I hope you're hungry, Jesse. I've been cooking all day."

"Starved, ma'am," Jesse quipped, catching a glimpse of her surroundings as Winona offered her a chair at the kitchen table. "We could smell the food a mile away!"

"Where are the boys?" Charlie asked, getting a bowl from the cupboard and filling it with water for the wolf. "I thought they'd be here by now." He put the bowl down on the floor, but Shadow stuck close to Jesse for the time being, not quite sure of the new surroundings.

"Frank is out back feeding the chickens for me," Winona said, returning to her stove. "Mary is working late at the store, so she won't be here 'til later." Winona glanced at her husband at the sink. "Get Jesse some iced tea from the refrigerator, please."

"And Johnny?" Charlie asked warily, following his wife's instructions. He poured the iced tea before he sat down across the table from Jesse.

"Haven't seen him all day, as usual," Winona sighed. "But he'll be here."

"There you go with your blind faith," Charlie grumbled. "That damn fool kid has you wrapped around his little finger." Jesse concentrated on Shadow for a second, hoping their discussion wasn't going to turn into an argument.

"The day he lies to me," Winona stated righteously, "then maybe I'll change my mind. But he hasn't yet, so close your mouth and entertain our guest."

"Now, how can I do that, woman?" Charlie snickered. "If I can't talk, it's gonna' get pretty quiet around here and Jesse will fall asleep at the table."

Jesse smiled at the Native American when he cast her a wink across the table. She picked up her iced tea and drank.

"So, Jesse..." Winona ignored her husband. She was a small woman with long dark hair, highlighted with strands of pure silver, and exquisite turquoise-blue eyes. Although advanced in years, she was still quite beautiful. Her smile brightened the room and especially Charlie's face. "...Tell us why you've come to Montana." The food preparation complete, she joined her husband and the young woman at the table.

"I guess the simple answer," Jesse said, quickly swallowing another drink of her iced tea, "is to give my wolf a normal life."

"Hmmm," Winona hummed. As she looked at Jesse with those vivid blue eyes, Jesse was charmed. There was wisdom and a sense of clarity that Jesse wondered if she, herself, would ever possess. "I think there must be more to your story, now isn't there?" The woman's smile was infectious.

"Well, I suppose so," Jesse answered, "but I don't have a clue what that is at the moment." Shadow trotted under the table and over to the water bowl. His tongue lapped at the water noisily. Winona and Charlie both turned their heads a quick moment to see the wolf drink. "Maybe it will come to me now that I'm here and have some time to think about it."

"Our paths take us many different ways," the Native American woman continued. "I hope you will find some happiness here."

There was a clamoring at the back of the house, which startled Jesse. She looked up in time to see two men entering from the back of the living room into the kitchen. "You're out of your mind, brother," the eldest was saying to the younger one. "It would never work."

"Especially, if it was your idea, Johnny," Charlie jumped in, completely clueless to their conversation but anxious to stir things up. The younger man glared at his father before turning to do the same to Jesse. She felt his anger before he showed it. She looked quickly away from Johnny's brooding eyes and concentrated on the other man beside him.

"Hi, I'm Frank," the eldest son announced, offering his hand to Jesse. "You must be the city girl dad's been telling us about."

"Jesse Harless," she said rapidly, shaking Frank's hand. "Pleased to meet you."

"So, where's this wo…of," Frank had started to say *wolf*, but when the animal—also startled by their abrupt entrance—turned and faced them with a hint of a snarl, Frank was suddenly stunned into lowering his voice. Johnny also seemed momentarily mesmerized by Shadow's glower. Jesse was glad to be out of the spotlight. "Jesus," Frank murmured, "It *is* a wolf."

"And I think it grew a few more inches since I saw it this morning," Charlie threw in, holding his hand out to the wolf, who cautiously approached it. The animal kept its alert eyes trained on the newcomers.

"Christ!" Frank said, awestruck, "that's amazing." He took a seat in the chair next to Jesse. "I was expecting some German-Shepherd or something."

Winona got up and poured some iced tea for her boys. She handed one glass to Frankie and set the other on the table, indicating that her younger son should take a seat. Jesse noticed the silent exchange between the two of them, expressed only with their eyes. Johnny's were the same turquoise-blue as his mother's. They were particularly striking against his shoulder length black hair. Oddly, the young man was compelled to sit down.

"That is so cool," Frank continued, tearing his attention away from Shadow and turning back to Jesse. "So, how do you raise a wolf?"

"I haven't the slightest idea," Jesse smiled weakly. "I guess I'll learn as we go along." She was grateful that at least one of Charlie's boys appeared to accept her. She felt the icy stare of the other one upon her, but refused to return it.

"I understand you gave up being a secretary to come here and raise a wolf?" Frank asked.

"An Office Manager/Assistant, actually," Jesse gently corrected him.

"Must be nice to be rich," Johnny hissed from across the table. "Just up and take a vacation in the wilderness for a while until you get bored with it all and go back to your fancy house in the city."

Jesse's skin crawled at the tone of the younger man's voice. He reminded her of every man who had belittled her in her life. Suddenly tired of the verbal abuse, she spoke before Charlie had a chance to admonish his son. "I quit my job after working there for fifteen years," she stated firmly, slowly turning to face him. She met his gaze coldly. "And I sold everything I owned to come up here. So, I'm sorry to disappoint you. I'm not rich, and at this point, there's no going back to my job or my home."

Johnny blinked and looked quickly at his mother. "Well, we're glad to have you and Shadow here," Winona interjected. "And I know you're all hungry. Johnny, help me get dinner on the table." Her son seemed somewhat relieved to have something to do. Jesse drew in a deep breath. Perhaps she had won the first round.

"So, how long have you known Joe?" Frank went on, making small talk. "We didn't think he knew any women."

"Frank!" Winona chastised him.

"You'll be happy to know," Jesse smiled, "Joe's got several friends. And I'm not the only female he hangs out with."

"Cool," Frank smiled back. "Good to hear it. I just got married two months ago. I was tired of waiting for my *older* cousin to tie the knot first." He took the plate his mother offered and put it down in front of Jesse. "Are you married?"

"Frank!" Winona snapped.

"What?" Frank asked innocently.

Jesse laughed. "No, I'm not married, Frank. Never got that close." The smell of the food was glorious. She could hardly keep from tearing into the chicken on her plate, but she waited until Winona had finished serving and sat down with her own plate, before she began to eat. Smelling the food being passed over his head, Shadow returned to Jesse under the table. He put his front paw up on her leg and she squeezed it tight. "Right now, I think I'm better off with my wolf."

"Well, there's something to be said for the four-leggeds," Charlie offered, accepting his plate from his son. "At least they can't talk back. And they're probably cheaper to feed." He was watching Frank *wolf* down his food as he spoke.

"Charlie!" Winona sounded exasperated. "Let's just let Jesse eat, all right?" She sat down next to her husband with a thud and Johnny did the same. "I look at the three of you and wonder why I got married myself." She looked at Jesse and smiled. "Eat, young lady. You need some meat on those bones."

Jesse dove into her food ravenously as did the others. She snuck a piece of chicken off her plate and gave it to Shadow, who gulped it down.

Charlie turned his attention to his sons. "So, what new plan have you come up with now, son?" he asked Johnny, after swallowing a mouthful of food. "And how much is it going to cost me?"

"He thinks he can talk old man Red Cloud out of his truck," Frank intervened, betraying his younger brother. "Then he's gonna' high tail it to Billings."

"And do what?" Charlie demanded.

"Shut up, Frank!" Johnny spat at the same time.

Jesse kept her eyes lowered to her plate. She sensed an argument brewing.

"As if Red Cloud would even think about giving you that truck," Charlie went on. "All you're doing is fixing his barn door. Any idiot can do that. You gonna' steal it? And what in the hell are you going to do in Billings? Panhandle?"

"Charlie..." Winona warned with her eyes trained on their guest. "Can we talk about this later?"

"Maybe I'll get a goddamn job down *there*," Johnny fired back. "I'm tired of hearing you bitch!"

"You can't hold a job *here*," Charlie's jaw tightened as he spoke. "You think some white man's gonna' put up with your crap?"

"Well, if we've got to put up with them *here*," Johnny snapped, "I'll be no worse down *there*!"

"There's no place in Billings to live and eat for free," Charlie hissed. "Unless you want to rot in jail."

"Jesus," Johnny muttered, throwing down his fork and shoving his plate away. "Maybe I'll go to Joe's. He seems to be taking in strays. Give me a goddamn break!"

"I'll give you a break," Charlie started, throwing down *his* fork and pushing back from the table.

"All right!" Winona interrupted. "That's enough." The others at the table fell silent. Jesse kept her head down and ate hurriedly. Shadow's ears pricked up at the tone of her voice. "Johnny, you're not going to take Red Cloud's truck and you're not going anywhere," his mother ordered.

"Hey, Jesse," Frank murmured. "Hand me Johnny's plate, will you?"

Jesse looked at the man in disbelief.

"May as well not let it go to waste," the Indian smiled.

"If you three can't sit here and eat in a civilized manner," Winona retorted, giving her older son the evil eye, "you can go eat someplace else."

"Fat chance," Charlie muttered. "I'm sure he doesn't have a cent to his..."

"Charlie!" Winona cut him off. "That's *enough*!"

"It's like this all the time," Frank whispered into Jesse's ear. "Don't worry about it."

Johnny got up, knocking his chair to the floor. "I've got plenty of cash," he barked at his father. "I stole your wallet last night," Johnny laughed sardonically as he stormed out the door. "You must have just got paid, pop! There was a whole five dollars in it." The door slammed shut behind him.

Charlie started to get up, feeling for his wallet. Winona grabbed his arm and forced him to sit back down. "Let him go, Charlie," she pleaded. "We've scared Jesse enough."

"I'm fine," Jesse said, finishing her meal. "Don't worry about me." She waved them off and finished her iced tea with a gulp. She wished it had been something a little stronger, like a shot of gin.

"Apologize to Jesse," Winona snapped at Charlie. She rose from the table and picked up Johnny's plate. "Come here, Shadow," she spoke softly. "Here's some dinner for you."

"Ma!" Frank cried. "I'm hungry too, you know."

"You eat too well as it is," Winona said. "Mary's not going to keep you if you get any fatter."

"I'm not fat!" Frank observed, looking down at his stomach. "Am I fat, Jesse?"

"Thin as a rail, Frank," Jesse answered quietly. "You're just fine."

"See?" Frank looked up at his mother. "You don't have to pick on us, just because *Johnny's* such a pain."

"Charlie, the apology please!" Winona was not going to let up. Shadow walked underneath the table to the plate of food Winona had placed on the floor. He sniffed twice at the concoction of chicken and potatoes before gobbling it up.

"I'm sorry my son's an ungrateful, selfish, hateful bully who despises everything and everyone in his small little world," stated Charlie, indicating with a turn of his hand that Jesse should join him in the other room. "His behavior was, as usual, out of control. On the bright side though, now that he's had his tirade and disappeared, we can have a nice evening."

"Charlie…" his wife warned as he left the kitchen.

"And," Charlie got the hint, "I also apologize for me, too. He does get my blood going."

"I'm the one who should apologize," Jesse reasoned after they were well into the other room. "Apparently, it's people like me whom he hates the most."

"Naw," Charlie offered. "It's pretty much everybody. White and Red alike."

Jesse was still reeling from the onslaught of the younger Indian's words. She had not won any battles with him. She probably made him angrier when she snapped back at him earlier. "I kind of wish you'd given me a little more background before he came in," she suggested timidly.

"It wouldn't have made a difference. Johnny's a very miserable young man. Sometimes I think he'd kill us all if it wasn't for his mother."

"I should help Mrs. Stillwater in the kitchen with the dishes," Jesse suddenly realized, hearing the clink of the plates as her hostess cleared the table. She glanced back into the kitchen and saw her at the sink. Shadow was sitting next to her waiting for more handouts.

"You sit yourself down, Jesse," Winona called out from the kitchen. Jesse was surprised to learn that Winona could still hear them in the next room. "Frank will help when he's finished and we'll join you in a little while."

"Aw, ma," Jesse heard Frank complain.

"You just get comfortable, Jesse," she ordered.

Jesse reluctantly did as she was told. Charlie sat down in his well-worn chair and carefully removed his pipe from a handmade holder that rested on the table beside him. "I just need to learn to keep my mouth shut when we have visitors," Charlie said, filling his pipe. "But it's better he screamed at me instead of you."

"He doesn't like me moving up here, I take it," Jesse mentioned quietly. "Joe should have warned me."

"Joe hasn't been around for a long time," Charlie reasoned. "He doesn't know how bad Johnny is." He put the stem of his pipe to his lips and lit up. He inhaled the smoke of the tobacco and smiled. "We're not bad people, Jesse. We just have problems like everybody else. Now you know our secret, so welcome to the family."

"Thanks," Jesse sighed, resting back against her chair. The food she had eaten was sitting like a lump in her stomach. She wondered what the hell she had gotten herself into. An isolated cabin in the woods, complete with a maniac Indian who hated white people living next door. Her only protection, besides a gun she was afraid to shoot, was the wolf pup who was now wrestling playfully in the kitchen with the madman's brother. If the winter didn't kill her, she was sure the Stillwater boy would be happy to give it a try. She felt a myriad of emotions, but security was definitely at the bottom of her list. She had fully accepted the fact that she would eventually have to stand up to angry ranchers and folks who did not like wolves. Unfortunately, she had not planned on facing angry Indians.

Jesse was surprised to find, while Charlie bantered on about raising sons, that she was not paying much attention to him at first. Instead, her mind raced. So much for the peace and solitude of wilderness life. It was time to get some shooting practice in. If she was planning on staying in this *wild* territory, she needed to start recognizing the dangers and learning how to protect herself. She wondered if there even was a 9-1-1. Joseph and his wild animals be damned, there were other threats that could prove to be far more disastrous to a female living alone in the woods. It was high time to get over being afraid of those darn guns she owned.

CHAPTER 12

Jesse woke up the next morning with a headache. She was sprawled out on the couch and Shadow was licking her face. It took her a moment to remember where she was and what had happened the night before. "Okay, boy," she grimaced, slowly getting up. Her back was aching from a couple of nights without a bed. Like it or not, tonight she had to sleep upstairs.

She shuffled over to the front door and unlocked it. She opened the screen door and Shadow scurried out. The day was well underway; the sun already high in the deep blue sky above her. The clouds were building into billowing masses of white velvet just over the tree line. The tall grasses were emerald green and dotted with yellow, purple and white wild flowers. The little wolf bounded off the porch and into the grass to explore his new domain. Off of the path, Jesse could just make out his head as he snaked through the greenery, sniffing the air and a flower or two as he meandered.

Jesse slipped into the kitchen and grabbed a Coke out of the refrigerator before stepping out onto the porch and taking a seat on the wooden porch swing where she could keep a wary eye on her little charge. She knew she'd have to let him do his own thing eventually, but at the moment she felt like he was her only true friend.

Not that the previous evening had been totally ruined by Johnny Stillwater, but it sure had put a damper on her mood. Winona, Frank, Charlie, and later, Frank's wife Mary—a full-blooded Blackfoot Indian—had done their best to make her feel at ease. Unfortunately, every creak in the floorboard or slam of a door made the young woman jump in her seat.

The conversation was lively, although Jesse barely uttered a word. She heard the tale of Frank and Mary's wedding and funny stories about Joseph when he and the boys were growing up. They filled her in on the neighbors, although she found it hard to call any of them neighbors when Charlie and Winona were the closest at three miles away. The Rancher/Marshal Clayton Phillips and his son lived up the road apiece. Old man Red Cloud was just around the bend on the Blackfeet Reservation. Arleen Stewart had a little place about ten miles south of her own, and there were a few out-of-staters who had ranches and getaways to the east. As she had readily seen on her walk to Charlie's, the mountains were just to the west and that property was preserved for the wildlife. She was also told she was not to be surprised if some of that wildlife came down for a visit from time to time. Charlie promised to help her with some needed repairs to the cabin. Winona expected her to come for dinner at least once a week. Jesse absorbed it all, laughing when something funny was said, and listening carefully when the conversation turned serious.

When it was finally time to call it a night, Charlie warmed up his rusty old 1966 Chevy pickup while Shadow ran around in the dark marking territory and Winona loaded Jesse up with some leftovers before giving her a warm hug. The road trip home took a lot longer than it took to walk. It was forty-five miles of manmade road versus three miles through the woods, as the crow flies. A few times Jesse felt they may have been safer walking because when the truck hit a bump in the road, a short in the headlights caused them to go out, and they were forced to drive in total darkness until another bump brought the lights back to life.

Alone in the cabin, with the headlights of Charlie's lights flickering on and off in the distance as he drove away, Jesse tried not to notice the shadows that seemed to be moving outside her windows. She resolved to get curtains as soon as possible. When the light switch that was supposed to turn on the light upstairs did not work, her mind started to race with thoughts of every horror movie she'd ever seen. Refusing to give in to her fears, she found a bottle of wine in the kitchen and popped the cork. She pawed through her box of CD's until she found her precious Wolfsheim; put the CD in the player and turned the music up loud. Shadow, perplexed at her actions but intrigued with the German music, howled along with Peter Heppner, the lead singer. Jesse joined them in their singing.

Feeling the wine, she sat down on the floor and unpacked a few more boxes, with Shadow trying to help. Everything in the boxes became fair game for the pup and Jesse had a heck of a time keeping him from running away with each item he got a hold of. She found the boxes Eric had given her after their last day of shopping. Opening them, she cried when she saw the little black designer dress and the fabulous stiletto heels he had purchased for her. The other box contained a sparkling necklace with earrings to match. She sobbed, realizing she'd never have a place to wear them and everything else she had given up. Apparently, sometime after that tearful scene, she had curled up on the couch with her wolf and had mercifully passed out.

Now, in the light of day, sitting lazily on the porch swing, her fears subsided and she forced herself to think positively. Shadow was romping in the grass, literally hopping on all fours as he pounced on field mice or whatever chanced to move.

She wondered if she could find her way back to the general store where she could pick up some more supplies. Perhaps Arleen Stewart would know where she could get some curtains or blinds or something to block out whatever or whoever might try to use the pitch black of the night to watch her unnoticed.

Shadow eventually scrambled back to the porch, squeaking at her to join him. She finished her Coke and followed him out into the yard. They played tag for a while and Jesse tried to teach him how to fetch sticks. Unfortunately, he liked to chew on those, too, and she had a heck of a time getting them back in one piece. They explored some of their property, venturing into the dense line of fir trees and cottonwoods that surrounded the cabin. They found a path to the lake and Jesse skipped stones across the water while Shadow yipped and squeaked some more when his paws got wet. After a few trials and errors, he figured the water was a good thing and plunged in after the stones his mistress was tossing. Jesse laughed at his antics and tossed another stick so he could actually catch something. Proud of his accomplishment, he strode out of the water with his head held high and the stick clenched between his teeth. He shook his fur briskly and lay down next to Jesse, teething on his prize.

Jesse stretched out on her back with her head resting on her hands and watched the circling hawk, or perhaps it was an eagle, for upon closer inspection she wasn't exactly sure what kind of bird it was. The size of the bird, together with it's white head, resembled what she thought was an eagle. But she'd never actually seen one before, except in the zoo, so she could not be sure. It was majestic enough to be an eagle. She was enthralled by its grace and beauty.

In due course, the woman and her wolf pup found their way back home. After a hearty lunch of cold cuts for her and puppy chow for him, Jesse tackled the rest of the boxes and put everything away while Shadow took a nap in front of the screen door. More books went on the shelves. The pictures went on the mantelpiece over the fireplace. She stashed the clothes under the staircase, not ready to venture upstairs quite yet. The candles were placed strategically around the house. Finally, she took some bed sheets and nailed them up over the windows, using string to tie them open during the daylight hours.

Late in the afternoon, she sat down with a pen and paper and made a list: curtains, curtain rods, white paint (the bedroom was so dark up in the rafters), more lights and some rugs. Tomorrow, she and Shadow would get in the truck and do some shopping. She also needed to find her bank, get cable or a satellite dish and find out if there was Internet access. She had to get settled if she was going to stick this out. And with Shadow as happy as he was, she was determined to do it.

Jesse was making some supper, with Shadow nipping at her heels for his own, when they heard the vehicle pull up out front. She fought the nervousness that hit her stomach as she considered who it could possibly be. Shadow ran to the door and pushed at the screen. Jesse took a deep breath, wondering where she had put the gun. She approached the door with trepidation, but was pleasantly relieved to see Arleen Stewart coming to the porch, laden with boxes.

"Hope I'm not intruding," Arleen declared as Jesse opened the door wide to let her in. Shadow sniffed at the woman, inspecting her briefly before he took the opportunity to get out of the house. Arleen had to watch her step as he scooted by her.

"You'll never be more welcome anywhere than you are here," Jesse smiled, taking one of the boxes from her and placing it on the kitchen table.

"I take it, that was Shadow," the woman noted, entering the house. "I guess I'll meet him later." She put her box down next to the other one and smiled at Jesse. "I thought you might need a few things, so I took the liberty of opening up an account for you."

"You're an angel!" Jesse said, perusing the contents of the boxes. Arleen brought bacon, hamburger, other foodstuffs and, tucked into a corner of one of the boxes, a bottle of Scotch. "Just what the doctor ordered!" Jesse laughed, pulling the bottle out.

"There are some glasses in there, in case you don't have any," Arleen said, giving the cabin the once over. "Hey, I love what you've done to the place." She walked into the living room, eyeing the windows. "But, we should probably work on those curtains."

"I suppose you didn't bring any, did you?" Jesse responded, pulling out a bag of ice from one of the boxes. "It looks like you brought everything else."

"Tomorrow," Arleen laughed. "I can even get you some blinds, if you'd like."

Jesse poured two stiff drinks into the glass tumblers Arleen had provided. "That would be fabulous!" Jesse gave one of the drinks to Arleen and took a big swig from her own. "I seem to have a problem wondering what or who may be outside looking in, especially since I can't see anything but black when I look out at night."

"You'll get used to it," Arleen assured, helping Jesse empty out the boxes. "After a while, you'll be able to see things quite clearly in the dark." She put the food into the refrigerator while Jesse pulled out the other items, which included a meaty dog bone for the wolf.

"It's very quiet up here," Jesse remarked, ogling her new treasures. "Cool! A flashlight."

"That'll change, too. There's really a lot of noise when you recognize the sounds." Arleen eyed Jesse surreptitiously as they worked. "So, other than the night vision thing, how are you settling in?"

"Okay, I guess," said Jesse quietly. She took another sip of her scotch, reveling in the familiarity of the taste. The last time she'd had a scotch, she was sitting in the club with Eric, depressed and feeling out of sorts. She had to wonder if things had actually changed that much. "Would you believe I'm afraid to go upstairs?" she finally spouted out, deciding to be honest with her guest.

Arleen put the last of the food away and gave Jesse her full attention. "And why is that?"

"I went upstairs for a bit yesterday and it seemed so dark, because none of the lights seemed to work. There's a bed, I think. And a window facing south."

"Have you been up there since?"

"Nope," Jesse answered. "I started to go last night, but when I flipped the switch on the stairs, now *that* light seems to be out. I gotta say it freaked me out a little bit."

"Well, then," Arleen took control, "let's take our drinks and do some exploring, shall we?" She headed toward the stairs. "I've always wondered what this place was like inside."

Jesse followed her new friend, with her drink in one hand and her new flashlight in the other.

"Did you know Joseph, Charlie, Johnny and Frank built this place?" Arleen tried the light switch at the bottom of the stairs. She looked at Jesse with a crinkle in her brow when the feeble light at the top of the stairs came on.

Jesse looked stunned. "That did not work last night!" Now she was really nervous. She jumped when Shadow started scratching at the screen door. She rushed over and let the pup in, but instead of joining the women, he headed for his food bowl instead. "Some attack wolf, eh?" she smiled weakly, returning to Arleen who had started slowly up the stairs.

"There must be a short," Arleen surmised, taking the flashlight from Jesse when she caught up with her. "Charlie can fix that."

"So, Joseph's a carpenter?" Jesse asked, keeping the conversation going.

"Not as good as Charlie," Arleen went on, "and Johnny's the best of the lot. He's built some amazing stuff."

"Like what, crosses to burn white people on?" The thought of the young man still upset Jesse.

"So, you met him, eh?" Arleen reached the top of the stairs and inspected the room with the shining flashlight.

"Last night at Charlie and Winona's. He's a real piece of work."

"You could say that," Arleen agreed. "But he's really okay, once you get to know him."

"Yeah," Jesse sneered, "I bet." With Arleen at her side, Jesse felt bolder. She looked around the room.

"You'll need a new bed," Arleen noticed. The mattress was drooping in the center and the brass headboard was broken.

"God knows who slept in it," Jesse grimaced.

The bed was placed against the east wall and with the help of the light, the girls discovered the two dormer windows that showed clearly from the outside. They were heavily curtained, allowing very little daylight to seep through.

Arleen trudged across the room and pushed the curtain to the side to let in some light. The heavy curtain, laden with dust, came down on top of her.

"Oh God, are you all right?" Jesse yelled, running to help her.

"Yeah," Arleen coughed, swishing the dust away from her face with her free hand. "The maid must have missed this room."

Jesse laughed and went over to the other window, yanking that drapery down as well. When the dust settled, there was more than enough light to see the rest of the room. "Look, there are curtains over there, too." She pointed to the opposite wall. Next to the opening for the staircase, there was another pair of heavy, dark curtains hanging all the way to the floor. They were draped on a heavier rod. Arleen walked back across the room, found the pull cord and slid them open. They covered French doors that led to a very wide balcony.

"Whoa!" Jesse cried out, joining Arleen quickly. She turned the deadbolt lock and opened the doors wide. The view of the mountains through thousands of trees was spectacular.

"Now, this is pretty neat," proposed Arleen, carefully stepping outside. Shadow climbed the stairs noisily, ran past Jesse and out the doors. "Hey, boy. How are you?" Arleen extended her hands for the wolf to sniff. He did so, before allowing her the privilege of scratching his head.

"Okay," Jesse decided, "this is very nice!"

"We'll replace these curtains also," Arleen suggested. "But we'll keep them a heavy fabric. I bet you need them to keep it warm up here."

"What is this balcony made of?" Jesse wondered aloud. It was wide, like a patio.

"There's another room downstairs," Arleen observed. "Didn't you notice?"

"Just saw a little bathroom and a storage room, but they're over there." Jesse pointed to the left of the house from where they were standing.

"More exploration," Arleen noted. "This gets more interesting by the second."

They left the doors open and ventured back in the house with Shadow at their heels.

"Here's a closet," Jesse said, turning on the light just inside.

"A walk-in," Arleen commented, looking over her shoulder. "That's nice."

Jesse looked a little further and found another door directly opposite the closet. She opened it and turned on the light. "Oh, this is heaven!" she exclaimed, stepping into another bathroom. "A bathtub!" The upstairs bathroom was much larger than the three-quarter one downstairs. Jesse was positively beaming with excitement. She turned around in a circle, taking it all in. "And to think I almost threw my bubble bath away."

"We can fix this up, Jess," Arleen said. "It'll be cozy and nice." Arleen checked out the water in the sink, tub and toilet. The plumbing was turned on and the faucets ran properly.

"Can we start today?" Jesse was thrilled with her discoveries. "Now I've got something to do!" Shadow watched the toilet refill with a cocked head.

"How about first thing in the morning," Arleen acquiesced. "I'll have my friend Fran watch the store tomorrow and that way I can show you around town, too."

"It's a date," Jesse smiled. "I'll be ready at the crack of dawn."

"Come on," Arleen ordered, "let's go find that other room downstairs."

"I feel so stupid," Jesse sighed, standing with Arleen in the big empty room, filled with windows, that she thought was a closet. "Why didn't I open that door?"

"From what you've told me in the past few minutes," Arleen commented softly, "I guess the past 48 hours have been pretty stressful for you. If I had driven some 900 miles in one day, almost landed in a lake, slept outside with only some candles and a wolf for company, dined with an interesting, to say the least, Native American family, and been scared to death that one of those Indians might be watching me from outside or even upstairs last night, I don't think I'd have cared what was behind this door, either." The woman turned and directed Jesse back into the living room. "And we haven't even discussed what drove you to do all this in the first place."

"Oh, that's an even longer story," Jesse said, plopping herself down on the couch. She pulled her feet up under herself and got comfortable. "We'll save that for tomorrow."

Arleen retrieved the bottle of Scotch and sat down next to Jesse on the couch. "Now, your dinner with the Stillwaters. What set Charlie and Johnny off?"

"Something about somebody named Red Cloud and Johnny taking his truck," Jesse remembered. "Johnny said he was better off in Billings working for the white man, since the *whites* were moving in here. I took that to mean me, of course."

"More than likely," Arleen agreed, filling their glasses again.

"He also called me one of Joseph's strays," Jesse continued. "I don't think he's happy that I'm living here."

"No, he wouldn't be," said Arleen, her blue eyes shining. "He always thought Joseph would let him have this place, since he did most of the work."

"Shit," Jesse murmured. "Talk about the proverbial bee's nest."

"If you promise to keep it between us, I can fill you in on the details," Arleen offered. "If you're interested, of course." Shadow lay down in front of the couch between the two women as they talked. It was a good time for another nap.

"I am," Jesse admitted, giving her new friend her complete attention. "I don't think I've ever met such an angry man."

"None of the Indians have had an easy time around here," Arleen began. "The government shoved them onto the reservation and has pretty much left them to fend for themselves."

"Joseph has hinted at that," Jesse said. "And I've been reading some books on the subject that he gave me."

"Well, the books tell only half the story," Arleen continued. "But some day Charlie will probably give you the history, if you ask him. Suffice it to say, most Native Americans live well under the poverty line and have no resources they can count on. In some states where gambling is allowed, little of the revenues go where they're supposed to, but the white man is still very much in control.

"Joseph was one of the lucky ones. Clayton Phillips, our Marshal—you'll meet him eventually—gave Joe a break and hired him as a deputy. He was a punk, a lot like Johnny is now. But Johnny has his reasons too. He was pretty young when a couple of white guys, up here hunting, got a hold of Winona and roughed her up pretty badly. Johnny was a little boy and saw the whole thing happen. When Charlie found out, he was powerless to do anything about it. The white men were never caught and Winona wouldn't let Charlie find them himself. She was terrified he'd end up in jail or worse, so she picked herself up and got over it. She's a strong woman, Jess," Arleen sighed. "I respect her very much."

"I could tell that," Jesse concurred. "And I could tell *all* her men love her very much."

"Well, Johnny has never forgiven himself for not being old enough to do anything and never forgiven his father for letting it go. He is fiercely attached to his mother. She's the only one who has any control over him, but thank God, somebody does. Because I do believe if she didn't, Johnny would scalp every white man who got within fifty feet of her."

"I had no idea," Jesse said, truly concerned. "That explains so much."

"A word of advice," Arleen countered. "Do not let him know you know this. Johnny hates pity more than he hates whites."

"I doubt I'll get that close to him, again," Jesse stated. "There's no need to feed the fire."

"Speaking of fire," Arleen said, "I brought some steaks. You're not a vegetarian or anything like that, are you?"

"Absolutely not!" Jesse laughed, getting up from the couch. "Let's cook!"

The women chatted on, enjoying each other's company, well into the night. Whether or not it was attributable to the Scotch, they were openly honest with each other and found they had a lot in common. They bonded instantly.

They ate well and discussed everything, from their pasts and the characters who had crossed their paths, to what they expected and looked forward to in the future. Arleen was Montana born and raised, with a husband who lived in Helena when he wasn't on some wilderness trek in the mountains. He was an outspoken natural scientist, so she understood Shadow's plight and applauded Jesse's efforts. They saw each other rarely, which was Arleen's secret to a good marriage. When they were together, there was no time for petty arguments and they always had something new and exciting to tell each other. They missed each other terribly and Arleen had several steamy love letters to prove it. But Arleen had wanted more stability and a roof over her head rather than a tent, so she opted for the store and a cabin a little closer to civilization. She had owned her store for ten years now and was very happy with her existence. The only flaw was not having a friend to carouse with once in a while. She was convinced her prayers had been answered with the arrival of Jesse.

It was after midnight when they finally shared a hug and said good-bye. Jesse was thrilled to have Arleen's company and especially pleased to discover what promised to be a soul mate.

That night, undaunted by the lack of electricity, Jesse took several candles upstairs and took a long, hot bath. Somewhere in the middle of the bubbles and the hot steam, Jesse admitted that she might be able to stay here for a while. It would take a lot of hard work and a good chunk of money, but for the first time since she had arrived, she actually saw herself doing it. "To hell with it!" she murmured, lulled half to sleep by the hot water and the Scotch. "Welcome to Montana, Jesse. Get your ass in gear and make this work!"

CHAPTER 13

Jesse collapsed onto the porch swing and wiped her brow with the icy cold bottle of water. The work of the past couple of weeks had been hard, but very satisfying. Her little cabin was almost complete. Once Arleen had shown her around, Jesse was able to get everything she needed to make the cabin into her new home.

She had cleaned out the upstairs and painted it. She bought herself a new king size bed, a chest of drawers, bed stands and plenty of lamps. She hung new curtains on sturdy rods and found some beautiful paintings of wolves by some regional artists to cover the walls. She cleaned out the fireplace and filled it with candles. On another trek with Arleen she found a hand loomed rug. She bought a comfortable reading chair and another bookcase for knickknacks and more books. The electrical was still a little shaky upstairs, but Charlie had promised to drop by soon and get it fixed.

In the back room, she scrubbed down the windows and marveled at the beautiful scenery. She bought sheer, floor length curtains that completely covered the walls and the windows when they were closed, but when opened, they allowed access to every inch of the scenery and the light. Just outside the back door, she squared off the area that the L shape of the house surrounded and started to work on a small sitting area and garden. She bought a fountain and some garden furniture. She had a pallet of stones delivered to make a patio and a rock garden around it.

She cleaned out the storage room and built shelves for supplies and canned goods. She bought a washer and dryer and forked over the extra cash to have it delivered and set up. She even purchased a wine rack and stocked up some fine bottles of wine for the winter months.

She purchased two satellite dishes and now had T.V. as well as Internet accessibility. She had a new flat screen television, complete with surround sound, and a great stereo system. Levelor blinds now covered the living room and kitchen windows. She had privacy when she wanted it.

She was settling in quite nicely. And with all the work, as well as play time with Shadow, she had been anything but bored. Arleen was a regular visitor and even stayed over a couple of nights a week. Jesse contacted Nancy Middlesex by email and kept her up to date on Shadow's progress. She called or emailed Bianca and Eric regularly.

Shadow had grown like a weed, his black fur now mottled with a few brown and white guard hairs around his snout. He weighed in at about 60 pounds and his eyes were more greenish-yellow, rather than the blue color he had been born with. With his claws and teeth, he had cleverly slit the screen adhered to the wood on the screen door along the side and the bottom, which allowed him access to the inside of the cabin or to the outside world on his own terms. He spent a lot more time outdoors now and his explorations took him further and further from the cabin. But he checked in regularly and insisted Jesse join him on his excursions at least once a day. At night, Jesse liked to keep him inside, although on one or two occasions he was not ready to go in when she was. But for the most part he seemed content to do his howling at dusk while Jesse kept close guard from the porch. Jesse could now hear the other wolves that he conversed with. She thought she saw one just inside the tree line on one of those nights. She was grateful Shadow did not run after it when the blur of white fur headed back into the trees. Jesse was a little apprehensive, knowing they would eventually meet.

They had met quite a few other animals in the evening. A pair of raccoons lived close by, and the family of deer hardly gave them a second look when they passed through the edge of the trees. She saw a bobcat one night and both she and Shadow headed into the cabin quickly when on another night they came across a medium sized black bear. The smaller animals, like hares and mice, took their chances in the area because Shadow had no qualms about hunting them down for a snack.

But once the heavy wooden front door was closed for the evening, Shadow would eat his dinner and lay down at Jesse's feet by the fire with his beloved Prada shoe. He was almost too big for her lap, but she never complained when he wanted to curl up on it.

As Jesse sipped her water, wondering how much more stone she could get into the back patio before dark, the afternoon clouds were starting to turn from white to pink and purple hues, announcing another spectacular sunset. The clouds were building up and looking heavier. Perhaps later there may be rain, not that the land needed it. The ancient pines and trees stood guard, dark and lusciously green. The fields were filled with wild flowers in the rich, dark soil. She could smell the land in the breeze that wafted around her.

Gazing across the acreage she lovingly referred to as her front yard, Jesse suddenly spied a curious sight. She saw a horse with a rider and they appeared to be heading her way. At first, she could not determine what was tethered to a rope and obviously forced, against its will, to travel along side them. But after a few minutes of contemplation, her eyes widened in disbelief and her heart jumped into her throat.

She peeled her eyes from the unfamiliar scene and looked frantically for Shadow. He wasn't in his usual spot in the clump of trees by the porch, nor was he exploring anywhere near the cabin. The horse and rider were coming closer and eventually she was able to discern what the rider had tied at the end of that rope. She stood up and craned her neck to get a better look. Her beautiful black wolf was straining at the makeshift leash, unable to get away from his captor. The man was determined to keep the wolf in tow.

Jesse dashed into the cabin and grabbed her rifle, then headed out to meet them. Shadow whined and yipped and pulled harder at the rope when he saw her. The horse was forced to speed up to keep pace with the wolf when the lupine took to running toward his mistress.

"Does this animal belong to you?" the rider called out as he and his horse, now at a gallop, approached her.

"Yes, he does!" Jesse shouted back, aiming her gun at him, just in case. "And I'd appreciate it if you'd let him go, now!"

The rider loosened the knot of the tether and Shadow took off like a shot. The man yanked his hands away from the rope just before the end snapped against the saddle horn. Shadow was at Jesse's side in seconds. She removed the rope from his neck and checked him thoroughly for cuts while he cavorted around her, licking her face.

"Wolves aren't welcome on my land, young lady," the rider announced, bringing his horse to a halt in front of her while sliding off the saddle. "He would have been dead if I hadn't seen Charlie Stillwater a week ago. He told me you'd moved in."

"And who are *you*?" she asked coolly, not fully lowering her rifle. "Apparently not the welcome wagon, I guess."

"Clayton Phillips," the rider said. He was of medium size, with short, blond hair and bright blue eyes. His face was ruddy and he looked like he'd spent most of his life in the saddle. "I own the ranch to the northeast of you and I'm what they call the law around here."

"So, what law did my wolf break?" Jesse was not afraid to look the man in the eye, lawman or not.

"He was staring at my chickens," Phillips stated, nonplussed by her stance.

"Excuse me?" she demanded.

"The damn thing was staring at my chickens and it felt like he was watching me too."

Jesse could not answer right away because she might have burst out laughing. The lawman's stern look dissipated slightly. They both realized the absurdity of the comment at the same time. "I didn't know staring was against the law."

"You know what I mean," Phillips shot back. "He was after some easy prey."

Shadow leaned in close to Jesse, almost knocking her off balance. She put the rifle down, stooped down and rubbed her hands into his fur. "Did he attack them?"

"No, he just sat there inspecting us."

"And he was close?"

"No, he was out about 200 yards," Phillips added. "But you just saw how fast he can run. He could have caught them in a split second."

"But he didn't, did he?" Jesse queried. "As a matter of fact, I bet you called to him and he came right up to you."

"Well, yes," the cowboy murmured. "That's how I got the rope around his neck."

Jesse took Shadow's snout into her hands and looked into Shadow's eyes. "Do not trust these people, boy," she said sternly. "You could have gotten hurt." She nuzzled him on the forehead and straightened up. "So, you probably considered shooting him, but you thought twice about it, thank God, and brought him home," she spouted at the man standing in front of her. "I apologize for my wolf's behavior," she swallowed hard. "I'll make sure he stays away from your precious ranch."

"Look, lady. We haven't seen a wolf around here for years," Phillips reasoned. "You're damn right I thought about shooting him. I'm not about to lose any of my livestock."

"I would have to say," Jesse retorted, "if my wolf met up with one of your cows, he'd beat feet and head out of there pretty quickly. They're a lot bigger than he is, you know. And he's used to eating his meals out of a dog dish, or something smaller, like a mouse, that he can catch."

Phillips eyed the area furtively. The wolf was trying to play with Jesse, tugging at the leg of her jeans. It was acting like a very big puppy.

"Shadow is a good soul, Mr. Phillips," she continued, following his eyes as he looked at the grounds and the cabin. "I feed him very well. And while I realize as well as you that he is a wild animal, he behaves himself as most wolves do when they're not harassed."

"Well, I'm sorry," the cowboy said, "but that kind of behavior is a little hard to believe around here."

She wanted to be angry with the man, but she couldn't. Behind that gruff exterior, she could see his kind eyes. If Shadow went to him willingly, there had to be good in him somewhere. "Please forgive me," she went on. "I'm forgetting my manners. I was just about to get a drink. Can I offer you one as well?"

"I should be getting back," Phillips said, although a cold drink sounded appealing.

"It's cooler up here on the porch," Jesse extended her hand invitingly toward the cabin. "As we're neighbors, we should probably try to come to an understanding, don't you think?"

Phillips took off his cowboy hat and slapped it against his hip to remove some of the dust. "Yeah, maybe you're right." He followed her onto the porch and sat down on one of the chairs. Jesse went inside and quickly returned with two glasses and a pitcher of iced tea. Shadow had taken his place on the top step of the porch and lay down. Worn out from his ordeal, he watched the stranger with half closed eyes. Phillips returned his gaze.

"There now," Jesse said as the screen door slammed behind her. "It looks like you two are at least tolerating each other."

"Just barely," Phillips took the glass and let Jesse fill it. He was thirstier than he had thought and downed the cold liquid quickly. Jesse set the pitcher on the table between them so he could have as much as he wanted. "This is just not normal," he commented. "I raise horses and cattle. The wild dogs and the coyotes do enough damage. Seeing your wolf at my place today was pretty unsettling."

"As I understand it, Mr. Phillips," Jesse began, "wolves prefer deer, elk, snowshoe hares and moose to cattle and horses. And with any of *those* animals they tend to go for the sick or helpless. They'd have a heck of a time tackling a healthy one." She took a sip of her iced tea. "Wolves are not stupid, Mr. Phillips. They don't carry a death wish. After all, most of them have families to return to; and they prefer to hunt in packs."

"Yes, but like any wild animal," Phillips stated, "they're unpredictable."

"Just as a stampeding horse can be."

"Any animal in a challenged situation may kill, Miss Harless."

"That's the way of the world, Mr. Phillips," Jesse smiled. "But please call me Jesse."

"I'm Clayton," he smiled back.

"So, tell me about yourself, Clayton. What brought you here to Montana?" she asked casually.

"Oh, that's a long and boring story," he quipped, refilling his glass. "It puts me to sleep just thinking about it."

"The one thing I've noticed in the past few weeks," Jesse smirked, "is that the sound of a human voice can be quite exciting, no matter what it has to say. Most of my monologues are answered with a howl."

Clayton chuckled quietly and turned in his chair to face her. She was a pretty little thing, he thought, and she seemed appreciative of his company. "I was a cop for twenty years," he finally began. "I had the house in the suburbs, the wife, the cars and the debt. The job was demanding and never quite paid well enough to cover the bills. The stress almost killed me a few times and the bad guys tried to get me whenever I turned my back. The wife left me because I was never at home. When I was home, all I wanted to do was sleep. I was chained to a pager and even vacations were filled with constant interruptions.

"I truly didn't think I'd live to see retirement, so when I surprised myself and did, I sold everything, bought my land up here and settled in for the long haul. I bought a pair of horses and some Corriente cattle and I've never regretted it. I didn't like the idea when the folks around here asked me to be Marshal, but the extra pay comes in handy and the only crimes involve the occasional bar brawl; the errant bear; and coyotes or wild dogs taking down some of the livestock.

"So, I hope you understand, when I looked out today and saw your wolf staring at me, it gave me a bit of a fright. We haven't seen wolves up here for years and the thought of them tearing up the place is not good news. We've got enough troubles with the other animals I mentioned without adding wolves to the list. It's peaceful up here. We just want our own space." Clayton leaned back in his chair and observed the young woman casually. She returned his gaze kindly and did not appear to be bothered by his opinion.

"I can understand that," Jesse empathized. The sun's rays had turned the horizon and everything they touched into colors of golden red and purple. "It's funny how similar our stories are, to a point. The firm where I worked for fifteen years was *killing* me, too. I worked all the time and had no life outside of those office walls. While I made pretty good money, I wasted it on frivolities like clothes, shoes and stuff of little importance. I lived in the city. I thrived on the noise because it helped me feel like I wasn't alone. Oh, I had friends and even an occasional boyfriend or two, but something was always missing. I cried a lot. I felt pretty sorry for myself and my lot in life."

"And then I was given a present," she continued. "An eight-week old Timber Wolf that nearly drove me insane. I couldn't believe I suddenly owned this peeing, howling, starving ball of fluff that chewed up everything it could get its teeth into, and demanded all of my attention. As with every other problem in my life, the boss didn't care, nor did the landlord, and I found myself in pretty dire straits.

"Nobody seems to care too much for wolves, Clayton. It seems they've been saddled with a bad reputation from the start. Wolves have been hunted and destroyed as long as they've been alive. In parts of Europe there's still a bounty on their heads and in Alaska they can shoot them from a plane. The folks in Denver condemned Shadow immediately. Everybody said the city was no place for a wolf, and I knew they were right. So, I took him to the mountains to a refuge where the people who care for them are forced to keep them separated in pens and have to rely on donations to feed them. They're not allowed to run and live the way of the pack. They're threatened the moment they step across the refuge border.

"When I was there I looked into the eyes of a full-grown wolf. Her heart was strong, but there was so little of her spirit left. I couldn't condemn Shadow to the same fate. And when I got back to my pup and held him in my arms, it suddenly all made sense. I stopped feeling sorry for myself and decided to do what I could to help.

"I quit my job, sold my condo, sold everything else or gave it away; traded my beautiful BMW in on that Dodge truck, and Shadow and I came here. We've been here for a short while now and until today our life has been pretty good." She took a sip of her iced tea and set the glass on the table.

"Here's the dilemma, Clatyon," Jesse sighed. "You say you came here for a little peace. You bought your land, you built your house and you're raising your horses, cattle and chickens and life is good. I came here to provide Shadow the peace and freedom he deserves. Who has the rightful claim to this land? Who's been here the longest? Did you ever stop to think that when you moved here for your freedom, those wild animals you complain about lost a lot of theirs? The wild animals just can't pack up and move, you know. If they move to a more populated area, they'll be destroyed for sure. If they move to a more remote area, they could lose their food source and die." She rose up from her chair and joined her wolf on the porch step. She sat down cross-legged and Shadow, who was roused from his nap, rested his head on her leg; his interest once again piqued by the stranger sitting on their porch.

"If Shadow can't live here, I don't know what we're going to do. After all, this is where his ancestors lived. You've brought your livestock here to this wilderness and expect a rolling hills, Kentucky farm life existence. Man may not know the difference, but I bet the animals do. I have to wonder, if given the choice, would your animals have come here voluntarily? Personally, I think they'd sleep better on that farm in Kentucky or Kansas. Nowadays most of the world is a pretty safe place for livestock, Clayton. Why can't there be just a few places were wild life can be safe too? And I'm not talking about shelters or zoos."

"You make a strong case, Jesse Harless," Clayton stated, slowly getting up. "But I still believe just as strongly in mine." His joints were a little stiff from sitting still for a while. He shook one leg, then the other, to get the blood moving again. Shadow was standing on all fours in a heartbeat. A growl rumbled deep inside his throat. "So, what do you recommend we do about this?"

Jesse got up and shooed Shadow from the porch step. The sun was just about to disappear behind the mountain range and the temperature was dropping quickly. "I hope we can work together on it," she said optimistically. "I know you spend a lot of money on your animals and I spend my share to keep this animal well fed. I figure if he's not hungry, he won't need to go looking for food."

Shadow, rejuvenated by the colder air, wanted to play. He rushed at Jesse and she faked a lunge toward him. He jumped back, braced his legs and waited for her attack with his tongue lagging out and his tail wagging. "Unfortunately, he's very friendly and thinks most strange people are family he hasn't met. If I'm not careful, obviously, that could hurt him someday." She started for him again and he ran a few feet away into the dark with a yip. "I'll try to watch him closer and keep him from going onto your land."

When Clayton Phillips stepped off the porch and onto the ground, Shadow came around from behind him, brushing his side against the cowboy as he passed by. "Whoa!" Phillips called, surprised. Still wagging his tail, Shadow stopped and turned, looking back at the man. Clayton looked at Jesse for advice.

"Put your hand out, palm up," she suggested. "He'll come to you, if you want."

Clayton put his hand out and Shadow, cautiously, came closer. The man touched the wolf's head and when the animal moved closer, he was able to sink his hand into the wolf's thick fur. "Never touched one of these before," he said quietly. "There's a lot of fur in there."

"The guard hairs protect the fur underneath," Jesse said, watching the interaction. "It's so thick, you can't touch skin. It protects him from the cold."

Eventually, with Shadow's prodding, Clayton was on his knees and the wolf was playing and nudging against him. A couple of times, the animal almost knocked the well-built cowboy down. Jesse stepped into the cabin, where she grabbed a jacket and turned on a light before coming back outside. Clayton and Shadow were still playing when she returned. She joined in the romp for a while until Shadow found something more interesting in the sagebrush.

"Okay," Clayton laughed, quite out of breath. "I guess Shadow wins this round." He looked at Jesse and squinted. Suddenly, he realized it was dark. "That's some wolf you've got there." He stumbled around looking for his hat. "And, I guess I can try to cut him some slack."

"You're too kind, Mr. Phillips," Jesse smiled. She found the hat and brushed the dust off before handing it back to him.

"I'm sure, if we put our heads together," he added, nodding his thanks, "we can come up with some kind of solution. But right now I'd better be getting back."

When Jesse heard a rustle and a squeal in the bushes, she cringed. "I hope we can."

Clayton walked over to his horse, apparently not aware of the tussle. "And thanks for the drink. That was right neighborly of you."

"Any time!" Jesse said, walking with him to hurry him along.

Clayton jumped into the saddle and extended his hand to shake hers. "It was a pleasure meeting you."

"And I look forward to seeing you again," Jesse said cheerily. Shadow picked that moment to come from the bushes with a rabbit firmly locked between his jaws. "Damn," Jesse winced, seeing the look of shock on Clayton's face when he saw what had happened. "I hope that wasn't your rabbit."

Clayton looked from Shadow to Jesse's face and after a brief moment broke out into a hearty laugh. "Hey, they eat the damn lettuce, anyway." He kept his hand extended and Jesse accepted it gratefully, laughing herself. Shadow carried his prize back to the porch and started munching on his feast.

"By the way," Jesse called out as the cowboy turned his horse and started off, "you said you haven't seen any wolves around here for some time, was that right?"

"For as long as I've been here," he answered back, reining the stallion in a bit and looking back at her.

"Well, I guess I should warn you, there's at least one more out there," she figured she might as well lay all the cards on the table. "Shadow seems to have found an acquaintance. I saw a white one a few nights back, and by the sound of it, she's got a friend."

"That's enough information for one night!" the cowboy yelled back. "I'll check again after I make sure my rag boxes are all plugged in and working right."

The cowboy turned his horse and trotted off. Jesse watched them for a few minutes, outlined by the rising moon, before she headed back to the house. She ignored Shadow's warning growl in case she might be the least bit interested in his bunny, and sat down on the porch steps with a concerned look upon her face. She wondered to herself, recalling Clayton Phillips' concerns, just how safe her wolf would be here in Montana. Especially if there was a wild wolf pack some place close by. If they attacked his cattle, Shadow would be the obvious scapegoat and a lot easier to kill, knowing where he lived. She could not pen him in. That is why she brought him up here in the first place; so he would be free like he had the right to be.

She resolved to keep a closer eye on him, and hoped he would be content to live by her rules. But by giving him the wilderness to grow up in, she knew in her heart he would eventually become a part of that wilderness. No matter how good she was to him or how hard she tried to keep him safe, he would always be a wolf; and because of that, his life would always be at risk. She cursed the world under her breath for vilifying one of nature's most perfect creatures. Because these animals cast doubt upon man's claim to be smarter than, and superior to nature, they were hated and destroyed for it.

Jesse's attention was drawn, subtly, from her odium for the human race to a rustling just inside the tree line. She peered out into the darkness and saw a sliver of something white between two conifers. Shadow saw it too. He left his rabbit carcass, climbed stealthily down the stairs and sat on his haunches at Jesse's feet. She rested her hand upon his backside, just below his neck, knowing if he bolted she could do nothing to stop him. Instead he slowly raised his head and howled into the darkness. The reverberation of sound traveled up Jesse's arm and coursed through her body. She involuntarily shivered at the intensity of this magnificent feeling.

There was a second or two of the sound of the wind passing through the trees before the white wolf answered Shadow's call. Every other creature was silent. Shadow howled again and the white wolf responded. In the distance, another wolf call added to the harmony. Jesse was transfixed by the beauty and listened in rapture as the three voices joined into a chorus. The wolf song grew loud and boisterous, one of the wolves barked and yipped and whined until their howls culminated into a crescendo at a fevered pitch.

As the sound of their cries echoed into the night, the white wolf stepped carefully into plain view. It was about the same size as Shadow, Jesse noted, careful not to move an inch for fear of frightening the animal. It, too, was a small adolescent. The white wolf was much thinner than Shadow, due, no doubt, to the rigors of finding food in the woods. Jesse wondered where its family might be and why it appeared to be on its own. Shadow took a few steps toward the other wolf. Their eyes did not stray from each other as they drew closer.

Jesse made a decision. Using her hands and feet, she edged backwards up the porch stairs toward the cabin door without getting up. Perhaps, if she was able to get some food to the wolf, they could come to some sort of understanding. Luckily, by the time she reached the screen door, the wolves were engrossed in a greeting of sorts and paid no attention to the crawling human entering the house. She opened the door carefully to minimize the squeaks and slipped inside. Once there, she extinguished some of the lights and hurried into the kitchen. She grabbed Shadow's puppy chow and poured a heaping mound of it into a plastic bowl.

Stepping gingerly outside, Jesse paused on the porch. Shadow and the white wolf were nose to nose. They yipped a bit and checked each other out. The white wolf bowed its chest and tilted its head. Shadow stood taller and nuzzled its snout. Like children, they examined each other and effortlessly began to play. By the looks of their behavior together, the white wolf was a little female.

Unfortunately, as quiet as Jesse was, when she stepped off the porch, the white wolf gave her notice. With a whimper she tore herself away from her new playmate and headed back toward the woods. Shadow started after her and Jesse's heart leapt into her throat. "Shadow," she called out. "Come on, boy. Time to come in."

Shadow stopped when he heard Jesse's voice and turned to look at her. "Come on, sweetie," she pleaded, "it's dinner time."

The white wolf was still watching when Shadow decided he'd rather inspect what was in the bowl that Jesse was carrying. In a flurry of rippling fur, he bounced up to Jesse and tried to knock the bowl from her hands.

"That's a good boy!" Jesse sighed, realizing the food was her saving grace. She kept it just high enough so he could not reach it. "Come on, let's go in." Shadow followed Jesse at her heels, jumping up and cavorting like the puppy he still was. She got him into the house and shut the wooden door before giving up her prize. She poured the puppy chow into his bowl and he attacked it eagerly. While he ate, Jesse poured some more chow into the plastic bowl and quietly snuck back outside.

"Here, girl," she called out to the white wolf. She could not see the animal, but she knew the animal was close by. She put the bowl of puppy chow down where the two wolves had met and then quickly backed away. "There's more where this came from if you like it." Jesse scanned the tree line and thought she saw a shadow move in the trees. When visible, the wolf was easy enough to spot because her white fur glowed in the moonlight. "Have a good night, Cheyenne," she proclaimed softly, giving the animal a name on the spot. "Come back tomorrow, okay?" She walked slowly back to the cabin, taking in the cool night air and the star filled heavens above her, yet careful not to look over her shoulder, where she'd left the food. Shadow waited impatiently—at the kitchen window one second, at the living room window the next. She stepped up her pace. She was lucky this time; Shadow was still more interested in food than he was in the opposite sex. But that phase would not last forever and Jesse knew that soon nothing she could offer would be enticing enough to lure him home. The work around the cabin could wait a few weeks. The determined woman was now going to spend some quality time with her little wolf.

CHAPTER 14

Jesse rose with the sun—and her wolf—every morning. She dressed and prepared their respective breakfasts before they ventured outdoors. It had taken time and patience, but Cheyenne's food dish was now located very close to the porch. Jesse moved it one step closer to the cabin every evening when she filled it. It was hardly necessary now because Cheyenne and her brother, a smaller gray wolf Jesse named Mesa, joined them regularly on their walks. They were almost close enough to touch, even brushing up against Jesse's legs as they rushed by chasing and playing with Shadow. Jesse always carried a generous plastic bag of dog chow with her for such occasions. Mesa was eating out of her hand and Cheyenne was close enough to catch each piece in her mouth when Jesse tossed it her way.

The two wolves hung around the cabin now, not quite brave enough to take a step inside when Jesse held the door open for them but content to sit on the porch when Shadow had to go in. Jesse's wolf was elated with his new companions and they were slowly, but definitely, forming their own little pack. They felt comfortable with Jesse and because of that, Jesse felt more at ease letting them socialize with and occupy more of Shadow's time.

Also, in their travels, which took them to every inch of the property as well as to many points beyond, they amassed another wild creature who eventually settled into the area around the cabin. A young bobcat, Jesse called Kitten, enjoyed the hassle free morsels the woman provided her and seemed to have a bit of a crush on Shadow. She followed him, at a safe distance from the other two wolves, teased him, and constantly prodded him to play with her. Lately, Jesse had noticed Cheyenne and Mesa were also tolerating her. Jesse made sure everyone was well fed, so the deer and raccoons heeded the menagerie less and less, as they carried on with *their* day-to-day existence.

After studying the Internet, Jesse discovered that the bird, which always seemed to be flying over their heads, was in fact a bald eagle. There were owls and hawks as well, and scores of other birds in the trees that surrounded the house.

On the day when Johnny Stillwater finally complied with his mother's request—after ignoring his father's demands for a month—to go fix the electrical problem at Joe's cabin, the young man was not in a good mood. He hated the thought of helping this woman, who had taken over the cabin he had practically built with his own two hands; the cabin he thought his cousin would give to *him*. No one, except his brother, who was sworn to secrecy, had any idea that Johnny had lived in it up until the day his father got the call from Joe telling them Jesse was coming. He resented having to remove his belongings in a panic as his father came over to inspect the condition of the place. Johnny had snuck out of the back door with the last of his things just as his father walked into the front door. What had been just fine for Johnny, looked like a dive to his father.

Johnny's stuff was still in a burlap bag, buried about 1,000 feet from the back of the house. It didn't matter, because he had no other place to put it. He would certainly not put it in his parent's house. It was bad enough that he had to live there now. His parents had thought he had shacked up with some girl and that lie had worked just fine, because when he wasn't around, his old man tended to stay off his case. But now that he was back home, his mother was certain he was nursing some kind of a broken heart and he was tired of having to make up stories to keep her from trying to help.

He trudged along the path with his work belt and tools, furious about the whining of a fancy white woman over a defunct light switch. He was going to fix it a while back, but then she came and the opportunity had slipped away. *What would she want next*, he asked himself. *A Jacuzzi and a garage?*

He forced a tree branch out of his way and it snapped back, almost cold cocking him on the back of the head. *Keep your cool, man*, he told himself, trying to control his temper. She had already seen him in action once. That incident, he was sure, got the message across. He didn't like her and there was no need for her to like him. He'd be in and out of there in a few minutes.

Up ahead, through the trees, he caught a glimpse of the cabin. *Almost there*, he thought. He mused whether he'd have the chance to dig up his stuff, but doubted it. She'd probably never let him out of her sight. And, of course, if he took the bag home, his mother would start in with a whole new barrage of questions and sympathy.

He stepped into the clearing and stopped short, his hand taking hold of a young sapling for support and cover. He was astonished by what he saw, and he needed a second to take it all in.

There was Jesse wrestling in the grass with two wolves while another wolf and a bobcat looked on from the porch. He stood there for a moment, riveted. It was the most amazing sight he had ever seen. *That chick is not right*, he thought as he shifted his work belt over his shoulder. The insignificant sound he made in doing so put every animal on alert. A raven cawed, the bobcat hissed, the white wolf growled and the rest of the party stopped playing instantaneously, their attention now focused on him where he brazenly stood in the pathway.

Jesse recognized his face and stood up quickly, brushing herself off. She had not seen Johnny Stillwater since their ill-fated introduction several weeks ago. On the few occasions she had visited the Stillwaters since then, he was never around or had always just left and Jesse liked it that way. She certainly did not like the fact he was visiting now, without Charlie, Frank or Winona around to keep an eye on him.

Kitten and Cheyenne headed, in a bolt, to the safety of the woods. At Jesse's side, Shadow growled and Mesa, hearing his stepbrother, joined in. Jesse stood her ground and placed her hands on the ruffs of the wolves' necks. If Johnny wanted trouble, she'd be happy to let him have it.

"My dad said you had a short in your wiring upstairs," Johnny yelled out with no hint of friendliness in his voice. Hearing Jesse's companions and seeing the look upon her face, Johnny suddenly felt it was in his best interest to announce his intentions before he got too close. "He told me to come fix it."

Jesse eyed him coldly but allowed him to approach her. She tried to shoo the wolves into the woods with Cheyenne, but they would not budge. Shadow lowered his head and bared his teeth, staring at the stranger. Mesa, with one eye on Shadow and the other on Johnny, just kept growling. "I'd recommend you go into the cabin," Jesse suggested straightforwardly. "I'll be there in a second."

"I know where everything is." Johnny obeyed her orders and hopped up onto the porch. "I'll be out of here before you know it."

Jesse nodded okay and let him go. She ran through the house mentally, hoping there was nothing lying out in the open that he might steal. *Whatever*, she decided. She knew where he lived if anything happened to turn up missing.

Johnny stepped quickly inside, casting a sidelong look back at the woman and the animals. He still couldn't fathom what he had witnessed just before they had noticed him, but once inside the cabin, his thoughts quickly turned elsewhere. He was now stunned to see what the woman had done to the cabin. There was new furniture, carpets, curtains and one hell of a television perched above the immaculately clean fireplace. In fact, the whole place was a lot cleaner than he'd ever seen it. He stood in the middle of the room and absorbed it all, even more surprised than when he had seen the wolves and bobcat outside. Through the screen door he caught a glimpse of Jesse bribing her wolves into heading for the woods. He also noticed the white wolf and the bobcat loping after them. He shook his head, mystified, and went upstairs to check on the lights. Equally impressed with the upper floor he explored a bit before settling down to do his work.

"Jeeesuz…" he muttered, checking it all out. "How the hell did she get that bed up here?" He looked in the closet and the bathroom. No clothes on the closet floor. The bathroom was clean and even sparkled when he turned on the light. There were clean towels hanging neatly on the racks. Johnny did not like to admit it, but he was impressed. He heard a noise downstairs and jumped. He worried she might sic the wolves on him if she caught him snooping around. It was time to get to work.

Jesse had walked through the cabin and, seeing that nothing appeared to be disturbed, she left by the back door. Her latest project was the patio floor. Thinking it best to look busy, she picked up a flat rock from the stack and threw it down on the dirt making a dull thud. It was heavy and it took a bit of work, but she eventually slid it into position next to the others. Someday, she knew, she'd have a lovely patio area here in the "L" of the cabin. The fountain gurgled behind her, thanks to the strong water pressure of her own well pump. The wolves had come around and romped in and out of the trees. An occasional hiss and spat told her Kitten was mixing in nicely.

She was curious as to what was going on in her house, but she refused to show it. She worked on the patio stone like she was all alone, denying to herself there was a crazed, white man-hating Native American upstairs in the sanctity of her bedroom, doing God knows what. When she heard him descending the stairs, she intentionally turned and faced the other way.

Johnny had to come out back to turn off the circuit breaker. He would have told her what he was doing if she had looked up from her work. She didn't, but the wolves did. He switched off the breaker and headed quickly back inside. Jesse smiled to herself. All her babies would get treats tonight. Of course, in the back of her mind was the story Arleen had told her, but stronger still were Arleen's words of warning against letting him discover that she knew what was fueling his resentment. It was a quandary, to be sure. But it was easiest just to ignore him all together. That, apparently, is where *his* intentions led in reference to her.

Shadow stepped over Jesse's work, rubbing against her as he passed. Mesa, as was becoming the norm, followed the leader. They went to the back door. Shadow wanted to go in.

Jesse sighed and got off her knees. She was thirsty anyway, so she really didn't mind getting up to let them in. As she rose, her eyes naturally traveled up the side of the house. With an unintentional glance upward, she thought she saw Johnny watching her from just inside the French doors.

"Ridiculous," she said out loud, grabbing the door latch and opening the door for the wolf. She refused to let her mind play tricks on her. And it didn't matter anyway, because to her surprise, for the first time Mesa followed Shadow right into the house. Although she was blown away by the action, she played it cool. As far as Johnny was concerned, she wanted him to think it happened all the time.

Shadow jumped up on the couch. Mesa did the same. Shadow jumped over the back of the couch, slid on the rug and ran into the kitchen to his food dish. Mesa was right behind him. Jesse got another bowl from the cupboard and filled it with Shadow's dog food. She set the bowl down next to Shadow's, so both animals could eat. Mesa watched Jesse and the bowl. Seeing Shadow eating his food, Mesa started on his own bowl. As she stood at the kitchen sink, washing her hands, she noticed that Mesa's tail was low and the tip was wagging.

The woman got two glasses down from the cupboard and retrieved a pitcher of freshly squeezed lemonade from the refrigerator. She filled both glasses. As the wolves devoured their chow, Jesse took one of the glasses and walked slowly upstairs. On the landing, Johnny was busy working on the light switch.

"Thought you might be thirsty," she said quietly, setting the glass on the top riser. She couldn't help but notice as he concentrated on his work, how incredibly handsome he was. His hair, hanging down to his shoulders, was silky and looked black in the shadows. His high, sculpted cheekbones and brooding lips framed a perfect nose. His eyes were the same turquoise blue as his mother's. When he turned and looked at her, she suddenly felt weak in the knees. They stared at each other a moment before she turned abruptly on the stairs and headed back down, holding the banister for support. Too bad he had the attitude of an angry badger.

Johnny's eyes followed her as she retreated to the first floor. He had noticed her as well. "Thanks," he finally uttered. "I'm, I'm almost done."

"Take your time," Jesse called back up, now hearing Cheyenne whining just outside the back door. "We're not going anywhere." She stood at the door a moment and then slowly opened it. Cheyenne took a nervous step back. "Come on, girl," she cooed. "Everything's okay."

Cheyenne paced back and forth in front of the open door with trepidation. She knew Shadow and Mesa were in there, but she was too afraid to go inside. Jesse kept her eyes on the white wolf, not wanting to scare her. She crouched down so she was at Cheyenne's level of sight. The wolf whimpered and continued to pace until she noticed something move behind Jesse. Shadow appeared from around the kitchen corner and Mesa followed suit. The female wolf, seeing her companions, took a leap of faith and bounded into the house. She rubbed against Mesa and nuzzled into Shadow's neck. He turned and bit her snout playfully. She lowered her chest and pressed against him. Shadow placed a front paw on her back and held her down for a bit. Then, with a bounce, he headed out the door that Jesse was still holding open. The other two wolves followed him, almost knocking her to the floor as they tried to get out the door at the same time. Outside, Shadow wrestled a bit with the bobcat who was waiting for his return. The four animals pranced across the unfinished patio into the woods.

Excited, Jesse grabbed the pitcher of lemonade and her drink and left the house. She sat down at the wrought iron table she had purchased recently and drank her lemonade with gusto. She couldn't believe she had had all three wolves in the house at once.

Johnny had watched the whole affair from the landing and had noticed her excitement. Suddenly, it struck him how kindhearted she must be. She certainly loved those animals very much. He affixed the switch plate back on the wall and took a drink of the lemonade. It was surprisingly good. He could have yelled down and asked her to turn on the circuit breaker, but he decided to go down and do it himself. He saw the smile of contentment on her face when he met her outside.

Jesse turned, still smiling, to see Johnny come out. "Gonna' turn on the juice," he offered as an explanation with a quick nod toward the fuse box. "I think it's fixed."

"That's great," Jesse answered. "Thank you very much."

He flipped the switch and turned to look at her again. Her brown hair framed her face and her eyes were the color of her wolves' eyes. "Why don't you come up and try it?" he finally suggested, breaking the silence.

"Sure," she said, suddenly realizing that he probably wanted to get out of there. She jumped up and did not show her surprise when he held the door for her. "Tell me it was more than the light bulb," she asked as she climbed the stairs ahead of him. "I hope you haven't wasted your time."

"No," he said, intrigued by the sound of her voice. It was soft and melodic when she was not angry. "One of the wires was loose. It should be fine now."

Jesse climbed to the top of the stairs and flipped the switch. The light overhead was bright and clear. Johnny came up behind her and they shared the landing, standing very close. He flipped the switch several times and it functioned properly. "Yeah, that's got it."

"Thank you," she breathed, embarrassed to be so close but not anxious enough to move away. "I know you're very busy."

"No problem," Johnny said softly. "I should have fixed it a long time ago." He could smell the scent of flowers in her hair. He wondered if it was as soft as it looked.

"Do you have time to finish your lemonade?" she asked, shyly.

"No," he said too quickly, for the look in her amber eyes somehow made him want to change his mind. "Well, I guess I got a couple minutes." He slowly turned and headed back down the stairs with Jesse following behind him. "You've really fixed this place up. It looks nice."

"Thank you," said Jesse. "I've got a long way to go."

They stepped back out onto the unfinished patio and Jesse offered him a seat at the table. Johnny watched her as she poured him another glass of lemonade. The wolves had appeared again. Mesa was drinking out of the fountain. Shadow and Cheyenne were resting under one of the trees. He chanced a glance in their direction. "I thought you only had one wolf."

"I did," she said, smiling again. "Funny, I seem to have three now."

Johnny saw that look again in her eyes. She truly loved those beasts. It was quite obvious when she talked about them. Johnny studied her closely as she coaxed Mesa over to the table and scratched his head behind the ears.

"I think Mesa here and Cheyenne, the white one, are brother and sister," she went on. "I don't know where their parents are. They're close to Shadow's age, I'm pretty sure. So, they were born just this year."

Johnny was somewhat mesmerized, watching Jesse's fingers caress the animal's fur. "How do you know that?" he asked finally, snapping out of it.

"Their eyes have just turned and they act like Shadow. For him to become the leader so fast is a clue that they've been without supervision."

Johnny's eyes snapped to attention and found the bobcat up in the tree after he had heard it hiss.

"I call her *Kitten*," Jesse grinned. "I think she's an orphan, too. She sure latched on to Shadow in a hurry." She looked up into the tree. "She follows him like he's her mother."

The pair fell silent and drank their lemonade. Johnny sat back in his chair and gazed at the scene unfolding around him. The water trickling in the fountain was relaxing. The birds called out from the trees. Mesa strolled over to the other two wolves and settled down for an afternoon nap. Johnny was surprised to find he felt like joining them.

Jesse noted that the young man was not a big talker, but she did not feel uncomfortable in his company. Her own father had been like that. Not a lot of words, but there was comfort and a feeling of safety in his presence. She did not need conversation. She had spent so much time alone lately; she had grown accustomed to silence. And she had Arleen if she wanted to chitchat. She sat back in her chair. Living the life of a wolf lately, which meant eating, playing, hunting and sleeping when they did, she knew exactly why she was feeling a little drowsy. When the wolves napped, she napped. She closed her eyes and let the sun beat down upon her face.

Johnny watched her covertly from the corner of his eye. He was not supposed to like it here. Preparing himself for this day, he had conjured up every bad experience with white people in his past, and he had resolved to keep them foremost in his thoughts. He did not like this white woman. He did not like what she represented.

So, he had to wonder why he did not want to leave. He wished he had something to talk about, but he couldn't think of a thing to say. He liked the fact that she wasn't gabby like the other women he knew. Always babbling on about something that didn't matter. She was a lot like her wolves. He thought about how nice it would be to have a hammock over in the trees. What would it be like to nap with this brood, holding this woman in his arms as they rocked gently back and forth in the afternoon breeze?

That's not very hateful, he reminded himself. However, the house was so cozy and this patio area was a great idea. He wondered what it was like to watch television on that flat screen T.V.. He was not supposed to be sitting here. He was supposed to be hanging out at his brother's house wasting time. Suddenly, he didn't want to waste so much time. He wanted her to ask for more help. God knows she needed it. It wasn't his way to offer help to a white person. That was against all his beliefs. But if she would just ask, he would swallow his pride and get a lot of things done for her.

"I saw a couple of other things that should be fixed," Johnny startled Jesse when he spoke some time later, "…when I was upstairs."

"Yes," Jesse agreed quietly, not opening her eyes. "There's that leaky faucet."

"Yeah," Johnny lied casually. He actually hadn't seen that, but he was pleased that there was actually some work that could be done.

"And the closet could definitely use a better light than just that light bulb hanging from the ceiling," Jesse said as she stretched and sat up. Her golden eyes met his and she almost smiled.

"Are you doing this stonework all by yourself?" Johnny inquired, making up a list in his head.

"When my back lets me," she sighed. "This area needs a lot of work."

"Well," Johnny announced, satisfied with her pseudo request. "I could probably free up a little time and give you a hand, if you need it."

"If it's not too much trouble," Jesse said softly, looking curiously into his eyes. They were guarded, but his malice had dissipated. *Perhaps this guy is all right,* she thought. Unfortunately, it would take a lot more than an offer of help to convince her. She decided to give him the benefit of the doubt. "We'd appreciate it."

Johnny returned her gaze skeptically for an instant before the meaning of *we* dawned upon him. "More time for the wolves, right?" he asked.

"Right," Jesse smiled. "They come first in my life, for now anyway. More lemonade?" She offered to pour.

The Native American did not have cause to believe anything the white man said, but he knew this white woman had just told him her truth, which impressed him. He agreed to stick around and have another drink.

CHAPTER 15

Jesse pulled the truck up to a spot in front of the general store and parked. The sun was out and it was a beautiful day. Shadow, almost too big for the front seat, turned from gazing out the window and looked at her with a panting grin on his face. Jesse had had a heck of a time getting him to come along for the ride. "You stay, boy," she announced, making sure the windows were just low enough to allow the air to flow and yet keep the wolf in. "I'll be right back and we'll head for home, I promise." She had completed all her errands—gone to the bank, filled up the truck with gas and mailed the bills. Once she'd picked up the supplies from Arleen, they'd be on their way home and Shadow would be much happier. The days of Shadow tagging along were ending, Jesse knew very well. The wolf preferred his playmates and the wide-open spaces of home to the cab of her truck.

Jesse slid out from the driver's seat and locked the doors. Shadow took her spot behind the wheel. His nose was wet against the glass when he touched it. "Just a minute, baby," Jesse smiled. "Gotta' get food. We've got a lot of mouths to feed at home." She went quickly into the store.

"Well, if it isn't the curator of our famous Harless Zoo," Arleen called out from behind the counter. "What brings you into town today?"

"Bones," Jesse laughed. "I need bones...and dog food, and cat food, and if there's any money left, some food for us. You're coming over tomorrow night, right?"

"Of course," Arleen said, walking out from behind the counter to help.

"The grocery store gave me all their scraps," Jesse said, "but the kids prefer your delicacies to theirs."

"I've got a new stash back in the refrigerator," Arleen stated, heading toward the back of the store. "I was going to bring them out tonight."

"Well, with me picking everything up today, you won't have to worry about it." Jesse roamed the shelves for other things she needed. "You can relax and be a guest for a change."

"Who all's coming?" Arleen lumbered out of the back room with a rather cumbersome box, overfilled with packages of bones and raw meat. She headed straight for the front door. Jesse ran over to open it for her.

"I invited everybody I know," she quipped, reaching the door just in time to prop it wide open. "Of course, nobody seems to RSVP around here."

"As long as there's food and booze, they'll come," Arleen said, walking quickly to the truck. Shadow whimpered at her from inside the cab. Jesse ran on ahead and pulled down the tailgate. "We don't have many fancy dinner parties around here." She set the heavy box down in the bed with an, "Umph."

"It's not a dinner party," Jesse sighed, feeling a bit embarrassed. She just thought it might be nice to get everyone together. "No big deal."

"Hey, it'll be fun," Arleen said, sensing Jesse's apprehension. "Jack said he's bringing the booze."

"Yeah, I saw him when I went to the post office," Jesse noted. Jack Miller owned the Bar and Grill, located just two doors down from Arleen's store. Jesse met him on one of her *nights out* with her girlfriend. There was not a lot to do in this part of Montana. The little bar was an oasis in the desert as far as Jesse was concerned. "His son's gonna' watch the bar for him."

Arleen brushed off her hands as the two women headed back into the store. She stopped briefly and stuck her hand in the opening in the window and Shadow licked it. "There's my boy," she smiled. "You're getting too big for this truck."

"I think our trips to town are about over," Jesse murmured. "He likes it better at home." She noticed the three men coming out of Jack's bar when she saw Arleen looking in their direction.

Arleen's eyes perused the men coldly. They were pretty drunk. "He's probably better off there, anyway." She ushered Jesse back into the store and shut the door. "Okay, what else do you need?"

The girls chatted while they packed up a few more boxes. "I saw Johnny earlier today," Arleen offered, grabbing some sugar and coffee off the shelf. She looked slyly in Jesse's direction to see how she'd react to her comment. "He says he's been doing a little work up at your place."

Jesse smiled to herself, thinking about his visits, which now totaled three. A number of things were working better, thanks to his labor. "He got that light fixed in the hallway and the tub's not leaking anymore."

"So, will we be seeing him tomorrow?" Arleen asked, almost too innocently. She set the last box up on the counter and tallied up the bill.

"Maybe," Jesse mentioned. "I asked him to come."

The door to the shop opened and an elderly woman ambled inside with her shopping bag. Arleen looked up and smiled, "Mrs. Wolsey. Nice to see you today."

"You know," Mrs. Wolsey said, closing the door behind her. "…These hooligans nowadays drive me crazy. They're out their teasing that big dog in that truck. Don't they have anything better to do?"

Jesse had smiled at the woman when she entered, but her glimpse instinctively focused over her head where she noticed there was somebody by her ride. She glanced back at Arleen, who motioned her on ahead. "I'll be right back."

"I'll be there in a second," Arleen stated with straight lips. She saw the men at the truck, too. "What do you need today, Mrs. Wolsey?"

Jesse was out of the shop in a heartbeat. The three men who had come out of Jack's bar were now surrounding the cab of her truck. "Pete, go get your gun," one of them said as she walked toward them. "It'll be like shootin' fish in a barrel."

"Can I help you gentlemen?" Jesse asked, her heart pounding. She moved quickly to the driver's side, making the man on that side step out of the way. Shadow sat in the middle of the seat, growling.

"Well, I could think of a way," the man slurred as he stepped back.

"Hey, you got a damn wolf in that truck, lady," one of them shouted. "We'll kill it for you for fifty bucks."

"How'd ya catch it?" another one asked, peering into the passenger side window and tapping at the glass. "Those things'll eat you alive if they get the chance."

"Goddamn things, killin' the livestock and all."

"Damn bleedin' hearts is what brought them back up here."

Jesse was overwhelmed by their comments. They weren't giving her a chance to speak.

"Pretty little thing like you taking a big chance with that thing in your truck."

"That fucking thing's got the devil's eyes."

"I'm quite all right, thank you," Jesse finally got a word in. She started fumbling in her jeans pocket for her keys.

"Hey, you want me to help you get those keys, darlin'?" the man leered, closing in.

"No thanks," Jesse stated, sorry her revolver was in the glove box. She really wanted to get into the truck. Shadow was now standing on the seat, his tail down and his gaze staring past her. "I'd like you to get away from my truck."

"Naw," the ruffian stepped closer, "you don't know what you want, honey. I can give you something you need real bad…"

"And we can kill that wolf just like we killed those others." The man with his hand on the window tried to open the passenger side door. Jesse thanked God it was locked. Her city girl attitude had saved the day. "We got five of 'em earlier this year. Two big ones and three pups."

Jesse's heart sank. She suddenly realized, horribly, what happened to Cheyenne and Mesa's family.

"Hey!" Jesse heard the voice coming from somewhere behind her. The man, with his alcoholic breath breathing down her neck, was way too close. Luckily, he turned, distracted, as he grabbed Jesse's arm. "Leave the lady alone," Johnny said, coming towards them from down the street.

"Goddamn, fucking Indian!" cursed one of the men on the other side of the truck. He started to come around the truck to where Jesse stood. "This ain't none of your business, boy!"

"Oh, it's my business," Johnny snapped as Jesse broke away from the man's grasp. He saw the frightened look in her eyes and gave her a quick wink. Jesse smiled gratefully at him and ran to his side. "Get away from the lady's truck."

"Who and what tribe is gonna' stop us?" the man who had been so close to Jesse sneered. "We beat all you Injuns down once and we can do it again."

"I don't think you want to try that," Johnny said calmly. "But, if you're really stupid, like I think you are, I'll be happy to teach you a lesson."

"Johnny," Jesse whispered, "please, don't."

"Yeah, listen to your squaw, Johnny," the man leered, coming toward them. His cronies were now right behind him.

"Go on back to your reservation where you belong."

"Why?" Johnny asked sardonically. "You think you're gonna' kill me like you killed those ferocious pups?" He gently pushed Jesse behind him. "The odds are better here. I'm a little bit bigger than they were."

The closest man lunged at the Native American, while his friends stood by—ready to help if he needed it. Jesse, feeling the strength of Johnny's arm when he pushed her out of the way, stepped back, incredibly frightened. Johnny let the man throw the first punch. He missed and Johnny grabbed his arm, wrenching it painfully behind his back. The other two started in on the attack, but stopped short. In an instant, Johnny had produced a knife and was now holding the blade against the drunken man's throat.

"Jesus H. Christ!" the man trapped in Johnny's arms, stuttered. "Get the fucking Marshal!"

Arleen stepped out of her store with her rifle cocked and pointed at the other two men. "He's on his way, fella'! Everybody just stay put."

Mrs. Wolsey peered out through the store window with an excited look upon her face.

Jack Miller came out of his bar with a gun in his hand. "And I got your back, Stewart," the burly saloonkeeper called out. "Don't you boys even think about scratching your ass if you want to keep it."

The threesome was surrounded, when a few minutes later Clayton Phillips' marked SUV roared into town, the tires kicking up a dust cloud at least eight feet high behind the vehicle.

"All right, Johnny," Clayton said evenly, as he jumped out of his vehicle. "You can let him go."

"If you don't mind, Marshal," Johnny answered back, "I'll wait 'til I see your handcuffs."

"They were after Shadow," Jesse said to Clayton when he saw her behind the Indian. Under different circumstances, Jesse would have laughed at the perplexed look upon his face. "Johnny saved our lives."

"And just who are you boys?" Clayton demanded, walking up to Johnny and placing the handcuffs on the man he held. Johnny's knife disappeared as quickly as he had produced it. "I haven't seen you around here."

"They've been here off and on since spring," Jack offered. "Never did get their names. But they do like to drink."

"It ain't none of your business who we are," the man in handcuffs said. "This is a free country."

Clayton shoved the man down on his knees a little too harshly. "Oh, not in this town, it isn't." He walked briskly over to the other men and locked them together with his spare pair of handcuffs. He instructed them to sit down next to their friend with a nod of his head and a glare. They grudgingly obliged. "Let me introduce myself. I'm Marshal Phillips and you happen to be in my town." He looked down at his charges and smiled mockingly. "Now, if you don't feel like being friendly, I can take you over to the jail in Conrad and let my buddies over there play a round of twenty questions with you." Clayton glanced furtively at Johnny, who stood protectively next to Jesse. He was inwardly thankful he had arrived there when he did. Johnny could have done a lot more damage to the men if he had been a minute later. At the moment, surprisingly enough, the young Indian seemed relatively calm. "As I see it, I've got plenty of charges to keep you there for a long time. Assault, harassment, ethnic intimidation, and drunk and disorderly to boot." He turned his gaze back to the intruders. "And I wonder what else I'd find if I go take a look in that truck over there. I take it, that's yours?"

"Yeah," one the men answered begrudgingly.

"Arleen," said Clayton, "keep an eye on our friends here while I grab their wallets."

"Got 'em in my sight," Arleen announced, taking a menacing step forward.

After a search of the truck and their pockets, Clayton faced them down. "Most people put tools in a tool box," he stated coldly, perusing their driver's licenses and the truck registration. "You boys up here hunting?"

Jesse wanted to scream out that they had killed the wolves, but Johnny put his hand on her arm and with a look, hushed her up.

"Ain't no law against it," the man who'd been after Jesse piped up.

"No, there isn't," answered Clayton, measuring the man against his driver's license picture. "Pete McClennan, is it?" He looked intently at the individual.

McClennan did not answer him back.

"But here in these parts, we frown upon it. Unless, of course, you've got the proper hunting licenses and credentials." He looked at another piece of identification. "I would think you'd know that, Larry Russell, seeing you live pretty close—just over the Interstate."

"We ain't hurting nobody," Russell contended. "As I see it, we're helping out. The animals we kill would kill us if they had the chance."

Clayton sighed heavily. Jesse, behind him, was not going to like hearing that. "Well, tell me Jim McClennan," he had made note of the final license. "Do you think you might consider finding another place to do whatever it is you're doing?" Jim McClennan looked over at his brother before he opened his mouth. "Because I really just don't want you in my town or anywhere around here for a long time." The Marshal bent down on one knee in front of the man. "What do you say to that?"

"I guess so," Jim McClennan answered awkwardly.

"And that's a good answer," Clayton snapped back, startling everybody. "Because I will arrest all of you if I see you again in these parts. Got it?"

"But, Marshal," interjected Jesse, troubled that he might let them go. Johnny clasped her arm tighter, but to no avail. "They threatened Shadow and scared the hell out of me. If Johnny hadn't showed up, I don't know what would have happened."

Clayton sighed again and stood up. He continued to concentrate on the three men in front of him and did not turn to face the young woman. "It's okay, Jesse. I'm sure these gentlemen would be glad to apologize and get on their way. They've got some driving to do if they're going to get out of this county before nightfall, right?" He motioned for the three men to get up off their knees.

"Sorry if we scared you, ma'am," Larry Russell mumbled. "Guess we just had too much to drink."

"And don't be coming back to my bar," Jack burst out. "You're not going to get in if you try." He turned on his heel and headed back into his establishment.

"You're not welcome here, either," Arleen added, still pointing her rifle. "Just don't come back to this town. That should cover it."

Mrs. Wolsey had come outside sometime during the event and now took the time to put her own two cents into the conversation. "I told you they were hooligans. Picking on that poor dog like that." She clutched her purchases close to her chest and hurried down the street and around the corner.

Clayton took the handcuffs off the three men and directed them to their truck. Jesse's mouth was agape from her vantage point just behind and to the side of Johnny. She couldn't believe that Clayton was letting these thugs go. Johnny squeezed her hand one more time and firmly conducted her over to Arleen.

"The vote's unanimous, boys," Clayton observed, directing them with a nod of his head toward their truck. "Find a new place to haunt." They begrudgingly obeyed his order. He watched them, muttering to themselves under their breath, climb into their pickup and slowly drive out of town. He had memorized their names, birth dates and the license plate on the truck. He went over to his SUV and called the information into the County Sheriff's Office, who would run a check. He also called the State Patrol and let them know the way they were headed. They'd get them off the highway and into the drunk-tank within the hour.

Arleen put her gun inside the door and enlisted Johnny's help to finish loading up Jesse's truck. Jesse stormed over to the Marshal, who was sitting in his SUV.

"I can't believe you let them go like that!" she shouted at him, waving her arms about. "They killed a family of wolves and they probably killed Kitten's parents, too!"

Clayton raised an eyebrow. "Kitten?" he asked, almost afraid of the answer.

"Did they have licenses for those guns? They threatened to kill Shadow! Jesus, they wanted a piece of me!"

Clayton eased out of his vehicle. "They didn't break any laws, Jesse," he tried to soothe her. "They were just..."

"Drunk!" Jesse interrupted him. "They arrest people for that in Colorado, Clayton! You just let them drive off!"

"The State Patrol will pick them up as soon as they get on the highway," the Marshal reasoned. "We don't have any place to put them here. Haven't you noticed? We don't have a jail."

"That's no excuse!" Jesse was infuriated. "How many other animals have they killed? You're telling me they can come onto my property and shoot everything that moves?"

"No, Jess," Clayton sighed. "If they come on your property, that's another story." He tried to take her arm to comfort her. She snatched it away from his grasp. "Jesus, you just let these people come up here and let them do what they want? No wonder you don't see any wolves. They don't have a chance around here."

"Now, Jesse, please," Clayton tried again, "there was really nothing I could do."

"They were gonna' kill Johnny," she added, still fuming.

"But Johnny's the one with the knife," Clayton warned. "I could have arrested him, you know."

"My God!" she screamed. "The one person who stood up for me?" She spun away from him and stomped angrily back to the store. "Justice is so fucked up!"

Hurriedly loading the truck, Arleen managed a weak smile at the Marshal, who threw up his hands in frustration and climbed back into his vehicle. Johnny kept his head down and kept busy inside the store. Clayton Phillips drove off a little bit faster than he should have.

Jesse took her keys out of her pocket and opened up the driver's side door. Shadow looked at her tentatively before he lumbered out. He brushed a paw against Jesse's leg while she reached in and put the keys into the ignition. Realizing she was upset, he left her alone and sniffed for a spot to relieve himself.

"It'll be okay, Jess," Arleen commented to her friend. "They won't be back."

"How can you be sure of that?" Jesse asked incredulously. "What if they come back at night when you're alone in the store? What if they decide to pick off Jack too?"

"Okay, big city girl," Arleen stated firmly, "trust me. That will not happen."

"I don't know how you can be so calm," said Jesse, trying to catch her breath. "All I can see is *Deliverance* and you guys are living in the *Little House on the Prairie*."

Arleen snickered. She took Jesse's arm and looked at her intently. Jesse was a little embarrassed to look back. "They won't be back because Clayton has warned them. There's a different code up here, Jess. It's not like *Tombstone*. There are no shootouts and there's no LAPD. If you make a mistake, you get the chance to make it right. If they come back here, Clayton will be on them like ants on ice cream. You gotta' trust him…and us."

"Could Johnny really have gotten in trouble?" Jesse questioned her friend, sitting down on the running board of her truck.

"Yes, unfortunately," Arleen sighed. "He's not supposed to be carrying a concealed weapon in town. You noticed, those clowns didn't have any weapons on them."

"Shit," Jesse hissed, "I'm sorry for making such a scene."

"Hey, Johnny!" Arleen called out to the Native American, who was bringing out the last box of supplies. Shadow leapt over to him and followed him to the back end of the truck. The Indian crouched down and rubbed the animal's neck robustly. "Maybe you'd better drive these two home. Jesse's pretty upset."

"Yeah," he agreed. "I should probably do that." He got up and Shadow followed him. They walked around to the cab of the truck and he ushered the wolf in. Shadow licked Jesse's face as he plodded around her to get into the cab.

"Johnny can answer your questions for you," Arleen suggested, stepping back from the door to let Johnny climb in. Jesse scooted in first. "Trust me, kiddo. Everything is all right."

"Thanks for everything," Jesse handed Arleen a signed blank check and slid over to the middle of the seat. "We'll see you tomorrow, right?"

"With bells on!" Arleen shut the truck door and stepped clear of the vehicle. She waved to them as they drove away.

"I'm so sorry," Jesse finally said, halfway home. "I didn't want you to get in trouble."

"I didn't," Johnny replied. "It's okay."

"Everybody says that a lot around here, don't they?" Jesse retorted, absent-mindedly petting Shadow's back. The wolf was thrilled to be headed home. His head was out the window, enjoying the wind butting up against it. His fur was flying and his tongue was lagging out the side of his open mouth.

"Well," Johnny noted, "for the most part, it *is* okay." He cast her a sidelong glance as he sped the truck down the road. He was impressed with the new truck's performance.

"It's okay to kill animals for the thrill of it?"

"That's what you call a white man hunter."

"It's okay for people to talk to you the way they did today?"

"That's what you call our history."

Jesse looked at Johnny, who kept his eyes on the road. He was so beautiful, she thought. His chiseled features gave him a strong look, yet his golden skin looked so incredibly soft. Shiny and pitch black in the cab of the truck, his hair floated listlessly around his face. "That makes me angry," she murmured.

Johnny looked at Jesse with a tiny smirk upon his lips. "Welcome to the club," he muttered back.

"So how do you deal with it?" she demanded, turning toward him. She resisted putting a hand on his knee, even though she wanted to very much. Of all the events of the day, she remembered how strong his hand was when he kept her at bay from the Marshal. She liked how she felt with her hand clasped in his—amazingly safe and secure.

Johnny stated matter-of-factly, "Well, if you were me, you learned how to fight. You also learned how to shoot a gun, a bow and arrow and how to work with a knife. You pick your battles according to the enemy's strength. Walk away if you're not sure you can take them down in the first five seconds." He turned the steering wheel and guided the truck onto Jesse's property. Shadow was beside himself with excitement; his heavy paws clawing into Jesse's jeans and thigh as he tried to move about in the cabin.

"Johnny," Jesse winced for the second time. "Can you stop a second? I think Shadow would like to run a bit."

"Sure," Johnny slowed the truck to a stop and Jesse opened the passenger side door. Shadow was out like a shot, free from the truck at last. Johnny drove not too slowly down the road to the cabin. Like the wolf dog, Max, Shadow ran blissfully behind them.

"So," Jesse wanted to continue their talk, "have you ever killed anyone, Johnny?"

"If I killed everybody I was mad at in my life, I'd be the sole occupant of Montana." His turquoise-blue eyes sparkled when they looked at Jesse. "I'd have to say *no* to that question."

"I would have killed those three today," Jesse smoldered. "And laughed while I did it."

"Well," Johnny remarked, "then, you'd have to face my father. Charlie White Feather doesn't take kindly to violence no matter what the cause is behind it." He pulled the truck up in front of the cabin. Cheyenne and Mesa, who were lying on the porch, scattered toward the woods. When they spied Shadow behind the truck, they guardedly changed course and converged with him instead. After their customary greeting, play began in earnest. "Now, if you're my father, the way you handle it is by doing nothing. He says his prayers, turns the other cheek and walks away. He says the Creator will protect us and defend us. What goes around comes around. And about a hundred more old wise sayings that would drive you crazy if you had to hear him spitting them out all the time."

"Then, that explains you," Jesse smiled, getting out of the truck. Johnny looked at her with a curious stare. "Why you're crazy, that is."

"Yeah," Johnny laughed out loud, "pretty much psychotic, to hear him talk." Kitten hissed from her cool spot underneath the porch.

"Well," stated Jesse, pulling the tailgate down on the truck and grabbing the first of many boxes loaded with supplies, "I wish I could say I was like your father—with all the forgiveness and stuff—but when it comes to my animals, I might as well be your sister. I was a pretty big wimp when it came to standing up for myself and I deserved to get stepped on because of it. But when it comes to my babies, as far as I'm concerned, if I had had the chance to get to my gun today, which I will now carry with me at all times, there'd be three idiots who wouldn't be able to sit down for a couple of months."

"Way to go, Sis," Johnny said, still smiling.

"I can't turn the other cheek when it comes to those wolves," she said seriously. If I did that, they'd all be dead by now." She glanced over at the wolves, who were busy stalking and pouncing on some poor creature, probably a field mouse. She smiled winsomely. Her babies were safe *here*, at least for now. "Hey, if you help me with these supplies, I'll make you the best dinner I can muster," Jesse suggested, turning away from the beasts and heading for the house with the first box. "Because I'm glad *you* were there today instead of your father."

With a smile, Johnny grabbed the next box and followed Jesse into the cabin.

CHAPTER 16

❀

Clayton Phillips' thoughts were not on the task at hand. Jesse's heated words from the afternoon before played over and over again in his head, which in turn distracted him and led to more than one mistake in his fence repair project the following day. The hammer hit his thumb, rather than the nail, for the third time in less than two hours, causing him to curse out loud and lose another nail in the weeds while he shook his hand to get the blood flowing once again.

"Damn that girl!" he muttered. "What does she think I can do about this?"

Yes, it was wrong to just up and shoot a pack of wolves, pups and all, but it was not against the law, at this point. If they were on protected land, that was another story, but according to the men he talked to, the pack was not on the wildlife preservation, so they had done nothing wrong. Of course, that was only if one did not consider killing a mother, father and three helpless pups in cold blood to be wrong.

Clayton's sensible side was happy—five more wolves out of the equation, which kept that many more of his cattle alive. Yet, in his heart, he was angry. Three pups, for God's sake. What were they thinking? He looked out over his property and the mile of fence that was always in need of some repairs. Why couldn't everybody just live together in peace? "Because cattle costs money," he snapped, rummaging through the tall grasses and weeds for the nail he dropped. "And wolves don't." He concentrated on his repair work. No city girl was going to change his mind. There would be no preferential treatment for any of the animals out here. He'd never have time to do his own work if he was always chasing after somebody who'd injured or killed a wild animal.

An hour passed and the heat of the day was intensifying. He stood up straight and stretched, removing his cowboy hat to run his fingers through his hair, which was wet with sweat. He thought he heard an odd sound from somewhere behind him, but he dismissed it. His eyes traveled back along the fence and the work he had accomplished. After forcing Jesse and her wolves out of his mind, he was finally getting something done.

The next growl was unmistakable. There was something behind him and it was very pissed off. Clayton turned to check on his horse that had been casually grazing when he last checked. Now, in a blink of an eye, the horse was whinnying and pulling at its tether fastened to a fence post several hundred feet away from the cowboy. Closing in on them, from out of nowhere, was a large black bear running on all fours and hell bent for one of them. The bear stopped, barring Clayton from getting to his horse or his gun lodged in the horse's saddle, and reared up on its hind legs. There was blood coming from the animal's mouth. There was blood oozing in his fur.

"Damn!" Clayton cursed, temporarily immobilized by his dilemma. The bear was injured. To Clayton it seemed to have been shot. But it was only wounded and nowhere near dying. It was furious and wanted Clayton's and/or his horse's blood in retaliation. The bear glared at his options—a man or a beast. It made a decision quickly and took its first steps toward Clayton.

They were in the middle of a field. There were no trees or cover to run to. Clayton was out of luck and for the first time since he was a cop, he actually felt fear. He turned and started to run; scared to death and knowing he was very close to facing his own firsthand. As he dug his heels in the ground and sprinted, he stopped short again. Coming at him from the opposite side of the field was Shadow, or what looked like Shadow—in other words a big, black wolf. But the wolf was not in his usual playful mood and was not interested in Clayton at all. It passed him in a flurry of fur and when the man turned he saw two other wolves, one white and the other mottled gray, bearing down on the same subject. They were growling and nipping at the bear, taking rare chances and coming in way too close. The bear swatted at the smaller animals and actually hit the gray wolf, sending it flying back with a yelp and a whimper. The white wolf renewed its charge and Shadow, the biggest of the three, tore at the wounded bear from behind, ripping flesh and fur.

The gray wolf got up and shook itself off before entering the fracas again. Clayton stood still, transfixed by the event that was taking place before his eyes. He then realized the danger. The wolves really had no chance against the bear if they were careless. The bear could kill all three if they didn't bring him down in the next few seconds.

He ran around them and got to his horse as quickly as he could. He pulled the rifle from his saddle, bolted it forward and cocked it, ready to shoot. He took a few cautious steps, getting as close to the melee as possible. He took precise aim and shot the bear in the head, felling it instantly. The wolves still growled and hissed at the beast, but broke off the attack. Shadow pawed at the body as if to check whether it was truly dead.

Clayton sat down with a thud in the grass and took a couple of deep breaths. His heart was racing and his hands were shaking under the duress. Shadow came warily up to the man as the other two wolves paced around the kill. Shadow's growls kept them at bay and from attempting to chow down on their newly fallen prey.

"Thanks, boy," Clayton sighed, rubbing his hand against the wolf's neck. Shadow came up close and nuzzled his shoulder. "Jesus, I didn't see that coming." He got up from the ground and started toward the carcass. The other two wolves lowered their heads, bared their teeth and began to growl. "These must be your new friends," Clayton said evenly. He eyed the two wolves and slowed his pace. Shadow hunched his shoulders, growled back and lunged toward them. The wolves yelped and took a few steps back. "That's okay, Shadow," Clayton murmured. "I can see from here that bear was shot." His keen eyesight studied the carcass from a few feet away. "There, near the shoulder," he pointed. "Probably missed any vital organs." Content that the other wolves were behaving, Shadow rejoined Clayton by the body of the bear. "Who did this, boy?" he asked. "Who the hell would be so stupid?"

Clayton stood up and looked over his land again. "Hopefully, this big guy killed the bastard who shot him," he said boldly. "I'd hate to think something like this might happen again." He looked over at the wolves and realized the white and gray ones wanted a piece of the dead animal. He stepped clear of the bear and walked back to his horse. "It's all yours, guys," he said. "I'm heading home. I need a drink."

Johnny laid the last stone of the patio into place and pounded it down into the dirt. "There," he announced, sitting back on his knees. "How does it look?"

Jesse looked up from the rock garden where she had just finished deadheading the petunias. She surveyed Johnny's work with a critical stare. "Hmmm," she pronounced, "I believe that might do." Her eyes betrayed her folly. She smiled warmly at her new friend.

Johnny smirked, "Good enough for who it's for, that's what I say." He stood up and took a look at the completed project.

Jesse came up from behind him and touched his shoulder gently. "It's beautiful," she whispered. "I'll sweep it off and get it ready for tonight. It'll be like a fairyland when the candles are lit."

"Speaking of fairyland," Johnny mentioned, heading over to the table to pour them each a drink of water from the pitcher. "I haven't seen, nor have I heard the creatures for a while. Do you think they're okay?"

Jesse was touched by his concern for the wolves. It warmed her heart to hear him speak the words. "It's funny," she told him. "When I think that..." she looked to the north. Like clockwork, from under the conifers the three wolves were heading home in single file. "It must work for you too. Every time I start to wonder about them, it's like a switch goes off and they show up." She took the glass of ice water he offered her and took a drink. "Here they come now."

Johnny gulped down his water and traced Jesse's line of sight. "That's good," he said simply and poured another glass of water for himself. "I should probably get some propane for the barbeque, don't you think?"

"It looks like the weather is going to hold out." She started to sweep up. "Take the pickup. The keys are on the table. I'll finish up while you're gone."

Johnny finished his ice water and covertly studied the woman over the rim of his glass. *She trusts me*, he thought. After being such a pig the first day they had met, she was willing to take a chance and give him the keys to her very expensive truck. Nobody trusted Johnny Stillwater—nobody. Hell, there were times his mother had her doubts about him. He liked it that way. It gave him an excuse to express his anger whenever he wanted to. And up until a couple of days ago he was angry a lot. Nobody understood him or why he was so pissed off all the time. He hated the cards he had been dealt. He hated being poor and being a minority. He could never rise above it all like the rest of his family did. And of all people, his mother should understand that. He knew she'd gone through hell, because he had watched it happen. Why didn't she understand *his* hell? That he'd been too young to do a thing about it.

That was one of the reasons, when he left Jesse's last night that he didn't go home. He crashed out on the newly hung hammock, just in case those thugs had decided to cause more trouble. He had heard Arleen's words too, but like Jesse, he didn't trust them either. The white man, especially when he was drunk, could show some pretty sadistic behavior.

Had Jesse figured him out? Did she have any idea that he liked hanging around the cabin and that he liked to be near her? He couldn't understand it, but for the first time in his life, he decided not to worry about it. "I'll be back in a few," he said, going into the house.

The wolves arrived just as Johnny drove off in the truck. He slowed down and stuck his hand out the window, petting Shadow when the wolf put his front paws up on the cab door. Jesse watched them from inside the cabin. She briefly considered whether the man would actually return and just as quickly dismissed it. She knew he would come back. She saw it in his eyes when he looked at her before he left.

She washed out the water glasses and tidied up the kitchen. The rest of the cabin was in pretty good shape. She had planned to check her emails before she went upstairs to take a quick shower and get ready for her guests, but Shadow and Mesa came in through the hole in the screen door, tentatively followed by Cheyenne, and Jesse assumed they'd want something to eat. She gave them three big bowls of dog chow and tossed a fish filet out to Kitten who was resting under the porch. When the wolves just picked at their dog chow and did not show a lot of interest, she gave them each a meaty bone. They took their treats out into the backyard.

In the shower, she thought about the emails again. "Damn, I haven't checked those in days," she commented to no one in particular. As far as she knew, no one had called lately, so there probably weren't any emails either. Jesse also remembered that both Joseph and Eric had demanded she get an answering machine. "I really need to do that, soon," she agreed with herself.

The hot water felt good upon her skin. It always felt good to get cleaned up after a hard day's work in the Montana sun. She dressed casually in jeans, cowboy boots and a white shirt. She piled her dark hair up on her head and took the time to put on a little makeup. She was looking herself over in the full-length mirror when she heard the truck pull up. "Good enough for who it's for, I guess," she sighed and headed downstairs.

She was surprised to see Clayton's truck instead of hers when she stepped out onto the porch. Clayton Phillips lumbered out of the vehicle along with two younger men.

"Hope we're still invited to the cook out," Clayton said at the bottom of the porch stairs. Kitten hissed from under the porch, startling him somewhat. The two young men stopped in their tracks.

"Of course you are," Jesse smiled. In the distance she could see another vehicle's dust wafting toward them. "Don't mind Kitten. She doesn't like to share her dinner."

"Bobcat?" Clayton asked, peering under the porch.

"Bobcat," Jesse answered. "Your friends probably killed her parents too."

"Jess," Clayton sighed exasperatedly, "this is my son Tim and my ranch hand Mike." He walked slowly up the stairs.

"Good evening, gentlemen," Jesse waved them up to the porch. "Kitten won't bother you, if you don't bother her." Tim Phillips was a strapping young man, tall and slim, with blond, shoulder length hair, blue eyes and a beautiful smile. He tipped his hat to the lady and murmured a quiet hello. Jesse could tell he was a little shy.

Mike was a little shorter and stockier, with a mop of brown hair and large, dark brown eyes. He was ruggedly handsome. "Thank you, ma'am, for having us," Mike said quietly, when he shook her hand.

"There's beer in the refrigerator," Jesse offered, holding the screen door open for them to go in. "Please make yourselves at home." She looked back out to the road. Johnny was right on their heels. He slid the truck in next to Clayton's and hopped out, giving her a wink before grabbing the propane tank from the truck bed. Jesse smiled back and went inside.

"So, how's your wolf?" Clayton inquired, accepting the beer Mike gave him and looking around the cabin. Everything must have been all right, he surmised to himself, because if it hadn't been, she probably would have shot him when he pulled up.

"Fine," she answered, now opening the door for Johnny. "Why do you ask?"

Johnny greeted the newcomers. "Hey, Mike! Hey, Tim!" He walked through the cabin and out the backdoor with the tank.

The young men replied, "Hey," in unison and followed him, not wanting to be around when Clayton told his story. They had already heard she had a temper when it came to her pets.

"Boys," Clayton warned, "I'm going to need your help in a minute, so don't disappear."

"Clayton," Jesse asked deliberately, her golden eyes fixed on his, "what's up?"

"I suppose you know Shadow's got playmates," he sighed, avoiding her stare.

"Of course," Jesse quipped. "The white one is Cheyenne and the gray one is Mesa."

"And Mesa's okay?" Clayton asked. "He's not limping or anything?"

Jesse's tone of voice was even, but showed obvious concern. "I just tried to feed them but they didn't appear to be overly hungry. Other than that, they're okay. What happened?"

"I was working on my fence earlier today and I got attacked by a wounded bear."

"A wounded…"

"It had been shot," Clayton admitted. "Probably by those goons I let go. I've called the Sheriff. There's a warrant out for them as we speak."

"Are you all right?" Jesse wondered, looking him over from head to toe.

"Just a little shaken," Clayton retorted. "Your wolves actually saved my life."

"My wolves?" Jesse asked dubiously.

"They came out of nowhere," Clayton continued. "Just like the bear. Never seen anything like it. They distracted it so I could get to my horse and grab the rifle. It slapped Mesa around a bit, so I was a little worried."

Jesse tore through the cabin and out the back door. Mike and Tim had been filling Johnny in on the details as he hooked up the tank, so when she flew past them they knew to get out of her way. Her eyes searched frantically for her babies. They were over by the hammock, chewing on their bones. Jesse took a deep breath and walked slowly over to Mesa. Shadow hopped up, with his bone still gripped between his teeth, and trotted over to her. Mesa growled when Jesse got a little too close to his bone. "That's okay, boy," she spoke softly, kneeling down to get a good look at him. He seemed to be fine. She couldn't see any blood.

"I learned a big lesson today," Clayton murmured, coming carefully up behind her. "I'm grateful for their help."

"Hey, Shadow. Come here, boy," Johnny passed behind them and grabbed Shadow's attention. The wolf followed him out into the open area away from the patio. They played a bit—Johnny chasing the wolf and the wolf chasing Johnny.

"Pop was a little distracted," Tim offered. Mike stifled a snicker. "He was a good 300 feet away from his horse when the bear came at them."

Mesa, still gnawing on his bone, watched Johnny and Shadow with interest. It did not take long for the gray wolf to get up and go over to them. Johnny was careful, but studied Mesa and watched his behavior. Jesse stood up and watched them, too.

"He's good," Johnny finally proclaimed. "He's not favoring any leg. I think he just got bumped."

"Glad to hear it," Clayton stated, turning back to Jesse. "I'm sorry and I just wanted to tell you that as far as the Clayton ranch is concerned, your wolves are welcome. We'll figure out some way to get along."

"My God, Clayton," Jesse observed. "You could have been killed."

"Do you want Mike and me to go get the meat?" Tim asked his father. Jesse looked at Tim and then back to Clayton with a puzzled look upon her face.

"We stripped the hide and cut him up. There's a ton of bear meat and bones in the back of the truck for the wolves. They helped me kill him and they deserve the spoils."

"Thank you, Clayton," Jesse murmured, giving the man a hug. He wasn't used to that gesture and hugged her back stiffly. "There's a freezer in the storage room, guys. Go ahead and load it up."

"Hey, Clayton," Arleen heralded, entering the patio with Jack, the bar owner, who carried a box full of booze. "You've got a dead bear in your truck. Did you know that? You gotta' slow that truck down—you knocked that animal clean out of his skin."

"Very funny, Arleen," Clayton mused, grabbing another cold beer from the box as Jack set it down on the patio floor.

Tim and Mike headed into the cabin to complete their chore. Winona, Charlie, Frank and Mary arrived on the patio a few minutes later and the party was complete.

"There's our boy," Charlie's voice boomed to his wife when he saw Johnny playing with the wolves. "I told you he'd show up sooner or later."

Jesse looked at Johnny and smiled, waving him back to the house.

"Jesse," Charlie continued, "that bobcat is a menace. It scared the daylights out of me when I got out of the truck."

"I'd say you're the menace, pop," Johnny sneered. "That cat is just protecting the property. He's fine with us."

"Well, if you..." Charlie started to cut his son down with a quip of his own but Winona touched his arm and exchanged a look with him, which put a quick end to it. Obviously, to Jesse, Winona and Charlie had been having some talks regarding their son. Charlie recovered quickly, "...I was going to say, if you would get your father a beer, I might be inclined to forget about it." With the truce declared, the party began.

The neighbors laughed and talked and enjoyed each other's company. Johnny cooked and Jesse served drinks. The wolves kept their distance, enjoying their bones and watching the medley of humans interact. Everyone had stories and jokes to tell. There were tall tales and serious discussions. Clayton related the bear story a few times. At every telling the bear became more ferocious, the wolves became more courageous and Clayton became a better shot. Tim razzed his father about some other close encounters that sent every member of the ranch running to save their lives—just to keep Clayton humble.

Jesse was the perfect hostess, doting on each of her guests to make sure everyone was happy. Winona noticed the exchanges between Jesse and her son. Johnny seemed quite friendly and happy to be a part of things. At first, Charlie tried to slip in a barb at him now and again. But Johnny was onto his game and refused to lose his cool. Winona was so proud of him and surprised to find that this young woman seemed to have such a positive influence on her son. Luckily, she noted in her thoughts, Charlie seemed oblivious to the whole affair.

Johnny's father was having a very good time, which was all that was important as far as Winona was concerned. As for this apparent closeness between her son and a white woman, a fling would surely do no harm if it cured Johnny of his anger and depression. Once the young woman moved on, then Johnny might be more apt to settle down with one of his own kind like his father wanted him to do. She dreamed for the day when that would happen. She hated seeing her son so miserable and always alone. Winona did not share Charlie's beliefs regarding the obligations of the Native American to keep their bloodlines intact. After all, her grandfather was a blue eyed, German military man who had married her grandmother because, as a female, she was a burden to her destitute family. Winona liked Jesse, but like her husband she did not think the young woman would stay in Montana forever. A young woman with a career and money had no reason to settle down in the wild country. It was a shame, she thought, as she watched the two of them, because they did seem to get along so well. So tonight she sat back and *pretended* that all was right with the world and that both her sons had found the women they loved and had settled down. Pretending never hurt anyone and she enjoyed the little peace of mind it gave to her; however brief that peace might be.

At dusk there were a few minutes of silence as everyone stopped and listened to the wolves' howls. The sun went down and the full moon rose. Jesse lit the candles, the women grabbed sweaters and the party continued into the night. Tim and Mike got out their guitars and filled the air with their music. Jack Miller told funny drunk stories from his bar and Arleen detailed the latest news from her wandering husband, the naturalist.

It was midnight when some of the guests started heading for home. Charlie and Winona left first, followed in short order by Jack, Frank and Mary. Arleen stuck it out a little longer, but she had to open the store early in the morning, so she was the next one to leave.

At one a.m. the five remaining revelers were feeling no pain. Jesse sat on the porch swing next to Johnny, while Clayton snoozed off and on in his rocking chair. Tim and Mike sat on the porch steps and worked on some new melodies, quite convinced by the accolades they had received throughout the evening that they had a future in country music. The wolves, now out front, howled every once in a while when the boys came to a chorus. Jesse leaned her head against Johnny's shoulder and closed her eyes for a minute. When she shivered a bit, Johnny put his arm around her and held her close. They all felt quite content.

"Five bucks says its Arleen," Tim said to Mike as they watched the headlights coming down the road through the trees. "She's always forgetting something."

"I'll take that five," Mike retorted. "It's probably Frankie or Charlie coming back to hang out a little longer now that the women are in bed." Their conversation intrigued Jesse enough for her to open her eyes and sit up.

"There's two sets of headlights," Johnny had also noticed them. "Maybe everybody's coming back."

"Those headlights in the back aren't off any truck," Tim noted as Jesse stood up and looked over the railing.

"Hey, maybe it's a UFO!" Mike called out, a little loopy. He had more than his share to drink.

The vehicles made the turn toward the cabin and pulled in side by side next to Jesse's truck. "Oh, my Lord," Jesse laughed when she recognized who it was.

"That alien's got some money," Tim snickered, observing the second vehicle. "That's a goddamn BMW."

The door to the SUV opened and Max bounced out. "Hey, Max!" Jesse yelled, skirting by the boys and running down the steps. "There's my good dog!"

Clayton was suddenly roused from his nap when Max barked. "Another wolf?" he asked, bewildered.

Joseph opened the driver's side door and slowly got out of the SUV, pressing his hands into the small of his back. "Woman, I will get a back rub tonight," he groaned to Bianca who had stepped out of the truck, making a beeline for Jesse.

The two women hugged each other tightly. "We'll see about that," Bianca scoffed back at him. She was beaming as she gave Jesse a kiss on the cheek. "I told you to stop in Great Falls!" Shadow pranced up to Bianca and rubbed against her with a wagging tail before falling into a *welcome to Montana* wrestle with Max.

The boys on the porch watched the welcoming scene with interest. Clayton recognized Joseph and got up stiffly from his chair. "Well, I'll be damned," he smiled. "The bad boy has come back home! Never thought I'd live to see this day."

Johnny was up too, happy at first to see his cousin. But as he walked across the porch to the stairs, the door of the BMW opened and a well-dressed city boy stepped out into the moonlight. The three young men on the porch stopped and stared at the city slicker as he took a long drag from his cigarette, exhaled slowly and crushed the butt out in the dirt with his very expensive boot.

Eric stared back at the cowboys on the porch and smiled sardonically. "I don't see any damsels in distress around here," he commented, winking at Jesse when she saw him. "Guess there's no shortage of *men* up here in the wilds of Montana."

"Jesus," Mike said, examining the man's expensive clothes and boots. "He looks like some country western star or something. Hey, are you famous?"

"Famous for getting myself into ludicrous situations," Eric retorted. "How about you?" He did not wait for an answer from the cowboy and turned his attention to Jesse. "Hey, where's *my* adulation? Where's *my* kiss?" Jesse broke free from Bianca and ran to Eric. She jumped into his arms and gave him a big kiss. Johnny, still on the porch, stepped back away from the light and watched the scene hidden by the darkness.

Clayton cast a sidelong glance over at Eric as the rancher and Joseph exchanged hearty handshakes and slaps on the back.

"Had to bring the woman's boyfriend," Joseph said stoically. "I tried to lose him on the Interstate, but that damn car must do two hundred miles an hour."

"German engineering and smooth pavement," Eric noted, finally putting Jesse down. She took his hand and led him to the cabin to meet her friends. "I guess there is a God, even in this forsaken country. The roads are great!"

"Bianca, Eric," Jesse announced, "These are my friends, Clayton Phillips, his son Tim and ranch hand Mike. And…" Jesse craned her neck, looking for Johnny. She couldn't see him on the porch. With a reserved stance, he slowly stepped back into the light. "…Oh, there you are," she smiled, locating him in the dark. "And that's Johnny."

Eric and Johnny's eyes met. Like two predators, they stared each other down. Eric was just the kind of white man Johnny couldn't stomach—rich, sarcastic and conceited. Eric didn't care for Johnny either. That brooding, dark haired vagrant was just Jesse's type. Somebody like that could make her change her mind about coming back home.

"Hey, cousin," Joseph interjected, breaking up the staring match between the two men. He bounded up the porch stairs, patted Mike on the head with a smile as he passed by, and forced a hug out of Johnny. "Good to see you."

"You too, Joe," said Johnny, returning Joe's hug stiffly. His gaze still followed the city boy as he fawned over Jesse. "Did you say *boyfriend*?"

In a heartbeat Joseph figured out what was going on. His cousin had a crush on the white woman. He took the young man by the shoulders and looked him over, confirming his theory. Johnny was too engrossed in the scene to even notice. If Jesse felt the same way, there was a problem that needed to be corrected immediately. Joseph realized he had taken care of the situation quite by accident with one misguided word. "Yes," he uttered, "boyfriend." Johnny slowly turned his attention to the man standing before him. Joseph refused to feel sorry for the younger man, because it had to be done. Joseph had broken enough rules when it came to his culture and family. He wasn't going to let Johnny follow in his footsteps.

"Did dad know you were coming?" Johnny asked, the spark gone from his voice and no hint of a smile.

"No," Joseph said. "I thought I'd surprise everybody."

"Surprise," Johnny said despondently. "Thanks." He walked away from Joseph and down the porch stairs. He stopped and looked at Jesse, who was still hugging and laughing with her friends. He wanted to say something to her. He wanted her to turn and see him standing there. Her *boyfriend* saw him and gave him a subtle smirk. The Native American refused to be baited. He turned and walked away into the woods.

"Hey," Eric interrupted the hubbub and chatter. "I need a drink and a place to lay down." He watched the Indian disappear into the trees before he took Jesse by the waist and spun her around toward the cabin. "I assume I may find both of my desires inside this wooden hut, right?"

"I guess it is last call, isn't it?" Jesse laughed, leading Eric and Bianca onto the porch and into the house. "The booze is out back on the patio. Get Bianca a glass of wine and I'll have one more shot of Scotch."

She opened the screen door to let Joseph, Tim and Mike bring in the bags from Joseph's SUV. The young men didn't bother to grab Eric's. They weren't especially fond of him, either.

"I better get my guys home," Clayton yawned, once Bianca and Joe's goods were delivered into the living room. "We've got a lot of fence work to catch up on in the morning."

Jesse gave the cowboy a hug and kissed him on the cheek. "Thanks for taking care of my wolves," she murmured. "I owe you one."

"Naw," Clayton decided, "I'd say we're even."

"G'night, ma'am," Tim Phillips smiled, shaking Jesse's hand before heading out the door.

"It was a great night," Mike added, also shaking her hand. "We appreciate it."

"And I appreciate you," Jesse said, taking a step back out onto the porch. She looked for Johnny but could not find him. "See you soon!"

Clayton, Tim and Mike climbed into the truck and sped off into the darkness. Shadow forced his snout into Jesse's hand, rubbing against her. She knelt down and scratched him on the neck. "Where'd Johnny go, boy?" she asked the wolf whimsically. "Did he leave without saying goodbye?"

The wolf cast a sidelong look toward the woods, but Max leapt up the stairs and distracted him. They yipped and chewed on each other in a frenzy of wagging tails and prodding paws. They almost knocked Jesse off her feet as they danced beside her.

"Good, God," Eric's voice boomed from inside the cabin. "Its dark out there, girl. Get inside where it's safe." Shadow and Max heard his voice and Shadow led the way through the slit in the screen, showing Max how to enter the house.

Jesse looked out into the yard and saw the silhouettes of Mesa and Cheyenne standing a safe distance away from the strange new people and their activities. "I'll be there in a minute," she said as she slipped into the kitchen and picked out some bones. Shadow and Max got two, because they insisted, and she took two more bones outside to the other wolves.

"Hey, babies," she murmured, sneaking out to them in the moonlight. Mesa stepped cautiously toward her and grabbed the bone quickly from her outstretched hand. Cheyenne stayed back, pacing back and forth in front of her. "I haven't had a minute alone with you guys for a couple of days. I think I know what happened," Jesse's voice was soothing. Cheyenne's eyes glowed when they met Jesse's. "I'm so sorry for your family and what you went through. I hope you know you're welcome here. And you don't have to be afraid anymore." Jesse stretched her arm out and tossed the other bone gently at Cheyenne's feet. The wolf jumped back, splayed her front paws and glared at the woman before letting her senses get the better of her. She pounced on the bone and carried it a safe distance away from Jesse and the other wolf.

"Please be careful and stay close," Jesse warned them before turning back to the cabin. "I can't keep you safe when I can't see you." She trudged back to the cabin. Kitten, like Johnny, must have escaped into the woods. That was the best place for them, Jesse surmised as she headed back home where the lights were bright and the voices lively. She breathed in the cool night air deeply, hoping to catch her second wind. It would be at least another hour before her new guests would settle down and call it a night.

"The place looks great, Jess!" Bianca remarked to her friend when Jesse finally came back inside. "And you've got all the comforts of home!"

"Except for an answering machine," Joseph quipped coming in from the patio with Eric. "When's the last time you checked your email?"

"Aaah…" Jesse started, bracing herself for the third degree. She took the drink Eric handed her.

"Obviously," Joseph cut her off, "not in the past week. You can thank Bianca that I didn't send out the cops looking for you." He looked quickly around the living room. "Who did all the work around here? I hardly recognize the place."

"Joseph," Bianca warned, "stop with the third degree."

"I did a lot of it, but Johnny and Arleen Stewart helped," Jesse jumped in. "And for a hefty fee, the delivery men did the rest." She sat down on the couch between Eric and Bianca.

"That patio area is really nice," Joseph continued. "But watch those candles. You could start one hell of a forest fire. And where'd you get those extra wolves?"

"Joseph," Bianca sighed, gulping her wine.

"Kudos for the T.V./stereo set up," Eric mumbled as Jesse leaned her head on his shoulder.

"Yeah," Jesse agreed quietly to her best friend. "Wait 'til you hear Wolf-sheim." To Joseph, she continued, "Cheyenne and Mesa are all that's left of a pack that was destroyed by some hunters. I've got plenty of food to take care of them."

"They're wild," Joseph insisted. "You could get hurt."

"They were wolf pups, like Shadow," Jesse voiced, placing her hand on Bianca's arm to delay her telling her lover off. "They deserve the same chance Shadow gets."

Joseph was now pacing in front of the threesome on the couch. Shadow and Max watched him for a few minutes before disappearing back outdoors through the screen door. "And, speaking of wild," he went on, "how much time has Johnny spent around here? He's a troublemaker, you know, and you're asking for it if you hang out with him. Indians don't make good house pets, especially Indians like Johnny."

"Joseph!" Bianca snapped. "That's enough! Good God, you scared him off five minutes after we got here. Jesse's old enough to choose her own friends without you scaring her to death."

"I was just saying..." Joseph tried to explain.

"I know," Jesse sighed, suddenly very tired. "We had a rocky start and, as I recall, it would have helped if you had warned me about him before I traipsed all the way up here all wide-eyed and innocent. We're getting along fine now, so don't worry about it." She looked at Joseph, who was seriously studying her face. "I'm doing all right. Okay?"

"I'm just..." Joseph interjected.

"Going to leave Jesse alone," Bianca finished the sentence for him. "Because, at this point, you're never going to get a back rub again."

"Hey!" Joseph cried, settling down immediately.

"I've been good," Eric murmured, under his breath. "Can I have one?" Jesse looked over and smiled at him.

Bianca got off the couch determinedly. "Where are we sleeping, Jess? Do you have enough room?" She picked up her suitcase and waited for Jesse's instructions.

"You guys go upstairs," Jesse said, getting up. "Eric, your room is back there." She pointed to the guest room/den at the back of the house. "I'll take you up, Bianca. I just need to get a couple of things while I'm up there."

"We're not taking your bed," Bianca retorted, eyeing Joseph, who was not lending his support.

"I sleep on this couch more than I sleep upstairs," Jesse answered quickly. "With wolves in and out all night, I like to keep an eye on what's going on."

"You're not locking that door?" Joseph asked incredulously, starting to rave again.

"Upstairs!" Bianca ordered. "You can talk to her tomorrow, if I let you." She threw his overnight bag at him, which he caught just before it knocked him in the head. "Eric," she continued without missing a beat, "if you get into bed real quick, I'll give you a quick massage before I go up." She was teaching Joseph a lesson and she was driving home the point.

"Yes, ma'am!" Eric was on his feet immediately. He realized his bags were not in the house and scurried out to the car to get them. "Damn! It's dark out here!" the rest of the group heard him say in the distance.

Joseph trudged up the stairs and Bianca made Jesse hang back. "We're all pretty tired," she apologized. "He just worries so. He's been a real bear the past few days because I couldn't get a hold of you. It will be better tomorrow."

"I'm just glad you're all here," Jesse smiled, giving Bianca a hug. "And the bickering is well deserved." The BMW beeped as Eric turned on the alarm. "It's so good to see you!"

"And damn cold, too!" Eric hurried back into the house, with Shadow and Max at his heels. "You'll be home by Christmas, Pumpkin," he announced, flipping her long dark hair as he passed by. "You hate the cold. And this is summer, for God's sake."

Jesse rolled her eyes and Bianca giggled, "Let's get this lot to bed."

CHAPTER 17

Jesse awoke to a cold, wet nose and whiskers tickling her face. Shadow was persistent and wanted his mother to get up. His front paw prodded at her shoulder until she finally opened her eyes. "Good morning, baby," the young woman muttered. "Are you hungry?" Max and Mesa crowded in, too. Sometime during the night, the three males had become friends.

Jesse rolled off the couch and was playfully attacked by her animals. "Okay, you win," squealed Jesse, covering her head with her arms. Shadow munched on her upper arm and Mesa was tangled up in her hair. Max's tail was wagging furiously, getting his licks in when he could. "Ouch!" The hair pulling was getting intense. Jesse shook her head and Mesa inched back. She put her hands on the sides of his neck and scratched him vigorously. He raised his head and reveled in the rubdown. "That's a good boy!" Jesse smiled. "You're all good boys!" She struggled to her feet, amidst her amorous attackers, and maneuvered Shadow up on the couch where she had spent the night. Side stepping Max and Mesa, she was able to make a dash for the kitchen. The wolves were surprised for a moment that she got away, but were on her in no time; Shadow traveling over the couch to get to her first.

She filled the food bowls with dog chow and some fresh meat. Max looked at his feast and then up at Jesse as if he wasn't sure it was actually his. "Go ahead, Max," Jesse murmured. "Its all yours unless you're too slow and the others get it before you do." Max dove in, gulping down the meat first.

She made up two more bowls—one for Cheyenne and another for Kitten. She grabbed a cookie out of the cookie jar for herself and then noticed there was hot coffee in the automatic coffee maker. "Hmmm," she mused, "somebody's already up."

Still in her sleepwear, which consisted of sweats and a t-shirt, she slipped her boots on and grabbed a sweater before heading outdoors. Opening the screen door with a swing of her hips, she walked out onto the porch holding the two bowls, and the cookie still in her mouth. "Mmmm," she mumbled, seeing Bianca sitting comfortably on the porch in a rocking chair. Her friend was wrapped up tight in a blanket and sipping on her cup of hot coffee. She was smiling when Jesse staggered out the door.

"Good morning!" Bianca laughed. "Do you need some help?"

"Nope!" Jesse's words were still muddled. She swallowed her cookie as quickly as she could. "I didn't expect anybody to be up, yet."

"How can you sleep with sunrises like this?" Bianca asked, pointing to the east. "It's so beautiful up here, Jess. The air is so crisp and clean!"

"Did you sleep okay?" Jesse eyed the grounds for Cheyenne. She was over by the truck, waiting for her companions. When Jesse stepped on the creaking porch step, Kitten's familiar growl emanated from somewhere underneath.

"Like a…" Bianca stopped short when she heard the bobcat. Her eyes grew wide with concern.

"That's Kitten," Jesse laughed, quieting her friend's fears. "She's harmless—just hungry." Jesse negotiated the rest of the stairs. Cheyenne took a hesitant step toward her, eager for her meal. The bobcat slinked out from under the porch, also smelling breakfast.

"They're beautiful!" Bianca whispered.

Jesse put the food bowls down in a hurry—Cheyenne's closer to the truck and Kitten's by the porch. The bobcat grabbed the lip of the bowl and dragged it under the porch where she could eat in peace.

"I was watching the wolves this morning," Bianca commented. "Their howls woke me up. The white one has the most incredible eyes. She could stare down a corpse."

"I must have been wiped out," Jesse mentioned. "I usually hear them, too." Jesse smiled at her friend. "It's sure nice to have you here. Let me get some of that coffee and I'll join you if you don't mind."

"Please do!" Bianca said eagerly. "I want to hear everything that's happened. From what I've seen so far, it must be a juicy tale!"

When Jesse came back out with her coffee, Shadow, Mesa and Max were crowded around her legs. They clamored down the steps and ran off to play. Cheyenne finished her meal before she joined them.

Jesse pulled up a chair close to Bianca and sat down. She filled her friend in on most of the details of the past two months as the sun rose over the lodge pole pines and warmed the morning air.

Bianca listened intently with only an occasional question, as Jesse regaled her with how Cheyenne and Mesa came to be her charges, along with the bobcat, and various other wild things that crossed her path. She heard about Clayton Phillips, the Town Marshal, whom she'd met last night. She heard about the drunken hunters, the fiasco in town and the wounded bear. Jesse talked about Arleen Stewart, Winona Stillwater and Joseph's Uncle Charlie. She explained about the work she'd done on the cabin and the plans she had for making it even better.

While Jesse talked, Bianca watched the wolves and Max, their new companion, as they romped and wrestled in the tall grass. She saw the ravens pick at the playmates and an owl asleep in one of the tall trees. She looked in awe at the eagle as it circled the area for a few minutes, then swooped down and took off with a small creature locked firmly in its talons.

But, even with all this, Bianca slowly realized that there was one subject her friend did not touch upon in great detail, and with every other tale it became more apparent. There was more to Joseph's cousin Johnny than Jesse was willing to admit. The hints were subtle at first, but Bianca's intuitive side could tell something was up. When Jesse ran out of news and got up to get them more coffee, Bianca was glad Joseph and Eric had not yet gotten up.

"So, tell me," Bianca suggested, warming her hands around the cup of steaming hot coffee, "the young man who was here for a little while last night, that's Joseph's cousin Johnny, right?"

Jesse feigned interest in her wolves. "I'm sorry, what?"

"Johnny Stillwater," Bianca countered, "he was the one who was here for a few minutes last night."

"Yeah," Jesse stated flatly, taking a sip of her coffee. "What a pain he was when I first got here."

"But not so much any more, eh?" Bianca asked casually. "Sounds like he's been helping you out."

"He's a very good handy man," Jesse murmured. "He can fix anything. Did you know that Joseph, Charlie and his sons built this place?"

"Joseph told me that," Bianca cracked a smile, no longer interested in playing cat and mouse. She gently touched Jesse's arm and made Jesse look at her. "Jesse, tell me about him. He's important to you, isn't he?"

Jesse looked away from her friend and back out to her wolves. Poor Max was having a heck of a time keeping up with the 65 lb. pups. "He is important," she finally sighed. "I guess I forgot that was a no-no until you guys arrived last night."

"Joseph has it in his head that he's responsible for what happens to you, Jess," Bianca offered. "He doesn't want you getting cozy with his cousin."

"I was wondering what happened to Johnny last night," Jesse thought out loud, apparently not paying attention to Bianca's words. "I hope I didn't piss him off."

"Don't end up like me," Bianca stated. "Mine is not an easy life." Jesse returned her gaze to Bianca. "Do you know Joseph tried to make me get out of the SUV and get in with Eric just outside of Dupuyer? He was afraid *one of the family* might notice I was riding with him." Bianca drank some of her coffee before she continued. "I was incensed. And then when he started in on you…"

"The last time I saw Johnny, he was talking to Joe," Jesse remembered. "Do you think Joe said something that made him leave?"

Jesse was involved with this guy; Bianca could see that plainly now. Any advice she tried to give her would fall on deaf ears. "We'll give him the benefit of the doubt, okay?" Bianca answered cautiously. "I guess if he did and I have to kill him, though, this would be the place to do it. Far less people asking questions." Jesse laughed, but Bianca could see the concern in her eyes. "It will be okay, Jess," she said in a calm voice. "What will be, will be—and nobody, not even Joseph, can change that."

"Change what?" The screen door opened and Joseph stepped out onto the porch with a cup of coffee in his hands. He was instantly distracted when he saw the wolves playing out in the field.

"Incredible, isn't it?" Bianca volunteered, following his gaze. "They've been out there all morning."

Joseph took a step closer to the edge of the porch and was greeted by Kitten's warning hiss. He stepped back and looked down, startled by the unfamiliar sound.

"Oh, that's just Kitten," Bianca smiled. "I don't think she cares for strangers."

"I don't want to know," Joseph sighed, finding a spot to sit on the swing. His coal black hair was disheveled and he still appeared a bit groggy. He nursed the coffee like it was medicine. "Winter's coming," he observed with a shiver. "You never forget that first chill."

"Tell me I've got another couple of months at least," Jesse moaned. "I don't know if I'm ready for that."

"You'll be ready," Joseph said evenly, "or you won't survive."

"That makes me feel so much better," Jesse sighed. The wolves were preparing for their daily excursion. Jesse could tell by their movements and their vocalizations. She stood up and leaned over the porch railing, setting her coffee cup down on the ledge. "Hey, Max!" she shouted, leaving Bianca and Joseph in the dark. "Come on, boy! Come here!"

"What's up?" Bianca asked nonchalantly. Joseph sat back and drank some of his coffee.

"That's a boy!" Jesse smiled when Max ran up to her on the porch with his tail wagging. Shadow dropped his head, propelled his front paws in a fluid movement and followed the wolf dog up to the porch. "There's my two good boys!" Jesse said, petting them both. "We need to keep Max here," she mentioned to Bianca as she slipped a leash onto Max's collar. "The rest of the pack is about to take off for a while and I don't want to have to worry about Max keeping up." Shadow licked Jesse's face and rumbled back down the porch stairs. Kitten pounced out from underneath the porch and followed him over to the other wolves. The animals briefly nosed each other before falling in behind Shadow's lead and heading into the forest.

"Where are they going?" Bianca asked, confused. Max strained a bit on his leash and whimpered.

Jesse sat back down and lashed the other end of his leash to her chair to keep him put. "We don't know, most of the time," she said, making sure Max was getting plenty of attention. She rubbed her hand in his fur until he lay down at her feet. "I just have to trust the Creator and hope they'll be home by sundown." Joseph raised an eyebrow, listening to Jesse speak. "Of course, they're usually home for lunch and afternoon naps—barring any more bear attacks."

"The bobcat goes with them?" Joseph asked, stunned.

"Not always," Jesse remarked. "She's more of a night crawler. But sometimes she follows them for a little while during the day. She's usually the first one back, safe under the porch before the sun gets too hot."

"Which is a good idea, now that I think about it," Joseph agreed. He got up from the swing and headed to the front door. Max, dozing at Jesse's feet, did not get up. "I thought I'd go see Charlie today. You girls can catch up while I'm gone. Okay?"

"Okay," murmured Bianca, casting a quick glance at Jesse. "That'll be fine, dear." The tone of Bianca's voice was icy. She knew she was not to be included in his visits, but it bothered her now that she was so close to his family. The burly figure of Joseph, in his baggy t-shirt and jeans, dissipated into the cabin and was replaced by the svelte figure of Eric coming out. "It truly is magic up here, Jess," Bianca observed with a chuckle. "From a devil to a god with the opening of a screen door. Good morning, Eric."

Eric, clad only in a pair of sweats that hung low on his hips, stretched languorously as he peered out over the terrain. "Man, I slept like a rock," he yawned. "What's in the air up here?"

"It's what's not that counts," Jesse observed, smiling up at her friend. "Do you want a cup of coffee?"

"That would be tasty," Eric answered with a twinkle in his eye. "Do we have any food?"

"Bear meat and bones," Jesse retorted, getting up and going into the cabin. "But I can probably come up with something a little tastier if you give me a few minutes. Bianca?"

"I'm starving. Do you need any help?" Bianca asked, not in any particular hurry to get up.

"Nope," Jesse called out from the kitchen. "But you two better decide what we're going to do today, because I don't have the slightest idea."

"I suppose there's no bevy of cute cowgirls for me to seduce," Eric ventured, plopping himself down on the top of the porch steps. "Is there a mall in this state?"

"Not around here," Jesse commented. "Unless you're in the market for some cattle feed and a tractor." She handed a cup of coffee out through the door to Eric, who accepted it greedily.

"Just got my new John Deere on sale up at Bergdorf's last week," Eric sneered. "Damn!"

Bianca laughed. "How about if we just relax? I wouldn't mind trying out that hammock in the backyard."

"Got a deck of cards, sweet pea?" Eric asked so Jesse could hear.

"Your wishes are my command," Jesse answered cheerily from the kitchen. "As long as they're as easy as that." They could hear the clanging of the pots and pans as she prepared to cook. "If we really get adventurous, we can take a walk down to the lake."

Joseph decided to drive the forty-five miles to Charlie and Winona's place rather than walk the trail. Taking the long way through the reservation, or res for short, served as a reminder to him how conditions for his brethren had not changed and how lucky he was that he had gotten out. The decrepit shacks and beat up trailers, the rusted out vehicles and the junk along the road used to be so commonplace to him. Now, he saw it and felt sick. Children were playing in the dirt with broken toys and sticks as playthings. Packs of dogs scrounged for scraps in the piles of garbage strewn along the road. An old woman, who should have been resting under a vine-covered veranda, was beating the dust out of a tattered, threadbare rug. Unfortunately, she stirred up more dust off the barren ground every time she hit it. Inside the broken down shacks and trailers, television sets were broadcasting nonsensical cartoons and episodes of Jerry Springer, wasting everybody's time.

He turned the SUV right and drove toward the woods. At last, the air cooled down as he traveled into the groves of lodge pole pines, cottonwoods and fir trees. After another mile, he would see Charlie and Winona's place just up ahead. He never asked, as a child, why his uncle's home was a little better than the rest of his friends'. It took years to realize that never ending hard work, compromise and capitulation were the key ingredients to success on the reservation. The sad part was that he hadn't realized how nice he had it until after he was gone.

He was one of the lucky ones. His uncle had raised him as one of his own, keeping him from the clutches of an alcoholic father who eventually drank himself to death. Charlie was stern but fair. He allowed his boys to have minds of their own and weigh the options before them. He warned them how important the white man's school was and expected them to excel. *It's the only way to beat them at their own game*, he would drum into the boys' heads over and over again. *The more you know about the white man, the better off you'll be.* But he also taught them the old ways. He told them the stories and described their history in detail. Not the history the white man provided, but the way it really went down. He showed them the rituals and the way things were done. He instilled in them a sense of pride and respect for their own heritage.

With that pride and respect came Joseph's anger. He was harassed and rebuked at the white man's school. The teachers punished him if he spoke his own language or tried to explain his culture. He was ridiculed over the clothes he wore and more than one teacher took the scissors to his long black hair. Charlie demanded that he take it, so as a youngster, he was unable to fight back.

Joseph grew up confused and incensed—not knowing where he belonged. He saw the white men with their money and their big cars. He saw his own people starving and living in squalor. The older he got, the more frustrated he became. If he came from warriors, why couldn't he take up the fight? Why was he supposed to lie down like a dog when his spirit came from the wolf? Charlie's words, *the Creator will protect us*, rang hollow in his ears. The white men's words, *you must live like us but you'll never be good enough*, were even less palatable.

When it seemed like there was no way out for Joseph, a white man moved to a ranch not too far from the reservation. Clayton Phillips treated Joseph with respect, even though the lad was well on his way to becoming a juvenile delinquent. Instead of facing jail time, Joseph faced hard work on Clayton's ranch with Clayton letting him work out his frustrations on the land instead of people. While Joseph still resented the fact that a white man had given him the chance where his own kin could not, there would never be a proper way to express his gratitude to Clayton, who recognized Joseph as a human being and a good boy. The rancher also shared his skills and knowledge—and a helluva great letter of recommendation when he had needed it—giving him a positive opportunity to grow up and become a productive member of society.

Living in Colorado, with his house, job, cars and his woman, he did not spend a lot of time reminiscing about his past. Whenever he returned to the reservation, those memories came flooding back. Coming to Montana was never a vacation for him, but he loved his family and owed them some of his time. After all, they had never been stingy with the time they gave him. *Buck up*, he said to himself. He would swallow his resentment and make the best of this visit.

Joseph wheeled his vehicle around and drove through the clearing, up to his uncle's house. Winona was already standing at the open door, wiping her hands off on a dishtowel and smiling. He never could surprise her. She always seemed to know what he was thinking, ten minutes before he thought it himself. He threw the car into park and turned off the ignition, alighting from the vehicle and into his aunt's warm embrace.

"Did Johnny tell you I was here?" he asked as Winona escorted him into their home.

"Goodness, no," she responded, clearing off a chair at the kitchen table. "I just felt your spirit coming to me. It's very strong, you know!"

"I never could fool you, could I?" Joseph announced, as a glass of iced tea appeared miraculously in front of him along with some homemade fry bread, courtesy of Winona's magic hands.

"Not really," Winona smiled, looking up as Charlie lumbered through the door. "And you, old man," she said to her husband, "owe me one, brand new frying pan."

"Why do I doubt her?" Charlie queried, giving Joseph a bear hug around the shoulders and rubbing his head with his knuckles. "These bets are gonna' do me in!" He sat down next to Joseph at the table. Winona slapped her husband's hand when he casually reached for Joseph's fry bread. "When did you get in, boy? Where are you staying?"

"We're up with Jesse at the cabin," Joseph said. "Got in last night."

"And who's we?" Winona asked innocently, handing another piece of fry bread to her husband and taking a seat facing the men.

Joseph almost choked on his food. "Ah," he said, swallowing a bit of his iced tea to clear his throat. "Jesse's friends from Denver. I brought them up with me."

"That's so nice of you," Winona stated, reaching over the table and tearing a piece of bread off Charlie's. He scowled at her, but allowed her to do it. "Jesse's a nice girl, Joseph. Where ever did you meet her?"

"Through another friend," Joseph answered almost too quickly.

"Denver sounds downright *friendly*, doesn't it, Win?" Charlie asked, winking at his wife.

"It's different down there, Charlie," Joseph murmured, attacking another piece of his bread. "No reservations to keep us in line."

"Uh, huh," noted Charlie. "So, you've seen Johnny? How about Clayton?"

"They were both at Jesse's when we got in," Joseph answered. "Clayton looks good. Johnny looks like the chip on his shoulder is getting bigger."

"Just like his cousin's a long time back," Charlie agreed. "The sad part is, it doesn't look like Clayton's gonna' get through to him like he did to you."

"I've noticed a little light," Winona observed, quietly. She reached behind her and got the rest of the fry bread, putting it on the table. Both Charlie and Joseph looked at her with interest. "He's been spending a lot of time over at the cabin with Jesse. He's been doing a lot of odd jobs for her."

"Well," Charlie said, with a worried look, "now, I didn't notice that and I don't know if I'm real happy to learn about it...."

"Now, Charlie," Winona cut in, "there's no harm in it. They're both adults."

"That's what scares me," Charlie said.

"I'll talk to him," Joseph offered. "Although I probably fixed it last night, by accident."

"Oh, dear," Winona sighed, regretting that she had brought the issue up in the first place. "What happened?"

"Nothing," Joseph stated. "I just brought her boyfriend up here, that's all. At least I let him think it was her boyfriend. He's a friend, actually. But I didn't lie. That's a boyfriend, right?"

"I suppose that's for the better," Winona murmured.

"You're darn right it is," Charlie snapped. "There's been enough interracial marriages in this family. Joseph knows that—so does Johnny. The blood around here is too thin as it is."

"Well, now whose fault is that?" Winona shot back. "Certainly not these boys', old man."

"All right, all right," Charlie soothed his wife. "I'm just saying it would be best for all concerned if we stick with what's left of our own blood. That's all."

"I'll explain it to Jesse," Joseph offered. "Now that Eric and Bianca are here, she'll start to miss home and I'm sure she'll understand. I don't expect her to stay through the winter, anyway."

"She's resourceful when it comes to those animals of hers," Winona said. "I don't think you men give her enough credit."

"As long as it's just the four-legged ones—I got no problem with that," Charlie stated. "We'll let my boy here take care of it before it becomes a problem." Charlie got up and squeezed Joseph's shoulder. He ushered his nephew away from the table and into the living room. "Come have a sit and tell me what you've been up to. Your uncle gets some time with you before the rest of this clan does."

Joseph settled in to tell his story, cleverly noting that nothing had changed in Montana and that the rules were still the same. He was careful not to mention Bianca's name again in his uncle's presence. That part of his life was better left untold. There was no need to disappoint the old man with such a trivial matter as his love life. Joseph knew that no matter what he went through growing up, his uncle's history was much worse. Winona was right, of course. It wasn't Joseph's fault that Native American blood had been tainted co-mingling with the white man. But it was his responsibility to heed his uncle's set of laws, as long as he espoused them.

So Joseph painted a beautiful picture for his uncle with his words, weaving the tale around the cop shop, some close calls and some funny anecdotes. He told him about the Colorado powwows and what it meant to him to be an

Elder after these many years away from the reservation. Charlie was pleased and proud of his nephew. Joseph could see it in his uncle's eyes.

Was it a lie, not telling his family about the white woman he loved? No, he reasoned. Telling that story wouldn't do anybody any good. He'd make it up later to Bianca. Thank God she understood.

CHAPTER 18

Winona knew her youngest son was home before they heard the footsteps trudging up the gravel walkway and the door that slammed behind him. She always knew where her loved ones were. She always knew when they were in trouble. Joseph called it her *sixth* sense. She called it love.

She had cleaned the kitchen and kept out of Joseph's and Charlie's way while the two men talked. She added nothing to their conversation, keeping her opinions to herself. That's not to say she did not have any opinions, because she could *sense* Joseph was hiding something, but she chose to keep her mouth shut. She had nearly caused a full-scale war by simply stating that Johnny enjoyed Jesse's company. She wanted this to be a civilized visit. She wanted Joseph to come back, some day. She could see him sitting on the couch talking to his uncle. He looked healthy and happy, even though he wasn't entirely telling the truth. He had learned his tact from her, she was certain. He was a good man.

Her eyes met Johnny's when he came into the kitchen. She sighed inwardly when she smiled at him, weighing the innumerable cataclysmic scenarios that might come to pass with his arrival. "Everything okay?" she asked, already knowing the answer. He returned her smile and touched her shoulder gently as he passed by, grabbing himself a glass and some water from the sink. The young man spoke volumes with his silence. Winona's heart went out to him, for she could do little else.

"Speak of the devil," Charlie's voice was loud and clear from the next room. "Johnny, come greet your cousin."

Now it was Johnny's turn to sigh. He drank the water from the glass and put it back in the sink. He walked, like a condemned man, into the living room.

Joseph got up from the couch and gave his cousin a strong hug. "You look good, man," he said warmly. "Come join us for a while."

Johnny chanced a glance at his father, more as a dare rather than asking for permission. He realized in that instant that his father was in a good mood. Thanks to Joseph, there would most likely be a reprieve from the petty bickering and usual insults.

"You look good too, Joe," ventured Johnny. "Colorado must be good for you."

"Can't complain," Joe smiled. "Things are going pretty well."

"Well, I've heard the story," Charlie said, easing himself up from his chair. "Mother, let's get cooking. Our boys are pretty hungry, I'm sure."

"I'm sure they are," Winona called from the kitchen. "You can help shuck the corn."

"This looks like a setup," Johnny murmured as Charlie disappeared into the other room, leaving him alone with Joseph. "What's up, cuz?"

"Nothing, Johnny," Joseph smiled, resting back in the couch. "I just didn't get a chance to talk to you last night. Really, how've you been?"

"Well," Johnny decided to be straightforward, "I got no job, no place to live, no money and no car. Just another day on the res, Joe. Life's a peach."

"Hey, man," countered Joseph, "I was there once, remember?"

"I remember you were a lot younger than me when you got out." Johnny spoke firmly, but quietly. He didn't need his father coming down on him for picking on his perfect cousin. "I've got no skills, Joe. Clayton never thought *I'd* make a good cop."

"Hell, you practically built the cabin," Joe went on. "Your carpentry alone is outstanding, not to mention everything else you can do."

"Don't know if you've noticed," Johnny snickered, "but not many people around here can afford to build new houses, let alone furniture to put in 'em. And, speaking of the cabin, I thought you were at least going to give *that* to me."

"I had every intention to," Joe said apologetically. "Why didn't you remind me?"

"Oh, yeah," Johnny sneered. "I should have reminded you during one of our weekly Sunday morning phone calls when you checked in with the family." Johnny's turquoise blue eyes flashed at his cousin. "Oops," he whispered, "I guess *you* just forgot to call."

"Hey, man," sighed Joseph, exasperatedly. "I'm sorry." He studied his cousin's face. Johnny's eyes betrayed his anger and depression. "And, of course, your *white* friend needed it. Seems like they always come first, even before us."

"But you've been spending time over there, right?" Joseph wasn't sure what to say. Obviously, his cousin was not in the forgiveness mode. "Winona says you've been helping the woman out."

Johnny's eyes narrowed. "Yeah, what of it?" He sat back against the couch, hard. "I bet you're going to tell me that's against tribal law too."

"Damn it, Johnny," Joseph quipped. "I'm just trying to figure out what's going on in your head."

"Don't worry, bro," Johnny snapped back. "I know the rules. No fraternizing with the white folk. Leave the woman alone."

"God!" Joseph moaned. "I didn't say anything like that. I just asked..."

"Like you wouldn't have gotten around to it," Johnny cut him off. "I got some of mom's sixth sense, as you call it, Joe. I saw you checking me out last night. What? Did you guys talk about me before I got here? Did Dad tell you to straighten me out? I can't get any straighter, cousin. I know what's right and what's wrong." He smiled sardonically at the shocked look on Joseph's face. Johnny's nasty demeanor was his only weapon and he knew how to use it. "By the way, did you tell Dad about *your* white girlfriend?" He turned halfway around on the couch and shot a glance into the kitchen where his parents were busily cooking dinner, blissfully unaware of the banter in the living room. "By the looks of it, I'd say you passed on broadcasting that little news item, eh?"

"She's not..." Joseph started.

"Don't give me that crap, cousin," Johnny said lowly. "I got eyes too, you know."

"Look," Joseph groaned. "Jesse will never make it through the winter. You can have the place as soon as she checks out."

"Come on, man!" Johnny spat. "Don't you know anything? She's not going anywhere as long as that wolf's alive, and in case you didn't notice, she's picked up a couple more pets in the meantime."

"And you're one of them, right?" Joseph had had enough. He glared at his cousin and leaned in close. "Don't mess with me, Johnny. I'm probably the only friend you've got."

Johnny was taken aback by the tone of his cousin's voice. Not expecting it, he was momentarily stunned into silence.

"The way I see it," Joseph took advantage of the situation, "you've got two choices. Get over this *poor, nobody understands what it's like to be me* attitude, get a job and get on with your life. Nobody can take your nightmares from you, cousin. You're going to have to do that yourself. I'm sorry you saw what you did. Winona's over it—now, it's your turn to do the same. If you don't, and you keep this warrior thing up, you're going to end up in jail or someplace worse."

Johnny thought about mouthing off again, but decided against it. He let his cousin finish his speech.

"As far as Jesse goes, she's no concern of yours," Joseph continued. "She's a white woman who did a very foolish thing. Luckily, I was able to provide a place for her so when she screws up we can get her back home safe. I know she doesn't belong here, but she was adamant about providing that wolf a chance at a normal life. And I'm partly to blame because she got that wolf at one of our powwows. Another state or place would not have been half as understanding. Leave her be. She'll be gone before spring. And don't think hanging around a white woman is going to prove a point or pay somebody back or piss your old man off."

"Don't talk about her like that," Johnny hissed. "She's got more Indian in her, or at least Indian spirit, than most people I know. Those animals mean the world to her."

"Shit," Joseph murmured. He suddenly realized arguing with Johnny was like arguing with himself. He was an angry man with a chip on his shoulder and he was falling for a white woman. As the song said, *another one bites the dust.* "So, it's gone that far?"

"Nothing's gone nowhere," Johnny stated tersely. "She's been nice to me, that's all. Jesus, is your mind always in the gutter?"

"As often as yours," Joseph smiled weakly. He inhaled deeply, gathering his thoughts. He didn't want to argue with his cousin anymore. He didn't want to argue, period.

"And why are you bothering to tell me this if, like you said last night, she's got a boyfriend?" Johnny asked warily, Joseph's intentions suddenly resoundingly clear to him. "Were you lying to me, Joseph? Are you using the white man's way to get what you want?"

"He's a very good friend," Joseph sighed, rebuked. "I don't know any more than that, other than he's very protective of her and he wants her to go back to Denver with him. Bianca and I think she should go back too. Take what you want from that."

"I noticed..." Johnny started to give away a secret. He had slept in the hammock, as usual, behind Jesse's cabin last night. He saw where everybody bedded down, which is why Joseph would have had no case if he had denied his relationship with the woman. He also saw that Jesse slept on the couch with her wolf and the *boyfriend* slept in the back room. "...Never mind."

"Look, Johnny," Joseph offered. "I really don't want to fight. You're a lot like me, man. You're almost a carbon copy. Don't make the same mistakes I made. Get it together and get your life on track, that's all I wanted to say."

"I appreciate that," Johnny said calmly. "But it'll never be as simple as that. Our rivers have taken different courses, cousin. We're not as close as you think."

"Boys!" Winona called from the kitchen. "Come get something to eat."

Johnny looked at his cousin and smiled. He got up from the couch and held a hand out to help Joseph up. "Come on, old man," he teased. "Blood is blood—but yours is more like my father's than mine; old and tired."

Joseph got off the couch and tried to grab his little cousin in a good-natured headlock. Johnny was too quick and sidestepped Joe's grip adroitly. The young man did not want to be angry either. As a matter of fact, he was feeling pretty good. He had surprised himself when he stood up for Jesse. He had never stood up for anyone else before. He suddenly wanted to talk to her. He had to get a few things straight. He would break bread with his family before he snuck back to the cabin. On foot, he'd be at there long before Joseph could drive the SUV off the reservation. He had plenty of time to get the answers he needed, as Joseph had suggested, to get on with his life.

It had indeed been a lazy day around Jesse's place. In the morning after breakfast, Eric tried to entice her into returning to the city with some very expensive gifts from Denver. He gave her a beautiful new pantsuit, a diamond bracelet and a not very functional, but very fashionable, new winter coat. The fur along the collar and cuffs of the coat tantalized Max, which made Eric cranky and Bianca howl with laughter. Jesse laughed along with her, keeping the coat from the wolf dog's clutches while holding the bracelet close to her heart. Bianca and Eric exchanged casual glances as they chatted about the latest news from Denver. They both could see that Jesse was definitely feeling a little bit more homesick the more they talked. That's the result they were hoping for.

They played cards and watched a movie. Then they took a walk. They hiked through the dark green forest, down to the lake where Bianca took pictures and Eric skipped stones that rippled the still, blue water. They sat on the shore and talked some more, but this time it was Jesse's turn. She spoke about the night she arrived, much to Bianca's dismay, and pointed out some of the eagle and hawk nests she had discovered. After a while, it was Bianca who looked nostalgically across the lake, wishing she and Joseph had a home like this.

On their way back, the wolves joined them, returning from their morning journey—Shadow greeted each of the humans and Max, egging them on toward the cabin and some food. Cheyenne and Mesa hung back, trotting close to Jesse. Kitten was under the porch and the eagle soared high above the cabin clearing. The great gray owl, still asleep in one of the larger fir trees, opened one perfectly round eye to inspect the noisy conglomeration of animals and humans passing below. Satisfied there was no threat, he buried his head again under his wing and returned to his slumber.

Arleen Stewart dropped by to meet Jesse's Denver family. She brought sandwiches and homemade potato salad for a picnic on the back patio. The store owner also brought some elk meat for the four-legged brood. Following a leisurely lunch, Arleen returned to the store after insisting that Eric, Bianca, Joseph and Jesse meet her in town at Jack's place later that night. Eric was thrilled to have something to do. Jesse was relieved she didn't have to come up with another way to entertain him.

Bianca eventually made it to the hammock she had been eyeing since her arrival. She took a book and started to read, but the soft breeze and the sun filtering through the trees lulled her to sleep. Eric found a comfy spot on the couch where he stretched out and channel surfed the satellite T.V. until he found something suitable to watch. Soon, he was also fast asleep. Jesse attributed it to the clean Montana air.

She took the opportunity to play with the wolves and Max. They chased each other around the yard and played tug of war with a piece of rope. The bobcat hid in the tall grass, meowing, growling and hissing when one of the lupine creatures came too close. She pounced playfully on the rope every time one end was dropped and it was snaked through the grass. Jesse made the mistake of taking off her sweater when all the exercise caused a sweat. Shadow snatched it up in seconds and frolicked just out of her reach, the sweater dangling from his mouth. Quite exhausted after several minutes, Jesse sat down just inside the first row of the lodge pole pines to catch her breath. Mesa and Cheyenne grabbed opposite ends of the sweater, the bulk of which was still clenched between the black wolf's teeth, and pulled. The sweater was in shreds shortly afterwards. Jesse smiled and shook her head, her heart still pumping hard and her breath labored from the exertion.

One by one, her animals joined her in the shade, finding a spot to rest. Jesse lay back and watched the eagle circling lazily high above them. She noticed the owl was up and preening its feathers in the nook of the tall fir tree. The young woman was about to close her eyes for a minute when she heard the crack of a twig not too far off to her right. She slowly sat up and stretched; amazed the other animals had taken no notice of the sound. Turning ever so slowly she saw a shadow first, then the outline of a man. She knew it was Johnny. She smiled when he approached.

"What happened to you last night?" Jesse asked quietly. "You were there one minute and then you were gone."

"It got too crowded for me," he answered, sitting down cross-legged next to her. "Felt like the whole damn city of Denver landed on your doorstep."

"Yeah," she laughed. "It took the wolves a bit of time to settle down too."

"So," Johnny declared with a twinkle in his bright blue eyes, "I hear that's your boyfriend who showed up last night."

Jessed crinkled her brow and looked at him with narrowed eyes. "Oh? And who told you that?"

"Somebody who…" Johnny started.

"…Doesn't think you and I should be friends, I imagine," Jesse finished his sentence for him, looking back at the animals who were now slumbering not too far from them under the trees. Even Kitten stayed, deciding to find a spot close to Shadow rather than heading for her hiding place under the porch. "That was pretty clever of him, actually."

Johnny summoned up his courage and asked Jesse, "So, is he?"

"Is he what?" Jesse was confused.

"Your boyfriend." Johnny leaned back on his hands, closed his eyes and tilted his face up toward the patches of sun. The warmth felt good upon his skin.

Jesse watched him a moment before answering. She leaned back too, but on her side, braced by her bent arm, so she was facing him. "Well," she finally began, "Eric is my very best friend…and he's a boy.…So, I guess you could call him that."

Johnny's eyes opened slowly and he met her gaze. "Is he your lover?" he asked with a hint of a smile upon his lips. He already knew the answer just in the way she was looking at him at that very moment.

"If he was," she smiled back, "I wouldn't be sitting here in Montana talking to you."

"Good point," Johnny smirked, relaxing totally. "So, why not?" He enjoyed being here under the trees with Jesse. Her long dark hair danced gently in the breeze around her face. Her golden eyes, almost the same color as Shadow's, watched him intently.

"So, why not what?" Jesse asked, nonplussed.

"So, why is he not your lover?" Johnny clarified. "I mean it looks like he's got everything a girl would want—good looks, fancy car, expensive clothes and an attitude, which means he's got a lot of money. I don't think he's famous like the boys thought last night, but he's probably a lawyer or something like that." He picked a long blade of grass and stuck it in his mouth as he pondered the young man. "Hell, if I was a girl, I'd be after him. He's quite a catch."

"Hmmm," Jesse considered Johnny's statement, still smiling.

"And, he likes you." There was a slight catch in Johnny's voice.

Jesse leaned in close to the Native American and whispered, "He's not real crazy about guard hairs on his designer suits."

For a moment perplexed, a slow smile eventually came to Johnny's face; then he actually threw his head back and laughed. Jesse had never heard him laugh like that before. She was captivated by the sound and laughed quietly with him. Finally, Johnny leaned in close to Jesse. Their faces were inches apart. "Joe doesn't want us to be friends, you know," he stated, turning serious. "He had a little talk with me about it over at my folks' house."

"I can keep a secret if you can," Jesse murmured back.

"He can be tough."

"He usually is," she sighed. "He hasn't let up on me, yet." Jesse could feel Johnny's breath upon her skin. It felt like the breeze that came off the lake in the early mornings before the fog dissipated at dawn. He was awakening feelings she hadn't felt for a very long time. He was enticing and she found herself wanting to touch him, but he also looked dangerous, so she didn't. "He's been filling my head with rules since the day I decided to come here," she said. "And last night he started where he left off in Littleton." Johnny's eyes were mesmerizing. Gazing deeper, she could have sworn she could see into his soul. "You're Native American. I'm a white American." It was getting harder for Jesse to speak. "Never the two should meet," she proffered philosophically.

"I'm sure he'll give you the drill again before he leaves."

Their lips were a breath apart when Max jumped up and started to bark. Jesse and Johnny jumped, startled back into reality. Joseph's SUV was coming down the road, splaying a cloud of dust behind it. He would be at the cabin door in a few minutes.

"I gotta go," Johnny's voice was hoarse as he stood up, bringing Jesse with him. "Keep our secret, Jess." He brushed an errant lock of hair from her face. "I'll be back when they're gone."

Jesse moaned when Johnny sprinted off into the woods. He stopped and pressed his closed right hand against his chest, followed by his left closed hand against it. She smiled weakly and waved at him before she turned back toward the cabin to see Joseph pull up in his SUV. Shadow, Max and Mesa had surrounded the car. Kitten had bolted for the porch at Max's first bark. Jesse ran her fingers through her hair and dusted herself off. With Cheyenne at her side, she headed slowly toward the cabin and her guests.

CHAPTER 19

"There's my pups!" Max and Shadow had playfully attacked Joseph as soon as he got out of the SUV. Mesa was not part of the attack, but his tail was wagging and he danced in and out around them. The Native American stooped down and made sure he petted each one. He grinned when Mesa accepted the quick pat on the head.

"So, how was your day?" Jesse asked, coming up behind him. "Did you see Charlie?"

"Yes, I did," responded Joseph rather cheerily. Max had resorted to licking his face. "It was a good day, overall." Joseph shooed Max out of his way so he could close the door to the SUV. He walked with Jesse to the porch. "And how about yours?"

"We played some cards, talked a lot and took a walk to the lake," Jesse replied. "It was a good day here too."

"Where are those human companions of yours?" Joseph queried, climbing the porch steps. He decided to take a seat in the rocking chair on the porch rather than go inside. Jesse took the hint and sat in the chair beside him. As Johnny had just reported, it looked like Joseph wanted to talk if the others were occupied elsewhere.

"Bianca's in the hammock out back and Eric's inside on the couch. They've been sleeping for about an hour now." Jesse looked at the Indian and smiled.

Joseph nodded. "That's what this place will do to you." He returned Jesse's smile. "They're not used to the fresh air."

"I don't think Eric's walked that far in years," Jesse commented. "They both got plenty of exercise." Jesse could not stop a yawn that came on suddenly. "Are you hungry?"

"Winona force-fed me," he sighed, rubbing his stomach. Max placed his head, still wagging his tail, on Joseph's lap. He petted the wolf dog lovingly. "She slapped together some Indian Tacos. I forgot what a good cook she is."

"She's the best," Jesse agreed. She gazed out over the land. The sun was on the other side of the cabin and changed the sky to the reds and purples of another late afternoon. The wolves were resting by her truck. The gray owl spread his wings and took flight, circling once around the field before heading for the woods. The ravens were crowding around one of the wolves' discarded bones. Soon, she expected to see the deer pass by.

"You've done good, Harless," Joseph announced, looking out at the scenery. "Shadow is healthy and happy. And it is obvious other animals have benefited by your care." He concentrated a moment on the wolves before he continued. "So those other wolves, you said they were orphaned? How did you inherit a bobcat?"

"Some men were hunting, I guess," Jesse sighed. "It appears they got Cheyenne and Mesa's parents, as well as three other pups. I assume those guys shot everything they could find that had four legs. Kitten was also on her own. She's got a thing for Shadow. She followed us home one day and made a home for herself under the porch. She tags along with the wolves on their excursions and they don't seem to mind. Clayton thinks those hunters might have tried for a bear too, but only wounded him. One tried to attack him yesterday."

"A bear?" Joseph looked concerned.

"It was the craziest thing," Jesse offered. "The wolves showed up out of nowhere and kept it at bay until he could get his gun and kill it. Last night Clayton and the boys brought me a truckload of bear meat. The kids will have food for months."

"Amazing," Joseph remarked. "And it looks like you've picked up an eagle and an owl."

"The eagle has watched over us since we got here," Jesse said. "The owl nested in that tree a month or so back."

"So, the four-leggeds and winged ones have found a home here," Joseph murmured, shifting in his chair. "That is good."

Jesse knew where Joseph was going with this conversation. She sat back and allowed him to continue.

"Have you had enough of the wilderness yet?" he inquired. "Are you ready to go home?"

"In the short time I've been here," replied Jesse, "I've come to know *this* as home. It was tough the first couple of weeks, getting to know my way around and getting used to the quiet. But Shadow and I are happy."

"Bianca and Eric would like you to return before the snow settles in," Joseph related. "In fact, they've made a bet as to when you will return."

"And how about you, Joseph?" Jesse asked. "When do you think I'll give up?"

Joseph glanced over at Jesse, while he rocked slowly back and forth in the rocking chair. The clouds were building up and settling in over the cabin. "To be honest, I did not think you would last a week. I even doubted you would make it up here in the first place."

"Wishy washy city girl finds wolf, dreams of new life in wilderness, gets bored, dumps wolf, goes shopping, buys a new outfit and lives happily ever after, eh?" Jesse snickered.

"Well," Joseph uttered, "maybe not exactly like that."

"I'm sure there was a new outfit somewhere in the scenario," Jesse laughed. "What else do you want to know, Joe? Who I'm hanging out with? What are my favorite hangouts? What do I do with my days? How the hell did I get that fabulous bed upstairs?"

"Now, that's a question I *would* like answered," quipped Joseph. "That's quite a nice setup up there."

"Arleen helped me," Jesse filled him in. "Just two little helpless babes in the woods."

"Winona says my cousin Johnny's been helping out too."

"He's been a life saver," Jesse said, suppressing a smile. "He's fixed just about everything and even helped me with laying the stones in the back. I couldn't have done it all without him. This place would have been in shambles."

"I'm sorry I didn't warn you about him, Harless," said Joseph. "He's a very angry Indian."

"He has a right to be, as you all do," Jesse answered. "Your people got screwed, Joseph. I am well aware of that. And as far as I can see, it isn't getting any better. Unless, of course, you play the game of the white man and get the hell out like you did.

"The reservation is fraught with the usual problems—unemployment, lack of decent housing and, unfortunately, too much alcohol and drugs. Those with their own businesses work seven days a week, grateful for every customer in the short period of time when the snow and the frigid temperatures recede long enough for tourists to travel through town. They don't have the aid of the gambling casinos, not that I think that's the answer, because the white men have their fingers in those establishments too. There are few jobs for somebody like Johnny or anybody in this part of the state, especially if they don't want the white man paying their salary. It's hard to raise a family on minimum wage. To make matters worse, the Native American is still harassed and denigrated. If they'd been given the chance, those white goons who killed those animals would have killed Johnny too.

"Johnny's doing what he has to do to survive and it may not be pleasant. But while your old ways are beautiful and strong and the perfect rules to live by, those ways don't pay the bills or put food on the table. Thanks to the New Agers and those people who realize the earth is important, the Native American culture has grown in popularity and we can only hope it isn't a passing fad. The American Indian needs what is rightfully theirs—their land, their God-given rights and respect. Until then, they have little hope for that better life."

"I suppose Bianca told you about my relationship with her," Joseph said. "It is difficult for an Indian to have one with a non-Indian."

"Yes," Jesse answered. "There are rules that need to be followed, even though I am not allowed to know the reasons why."

"It is important to keep the bloodlines strong." Joseph caught Jesse's eye. "There are few full-bloods left."

"And yet, it was your ancestors who broke that rule first," Jesse returned Joseph's gaze. "So it must be hard for everyone."

"They had to do what they did to survive."

"Which makes perfect sense to me," Jesse said quietly. "What better way to win the war."

"What do you mean?" Joseph asked. "Almost all the full-bloods are gone. With them goes our history and our lineage."

"Why is it, that throughout history, when civilizations expand by incorporating new blood, they whine for the days when their race was pure? It seems to me that those races that tried to keep the *blood within the family* pretty much killed themselves off. Insanity and hemophilia are some of the biggest catastrophes that come to my mind. Look at it this way—say you've got ten Indians and 300 white people. If those ten Indians, who know and believe in their traditions, married ten white people who were taught those traditions and learned to respect the Native American way, and each couple had two children, you'd now have the equivalent of forty Indians and only 290 white people left to fight against them. Now, if each of those twenty children married twenty white people, and taught them the Indian way, who in turn taught it to their children, you'd now have even more Indians to even less white people. In two more generations, there would be more Indians than white people—enough to take back the land, the water and their rights."

"Good Lord," Joseph sighed. "So, what you're saying…"

"What I'm saying is, the more people you bring into the fold the more sympathizers you've got," Jesse continued. "What better way to destroy the enemy than to raise their children to be loyal to their foes. Have you ever stopped to consider that if every white man and woman carried Indian blood there would no longer be a distinction between the two? What better way to get back at the white men who perpetrated these heinous crimes on the Native Americans, than to have their ancestors carry Indian blood themselves."

"Harless," Joseph said, "you're crazy."

"Have you ever noticed how the *wanna-be's* are so captivated by your culture? They study the ways and respect the rules. They respect the old ways and are taking better care of the land. Environmentalists are doing their best to save the world before it's too late. A full-blooded Indian may have no chance in hell to become President of the United States, but a white man with some Indian blood could maybe do it. The more sympathizers you have, the more work you get done. Eventually, your people might even get back some of what was stolen from them two hundred years ago or at least the respect they deserve. It's time the vilification of these people and that of the wolves be stopped."

"You've developed some very strong convictions, Harless," Joseph countered. "I hope you realize that one white woman with a wolf isn't going to make the world right with a wave of her *magic wand*."

"That's for the generations after me, Joseph," Jesse stated. "The only thing a *white woman* in the wilds of Montana can do is to try to educate those around her. Maybe just get them to think."

"And Johnny is listening to you?" Joseph questioned.

"Johnny listens only to Johnny—nobody else," Jesse retorted. "Well, maybe Winona can get a message through on a good day, but for the most part, Johnny does what Johnny wants to do."

"Charlie wouldn't like the two of you fraternizing, you know," Joseph blurted out. "…You know, the blood line thing and all."

Jesse laughed. "Still afraid of the old man, eh?"

"That's not funny," Joseph snapped. "It's our custom and the laws that have been passed down through the ages. It's our heritage and identification."

Jesse considered starting an argument and if she had said what was on her mind, she certainly would have. There was no point, she realized. Apparently, he did not want to hear the ideas of a *white* woman. Some things were better left unsaid, at least for now.

"Joseph, I'm a little too busy up here keeping track of my animals, keeping them fed and cared for, and getting this cabin back together and ready for winter to have an affair with your cousin right now. I'm sorry if that disappoints you," Jesse snapped sarcastically.

Joseph eyed the young woman carefully. She was looking straight back at him, defiantly. If she had not just spoken them, he could not tell what her true feelings were. "I don't want to pry," he muttered.

"Then don't," Jesse sighed. "I know the rules, Joseph. I've talked to Bianca and I've been around here long enough to know such matches don't work up here."

"I just don't want you to get hurt," Joseph said quietly. "Johnny makes his own rules. You never know what he really wants. There's one warning I can give you. I do know he's got his eye on this cabin."

"That's good to know," Jesse responded with a raised eyebrow. Joseph's words would normally have stung the woman in the heart. She'd keep that last statement in mind, but whatever happened would be between her and Johnny—not anyone else—Indian or White. The screen door opened and Jesse was relieved to see Bianca come out onto the porch, which meant the conversation was over.

"Hey, you two," Bianca interposed. "How long have I been out?"

"Hours and hours," Joseph chuckled. "We've been sitting here since noon."

"Yeah, right," Bianca quipped. She bent over and gave her man a kiss on the forehead. "How's the clan?"

"Good!" Joseph announced. "Winona's still the best cook in the world."

"And you can move in with her at any time," Bianca jibed, "as you were so close to starving to death at our house." She patted his rotund tummy as she walked by and took a seat on the other side of Jesse.

"Speaking of dinner," Eric declared, joining everyone on the porch, "I could use some about now." The wolves stirred from their naps and started to stretch. Shadow rose up on his lanky legs and trotted up to the cabin. Eric stooped down and greeted him at the top of the stairs with a hug. "This poor animal is starving too," he kidded. "Come on, boy, let's go find some grub." Eric got up and reached for the screen door handle. Shadow let himself in through the slit in the screen.

"Jesse, go call Winona," Bianca said with an acid tongue. "Maybe she can bring us some doggy bags of her leftovers."

"Okay," Jesse said, rising up from her chair. Mesa was sitting at the bottom of the steps, considering whether to come up. Cheyenne kept her distance out by the truck. "Come on, Mesa," Jesse urged her wolf. "At least we've got plenty of meat for you guys." The clouds forming over the cabin were heavy and darkening. The last rays of the sun disappeared behind them. The wind was picking up.

"Looks like a storm is coming," Joseph observed, getting up from his chair. He looked shyly at his woman, wondering how much of his conversation with Jesse she had overheard. There was no way of telling by the look on her face.

"Hope it stays outside," Bianca said, heading into the house behind him.

The foursome's spirits were cautiously cheerful and they kept the conversation light while they all helped prepare the evening meal. Joseph grabbed a bottle of wine from the storage room, impressed with Jesse's collection. He had no problem finding his appetite again when the food was finally prepared and served. The others ate ravenously as well. The wolves were in and out of the cabin—Shadow and Max enjoyed the tidbits of food the human's were coerced to provide.

After dinner they cleaned up and piled into Joseph and Bianca's SUV. For the most part, the storm had come and gone, heading toward the eastern plains. They traveled the twenty miles into town, in a light but steady rain, to meet Arleen at the Ranger Bar.

Joseph couldn't help but smile when he saw Arleen perched on her favorite stool, and his old friend Jack behind the bar. Arleen let out a little shriek of delight when she saw him. She jumped off her stool and ran to Joseph's outstretched arms as Jack threw down his towel and stepped out from behind the bar to join them in a group hug.

"Still the same dive I knew and loved," Joseph smiled, letting Arleen give him a big kiss on the cheek. "Still the same clientele, too," he shook Jack's hand vigorously.

"That's 'cos I still let the likes of you in," Jack retorted, beaming at his old friend.

Eric, who had stopped in his tracks at the door, perused the shabby but cozy room with disdain. "Holy Shit," he declared. "Welcome to the netherworld."

"Shush up, smart ass," Jesse gently chided him. "Don't get us kicked out before we get in the door."

The bar was depressing. Dark paneled walls covered with tattered, old beer posters and neon advertisements from the sixties. There were battered tables and chairs, a beat up pool table in the corner and the brightest light came from an old jukebox shoved into one of the corners. The bar expanded the length of the right side of the room. The dusty bottles of booze sat precariously on warped wooden shelves that seemed to cling for their existence against a large cracked mirror, haphazardly attached to the wall. There were three other patrons sitting at the bar, lost in their beers and sporadic conversations. Two guys sat at a table close to the opposite wall playing cards. All of them stared at the newcomers for a very long minute or two before warily returning to their activities.

"Damn, Joe," Arleen said with a grin. "You look great!" She finally let go of him and gave him the once over. "Colorado becomes you!"

"And you're a sight for sore eyes," Joseph returned. "How's Richard?"

"Discovering new ways to piss off the government daily," she answered. "There's a lot of endangered wildlife out there, you know, and too many rich lobbyists who want to use and eventually destroy what's left of their protected territory."

"Progress—ain't it grand?" Joseph sighed mockingly.

Arleen motioned for her friends to join her. She gave Jesse a hug and tugged at Eric's jacket sleeve, bringing him into the fold. "You'll like it better after you get one of Jack's drinks in ya," she encouraged the young man. "This place'll look like a palace after three." Eric gave her a weak smile and sat down on a wobbly stool next to Jesse. Bianca sat between Jesse and Joe. Arleen touched Bianca's arm gently, giving her a warm smile while yelling to Jack, "First round's on me." She took the seat on the other side of Joseph. "Let's start out with a shot," she added.

Jack Miller was generous with his liquor, and the little group settled comfortably into their seats. The conversation was lively and rowdy at times and soon the other patrons joined in with their own quips and barbs. A few more stragglers came in, more introductions were made and more drinks were served. Eventually Eric headed for the jukebox, towing Arleen with him by the arm, to warm the place up with some music.

As the evening wore on, the foursome was regaled with tales of Joseph's history and the tall tales of the town's other residents. Eric danced with Arleen and Joseph danced with Bianca. Jesse sat at the bar and chitchatted with Jack and the others until Eric scooped her up and made her dance with him too.

With her arms around Eric's neck, Jesse gazed around the bar as Eric held her tight and twirled her slowly with the music. It appeared as though the whole town had suddenly shown up—now sitting, standing or also dancing in the tiny bar. She smiled, realizing how wonderful the evening was turning out for everyone. She was proud of Eric for not getting boisterous. She glanced over at Joseph and Bianca, happy to see them chatting quietly into each other's ears and smiling as they danced slowly around the room. It was wonderful to see them dancing together. For a while, they were free and clearly in love—not afraid of anybody noticing that they were together.

Jesse settled her head against her friend's shoulder while he guided her around the other dancers. It felt good to be in her best friend's arms. Her golden eyes casually noticed the door open and someone else come in. Eric turned her around and her gaze was temporarily shifted, but through her alcoholic haze she thought she'd recognized the newcomer. When they turned back around she was certain of who he was.

Johnny slid in the door and up to the corner of the bar. Jack shook his hand and got him a beer. He sat on the end stool and perused the room. He saw everything he wanted to see in ten seconds. His sharp blue eyes met Jesse's across the room.

Eric felt the subtle change in Jesse's body as he held her in his arms. He whirled her around expertly to see what had caught her attention and was not surprised to find the Native American he had seen the night before on her porch. For a few heartbeats he maneuvered her so she could not look back at the guy even though she desperately tried to. "Jesse," he warned, making her focus on him, "that's one too many strays. You're not the Dumb Friends League. Don't get involved in this."

Jesse met her friend's gaze defiantly. "Eric," she derided him, "if you're planning on staying here with me and helping me raise my wolves, then I'll consider it. Otherwise, it's none of your business." She grasped him tightly and turned around so she could see Johnny again. He was still watching her as he took a sip of his beer.

"Man, Bianca's warned you about it," he whispered into her ear. "And so has Joseph. I heard your conversation today and I know what you're up to. You may have fooled him, but you didn't fool me. You're my closest friend. I can see through you like a wrought iron gate in the French Quarter. Joe's right. He doesn't want you. He wants the land and everything else you're sitting on."

"Right now," she said boldly, "he can have it. You gotta let go, Eric. This is my decision. Nobody else gets a say." She broke away from him and headed for the bar. Bianca saw the exchange as well. Luckily, Joseph was enjoying their dance and paying no attention to what was going on behind him. Bianca held on to Joseph as tight as she could. She gave Jesse the break she needed. With a graceful sweep of his hand, Eric grabbed Arleen and continued to dance.

"You kids are pretty good dancers," the bartender smiled at Jesse when she sat down on the stool. He didn't notice that her concentration was somewhere else. "Can I get you another drink?"

"Just a glass of water," Jesse said quickly. She watched Johnny, who got up and walked toward the restrooms. He brushed against her as he passed. "Thanks," she said to Jack, grabbing the drink from his hand and gulping it down. She waited exactly one minute before she casually headed toward the restroom herself.

There were three doors—one marked *Men*, one marked *Women*, and the other emblazoned with *Exit*. She pondered her choices and picked one quickly. She opened the door to the women's bathroom. Inside the small room was a not too clean sink, a running toilet, an overflowing wastebasket and Johnny, who grabbed her, pulled her into the room, shut the door behind her and locked it. She had planned on saying something witty and clever but the words failed her when he pressed her body close to his. He looked at her with fire in his eyes.

"It looks like you're having a great time with your white man," he said, clutching her tighter. I have to wonder if you'll be sleeping on the couch tonight." Johnny's voice was deep and husky.

Jesse was surprised by his comment and it scared her. She was shocked to realize her initial fears may have been correct. He knew where she had slept and probably everything else she had done since she moved in. "I sleep where I want to," she snapped back angrily. "And why should you care, anyway?"

"Like I said before," he continued, his lips dangerously close to hers. "You're better off with him. Stick with what you know, Jesse Harless. There's danger in these mountains. Every tree becomes an Indian."

Her instincts told her to wrench away from him, but her soul wanted to kiss him hard. He took the guesswork away from her. He rubbed his head against hers, smelling the perfume in her hair. In an instant he left her and was out the door. Jesse grabbed the edge of the dirty sink for support, because she would have fallen to the floor if she hadn't. "Damn you!" she cursed into the mirror, more at herself rather than the Indian she had fallen for.

Bianca tried to keep Joseph on the dance floor, but once the song had ended he wanted a drink. She followed him reluctantly to the bar, keeping her eyes peeled for Jesse or Johnny. Neither one of them were in the room. Eric and Arleen also joined them.

"Another round, my good man," Joseph announced to Jack when he sat down, making sure Bianca sat down next to him. "Business is booming, eh?"

"This ain't my typical night," Jack laughed, grabbing more glasses. "I guess I need to play that jukebox more often. Seems to have brought in the whole town." He poured the drinks with an expert hand. "Even Johnny's here," he quipped innocently. "Have you seen him?"

Eric and Bianca tensed immediately. On either side of Joseph, they could feel the emotional change in him when he heard the words. The Native American looked up slowly and started eyeing the patrons in the bar. He turned on his stool to check out the dance floor, which allowed Jesse to slip in next to Eric at the bar. When she saw that Johnny was not in the bar, she knew he had slipped out the back door. Joseph scrutinized the room. Everybody was in their places as they should be. He ended his search when he turned once more and saw Jesse sitting next to Eric drinking her water. "No," he finally answered the bartender, "I didn't see him come in."

Jack glanced over the room haphazardly as he served the drinks. "Humph," he grumbled with a shrug of his shoulders. "He was here earlier." Bianca, Eric and Jesse played dumb and finished their drinks.

That night, when they all stumbled back to the cabin, Jesse was irate. She scrutinized the area for any signs of unwanted Indians peering out from behind the trees and was angry that it was impossible to tell. The wolves were off on one of their midnight treks. She could hear them howling in the distance. Bianca and Eric stood on the porch shivering, mesmerized by the sounds the animals made. After giving Bianca a sloppy kiss, Joseph went directly upstairs to bed.

Once everybody else was bedded down for the night, Jesse added another log to the fire and curled up on the couch next to Max. She had closed the blinds and drawn the curtains over them. There would be no peep show tonight, she determined. Her mind was muddled with conflicting thoughts. Had he really been watching her when she first arrived? Why did the thought intrigue her now, when it scared the daylights out of her then? It was a long time before she fell asleep.

The next morning Jesse awoke to Joseph trudging out the front door with Max in tow and his grunt of a good-bye when they left. She thought about sticking her head back under the covers and trying to get more sleep, but Bianca came down shortly afterward, thwarting that plan of escape. When she looked at Bianca with a puzzled countenance, Bianca shook her head with a sad smile.

"He got too close again last night," Bianca answered the question before Jesse asked it. "He'll be gone most of the day, brooding about his horrible existence." She walked into the kitchen and started the coffee.

"This still doesn't make any sense," Jesse said, getting up.

Joseph had closed the door, and Shadow, with his little pack close behind him, was scratching at it now, impatient because he could not just prance in. Jesse opened the door and got out of the way. The wolves were inside in an instant, making sure nothing had changed from last night. "I thought you guys had a great time, didn't you?"

"We did," Bianca sighed. "That's the problem. Now, he's afraid the news about our behavior will get to Charlie. And, from what I've heard about Johnny, it'll probably be in this morning's headlines. Joseph won't speak to me for days now."

"Is it worth it?" Jesse asked, feeding the animals. Shadow and Mesa did their best to get at the bag of dog food themselves, but Jesse had learned to be quick. Their bowls were down in seconds with only a couple of scratches on her legs and arms from their claws as they tried to help her.

"There's a big part of me that wants to say no," Bianca offered. "But somehow I always change my mind. I'm warning you, this is not an easy row to hoe, Jess."

"Don't worry about me," Jesse retorted. "Johnny did a great job of freaking me out last night."

"Well," Bianca said, "believe it or not, that'll make it a little easier for me. Joseph hates the thought of the two of you getting together."

"I just wish I knew why it has to be like this," Jesse wondered aloud. "I see white people and Indians together all the time."

"I cannot tell you," Bianca said sadly. "I made a promise and I am bound to it forever. For now, he's convinced me his reasons are sound and for those reasons I will live by his rules. It is their *secret* and they keep it well guarded. I love him, Jess. Until that changes, it's got to be his way or no way. I'm glad," she added, smiling, "that you have decided against trying it. You'll be better off for making that choice in the end."

"Hey," Jesse suggested, wanting to change the subject, "let's have Eric take us into Great Falls today. We can get there in an hour, the way he drives. It'll do us good, don't you think?"

"Yeah," Bianca agreed. "Let's spend some money. There's no better way to get your mind off stuff—just go buy more."

They roused Eric, ate breakfast, got ready and were out the door in record time. With Kitten and the lupines off on their morning adventures, the three friends were free to spend the day any way they wanted. The BMW purred into action and Eric was in his glory as they sped via 44 toward I-15. Jesse was right. They were in the big city in just over an hour. They shopped the mall. They went antiquing. They had a fabulous lunch at the Fairfield Inn and then picked up where they left off. They found bookstores and outlets and even did a little gambling in one of the casinos. Bianca, always lucky with games of chance, won $200.00. Eric lost about the same amount.

There was no talk of wolves, Native Americans or anything related to Montana. They reminisced about the old days and Jesse promised to come home to Denver for a visit. They filled up the trunk with treasures and they headed back—a little depressed. They put off the inevitable and stopped at the Lighthouse in Valier for a quiet dinner before going home. The BMW pulled up in front of the cabin at about 9 p.m. Joseph was home. The television was on and the volume was up.

It had rained again, Jesse noticed when giving her wolves their hugs and kisses. The weather was changing. It was getting downright cold at night. Joseph had somehow managed to feed the animals, although Kitten had proven to be a challenge. She was under the porch, chomping down on a giant trout that Joseph had tossed to her. Her customary growls let Jesse know she was happy with the treat.

"I think we'd best be heading home tomorrow," Joseph announced, after everyone had settled down around the television, wrapped up in blankets to ward of the chill. "I got the propane tank out back filled and the furnace is working. But, by the way my knee feels, it'll probably be snowing by week's end. If that BMW doesn't get out of here soon, it won't be going anywhere 'til the spring thaw."

"Are you sure?" Bianca asked, perplexed. "We've only had two days."

"Not that I won't miss you terribly," Eric mentioned to Jesse, "but that's been long enough for my tastes."

"Eric!" Bianca chided the young man while Jesse laughed at them both.

"Unless of course you've decided to come with us," Eric continued. "I'd say those animals are big enough to fend for themselves."

"Thanks for the offer," Jesse smiled. She looked up as Shadow came through the screen, opening the door wide. She jumped up and seeing no other wolves with him, closed the door quickly. It was definitely too cold outside to leave it open for long. "But I'm going to try and stick it out. When they stop coming home at all, then I'll think about it. I promise."

"I guess," Bianca said to Jesse, petting Shadow as he passed by sniffing the room, "you'd better come help me pack. You're the only person I know who can make a fur coat fit in an overnight bag."

"Sure," Jesse laughed halfheartedly. She was truly sad they were going to leave, but she knew they had to get back to civilization sooner or later. She did not really believe Joseph's excuse for leaving. After all, it wasn't even the first of August quite yet. She figured he was probably still upset about their evening at the bar and he wanted to get out of town as quickly as possible. She felt sorry for Bianca. The drive home would probably be pretty quiet. She followed Bianca upstairs with Shadow and Max behind them. Eric, packed in ten minutes, joined them a little later.

"I'm going to miss you guys," Jesse finally said, zipping up Bianca's overnight bag. "It does get a little lonely up here, now and then."

"Just say the word," Eric declared, lounging on the king size bed. "I'll buy a tank if that's what it takes to come and get you." He pulled Jesse down on the bed and hugged her close. "We can find you a place big enough for ten wolves if that's what you want. That's my promise."

"Don't do this just because they say you can't," offered Bianca, joining them on the bed. "I think you've already proven them wrong and I'm pretty proud of you for doing it."

"I'm going to get through this winter," Jesse said with determination. "Come spring, I'll let you know if I change my mind." There was a tear in everybody's eyes. "Just keep in touch, okay? I'll check my emails regularly from now on, and if Joseph's right, I won't be too far from the phone, as the cabin will be buried until March."

The troupe went back downstairs, made some popcorn and watched a movie before they finally went to bed. The moon was full and Jesse could not cover the window, despite who may be watching. She turned off the lights and sat on the couch, watching the orb move slowly across the black, star filled sky.

"Hey, Harless," Joseph's voice came from behind her. It did not startle her when she heard it. She turned and looked up into his big, black eyes. "I almost forgot," he muttered. "I wanted to give you this."

Jesse looked at the brightly wrapped present Joseph was holding. Bianca had obviously taken the time to make it so beautiful. "You didn't have to do that," she whispered. "Just bringing the kids for a visit was present enough for me."

"Okay, then," he said, turning on a light and sitting down next to her on the couch. "Consider it a necessity that I insist you have from now on."

She looked at him quizzically as she tore off the ribbon and paper. Inside was a telephone answering machine. She smiled when she saw it.

"You kept forgetting to buy one," he reasoned. "I had to get it for you, so Bianca would let me get some sleep." He took the box from her and opened it up. He wanted to get it hooked up and make sure it worked. "I told you earlier that I didn't think you'd be able to do this, but you've proven me wrong, Harless," he said, removing the plastic wrap from the machine. "I am starting to think you might make a pretty good frontier woman, after all." Jesse opened her mouth to speak, but Joseph hushed her with a wave of his finger. "I don't want to argue with you, but I've got to give you some advice and I hope you'll take it for what it's worth.

"Listen to Charlie. When he tells you to do something, do it. Stay inside at night and don't be rambling off in that truck of yours when the weather hits. You're a tough one, Harless, and I'm sure you're gonna' be all right. I know you're going to do what you want with Johnny. I can already feel that. But I can also tell he scared you last night. He's a good man, but he's angrier than I ever was and that makes him dangerous. You trust your instincts, little lady. Don't go where you don't want to go.

"If you did get together with him, it wouldn't be as tough as it is for Bianca. Johnny isn't an Elder. Johnny lives on his ancestors' land. But it wouldn't be easy for you, either. You're a white woman and my people don't trust you. Like your wolves, my people cannot forget. The white men throughout our history, and even today, have never kept a promise. They broke our treaties and they forced us from our homes onto uninhabitable land. When they found out that uninhabitable land held some of the country's most valuable minerals, they tried to force us out again, once again breaking their own treaties and binding contracts. They accepted our gifts and friendship and paid us back with whisky and guns. When the sword or the gun didn't work, they killed us with poisoned blankets in a game of truce. Their armies killed our women and children. They burned our homes, killed our horses and buffalo and tried to starve us to death.

"They forced us to split up our families. They pounded their rules and Christianity into our children's heads. They punished us for speaking our own languages, one of which saved them in World War II, when the Germans and Japanese could not decipher it. They have done their best to eradicate us, but somehow we just don't die…and they called *us* savages."

The answering machine put together, Joseph dug into his pocket and produced a couple of batteries that he slipped into the back of it. "Remember to change these once in a while. The electricity can go out a lot up here."

Jesse nodded, still listening. Joseph got up from the couch and put the answering machine on the table, where he hooked it up to the phone. The moonlight coming in through the window shimmered on his black, shiny hair.

"A girl like you cannot change over two hundred years of history and bad blood," he continued. "Do me a favor and don't get yourself killed trying to do it. Besides, the bigger those wolves get, the bigger your problems are going to be with those ranchers. I took the liberty of posting those *no trespassing* signs earlier today. Another thing you must have forgotten." He plugged the machine in and the lights came on. The machine started humming. A recorded voice gave instructions on what to do next. "Do you want to record a message?" he asked, looking over to her on the couch.

"Why don't you do it for me," Jesse answered quietly. "I'd feel better if callers heard your voice."

The machine prompted him further. When it asked him to speak, he said in a gruff tone, "This is 406-555-6576. If that's the number you wanted, leave a message." He hit the pound key and followed the rest of the instructions. Soon the message played back and Jesse giggled. "Is that okay?" Joseph asked.

"It's perfect. Thank you, Joseph," Jesse replied, smiling, "for everything."

CHAPTER 20

Jesse couldn't shake the feeling of loneliness that had crept into her heart. The wolves had sung at dawn, arousing her friends early. The car and the SUV were packed and ready in a flurry of minutes and suddenly Jesse was waving her good-byes as Joseph, Bianca, Eric and Max pulled out onto the road and disappeared in a cloud of dust.

She was all right while she fed the wolves and the bobcat. Thankfully, they played with her for a little bit, exuberant to finally have their home back with no signs of intruders. Shadow and Mesa ran in and out of the cabin several times, checking on Jesse as she took the sheets from the beds, the dirty towels from the bathrooms and started the laundry. Finding her busy, they left the house one more time, hooked up with Cheyenne and Kitten and were swiftly gone on their daily romp in the woods. This day they headed for the mountains. At least she didn't have to worry about them finding some new ranch to trespass upon.

But when the cabin was back in order, the beds remade and the towels almost dry, Jesse found she did not want to sit down and read a book or get on the computer or even watch T.V. She was alone and quite unhappy about it. She wondered if she'd ever see her friends again. She started to doubt why she had taken on this stupid challenge in the first place.

She grabbed a coat because the wind was blowing and the temperature was rather chilly. She walked out onto the porch with a mug of hot coffee, looked up to see her eagle take one long flight around the cabin before flying off after her animals and noticed the owl had yet to return from his nightly rounds. She sat down on the stoop of her porch stairs, took a deep breath and had a good cry.

After an hour or so, she toddled back into the house, took a hot shower and tried to disguise her puffy eyes with makeup. She dressed in her jeans and warm Irish sweater, grabbed her keys and got into the truck. She drove like a maniac into town, fighting back more tears. Jesse scared Arleen almost to death when she stumbled into the general store, quite the basket case. Arleen hugged the young woman, listened to her woes and then put her to work stocking shelves. It took a long day of hard work and a lot of discussion, but finally, by closing time, Jesse had calmed down and was pretty much back to her old self. The two women walked across the street to Jack's and ordered hamburgers and a good stiff drink for dinner. Assuring Arleen she'd be all right, Jesse eventually got into her truck and drove home.

When Jesse got there, she had some impatient wolves and a hungry bobcat on her hands. She also had a guest sitting on her porch. Charlie Stillwater was swaying in her rocking chair, patiently whittling on a piece of old wood.

"I fed the wolves, but that cat just won't have anything to do with me," Charlie yelled out to Jesse, who had quickly jumped out of her truck and found it difficult to keep her footing among the mass of wolf legs that surrounded her. "What do you feed that thing, anyway?"

"How long have you been here?" she asked, rubbing Shadow's ever expanding, furry neck. "I was over at Arleen's."

"Just a few minutes," the Native American lied. He had been sitting on that porch for about four hours when he saw the dust cloud of her truck making its way up the trail. "Thought you might be a bit lonely after your guests left."

"That's an understatement," Jesse sighed, finally reaching the porch. "Why didn't you sit inside? It's darn cold out here!" She opened the unlocked door and stepped inside to get one of Joseph's freshly caught trout he had left for Kitten. The bobcat, rather miffed at her mistress, jumped out from the bushes and trotted inside through the hole in the screen. Charlie, startled at the bobcat's behavior, decided to stay in his chair a little while longer to give the animal some space. Shadow leapt up the porch steps and nuzzled into Charlie's lap, expecting the Indian's attention while Jesse was otherwise occupied.

Kitten jumped up on the kitchen table and snatched the trout from Jesse's hand with one sweep of her forepaw. With the fish firmly lodged between her jaws she darted back out the door to her safe spot under the porch. Jesse opened the screen door and held it for Charlie.

"Come on in, now," she smiled. "The coast is clear. Shadow, leave Uncle Charlie alone!"

With some resistance from the rambunctious wolf, Charlie eased out of the rocking chair. Unfortunately, he dropped the piece of wood he was working on. Shadow grabbed it from the floor and took off running. "Hey!" the man yelped. "That was turning out to be a pretty good flute!"

"It'll have too many holes *if* I can ever get it back," Jesse said, helping Charlie through the door. "Sorry."

"Damn wolf!" Charlie muttered cheerfully, shaking his head. "Who'd a thought I'd ever know one good enough to curse at!"

"If you'd care to start a fire," Jesse offered, "I'll make you some hot chocolate."

"Don't tell Winona and you've got a deal." Charlie went over to the fireplace, rubbing his hands to shake off the cold. "I can't have chocolate at home."

"Our secret," Jesse promised.

"I brought the animals some road kill," the Indian said, stocking the fireplace with kindling. "A deer got hit up on the res. Figured I'd put it to good use."

"We appreciate that," Jesse called out. She put the kettle on the stove and started heating up some milk.

"For a minute there," he went on, "I thought you might have headed back to Denver with your friends. Just with it being so quiet up here and all."

"My friends," Jesse quipped, "are all right here, now. My babies would not fair too well if I left."

Charlie laughed. "Babies? Have you looked at them lately? Almost full grown, I'd say."

"By spring time." Jesse walked into the living room and leaned against the couch. "I spent the day working at the store with Arleen. I have to admit I was a little homesick after everybody left."

"That can happen real often up here now that winter's going to be settling in," noted Charlie. He put a log on the fire and reached in his pocket for his lighter. "But we're pretty used to having you around, so remember, you can always come see us." Shadow and Mesa bounded in the door and nearly tackled the old man, who was crouching in front of the fireplace.

"It's much better," Jesse laughed, watching the scene in front of her, "when you just drop by." She remembered the milk and tore back into the kitchen "I still get a little nervous on the path to your house," she called from the other room. "Never know if I'm following the right one."

"The wolves can get you there with no trouble," Charlie spat between wolf licks. "Shadow visits us all the time."

Jesse poured a generous heap of chocolate into the hot milk and turned down the heat, stirring constantly. "Better they travel to your house than down south or east."

Charlie held the wolves at bay long enough to ignite some paper and, in turn, the kindling on fire. He used Shadow's strong back to help him up from his crouched position and sat down on the couch.

"Don't you dare," Jesse gently warned Shadow, who had decided to *help* her with the steaming mugs of hot chocolate as she carried them to the living room. She had to step over Mesa who was lying down at the side of the couch.

Charlie stretched out his hand and took one of the cups from Jesse's grasp. The mug was very hot. He blew across the steaming hot liquid, knowing it was futile and downright dangerous to take a drink right away. "Have you had any trouble with any of the ranchers, yet?" he asked her.

"No, thank God," Jesse answered, also waiting for her drink to cool. Shadow sat on his haunches next to Jesse in her armchair. "Nothing more than a few strange looks in town."

"And how about my son? Has he been bothering you?" Charlie pretended to concentrate on his hot chocolate instead of looking in Jesse's direction.

Jesse smiled inwardly. How clever these men could be, subtly changing the subject in favor of their purpose. "He's helped me around here quite a bit." That was fast becoming her standard answer. "I think you'd agree this place was far from perfect when I moved in. It looks pretty good now, don't you think?"

"Very good," the Native American agreed.

"And you were the one who insisted he help, as I recall."

"Yes," muttered Charlie. "I just hope he isn't a pest." The hot drink had finally cooled down. Charlie took a sip, relishing the chocolate taste. "Winona and I haven't seen much of him lately. No telling where he's hanging out."

"Well, it isn't here." Jesse hoped she wasn't lying. That reminded her. Tonight would be her first night alone again. The blinds and curtains would be closed before the sun went down.

"He's a confused and angry man," Charlie related. "I thought he'd grow out of it like his cousin. As all families, we've had our share of problems. I guess I should have taken better care of them...and paid more attention to him."

"He's okay," Jesse assured him. "I think he truly loves the wolves and that gives him some peace. I think that's why he likes it here."

"*Walks with the Wolves,*" Charlie smiled. He noticed the curious look on Jesse's face. "That's his Indian name," he explained. "He was always hiding and never happy around people—much like the wolves that used to live in these parts."

"That's beautiful," Jesse said. "His mother gave him that name, didn't she?"

"Yes, she did. She's the only one who has ever been able to understand him. She tells me that you are good for him."

"Well," Jesse said hesitantly, "I don't know about that." It was Jesse's turn to feel a little nervous. She took a sip of her hot chocolate and savored it slowly. "You know," she finally added, "the *secret*. I have been warned about such a relationship and told that it isn't a good thing around here."

"That's Joe talking," Charlie chimed in. "He's got his principles he has always lived by. That the Red Man cannot live with the White Man in that kind of harmony is one of them."

"He learned it from you," Jesse declared.

Charlie laughed quietly. "Have you ever noticed that my wife has the most beautiful, blue eyes?"

"And Johnny also."

"There is a white, German grandfather in her family. He had yellow hair and blue eyes." Charlie had another sip of his hot chocolate and set the mug on the table. "There are so very few full-bloods left, Jesse. Like all races, we have mingled too."

"But you would like a nice Indian girl for Johnny, no?" Jesse asked. Shadow placed his big head on her lap, contentedly gazing at the mug she was holding. She scratched him behind the ears.

At one time, the Native American did feel his sons and his nephew would carry on the Red Man's tradition. As a matter of fact, he was quite adamant about it. But to be honest, lately, Charlie was getting too old to care. Frankie had listened and married a very nice Indian girl, so his legacy was safe. Joseph, of course, had taken up the torch and run with it, which was part of the reason Charlie sat on Jesse's couch at this moment. Johnny would probably never get married, nor raise a family. So it didn't matter whom he chose as a companion, because he would likely never do it anyway. It was sad for him to think of his youngest being alone forever, but if that was what Johnny wanted, that was the way it would be.

"I would like…" Charlie murmured, looking toward the fire, "…for him to have at least one happy day. I would like to hear him laugh."

Jesse considered whether she should tell him. Charlie looked a bit older in the firelight and a little tired. "He has a wonderful laugh," she conceded. "It is quite infectious."

Charlie turned to the young woman and smiled. "I bet it is." He picked up his mug and finished his hot chocolate. "But like an infection, he has a bad side too." He loved his son and he could now plainly see that this young lady had feelings for him also. He had to tell her everything in case his son did not. "He lies, you know. I cannot remember when he has told me the truth. The anger I spoke about earlier is strong in him and sometimes it clouds his vision. Please do not let it cloud yours. If he helps you, that makes me proud. His mother has hope he will come around." Did he see a glint of disappointment in the young woman's eyes? If so, he truly regretted it, but it had to be said. Jesse had to be warned. "Is there any more?" he asked innocently, holding out his cup.

"Of course there is," Jesse said. She moved Shadow off her lap, got up and grabbed the Native American's mug. "I've got plenty of chocolate for my special guests!"

Charlie got up and followed her into the kitchen. "There's quite a storm brewing," he mentioned, looking outdoors. Shadow was at his heels as he walked. "We'll probably get pretty wet in the next couple of days."

"How do you know that, Charlie?" Jesse inquired, warming more milk. "I can feel a temperature change, but that's about it."

"The eagles and the owls are fortifying their nests," he said nonchalantly. "I noticed it earlier today. The wolves' coats are coming in very fast. Your bobcat is hanging around under that porch rather than going out. And last, my knee is killing me—an old war wound that likes to act up. We'll get rain sometime tomorrow that won't let up for a while."

"I picked up some stuff at the store today," stated Jesse. "I should probably get it in the house."

"I'll help you after we drink," Charlie said. "We'll get you ready for this weather and then I better go home. Winona will start missing me pretty soon."

Later, after Charlie had left on his walk home through the woods, Jesse sat at the fire and thought about what had transpired between them. She wondered, although she wasn't sure, if Charlie had indirectly given his blessing if she wanted to see his son. It did not matter of course, for she had not seen him nor heard from him since their encounter at the bar. She did not expect to hear from him. Charlie had no need to remind her of Johnny's anger. She saw it in those turquoise blue eyes when he had held her so close. All her friends' warnings crowded into her head—*don't do it*. How could they all be wrong?

The wolves were all gone now, howling somewhere in the trees before their nightly romp. She closed the blinds and the curtains, despite the moon overhead. She took a hot bath and went to bed. She read a book, putting Johnny out of her head, and then went to sleep.

As usual, Charlie was right. The weather had practically changed overnight. The temperature was a good twenty degrees below what it had been just a week ago when her guests had come for their visit. After the first, heavy rainstorm, the days were suddenly crisper and clearer. The leaves were changing color rapidly on the trees. The tall grasses were turning sandy brown and the lake was always choppy, whether Jesse could feel a breeze or not.

Shadow's coat was filling in, as was Mesa's and Cheyenne's. They looked more like wolves with each passing day. Shadow's fur was still black, but now with a speckle of white and gray guard hairs here and there. His eyes were wild and the color of pure gold. Mesa's coat darkened as it filled out, but he was smaller than Shadow and not as dark. Cheyenne's fur and guard hairs were still all white. She was a vision running across the field toward the cabin. Her long, sleek fur rippled when she moved, like a silky scarf blowing in the wind.

The wolves stayed out later and later now. They thrived on the colder weather and were much more active for longer periods of time. Some days Jesse would not catch a glimpse of them all day until well into the night. She kept the front door of the cabin open a crack, for when they arrived home all three would now barrel in through the screen, single file, devour what seemed like tons of food and then settle in for a short nap before returning to the wild.

Kitten, meanwhile, preferred it indoors. She wasn't one to curl up on Jesse's lap, play with string or purr, but she did like to weave in and out between Jesse's legs as she puttered around the cabin. So at least the bobcat was home most of the time and Jesse relied on her companionship while her wolves were off on their daily expeditions.

Another storm was brewing one late afternoon as Jesse took some logs off the stack of firewood and set them inside the front door. She had driven to the general store earlier that morning and loaded up on supplies. As the temperature dropped even more, Jesse wanted to get the chores done quickly so she could get comfortable in front of a nice warm fire and relax. This impending storm had that kind of feeling—the kind where one just wanted to snuggle up on the couch under a blanket and read or sleep or do whatever came to mind as long as one did not have to go outside.

Jesse filled up the tinderbox with logs and kindling and put another stack into the storage room just in case it was too nasty to go out later. She lit some candles and placed them on the mantelpiece and the coffee table. The room was awash in a soft warm glow. She carefully prepared the fireplace using sticks and old newspaper for kindling, tucking it all under two nice sized logs of oak. The fire roared to life when she struck a match to the kindling.

Looking out the front door for any signs of the wolves, she howled twice into the wind. In the distance she thought she heard one of her children answer back. She closed the door partway, leaving the customary crack for easy animal access in case they might head home before the storm. But the rain had already started, darting and slashing horizontally in the wind and she knew she would not be able to leave it open all night. The charcoal gray sky was filled with a rumbling pattern of dark purple, heavy clouds and the wind was shaking the trees. The Eagle swooped down and landed in his nest, bracing for the ensuing storm. Jesse could not see any of her owls.

She picked up her sweater from the couch and slipped it on. There was not much for her to do now, except to wait this out. She contemplated whether to read a book or just watch T.V. There were probably emails she needed to answer too. Instead, she went into the storage room and got herself a bottle of wine.

In the kitchen, she was extracting the cork from the bottle, when she caught a glimpse of the front door opening. She was even quicker to note there were no furry beasts climbing on top of each other to be the first one inside. Rationalizing it must have been the wind, which was definitely growing stronger with every pass, she set the bottle down and headed for the door. She glanced at the clock on the wall to check the time. It showed 5:30 p.m.

The clouds were so dark and heavy she could not see the tops of the trees. The porch swing was sliding back and forth quite haphazardly, without human assistance. A torrent of rain erupted out of the clouds like a bursting balloon. When she stepped out onto the porch, Kitten scrambled up the steps, dashed into the house and past her through the open door. Jesse moved aside for the fur ball, but her concentration was elsewhere. Out in the field, about 300 feet from the house she saw Cheyenne. But what was even more amazing was the fact that the white wolf was sitting, quite contentedly, close to the figure of Johnny Stillwater, who was crouched down and petting her. They were both soaking wet. Johnny looked up at Jesse. She could barely make out his face through the rain, falling in sheets of water between them.

"Get your asses in here!" she screamed unceremoniously. "You've got ten seconds before I close this door!"

Johnny looked at the wolf for a split second and got up. The man and the wolf high-tailed it for the cabin, arriving on the porch in less than three. Jesse had already run inside and grabbed a stack of towels. She found the two drip-ping wet under the roof of the porch when she got back. She threw a towel at Johnny and tossed one gently over Cheyenne. When the wolf accepted it, Jesse got down on her knees and rubbed the towel over Cheyenne's fur. The wolf allowed her a minute before shedding the towel and shaking the rest of the water off herself.

Johnny seemed confused, holding the dry towel in his hands. Finally, he shook his head, à la Cheyenne. More water sprayed onto Jesse, who was stooped down in front of him tending to the wolf. It was immediately obvious to her that the towel would do no good. His jacket, shirt and jeans were soaked. No towel would help with that mess.

Jesse took the towel from him and used it on herself. Without saying a word, she got up, opened the screen door and indicated with a nod of her head she wanted everybody inside. While the Native American sheepishly followed her orders, Cheyenne passed on the offer, preferring to lie outside on the porch to keep a steady eye out for her companions. Jesse understood.

"You'd better give me those clothes," Jesse said matter-of-factly, once the two humans were inside. "I'll put them in the dryer."

"Ah," Johnny started, "I'm afraid I don't look as good in a dress as you do. And I know your jeans won't fit. How about if I just sit by the fire for a few minutes?"

"For God's sake," Jesse rebuked. She walked over to the closet under the staircase and pulled out an oversized, flannel shirt, along with a very large pair of jeans. "Here," she snapped, throwing it at him. "These are probably yours, anyway. They were here when I moved in." She cast a glance at him and wanted to smile, but didn't. He looked fairly ridiculous and helpless standing there dripping onto the carpet. "Change in the storage room," she went on, heading for the kitchen. "I trust you know how to turn on the dryer."

Out of his sight, Jesse leaned her hands on the countertop in the kitchen. She exhaled slowly, determined to remain in control. She grabbed a tall glass from the cupboard and filled it with red wine. She did not care how unladylike it was. She was downright thirsty and her stalker was in her storage room, probably naked, with everything but an engraved invitation in his hand giving him free reign to the house. She picked up the glass of wine and, with little contemplation, the bottle too, before leaving the kitchen.

She checked on Cheyenne again, who still wanted to stay outside. She plopped herself down on the couch and grabbed a blanket, wrapping it around her shoulders. She turned on the television to provide some needed distraction. She turned the volume very low because Kitten had curled up into a ball and was sound asleep by the fire.

When Johnny appeared from the storage room, Jesse eyed him skeptically. She noted immediately the dry clothes were not his own. They were more Joseph's size than his. The young man was holding his pants up as he walked barefoot across the wood floor.

"I suppose Joe didn't leave a belt around here anywhere, did he?" Johnny asked quietly.

Jesse moved over to the far end of the couch to let the Native American sit down as far away from her as possible. "I haven't noticed one," she answered curtly. "Sorry."

Johnny sat down at his end of the couch and rubbed his arms vigorously. Jesse could plainly see that he was shaking. She tossed another blanket at him. He wrapped himself up immediately. His eyes crossed over the bottle of wine, but dared not ask for a sip. He sat silently, watching the big screen T.V.

"Picked a lousy night for peeping in on me," Jesse finally stated, summoning her courage and her ire. "There's really nothing new to see."

"I was wondering if you were all right," Johnny's statement was short.

"Or if I was still even here," Jesse offered cynically, taking a sip of her wine. "I'm sure you thought I'd be long gone by now."

"Well, if you'd had half a brain you would have been gone." Johnny didn't like her sarcasm. He grabbed the wine bottle and took a swig, keeping it close. "Giving all that shit up to come out here. How stupid can you be?"

"At least I know when to come in out of the rain," Jesse retorted.

"But you leapt right into the fire," Johnny snapped back. "Maybe you just can't believe it could be so bad—as *everybody* has warned you. A guy once said that about the grizzlies. He just had to stay with the bears a few more days. They found him and his girlfriend in pieces the morning they were to be picked up."

"Gee," Jesse whined. "If you'd have resorted to horror stories earlier, I might have packed up and been gone by now. Then you'd finally have your precious cabin all to yourself."

Johnny stared the young woman down. She turned her gaze from him and concentrated on her glass of wine, which was getting low. "I don't give a damn about this cabin," he hissed. "It can burn to hell for all I care." He gulped another swig of the wine. "I haven't been spying on you. I've been keeping watch. I've frozen my ass off plenty of nights keeping you out of trouble. You keep that damn door open much longer and you'll find out. I'm surprised you haven't had a grizzly or a mountain lion in here already. There's been enough of them around. If wolves can pass through that door, they can too. God knows what would have happened if you ever had to fire that damn gun of yours. You'd probably blow yourself and the wolves sky high if you did." The sky outside had opened up and the storm raged all around them. The rain pelted the metal roof and roared past the windows.

"So don't come down on me, lady," he sighed. "You should have gone back to Denver with your boyfriend when you had the chance. 'Cos, now he won't be able to get back up here with that damn expensive sports car of his until spring. I'd say you've sealed your fate. And since my help's been such a burden to you, you can start taking care of yourself. I've got a lot more important things to be wasting my time on than looking after you."

"He's not my boyfriend," Jesse said quietly, moved by his speech. She turned and faced him again. His blue eyes were filled with fire. "Why don't you believe that?"

"Because you'd be a fool to turn him down. He's got everything—looks, money and power. Everything a woman could possibly want."

"I was told *you* wanted this cabin," Jesse went on cautiously. "He doesn't have that."

"He could have ten cabins like this," Johnny said lowly. "He could buy the whole stinking reservation, but nobody wants problems like that. Hell, he probably already bought this place from Joseph, just so you could play in the woods for a while. I couldn't have it if I wanted it."

"No, he didn't," retaliated Jesse. "I pay Joseph the rent. Only a Native American can own this land."

"This land's on the other side of the creek. This is white man's land, Jesse. You've got more right to it than any of us."

The door opened, startling them both. Cheyenne eased in the door and headed into the kitchen after giving them both a look. She drank some water and ate some food out of Shadow's bowl before heading back out the door onto the porch. The rain was pouring down steadily now. The brunt of the storm was above them.

Jesse got up without saying a word and went into the storage room. Johnny figured she be getting his clothes and throwing him out. Instead, she came out with another bottle of wine and went to the kitchen. She grabbed the corkscrew and another big glass and returned to the living room. This time she sat down in the middle of the couch, much closer to Johnny.

"I've always had the bad habit of letting my friends run my life. When I let them tell me what was best for me, I never had to worry about making my own mistakes. When I found Shadow, I found this strength I didn't know I had, and against *their* better judgment, I listened to myself instead of them. That's how I ended up here. Now, even here, they still tried to influence me—warning me about you and a friendship that should never be. Well, that's against *my* better judgment, Johnny. I'm sorry, but I just can't see what they want me to see." She offered him the bottle of wine and the corkscrew and set the glass next to her empty one on the coffee table. "I guess I should thank..."

"Don't!" Johnny cut her off. "Nobody needs to be thanked around here. Least of all me." He put the corkscrew in the bottle and began the slow process of pulling out the cork. "...If that's what you were going to do," he added awkwardly.

"Yes," Jesse smiled. "I was going to thank you for helping me to think for myself." Their eyes met. "But I won't, 'cos maybe you don't deserve it." Johnny gave her that sly, albeit confused look. "Of all the people I know, which isn't a congregation by any means, let me tell you only three seem to think you're okay. It just so happens that those three are the ones I trust the most. They're the reason I'm still here and will stay here—whether it kills me or not. Those wolves trust you, so it's time I got off my high horse and trusted you too.

"I may be naive, but it seems to me the people who think they know you best, actually don't know you at all. And the one who doesn't know you at all, has no right to comment." Jesse paused and drank some of the wine Johnny had poured into her glass. "You scared the hell out of me the other night," she finally continued, on a roll. "But I guess I needed it. I've been dead so long and living the way I was told to, it took something like that and someone like you to finally wake me up.

"If you want this cabin, I want you to have it. It isn't that important to me, either. As long as I can find a place where my animals will be somewhat safe and have a place to come home to, I'll be perfectly happy," she concluded.

Johnny laughed quietly, snuggling back against the couch under the covers.

"What's so funny?" Jesse asked warily, sipping more wine.

"I used to think this place was the most important thing in my life," he murmured, his eyes sparkling in the firelight. "My way out; my independence; my freedom. I built most of it and a lot of the furniture. It was my place to be alone. Now the rules have changed." It was Jesse's turn to look confused. He could not quite meet her gaze. "You've made it a home, Jess. If you and those wolves...and that bobcat lying over there next to the fireplace weren't here, I wouldn't want a thing to do with it." Jesse looked astonished. "The only reason I want to be here is just to be close to you."

Jesse started to speak, not entirely sure what to say. Those were the last words she ever expected to hear from his mouth.

"I've been told I was bad, by a lot of people, for a very long time," Johnny went on, instilling her silence. "I can still hear the school teachers and the preachers and the white men and even my father drumming it into my head. After a while, a kid gets the message, you know?"

Jesse nodded her head in agreement.

"Growing up, I guess I was lucky, but I sure didn't feel that way," Johnny continued, casting his eyes toward the fireplace. "I lived in a real house. I had both a mother and a father. But that didn't stop me from seeing the world through tainted eyes. Unfortunately, some white men attacked my mother when I was pretty little. I saw the whole thing and couldn't do a thing about it. My father didn't do anything about it either for which I've never been able to forgive him. My introduction to the white man's world was early and pretty repulsive.

"The few friends I had felt the same way I did. We were ostracized by the Christian teachers who taught at the white man's school. They didn't care if we learned anything or not. Their main purpose was to remind us how insignificant and stupid we were. We were considered savages and picked on at every opportunity. The girls were told they'd grow up to be streetwalkers. We boys were told we'd be dead or in jail by the time we were twenty-one. Some of the kids were abused; sexually and verbally.

"When we were little I remember a lot of drugs around town. It seemed like they were hanging off the trees and free for the taking. I, luckily, got sick the first time I tried them and didn't go near them again. Most of my other friends did not. Funny, how when they started out there was plenty to go around. Once they got hooked, the supply kind of dried up. Oh, don't get me wrong, it's still available—but it costs money now. Go figure. My friends lived in shacks, with maybe three or four people sleeping in one room. They didn't have money, but they were hooked. The things they'd do to get their stash. It wasn't very pretty.

"There was no money and no grade point averages for college. We had no trade or skills, so we couldn't get jobs. The jobs we could get were menial and grossly underpaid. So, we hung out. We did what was expected of us—we became useless alcoholics, drug abusers, petty thieves or bona fide criminals. We just lived up to their expectations."

Johnny took a break and sipped his wine, still not ready to meet Jesse's gaze. After a few deep breaths he carried on. For the first time, he was bearing his soul, so he figured he might as well tell her everything. "My grandfather told me to be proud of who I am. How can I be proud of a race of people who trusted the white man and believed their lies, or were murdered if they didn't? Of a race who crawled into a bottle and drowned in their own tears? The church calls us heathens. Derides us and outlaws our simple beliefs. My grandfather used to tell me the old stories. They were beautiful and full of meaning—to him, not me. No horse was gonna' save me. No buffalo was left to teach and provide for me. The stars in the sky could only teach me how small and insignificant I really am. The medicine never worked as far as I could see. If it worked so well, why did so many die? And if we refuse to stand by and let our children die of starvation, our women be abused and our homes be moved whenever the government finds another ore under our dry and dusty land—we pay and pay. And more history books are written to tell how bad we were. After all, we did kill that damned fool Custer. Of course, the *great white chief* wanted that to happen, so he set it up for us to take the blame. *We* had to pay for somebody's political aspirations. Those books never mention the thousands and thousands of innocent Indians who were killed just because they were in the way." Johnny emptied his glass. Jesse drank with him, riveted by his words. He now took the chance and looked into her eyes. They were glistening with tears. He smiled at her cautiously.

"But, then, just when my hatred was so strong for the white man that I could have spat fire and bashed some heads," Johnny concluded, "you, a white city girl, moves in and takes over my house. You didn't hate me, even though I did my best to make you. You were kind to me and offered me lemonade." Jesse looked at him, bewildered. "You trusted me alone with you. You even lent me your truck. Nobody does that, Jess," Johnny sighed, starting to get used to the wine. "Didn't they warn you about me? And don't be nice, 'cos I'm sure they did."

"Sure they did," Jesse smiled. "But I'm a sucker for turquoise eyes."

"Turquoise?" Johnny stuttered. "They're blue, like everybody else with blue eyes. I've got some white blood myself, you know."

"I know," Jesse said, pouring some more wine for both of them.

"Which is another problem," Johnny shot out. "You shouldn't look at me the way you do. That's really dangerous."

"Hey," Jesse defended herself, "turn about's fair play!"

"You should look at Eric that way," Johnny sighed. "He wishes you would and I was hoping you would. He can take care of you. He can give you everything you need and want. I don't have a job, Jess. I don't have a place to live. I'm not good enough. I can barely take care of myself, let alone take care of you."

"From what I've heard," Jesse said, getting up, "you've done an excellent job so far." She peeked out the front door. Cheyenne was now gone from the porch. Jesse went into the kitchen for some food. "I'm still healthy and the wolves are doing well. There's no bears hanging out and I have yet to see a mountain lion. The house is holding out the rain and we're warm and dry. We've got a fire and food. What more could a girl want?" They had forgotten about dinner—she grabbed chunks of cheese, ham and cold roast beef. She brought it all back with some home made bread from Arleen's store and plopped it down on the coffee table in front of them.

"I'm a poor Indian," Johnny rambled on. "There are racists up here who hate me. You got a taste of it the other day in town when those creeps tried to get to Shadow. You'd be branded a squaw in a heartbeat. That's why our friendship has to be kept secret." He dug into the food and ate hungrily, stuffing cheese and meat down like he hadn't eaten in days. Jesse was just as voracious. "They throw me in jail for the pettiest stuff. When Clayton isn't around, I'm treated pretty rough. I wouldn't want that for you. I'm uneducated and broke. Somehow I slipped by the drugs and I'm not an alcoholic, but I have nothing. I am nothing. I'm an outcast in my own world and the one outside the reservation borders. Like they say, I'm no good."

"Do you know what I see when I look at you?" putting her sandwich down, Jesse questioned the Native American. With his mouth full of food, Johnny shook his head no. She sat back and looked into his eyes. They were bright and full of interest. "I see a brave warrior," she murmured seriously. "When I read my books, of which I have many, and I picture Sitting Bull or Crazy Horse as young men, I see you. You believe in yourself, whether you know it or not. The wolves recognize it. They see your strength and your kindness. When I saw you outside tonight with Cheyenne by your side, I knew you were a good man. That wolf, of all my wolves, can tell the difference."

Johnny was surprised by her comment. It took him a second or two to swallow his food. "You think of me as an Indian warrior?" he asked in amazement.

Jesse smiled warmly. "Honey, if you ever rode up here on a horse with no shirt on and an eagle feather in that black hair, I'd swoon."

Johnny smiled that mischievous smile that Jesse adored. "Well, then," he declared, "maybe I'll just have to surprise you some evening…"

"Don't you dare!" Jesse laughed. Somewhat embarrassed, she turned her attention back to her sandwich and, aware that she really didn't need it, another sip of her wine.

They finished their meal and Johnny put everything away. Jesse couldn't help but giggle as he juggled the food and the empty bottles and still managed to hold up the oversized pants he was wearing. Jesse was falling hard for this man. She was having a difficult time thinking clearly because her head was starting to swim from all the wine. The Native American cleaned up the kitchen and then went into the storage room. When he came back he was fully dressed in his own clothes.

Jesse had lain down on the couch, snuggled under the covers. She was a little disappointed when she opened her eyes and saw Johnny, with his boots on, putting another log on the fire. Kitten mewed in her sleep and shifted ever so slightly to keep out of Johnny's way. He was pleasantly surprised when the bobcat actually let him pet her. He looked up, disbelievingly, into Jesse's eyes as she watched him from the couch. She smiled back.

"See," she murmured sleepily, "I was right. You are a good man."

Johnny rose up and walked over to the couch. "I should probably get going," he said quietly. "That rain doesn't sound like it's going to let up."

Jesse started to get up off the couch, but Johnny motioned for her to stay put. She defied his order and got up anyway, wrapping the blanket around herself to keep warm.

"That log should get you through the night," Johnny continued. "But keep one going for the next few days. I wouldn't be surprised if we see snow real soon."

Jesse, the blanket brushing the floor behind her as she walked, followed him to the door. She knew he had to leave, even though she didn't want him to. She had to let him go—for their own good. She said nothing as he prepared to depart.

Johnny opened the door to the cabin, the wind and rain still pounding on the other side of the porch. He stopped and listened into the night. "I can hear the wolves, can you?" he asked with a curious smile.

Jesse listened for a moment. "Yeah, that's Cheyenne. She's calling her men home." They listened together for a few minutes. "There," she finally whispered. "That's Shadow calling back." And a few seconds later, "there's Mesa. They're on their way."

"This is a good place to be," Johnny noted sadly. "Especially on a night like this." He looked down at her and dwelled on her golden eyes. "It's a good home, Jesse. I'm happy you're here."

Jesse reached up with her right hand and smoothed the hair on the side of his face. His hair was now dry from the warmth of the fire. It seemed shinier and black as coal. With both hands she pulled the collar of his jacket up around his neck. The blanket slipped off her shoulders and fell to the floor. She looked at him as though she was memorizing every line on his face. He did not look away but returned her gaze intently.

"I wish," she whispered, "we didn't owe so much to so many people."

"I wish," he murmured, "we were strong enough to say it just doesn't matter."

With her arms up already, she encircled them around his neck and drew him very close. "Stay with me tonight," she whispered into his ear. "I don't want to be alone."

He slipped his arms around her waist and held her very tightly. "That would probably not be good," he whispered back. "I can't get that Indian warrior idea out of my head."

She laughed and collapsed against him, letting him hold her up. "I don't need a warrior tonight," she finally sighed. "I just need my friend."

Suddenly, there was the sound of paws clamoring up the porch steps and in through the screen came three, not so wet—for their guard hairs shed most of the water—very hungry wolves. Shadow came in first, performing a quick sidestep to avoid colliding with his humans, who were unceremoniously standing in a huddle in front of him. Mesa followed Shadow, and after a brief pause to peruse the situation inside the cabin, Cheyenne came in also.

Smiling broadly, Johnny looked out into the weather one more time, sighed and with an arm still around Jesse's waist maneuvered them to the side so he could shut the door. "You're in for the night, kids," he announced, locking the door. "You were out past curfew, anyway."

Kitten raised her head sharply at the intrusion. Her investigation of the arrivals complete, she stood up stretched and repositioned herself out of harm's way under a chair. There she curled up and dozed off again.

"Can you get that bag of meat out of the refrigerator?" Jesse asked Johnny, who was already heading into the kitchen. Shadow was jumping up on her and wagging his tail. His tongue slobbered her with kisses. The wolf was now almost as tall as she was when he stood up on his hind legs. "That's my good boy," Jesse murmured, coercing him back into the kitchen. Cheyenne stood very close to Johnny as he dished up their food, and Mesa visited with wolves and humans alike as he wiggled in and out between the kitchen table and chairs.

Johnny put the food bowls down on the floor in seconds. Cheyenne got her dish first. Before the other wolves had time to get over to her stash, the young man had the other bowls down to placate them. Jesse served up the water dishes and within seconds the flurry had died down into the contented sound of chewing.

"Well," Johnny announced, satisfied the brood was happy, "that was exciting."

"I'm working at getting them to sit at the table and use knives and forks," Jesse smiled, helping Johnny take off his jacket. "But that opposable thumb thing keeps getting in the way."

Johnny just rolled his eyes. "How about some hot chocolate?" Without waiting for an answer he put a pot on the stove and grabbed the milk out of the refrigerator.

Jesse was going to say something like *wow, déjà vu,* but decided against it. Johnny sounded eerily like his father and she was sure he would not want to hear that.

"Dad says you make the best in the county," Johnny offered, noticing her silence. "I'd hate to think he gets special treatment around here."

Jesse stalked back into the kitchen and gently butted him away from the stove. "Special treatment, my ass," she quipped, tending to the task at hand. Johnny stood behind her for a while, smelling the perfume in her hair. She leaned, ever so slightly, back against him.

"You're sure you want me here?" he murmured into her ear. "Really, I can go if you want."

"I want you..." Jesse said lazily as she stirred the milk. Something else was stirring inside her also, but she was determined to keep her cool. "...to get the mugs out of the cupboard. There's nothing worse than burned milk."

A little while later they sat back down with their mugs of hot chocolate and a big black wolf spread out between them on the couch. Shadow resorted to licking his paws and giving himself a quick cleanup when his mother refused to give up her drink. Mesa curled up in front of the fireplace and Cheyenne settled down at Johnny's feet. Johnny searched the television channels with the remote, found an old western and settled in with Shadow's rump just about in his lap. Jesse thought how wonderful it all was. Her animals were home and safe and her favorite person seemed quite pleased to be a part of it.

It did not take long for the warm milk to take affect and soon Jesse was yawning and finding it difficult to stay awake. Shadow was already asleep with his head solidly on her lap, so she maneuvered herself carefully underneath him and rested her own head against Johnny's shoulder.

Johnny tried valiantly to keep watch, but soon he was nodding off, himself. Before it was too late, he eased Shadow off the couch and picked Jesse up into his arms. Shadow peered up at him with sleepy eyes. "It's all right, Shadow," he whispered. "It's time to put mother to bed." Jesse was a slip of a thing and Johnny had no trouble carrying her up the stairs to the bedroom. He knew the room well enough, but he was still relieved when he put her onto the bed without stubbing his toe on some new piece of furniture he did not know about. He lit the candles in the fireplace with the help of Shadow, who was now licking his face while Johnny was down at his level.

The young man slipped Jesse's shoes off, but stopped there. He put the covers over her and tucked her in. Shadow jumped up on the end of the bed. Johnny sat down on the side and brushed Jesse's hair away from her face with his fingers. When he started to get up off the bed, the woman's hand reached out and took hold of his shirt.

"Don't go," Jesse murmured, still asleep. "I'm cold." She turned on her side facing away from him, but held onto his shirt. He lay down next to her and put his arm around her, holding her close. He rested his head on her long, brown hair that trailed across the pillow. Shadow stretched out and lay across his feet.

He had every intention of sleeping on the couch downstairs, but the fatigue of the past several days was quickly overwhelming him. The candlelit room cast gentle shadows on the walls and ceilings. The rain fell steadily on the metal roof above their heads. Cheyenne and Mesa had ventured upstairs too. With Cheyenne on the floor next to Johnny and Mesa curled up in front of the candles on the hand-loomed rug, soon the warrior, the city girl and the rest of the household were fast asleep.

CHAPTER 21

Jesse woke up gradually. The sun was filtering through the windows and eased her gently from a restful sleep. She couldn't even recall if she had any dreams. All she remembered was how wonderful it was to have Johnny holding her. She turned slowly, sadly realizing in the light of day that she might have dreamt that happening, because she knew instinctively there was no one lying beside her now. She touched the side of the bed where he had lain and was comforted by the wrinkles in the blankets, which proved some one had been there for at least a little while. Jesse also noted, once she rubbed the sleep from her eyes, that there were no wolves in the room either. She appeared to be quite alone.

But all was not lost. There was something definitely different about this particular morning. Besides the shining sun, which she had not seen for days, there was the unmistakable aroma of something cooking. The smell of bacon and coffee wafted up the stairs and into the room. Perhaps, upon closer inspection, she was not alone after all. She got up from the bed and smiled. There on the chair next to the fireplace was Johnny's shirt. The shirt he had worn last night. She picked it up and held it close to her face. She could still smell his masculine scent. She slipped off her t-shirt and put his on. She couldn't help it. She wanted him close.

In her big, woolen socks she padded downstairs and saw a beautiful sight. The front door was open and Kitten was chasing a mouse just beyond the porch steps. In the kitchen, Jesse's handsome Indian was cooking breakfast, surrounded by three interested wolves who sat at attention around him, hanging on to every whisper he uttered to them.

"There, now," he was saying quietly, "we're almost done. You can have whatever your mother doesn't eat, okay? Because you've been good, you'll get your treat after she gets up." He reached up into the cupboard for some plates. Jesse's senses reeled in her head. He was, of course, not wearing his shirt, she was. The sight of him took her breath away.

She tiptoed into the room, unnoticed by its preoccupied inhabitants. Johnny gave each animal a strip of bacon. Their combined weight pressed the man's body into the edge of the stove. He did not seem to mind it at all.

There was an inch of space between the rears of Cheyenne and Mesa. Shadow, at Johnny's side, looked up and gave his mother a toothy smile, complete with a slight wag of his tail. Jesse edged a little closer from behind and wrapped her arms around the cook, pressing her head against his back.

"There's our sleeping beauty," Johnny replied, unfazed at her sudden arrival. "Two more minutes and *you* would have been getting the leftovers."

"It all smells delicious," Jesse smiled. "Thank you."

"Why don't you grab the coffee," he suggested, slipping the butter-drenched eggs onto the plates, "and meet us out back. I dried off the table and chairs. I thought it would be nice to eat outside."

"Sounds perfect to me," Jesse agreed, grabbing the mugs and the coffee pot. The wolves could not decide whether to join her or not. "Come on, kids," she persuaded them. "Let's go outside!"

Mesa and Shadow reluctantly followed her, knowing well who had the food. Cheyenne stayed with Johnny, waiting for his next move. Outside, the sun was high enough in the sky for its rays to filter down over the table. It dawned on Jesse she must have slept for quite a long time. She wondered how late in the day it actually was. The table was covered with a tablecloth, and in the center was a mason jar filled with wildflowers, which were perking up now that the sun had reached them. There were napkins and silverware. She sat down in one of the chairs and stretched her shoulders back. The air felt crisp and clean.

"I took a shower," Johnny said, carrying two plates heaped with bacon, eggs and toast onto the patio. Cheyenne followed behind him. "I hope you don't mind."

"I hope you don't mind that I haven't yet," Jesse apologized, her mouth starting to water. The food looked inviting, but so did his beautiful, brown, perfectly chiseled chest.

"As good as you look in my shirt, I'm not going to complain." He set his plate on the table and brought hers around to her side. He bent over her, bracing himself with his hands on either side of the arms of her chair. His smile was roguish. His hair, now dark brown in the sunlight, hung down, framing his face.

"I like your shirt on me too," she breathed. "Now, where the hell did I put that horse?" The way he was looking at her made her feel weak. She thanked the heavens above she was sitting down.

He leaned in close until their lips were just inches apart. "You still want me around then?"

Jesse's body ached to hold him. Her self-control was receding fast and her animal instincts were growing stronger by the second. "Cheyenne would be very unhappy without you," she muttered. "Her vote counts the most."

"That's a positive answer, I guess," Johnny stood his ground. "But what about Cheyenne's mother? How does she feel about it?"

"I told you last night," Jesse defended herself, afraid to say the words again. She did not want to appear weak in front of this rock hard pillar of a man bearing down on her.

"Tell me again," he demanded, "or I'll give your breakfast to the wolves."

"You wouldn't dare!" she asserted gingerly. She attempted to give him an evil stare. She knew it was useless under the pressure of the gaze he had leveled upon her.

"Wouldn't I?" Johnny reached over to take the plate away from her. Jesse's hand shot out to protect it. She touched the top of his hand, but in an instant his hand turned and captured hers instead. He pulled her up in one swift motion and held her tight against his body with her hand clasped in his behind her back. Other than a cockeyed stare from Shadow, the collision of these two different souls went unnoticed by the rest of the world. To Jesse, the moment was perfect.

"Okay," Johnny breathed heavily, "you can have your breakfast." Gently, he let her loose from his grasp, but she did not let go of his hand. He wanted to kiss her desperately, but they were friends, not lovers. Unsure what to do, he brought her hand to his lips and kissed it tenderly, instead. Jesse blushed. "And if you want it, you can have my breakfast, too," he conceded.

"Sit down and eat," Jesse laughed, letting him go as she collapsed into her chair. "Someday you may need all the strength you can muster." She was glad to see she wasn't the only one thrown by what had just happened. Johnny was a little shaky as he too sat down. Jesse picked up her fork and prepared to eat. She could not believe this handsome man, sitting across from her at the table, was actually going to be a part of her life. She was excited at the prospect. "After all," she teased a little more, "at your age, too much excitement may prove to be detrimental to your health."

Johnny's eyes traveled slowly from the bite of food he was about to take to Jesse, who was looking at him slyly. He gobbled down the morsel of egg and a piece of the bacon, and again he was up and out of his seat.

Jesse let out a yelp and got up too, running as fast as she could. The wolves studied the humans' antics, but were not particularly impressed. Jesse was easy prey. Johnny had a hold of her in seconds. She held onto him tightly when he picked her up and spun her around in his arms. They fell to the ground, laughing, and he tickled her unmercifully.

It was Kitten who took advantage of the humans' playtime. She had snuck around the house and watched as Johnny and Jesse rolled around out on the wet ground. She was on the table in a shot and before either of them noticed, she had eaten everything on Johnny's plate. By the time they got back on their feet, Jesse's plate was empty as well. The bobcat had pushed the flowers off the table and was now the centerpiece, giving herself a quick clean up with her tongue and front paws. Defeated, Johnny returned to the kitchen and Jesse took a shower. Afterward, they shared a quiet breakfast for two in the house, leaving the backyard to the animals.

"So," Johnny, finally satiated, wondered aloud, "what are your plans for the day?"

"What's left of it?" Jesse asked, recalling she had no clue what time it was.

"It's two o'clock," Johnny announced, looking at his watch. "You slept in, remember?"

"I promised Arleen I'd come into town sometime today," she said, sopping up the rest of the eggs with a last bit of toast. "She procured some horse meat for the wolves. You want to come with me?"

"Well," Johnny pondered the invitation for a moment. "As I don't have any pressing appointments today, I could probably tag along."

"Fabulous," Jesse smiled. "Don't let me forget. We'll need more bacon and eggs."

On the road to town, the pair laughed and teased each other, enjoying each other's company. Johnny filled Jesse in on the history of Joe's cabin and a few of the other homesteads they passed, recollecting past run-ins with some of her neighbors for whom he had done some carpentry. He also seemed to know the history of the general area and the surrounding landmarks. Jesse was impressed.

Once in town, they met with a typical afternoon. A beat up truck was parked in front of the Ranger Bar. The local mechanic was taking his time fixing a tourist's flat tire. Jack's old dog ambled across the street to greet Johnny and Jesse as they got out of the truck. There wasn't another soul on the street.

"Well, customers at last," Arleen greeted the pair at the door. "Man, I don't think a car has passed through this way for at least four hours. That storm last night must have scared everybody off."

"I slept in a little late," Jesse apologized as Arleen ushered them inside her general store. "Otherwise we would have been here earlier."

"No matter," Arleen said. "Hey, Johnny. What's up?"

"Same as always," Johnny answered, following Jesse. "Nothing but that big Montana sky."

"I got a ton of horse meat," Arleen noted. "Old man Aikens lost two." Arleen headed toward the cooler in the back. "Johnny, come give me a hand, will ya?"

"Sure," Johnny acquiesced. "You got any bacon back there?"

Jesse strolled down the aisles, picking up some other things she needed.

"Yeah, I think I got a slab or two." Arleen opened the heavy latch and heaved open the freezer door. "Are we upgrading the wolves' menu?"

"That darn bobcat eats everything that's not locked down," Johnny retorted.

Arleen laughed. "Go figure." She started to lift the packages of meat and groaned. They were very heavy.

"Hey," Johnny interjected, stepping in, "I got it. Jesus! Is the head in here, too?"

"Just old, tired, chopped up bodies." She stepped outside the cooler and grabbed a couple of boxes. "Here. Put some of them in here and I'll get that bacon."

"That's the mother lode," Jesse called out as Johnny staggered past her with the first box.

"And this is just the bacon," he teased her, shifting the weight on his arms. Jesse hurried to the door and opened it for him. "Do you ever wonder if the kids are worth all this? They could catch one themselves and leave us out of the mix, you know."

"And we'd all be dodging bullets from here to Colorado," said Jesse, holding the door open for Arleen who passed by with another box.

"We might all have to move to Colorado," Arleen called out, "if business doesn't pick up pretty soon." She handed the second box to Johnny who heaved it into the bed of the truck. "My numbers are way down this month."

Johnny shot the woman a concerned look. She smiled weakly and gave him a pat on the back as they strolled back into the store. "Actually, though," Arleen continued, "I've been mulling a couple of ideas around in my head. And it's funny you should happen to come into town today, Johnny, 'cos one of the ideas I had involves you."

"I didn't do it," Johnny said quickly. "Whatever it was."

"You're funny," Arleen quipped. "No, really. Come inside and we'll talk."

Jesse decided to look for a few more things before coming up to the counter. She listened intently to the conversation, just the same.

"I've been noticing that the other stores in the other towns have really been fixed up. You know, they look like old fashioned general stores and they've got collectibles and stuff as well as groceries and the occasional wolf chow." Arleen sat down on her chair behind the counter. Johnny toyed with the display of cheap pocketknives on the counter as she talked. "Have you seen the place in Lavina? It's a show place—and you could eat off the floor in the grocery section. Anyway, I thought I'd start simple—maybe a new coat of paint and some new light fixtures." She shifted in her seat. "And you know those rockers you made for the porch at the cabin? I was hoping I could talk you into making a couple for me, and also a wagon wheel table to sit outside. I'll pay for the materials and your labor. Richard's sending me some extra money. Maybe you could make a few extra chairs and I could sell them on consignment for you. I think they'd sell pretty quick, don't you?"

"They're just rocking chairs," Johnny dismissed Arleen's praise. "Are you sure you want them?" He cast a sidelong, questioning look over at Jesse. With raised eyebrows she just shrugged, leaving the decision up to him.

"If Clayton can fall asleep in one, anybody can," Arleen reasoned. "They're great chairs, Johnny. How long do you think it would take?"

"Ummm," Johnny tried to think, "a couple of weeks, I guess."

"And do you think you could help me with the lights and stuff?" Arleen went on. "I really could use it."

"I…" Johnny started.

"Come on," Arleen cut him off. "I've been to the cabin. I've seen your work. It's a job—for money. And you'll save *my* butt. General contractors cost a fortune up here."

Jesse came up to the counter and piled it up with the stuff she was going to buy. She smiled at Johnny, who looked rather perplexed, but said nothing.

"Well…" he mused, thinking about it a little more, "I'd have to get the wood, which is no problem. I'd need a place to work…"

"Why not use the back room of the cabin?" Jesse offered unassumingly. "I haven't really decided what to do with it yet and there's plenty of light in there. My computer won't be in the way, will it?"

"No…" Johnny replied, still thinking. "Actually, that would be a great place to work." He looked quizzically into Jesse's eyes. He could plainly see she was not going to offer as much as a hint as to what he should do. But he could tell she was intrigued by the prospect. He had to admit, so was he. "Sure, why not. I guess I can help you out."

"You're a saint," Arleen was grinning ear to ear. "How soon can you start?"

"Aaaah," he looked at Jesse again, this time pleading for help with his eyes.

"Can we pick up the wood today?" Jesse asked him, pulling out her wallet as Arleen rang up her purchases.

"I guess so," Johnny said. "I've got a stash over at Red Cloud's. My tools are over there too."

"Then is tomorrow too early for you?" Jesse turned back to Arleen.

"Perfect," Arleen sang out. "That'll be $57.37—with your discount, of course."

"You're the saint," Jesse laughed, paying the woman in cash. Johnny grabbed the goods and started for the door. "We'll be in touch. Stop by for a drink if you get a minute."

"I just might surprise you," Arleen called back. After Johnny had stepped outside, she added, "That'll be okay, right?"

"Anytime," Jesse laughed. "We're just friends!"

"Yeah, right," Arleen retorted. "I'll stop by during daylight hours, just in case."

"Good Lord, will you guys ever give me a break?" Jesse snickered, stepping outside. "We'll see you soon, Arleen."

"Red Cloud won't mind if I'm with you?" Jesse asked as Johnny turned the truck onto a rugged dirt road.

"He'll pay more attention to the truck than he will to you, Jess," Johnny said, steering the vehicle over and around the ruts in the road. "He's kind of a crazy old guy. Good man, though. He can't see worth a shit, but he knows a lot."

"Is he a Medicine Man?" Jesse asked curiously.

"Don't know about that," Johnny remarked. "A lot of people on the res say so. I, for the most part, don't believe in that sort of stuff. But, like I said, he's pretty smart with a lot of things. Kind of knows what you're thinking before you think it." He eased the truck over a cattle guard and into a junk filled yard.

In the midst of cords of wood, old car parts and other rusted out machinery, Jesse saw a beat up old shack with one of Johnny's rocking chairs perched just outside of the front door. Out back, behind the shack, she could see a fairly large barn, which was in a lot better shape than any other structure on the property.

"Tell me he lives in the barn," Jesse pleaded. "That shack looks like it's about to collapse."

"Sorry," Johnny snickered, driving the truck around the side of the house up to the barn door where he stopped and got out. "He only lets me work on the barn. Says there's nothing wrong with his house." He walked around to the passenger side and opened the door for Jesse. "He likes that *lived in* look," he whispered into Jesse's ear as he helped her out.

"Maybe he just doesn't trust you in his house," Jesse suggested.

"What?" Johnny asked, perplexed.

"Well, I seem to remember something about a truck," Jesse recalled. She stopped short and prevented Johnny from shutting the truck door. She reached up and got a small bag out of the glove compartment, then stuffed it in her jeans pocket.

"Oh, that," Johnny conceded, a bit embarrassed that she remembered the row he and his father had had the first night he met her. "It's that one over there." He pointed to a beat up old Chevy pick-up with two flat tires and the windshield missing. The driver's side door was hanging precariously from only one hinge. There was a chicken roosting in the front seat. "It's a beauty, isn't it?"

Jesse was about to make a wisecrack but was startled instead by a voice that came from behind them.

"Whoever the hell you are, you better have a reason to be on this property!" A very old Indian, with white, braided hair, faded jeans and a torn shirt stood at the back door of the shack with a rifle propped in his hands, ready to shoot. Red Cloud squinted out at the intruders by his barn trying desperately to see who had invaded his territory. His face was a maze of contorted wrinkles and his hands shook as he held his weapon.

"Shit!" Johnny muttered, half under his breath. "He's never seen your truck." He turned slowly with his hands in the air. "Red Cloud, it's Johnny Stillwater. I forgot, man. I got my woman's truck."

"Johnny? Is it you?" Red Cloud squinted harder and took a step closer. "What woman? What kind of truck is that?"

"Told you," Johnny said out of the side of his mouth. "This is a Dodge right?"

"Right," Jesse whispered back. "What's this about your woman?"

"Easier to explain than, *this is my white girl friend who moved here from Denver to raise wolves,* don't you think?"

"Good point," Jesse acquiesced, keeping her hands out so the older Indian could see them.

"Yeah, Red," Johnny called out, taking a few steps in front of Jesse to shield her in case there was a problem. "It's a new Dodge Ram Pick-up. You ought to see it up close. As for my woman, her name is Jesse."

"You scared the bejeezus out of me, boy," Red Cloud yelled, now recognizing the man's voice. He put the gun down to his side and hobbled toward them. "You know nobody messes with my barn."

"Yes, sir," Johnny agreed wholeheartedly. "I wasn't thinking."

"Thinkin' *more* about the young lady, you mean," Red Cloud snickered. Johnny walked toward the old man and closed the distance between them so Red Cloud could see his face.

"Now, Red," Johnny cautioned. He put his arm around the feeble old man and let the Indian lean against him as they walked. "It's all relative, isn't it?"

"Don't know about that, but I do know that's a fine truck!" Red Cloud exclaimed once he got close. He ran his thin, bony fingers gently across the side panel, checking the vehicle out. "New one, too. Bet that cost a pretty penny." He opened the passenger side door and looked inside. "Great day in the morning! Does all this stuff work?" He did not wait for an answer. He crawled up into the passenger seat and got comfortable. "Now, this is a nice ride!"

"Why don't you take him for a spin, Johnny?" Jesse suggested in a low voice. "Once around the property, maybe?"

"You think so?" Johnny considered his friend's offer. When she nodded her assent, he smiled. "Okay. We'll be right back." He squeezed her hand quickly and trotted around the front of the truck. "Buckle up, Red. Let's take a spin."

"Aho," the Native American smiled. "This day just keeps getting better." Jesse walked up to the truck and shut him in, closing the passenger side door. "And this is the pretty girl who gives me this opportunity. Aho, to you, too."

"Have fun you two," Jesse smiled. "Do I need to stay any place special while you're gone?"

"You go anywhere you want," Red Cloud yelled as Johnny revved the motor. "You are welcome here." The Indian was beaming with excitement. "Oh, the dog might sniff you out. Don't worry, he has a good spirit."

"Red," Jesse heard Johnny say, "you ought to see what she lives with—she can handle Rex." Johnny sped off, kicking up a dust cloud, turned in a big circle and headed up the road. Red Cloud's head was bobbing up and down like a rag doll and his arm was waving out the window as Johnny began to give him the ride of his life.

Jesse watched the cloud of dust until it settled little by little back into the ground. For the moment, she had plenty of time to look around the place. At first glance it was quite depressing. The shack the old Indian lived in was literally falling down. There were holes in the roof and a broken window with rags that were probably, at one time, curtains waving like tattered flags through the shards of glass. She meandered around the junk and remnants of what used to be machinery, now rusted and in pieces strewn about the land. She decided to stroll back to the barn. That was the only structure that seemed sturdy enough to withstand the slightest breeze.

She pondered the new door with its shiny latches and heavy-duty lock. That, she could tell, was Johnny's work. She felt proud of her carpenter. His touch was evident all over the building. He had really fixed it up. She was about to open the latch and see what was inside when she heard a shuffle and a low moan-like growl come from behind her. When she turned, there was an old dog, too old and too tired to put much effort into barking, slowly coming from the house to scrutinize the stranger.

Jesse stooped down to one knee and put her hand out. "Hey, Rex," she murmured. "I'm Jesse." The dog approached her warily. "That's a good, old boy. Come out of the sun, baby. It looks like you should lie down." The dog walked with a determined, yet rickety gait up to her. He sniffed her hand and looked her over with large droopy eyes. He fell over rather than lay down at her side and allowed her to pet him. She sat down next to him in the dirt and let him rest his head on her leg. "Why don't we just sit here 'til your dad gets back, okay boy?" Jesse's voice was soothing. "You just go back to sleep." That would be the safest course of action, Jesse decided. This place was an accident waiting to happen and there was no need for her to go looking for one. Jesse couldn't help but wonder, with all the rain that had fallen in the past few days and nights, how this land could still be so dry. She also wondered why people were forced to live like this—in filth and poverty. Jesse was damn lucky to have what she had. It was heartbreaking to think that people like Red Cloud and many others on the reservation had so little. No wonder Johnny was angry. Now she was feeling some of that anger herself. She leaned back against the barn door, stroking the old dog's mangled fur, and waited patiently for the men to return.

Soon the roar of the Ram's engine could be heard in the distance and the cloud of dust appeared just on the other side of the hill. Johnny sped back to the barn and locked the brakes, causing the truck to spin to the side with the passenger's side facing the barn as it came to a stop. Red Cloud was whooping and hollering like a kid on a roller coaster. The exhilaration and excitement he felt from the ride was plainly evident by the wide grin across his wrinkled face and the delight in his eyes.

"This is the best truck ever!" he called to Jesse, gazing down at her and the dog from his window high in the cab of the truck. Rex looked up fondly at his owner, but did not bother to get up. "Wanna' trade?"

"How about free rides whenever you need one?" Jesse returned the old man's smile. She got up carefully, trying not to disturb the dog. When the dog lost his lap-headrest, he just shifted his head to his front paws, only casually interested in the goings on. "That way you won't have to disturb your chickens."

Johnny came around from the other side of the truck and opened the passenger side door. He helped the old man out of the vehicle. "Come on, Red," Johnny laughed. "If we're not careful, he'll move himself right in," he added to Jesse.

Once out of the truck, it took a moment for the Native American to get his footing back. "Progress is a wonderful thing...sometimes. That pickup is proof positive."

"I'm glad you enjoyed it!" Jesse offered to help the old man, but he refused it. He motioned for her to follow him to the house. Jesse looked at Johnny for reassurance and the young man gave her a quick wink.

"Now, get your tools and whatever wood you can use, Johnny," Red Cloud continued. "I want to spend a few minutes with your lady friend." He stopped and turned, with effort, on his heel. "Bring that dog with ya', when you're done, okay? The darn thing's so old, he might lose his way back to the house." Jesse stepped in line behind the old man, slowly following his lead. "Yep, if I had a truck like that, I could rule the world!" Red Cloud bantered on. "And it's got heat and cold air or whatever you want. They call that climate control, don't they?"

Jesse nodded, while Johnny let himself into the barn. She realized, after seeing the two of them together, that they were pretty close friends. This was a far different theory from the one she made up after Charlie and Johnny's argument on the first night they met.

"I got a fan in the house," Red Cloud was talking on. "That's like climate control. You come on in and we'll have a talk." He finally reached the steps up to the back door. This time he accepted Jesse's help as he climbed them. She also opened the door for him.

"The boy says you're from the city," Red Cloud said as he passed her and went inside. "How's the country so far?"

"So far, so good," Jesse offered, looking around. For as filthy as the place was on the outside, the inside was surprisingly neat. There was one main room with a kitchenette and a bathroom off to the side. One of Johnny's rockers, well worn, was perched in front of a little black and white television set. The other furniture, which included an old couch, another chair, a table and an old single bed were all placed conveniently close together. There were clean Indian blankets on the furniture. The bed was covered and a furry one on the floor caught Jesse's eye. There were some handmade drums; a turtle shell rattle; and an assortment of herbs in a basket, which stood in the corner of the room.

"Had to close off the other room," Red Cloud stated, settling into his rocker and getting his pipe. "Broke a window. Haven't had the time to get it fixed. I like it better this way, I think."

"Very handy and organized," Jesse noted, taking a seat in the other chair. "But when winter comes, that broken window could be hard on Rex's bones. How about if I ask Johnny to fix that up for you? You can still keep everything just like it is."

"That's a good idea," the Native American agreed, searching for his tobacco in his basket.

"Oh," Jesse blurted, getting up. "I forgot. I brought you something." She searched in her jeans pocket and came up with the baggie from the glove compartment. It contained tobacco. "I hope you'll accept it." She handed the bag to the old man who, after eyeing it with a glint of surprise, accepted it willingly.

"Aho," Red Cloud said gleefully. "You are a good daughter." He opened the bag of Corsair Tobacco and inhaled the aroma for a moment before quickly stuffing some into his pipe. "You know our ways?"

"I just read that it is customary to bring a gift to a medicine man," Jesse proposed. "I've been carrying this around since I got here. And you're the first one I've met."

"There is *Red* blood in your veins. I can see it," The Native American's eyes studied her closely. "And it pleases me to accept your gift, daughter. Now, what would you like in return?"

"Ah..." Jesse stammered, "...nothing. I just thought it was protocol."

"A lady with no needs," Red Cloud smiled. "A good catch." He lit his pipe, filled with his new tobacco, and inhaled a couple of puffs. Rex halfheartedly scratched at the door. When Red Cloud nodded his consent, Jesse got up and let the dog in. She glanced out to the barn and saw Johnny loading up the truck. He gave her the thumbs up before he headed back for more wood. The old dog took his time coming in the house, sniffed Jesse as he passed by and let Red Cloud give him a pat on the head before he found his blanket and lay down.

"The boy tells me you came here to raise wolves," Red Cloud stated in between puffs of his pipe. He also leaned over and lit a tiny bundle of sage and other herbs while Jesse returned to her chair.

"I started with one," Jesse commented, watching the old man with interest. She thought it funny how he called Johnny *the boy*. "Now I have three."

"You are happy with your decision to come here."

"I'd be lying if I didn't say I had any doubts," Jesse sighed. "But Shadow is happy and healthy—and so are Cheyenne, Mesa and Kitten. That makes it all worthwhile."

"For them, yes. But for you." The Native American was persistent. "Your decision to come here was right."

Jesse looked at the man quizzically. He was not asking her a question. "I don't know yet. As they say, *the jury's still out*. I've got to get through winter, I guess." The smell of the burning herbs was pleasant. She felt a bit lightheaded. "Joseph says I probably won't make it. I'll give up or freeze to death trying to stick it out."

"Joseph does not know everything," Red Cloud smiled perceptively. "You'll make it through the winter. You'll be just fine." He puffed again on his pipe and rested back in his rocker, rocking ever so slightly back and forth. The smoke from the burning herbs as well as from the pipe filled the room. "Like I said. Your decision was right." He murmured some words Jesse could not understand. He was speaking in his native tongue, which sounded beautiful but made no sense to her.

"It is time to trust your heart and your instincts," the Indian finally said in English. "You must stop listening to those who do not know you or your heart's desire. Your heart called you here and now you have found it. The boy will watch over you. You are safe. There will be trials and some days will not be easy. But you made the right decision. You will suffer loss, but great happiness also. Your children will carry this desire too. They will make you proud."

"I don't have any…" Jesse started to say, but the Indian cut her off.

"Some day this will all make sense. Trust your strength. You have an abundance of it. Just follow the path that is right for you. You are well on your way. That is plain to see. Those who tell you that you cannot do it do not know themselves well enough to tell you anything at all. When they find their peace, they will recognize yours and fall in step behind you. Just like your wolves. There may be just one path in the snow, but through that path, many sets of paws have traveled."

"I am happy," Jesse drawled. "I just didn't know it. How can I see it now?"

"It's in your blood," the Indian smiled. "You just needed help to open the door. Do not walk, but run outside, daughter. Do not waste any more time trying to translate hidden meanings that don't exist."

There was a slight commotion on the steps and the back door to Red Cloud's shack opened. "Are you ready, Jesse?" Johnny's voice appeared to far off, like in a dream, to Jesse.

"Yeah," she said, getting up. Her balance was off and she faltered. The old Indian steadied her with his outstretched hand. "Thank you, Red Cloud," she murmured. "May I visit with you again if I fall off track?"

"You will not fall again," Red Cloud declared. "Johnny, come get your woman. She's not used to the smoke."

Johnny was at Jesse's side in an instant. His touch was warm and Jesse melted into his strong arms as he helped her out. "I don't know what came over me," she whispered, resting her head on his shoulder. "I'll be all right once I get outside, I'm sure." Johnny was watching her carefully as he guided her out the door.

"You're all right now," Red Cloud declared, getting up from his rocker. "Open your eyes, daughter. Your future is staring you in the face."

"I got her, Red," Johnny said. "Thanks for the wood."

"Come back any time," the old Indian offered, closing the beat up screen door behind them. "You and the boy are always welcome."

Jesse took a deep breath of clean air and exhaled. She turned in Johnny's embrace and waved back at Red Cloud, letting Johnny guide her to the truck.

"We should be getting that meat home," Johnny said, helping her up into the cab. "I didn't expect it to be this warm today. You're sure you're all right?"

"I'm fine," Jesse smiled warmly at her companion. She touched his arm gently when he reached over her and buckled her in with her seatbelt. "Arleen always packs everything in ice, so don't worry about the meat."

Johnny raced around to the driver's side of the cab and slid in beside her. He turned on the ignition and the Dodge Ram roared to life. "Just as well. Let's get you home, okay?"

"Are we close to your parents' house?" Jesse asked, looking around as though she had just woken up from a nap. She met Johnny's gaze and smiled sweetly.

"Pretty close," he answered with a puzzled brow. "Why?"

"Let's go get your clothes and stuff," Jesse said determinedly. "If we do it now, we won't have to make another trip."

"Jesse," Johnny acknowledged her warily, "are you sure about this?"

"Never been more sure of anything in my life," Jesse quipped, combing her fingers through her hair and pushing it away from her face. The wind from the open window was refreshing. For the second time in a year, the way was clear for her and she knew exactly what she wanted. She had her wolf and she had Montana. Now she needed Johnny to make her happiness complete.

CHAPTER 22

Shadow had Jesse down on the ground and was determined to lick every inch of her face. She giggled uncontrollably as she heaved, holding his incredibly heavy body, and rolled him over in a tangle of arms and paws. The wolf, now eight months old, was becoming a formidable force. His eyes were now the color of Jesse's, and his fur was thick and black. Jesse knew he still had some growing to do, and by year's end she would probably not have the strength to hold her own when he wanted to play.

The wolf got up with a bounce and danced around her as she sat up, his main goal keeping her down on the ground. He attacked again playfully, and Jesse had to grab his forelegs and hold on, lest he win the next battle. She rolled him over once more and got to her feet quickly, otherwise the game could have gone on forever as far as the wolf was concerned.

"Come on," Jesse insisted, keeping what control she could, "let's go see what Johnny's up to." Mesa now joined the duo. He had carefully stayed out of Shadow's way while he played with his mother. The other wolf knew when to behave. But he did not refrain from yipping and yakking at the proceedings, kind of like a play-by-play in wolf-talk. Jesse made sure Mesa got some attention too, scratching his head and rubbing her fingers into his now long, brown and gray fur. Shadow snarled a bit at his competition but was satisfied when Mesa bowed down to appease him.

Kitten, reclining on the top of the table on the patio, watched the event with a disinterested glance, preferring a tongue bath in the warm light of the sun. Now that everybody was up on their feet, she sprawled out, paws hanging languidly over the edge of the table, and closed her eyes to nap.

Through the row of windows in the back room, Jesse could see Johnny working on his latest project. In two weeks he had made four rocking chairs, a wagon wheel table, and was now working on a cabinet with doors. Each piece was unique, yet all tied together with a common theme. He had painstakingly hand-carved depictions of wolves in all of them. The backs of the rockers had wolves. There was a wolf in the center of the tabletop. The doors of the cabinet were cut out with wolves in the center of each. That piece was going to take a great deal more time than the others, for there were two opposing wolves and a half moon on each panel. When the doors were closed, if all went according to design, an elaborate scene would be created.

Cheyenne, who had become quite attached to Johnny, was lying on the floor of the room watching him work. Her head rested on her forepaws and her eye lids had started to close for her nap, but when she sensed the trio had arrived to look into the windows, her attention sharpened and she rose to her feet with a stretch. Johnny had not noticed his visitors. He was meticulously chipping away at one of his wooden wolf's ears. Jesse sat down on one of the stones just outside the windows and watched her friend work. She smiled at his concentration, especially with everything that was on his mind of late.

One of those thoughts, that had constantly plagued her also, recalled that day when she insisted they stop at his father's house. Charlie had not been very happy to see the load of wood and tools in the back of the pickup, undoubtedly sure his son had probably stolen them from somewhere. He was even less happy to see that Jesse was with him and had asked Johnny to move in. There was the expected quarrel when Johnny walked in and started cleaning out his room. Charlie even had a few harsh words for Jesse. As was their custom, the words turned foul and, at one point, Charlie made the serious gesture as if to stop Johnny from going through with it.

It was when Johnny raised a hand to his father that Winona had stepped in and quelled any further arguments. After silencing them with a few sharp words of her own, she picked up Johnny's meager belongings and ushered both Johnny and Jesse out of the house. Jesse could still feel the woman's hands when they grasped her by the shoulders, forcing her to look straight into Winona's eyes. Winona stared at her fixedly for a few seconds before she spoke. She told Jesse that *she* understood. She hugged the young woman and smoothed her long hair with the palm of her hand, and wished them good luck. She suggested they stay away from Charlie for a few weeks until she could make it right with him.

Johnny growled that he did not need her help, but willingly accepted Winona's embrace. They had whispered to each other in their native tongue. Johnny smiled at her and gave her a kiss on her cheek before he got back into the truck. His mother stood strong and still, watching them as they drove away.

That night at the cabin, Johnny was rather quiet. He played with the wolves for a while and Jesse stayed out of their way. To keep occupied, she put the meat in the cooler, and took his few clothes upstairs to put away. She cleared the backroom, making more space for Johnny's work. Then she cooked their dinner.

After their meal and a few glasses of wine, they settled down and talked. Johnny calmed Jesse's fears about the rift between him and his father and thanked her for giving him the opportunity to get away. She was not to think that she had brought this upon his family. This trouble had been brewing for most of his life. He was looking forward to working with the wood, he told her, because it would help him to work these problems out and hopefully gain some peace of mind.

During that conversation, Jesse noticed that her companion had found, probably while playing with the wolves, a small object that interested him immensely. It turned out to be a stone that he toyed with as he talked to her, rubbing it gently, sometimes vigorously, between his fingers or between the palms of his hands. When she asked him about it, he shrugged it off and said it was nothing. But she had noticed he kept it with him all the time. As she looked in the window now, it sat on the table next to his tools.

Still reminiscing, she thought about that first night they spent together as roommates. After holding each other gently and sharing a few quiet words, she fell asleep in his arms. When she finally lost consciousness and entered into her dreams, he was softly stroking her hair.

The following morning and every day for the next two weeks, his waking hours were occupied in the back room working. He spent time with her at meals and welcomed her company when she joined him in the workroom, but his attention was riveted to his craftwork and that attention had started to pay off. His pieces were constructed with exquisite care and were very beautiful.

Jesse smiled again, remembering one silly event that had also transpired. Johnny made sure he played with the wolves every day and had fallen into their routine easily. He learned how to feed them and spoiled them rotten. When one day they discovered a treasure hidden in the woods behind the house, Jesse had paid little attention to their digging and cavorting. She had been cleaning out the fountain and preparing it for winter, even though the bright sunlight and warm temperatures seemed a far cry from the impending snowstorm that, according to Joseph was due *any day*. Johnny had come out for a little break and a glass of water and Jesse casually mentioned the wolves' frenetic activity just inside the grove of cottonwoods over the crest of rocks.

When Johnny's gaze traveled to the spot she was talking about, his eyes widened. He put his glass down and hightailed after them. Jesse stopped what she was doing and stood up to watch. With a barrage of yips and barks, a tug of war was soon underway as Johnny tried his best to get a rather heavy burlap bag away from the furry pirates. Shadow, Mesa and Cheyenne were just as determined to keep it.

A compromise was eventually reached. Johnny came back to the cabin with one end of the bag and Shadow held the other end firmly between his teeth. Cheyenne and Mesa romped around them, nipping at the bag and Johnny's legs.

On the stone patio, the secret finally came out. Shadow shook his head forcefully and the material eventually ripped apart, spilling Johnny's personal effects that he had buried in the crag some time ago.

"I forgot," said Johnny guiltily, as the wolves snatched pieces of his underclothes and flung them about. "I buried this stuff up there right before you moved in."

Jesse stooped over and picked up a couple of shirts before the animals got to them. "It's a relief to me," she laughed. "I was hoping you hadn't spent your whole life with just three pairs of jeans, one sweatshirt and a couple of ratty old shirts. Now I don't have to do laundry every day." Those clothes, now cleaned and neatly folded inside the closet had made it official. Johnny was now at home and Jesse was very pleased about it.

Thunder cracked overhead and Jesse was drawn from her daydreams. Shadow scratched at the window and Johnny finally looked up, seeing the menagerie of faces peering in at him. He gave Jesse a sly smile and carefully closed the doors on his cabinet. The carved moon lined up perfectly. The carved wolves, surrounded by etched mountains and fir trees, appeared to howl in perfect unison up at it.

Cheyenne placed her head on Johnny's knee. He put down his tools and gave her a scratch. "I think we better go outside for a while," he smiled at her. "Looks like the other kids want to play."

Cheyenne perked up and headed out of the room toward the back door, checking briefly to see if Johnny was following her. He picked up his stone and walked to the back door. Opening it, Cheyenne was greeted by her comrades who instantly engaged her in sniffs and play. Kitten woke up at the noise, stretched and joined in the fracas, pouncing from the table into the middle of it.

"Want something?" Johnny asked, grinning at Jesse. He rubbed his stone briskly between his middle finger and his thumb.

"How about some attention?" she suggested, giving him a wink.

"And here I thought you wanted something important," Johnny sassed with a shameless look in his eyes. He ran over to her and picked her up in his arms. She put her arms around his neck and he spun her around. "You've been cheating on me," he said hoarsely into her hair. "You smell like wolf."

"All the better to eat you with," she replied lustfully, her head bent back enjoying his embrace.

Johnny held on tight, setting her on her feet. Jesse ran her fingers through his shiny, black hair. He was sorely tempted. He wanted her right then and there. He took a deep breath and stood up straight.

Every time they got so very close, one of them backed away. They had vowed to be friends, not lovers. His head was muddled with a thousand new emotions. It was so hard to know if Jesse wanted what he wanted now. They teased each other and liked to touch. But what would happen if he demanded more? Would she scream rape and catch the first flight back to Denver? Johnny did not want to lose her now. Jesse had never asked for anything else. She seemed content with the way things were. Unless she made the first move, he was bound and determined to hold his emotions and desires in check.

Jesse had never had such a relationship. It had always been a few drinks, some quick conversations and a couple of nights of passionate sex. The passion soon dissipated, the conversations turned to arguments, and it was over as quickly as it had begun. Before she knew it, she was looking for someone else. It was different with Johnny. She did not want to lose him. And for her, if they ever made love, there would be no turning away. She could not rope him in like some stallion, especially if he wanted to be free. She worried for Johnny's sake. He worried for hers. Neither one wanted to push the matter. Somehow, they both knew it wasn't right.

"I'm just about done," Johnny groaned, attempting to gain his composure. "I've just got to rub down the cabinet and it'll be ready to stain."

"We should get the chairs and the table down to the store," Jesse said quietly. "They're so beautiful, Johnny. Arleen's going to love them."

"It's going to rain," Johnny remarked assuredly, still gazing into Jesse's eyes. "I'll finish up the cabinet tonight and we'll take them in tomorrow, okay?"

"Whatever you say," Jesse answered. "Shall I fix us something to eat while you work?" She snuggled her head in the crook of his neck.

"That would be a good thing," Johnny smiled weakly, squeezing her close one more time before he let her go. "All this…" he paused, carefully choosing his words. Tempting her further with the words he wanted to say, would surely destroy their resolve. "…work," he finally said, "…makes me hungry."

Jesse made steak and eggs for dinner and served it in the workroom to save time. Afterward, he showed her how to polish the wood and she was eager to help. When the project was finally completed, late in the evening, Jesse cleaned up the dishes while Johnny toiled awhile longer. When she opened the back door to let the animals in for a late night snack, she noticed he was doing some kind of grinding on his little stone. Although curious, she left him to his work. She cuddled up on the couch in front of the fire and read a book. The rain had started, as Johnny had promised earlier. All her animals opted to stay in for the night.

It was very late when Johnny woke her up and ushered her to bed. Again, they talked and held each other close. Jesse was content that it appeared Johnny would finally get some sleep. He was out as soon as he laid his head upon the pillow.

In the morning, as usual, Jesse woke up alone. She took her shower and dressed, only to find a note on the table with a bowl of fruit when she got downstairs. Johnny had gotten up at the crack of dawn and loaded the truck with the furniture. The note said he didn't want to wake her up, so he was taking the stuff into town himself. It also said he had to go into Conrad for some supplies and that he hoped to be back by early that afternoon. There were three X's and his scrawled signature on the bottom. The P.S. said, *Eat the fruit—it's good for you!*

Jesse was disappointed that Johnny had gone to town without her. Lately, she did not like being alone. The day was gray but the rain had stopped. The wolves and Kitten were off on one of their rambles. The house was clean, so she pulled on a jacket, put on her boots and went for a walk. She walked down to the lake for a while and then headed for the woods.

She saw a fox and some rabbits and eventually found her pack, chasing mice in the field near Charlie's house. They greeted her happily with their customary licks. She ran with them for a while and they led her to a new spot. In the crags of the foothills she found a stream that led to a waterfall and a little pond. Trees crowded around the pool of water, so thick she could barely see the sky above. The ravens cawed and swooped down, skimming the top of the water. Shadow and Mesa churned at the water, stirring up the fish. Kitten waited patiently on a rock above and cleverly grabbed one of the fish when it popped up to the surface.

Jesse and Cheyenne explored the area. While gathering some wild flowers, Jesse found an eagle feather lodged in a rotted log. She examined it closely before carefully placing it in her pocket. Later, she and Cheyenne rested by the water's edge as Shadow and Mesa went exploring.

When the clouds finally dispersed, rays of the setting sun streamed down like golden stairways to heaven. From the angle of the light, Jesse could tell it was getting late. She took her flowers from the water where she had placed them to keep them fresh. She checked on the eagle feather in her pocket. She howled into the late afternoon air to summon her brood. In short order, Shadow howled back. They all met her along the path and headed home. Along the way, Jesse was glad to see her eagle flying in the clearing above the trees. If it was he who had shed the feather, it appeared to not hinder him at all.

Arriving at the cabin, she saw the truck filled with more wood, but Johnny was nowhere in sight. The ragtag group sauntered up onto the porch and Jesse opened the front door. The lights were on in the backroom of the cabin.

"We're home," she called out as the animals headed for the kitchen.

"I'll be right there," Johnny yelled back, sounding a bit mysterious.

Jesse thought about going into the room to see what he was up to but decided against it. She pulled some meat out of the refrigerator and plopped it into her animals' bowls. "How did Arleen like the furniture?" she asked, but Johnny did not answer. She pursed her lips, considering what to do next. She opted again to stay out of his way.

Jesse gently pulled the feather from her pocket and smoothed it out with her fingers. She thought about telling Johnny about her find, but instead she went into the living room and set it carefully on the mantelpiece. "Are you hungry?" she tried again.

"Starving!" Johnny answered back. "I'll be out in a second."

"Okay," Jesse sighed, kicking off her boots. She went into the kitchen and started dinner, conversing out loud with the wolves, as Johnny appeared to be too busy to talk.

"Sorry," Johnny's voice came from behind her. "I had to finish up a little project I've been working on." Cheyenne greeted him with a wagging tail. Mesa yapped at him with a mouthful of food. Johnny was surprised to see Jesse was alone. "Who were you talking to?" He walked up behind her and placed his arms around her waist.

"Nobody," she said. "I haven't said a word all day since you left me this morning, so I wanted to make sure my vocal chords were still intact."

"You got my note, didn't you?" Johnny asked.

Jesse felt bad, trying to make him feel guilty for leaving her. She turned in his arms and faced him, forgiving him on the spot. "Yes, I did. It was just kind of odd not having you around."

"I'll never do it again," Johnny vowed. "I was just anxious to get the furniture to Arleen and I had to go into Conrad. I wanted to get an early start."

"Did she like it?" Jesse asked, dropping her petty fears of abandonment.

He reached into his jeans pocket and pulled out a wad of cash. "She gave me three hundred and fifty dollars, can you believe it?" he beamed. "She said they were probably worth a lot more. But I said, *no way*. Geez, I've never held this kind of cash all at once—legally." He handed her the money.

"Why are you giving this to me?" Jesse asked incredulously, pushing it back.

"For rent and food," Johnny announced proudly, refusing to take it back. "I filled up the tank with gas too." He opened the refrigerator and grabbed two prime cuts of steak. "We're having these for dinner. Unless, of course, you'd like to eat out."

"Okay, okay, I'll take it," Jesse laughed. "Otherwise, you'll fritter it away in no time." She took a jar out of the cupboard and put the bills inside, setting it back up on the top shelf. "Let's just keep it there for emergencies, all right?"

"Good," Johnny said, unwrapping the steaks. Shadow and Mesa nosed around him, thinking the meat was theirs. "Let's get cooking."

Johnny put some potatoes in the oven and made a salad, all the while chattering about Arleen and her accolades. Jesse, proud of him, set the table while she listened. He suggested a candlelight dinner, so she put new candles on the table and retrieved a bottle of wine from the storage room. Johnny went on about some new ideas that he had and how he wanted to get started right away. He was animated and jovial. Jesse was elated and paid attention to his every word. He made her sit down at the table and do nothing. He put on some music, grilled the steaks and served a most delicious meal.

As he bantered on, she studied his face and his eyes as they danced in the candlelight. She wanted to tell him how much she was in love with him, but she held her tongue. There was no need to ruin a perfectly glorious evening with such a burdensome comment. He was light as air and she wanted him to stay that way for as long as the fates would let him.

After dinner, they did the dishes together and let the wolves out to roam. They cuddled on the couch and talked some more. As Jesse leaned against him, Johnny held her left hand and twirled the fingers of his right hand through her hair. More projects rolled out of his head. She offered some creative ideas of her own and he agreed with her suggestions.

The evening blended into the night as the wine and warm fire lulled them into a state of contentment and relaxation. The words faded, replaced by longing looks and gentle caresses. Those feelings were rising again and Johnny was in no mood to stop them. Jesse was in no mood to resist. Without warning, Johnny took Jesse's face into his hands and pressed his lips hard against hers. She reciprocated and their kisses turned feverish. Their passion rose and their hands suddenly began searching formerly forbidden areas of their respective anatomies. Their attempts were awkward and uncontrollable. They were making painful mistakes.

Jesse pulled away from Johnny first with tears in her eyes. "I'm sorry," she whimpered. "I haven't done this for a long time."

Johnny's eyes were smoldering, but a sense of relief crossed his face. "No," he whispered. "It's all right." He straightened himself out and planted his feet on the floor in front of the couch. "We shouldn't be doing this anyway. Friends don't *screw* friends."

"But Johnny…" Jesse was confused and upset, "I didn't mean…"

"I gotta' go out for a while, Jess," Johnny cut her off. "Go on to bed." He stood up and walked determinedly to the front door and grabbed his jacket from the back of the chair. "I'll see you in the morning, okay?" He did not wait for an answer. He stormed outside, slamming the door behind him. Jesse covered her face with her hands and cried.

Johnny did not take Jesse's truck. He headed, on foot, for the woods and cut across to the path that led to the reservation. "Damn it!" he cursed as he trudged hurriedly along. "Why did I do that? I'm so goddamn stupid!" He brushed one branch out of the way and walked straight into another. The other branch snapped back and hit him in the back of the head. "Shit!" he cursed over and over again for being so weak. He was stronger than that. Jesse didn't deserve to be treated that way. He loved her for Christ's sake. Why did he attack her like some wild animal? He was embarrassed. He had no excuse. She was used to city boys and their slick maneuvers. Of course, she was confused. How do you make love to a stupid Indian? Especially when the stupid Indian doesn't know how to make love himself. Oh, he had had women—plenty of them. But they didn't mean anything. They didn't give a shit about him either. It was just something to do on a rainy night after the bar closed or after a powwow when the stars were out and the air was warm and he just didn't want to go home. He did not know the first thing about romance and he probably never would. She wanted to be friends, damn it. Not groped by some country bumpkin with, at best, a seventh grade education. "Jesus!" he yelled. "Why did I have to fuck everything up just when it was going so good?"

Jesse cried for a good hour after Johnny left. She was devastated. She could not believe what she'd done—attacked the poor man like some common whore. They had made a pact to be friends. Why had she been so stupid and crossed the line? He had respected her. He had cared for her and watched over her. Now she was no more than an oversexed idiot who couldn't even finish what she started. She chugged down the rest of the bottle of wine and made herself sick. At least she got to the bathroom before she threw up. Thankfully, the wolves were out and Kitten was under the porch. She was embarrassed enough without having their inquisitive eyes staring up at her inanity. She left the door open a crack, just in case he might come back and literally crawled up the stairs to go to bed. Unfortunately, due to her drinking indiscretion, the bed was not what she needed. With her head still spinning, Jesse ended up sleeping on the bathroom floor.

In his present state of depression, Johnny headed for Red Cloud's place, where he was not surprised to see the old Indian patiently sitting outside on the front stoop when he finally arrived. He approached his friend, battered and weary from his nighttime journey through the woods. Rex was sleeping beside the man and did not give a wit of attention to Johnny's arrival.

"Don't ask," Johnny snapped when he walked up to the old man.

"Don't need to," Red Cloud quipped, getting up slowly from the stoop. He opened the door to his little house and ushered the young man inside. "You young kids," Red said, checking the boy out as he stumbled in and plopped himself down in the nearest chair. "Sometimes I wonder if this world has any hope."

"I lost control, man," Johnny spilled his guts, holding his head in his hands. "I tried to make love to my best friend."

Red Cloud grabbed a rag and ran some cold water over it in the sink. "As far as I know, making love has never been a problem for you in the past." He wrung out the rag and put it on the back of Johnny's head. The branch had sliced an inch long gash across his head and it was still bleeding. There were bloody scratches on his face. "I think you're just confused about the *friend* part."

"She wants to be friends," Johnny sighed. "I'm supposed to be her protector."

"You still haven't given me a problem to solve, boy," the Native American said, sitting down in his rocker. "You can be a friend, a protector and a lover. That's what life's all about."

"She trusted me," Johnny whined. "Then I let her down. She doesn't want that from me. She's too good for that. She just wants a friend to help her out. She's got better men back in Colorado for what I wanted to be."

Red Cloud lit his pipe and exhaled the smoke freely into the small room. "Calm down, boy," he said quietly. "You're not making any sense."

"I'm making perfect sense! I…" Johnny started angrily, removing the rag with a snap.

"Shush!" Red Cloud cut him off. "And keep that rag on your head. It's still bleeding, you big dummy." He smoked a little more before he spoke again. Johnny found it hard to meet his gaze and lowered his head so he wouldn't have to. "I'll never understand why you young people have to doubt everything. You can't accept anything for what it's worth."

"Because it's usually worth shit," Johnny muttered, half under his breath.

"Come over here and sit next to me, boy," Red Cloud ordered. "We're going to smoke this pipe."

Johnny reluctantly joined him. He sat cross-legged on the floor at the old man's feet. Red Cloud told him, with a turn of his finger, to face the other way. Sighing, Johnny complied. The old Indian took the rag and put the pipe in Johnny's free hand. Johnny smoked while Red Cloud pressed the cloth tightly against Johnny's head.

"The woman is not so hard to figure out," Red Cloud finally spoke. "If you pay attention to the signs she gives." Johnny knew better than to speak. He inhaled the smoke of the pipe again and Red Cloud felt him relax ever so slightly. "If she wants to be with you, she'll move heaven and earth to make you happy. Tell me, boy, does she make you happy?"

Johnny nodded his concurrence.

"And her intentions, that she wants to be with you, are pretty clear," the old man continued. "Leave it to a man to muddy the waters." He reached down and took the pipe from Johnny's hand and took a puff himself. "The man likes to be in charge. He likes to give orders, not take them. How can a *woman* tell him anything? How can she possibly know more than what his *superior brain* already knows? So most of the time her intentions go unread, or worse, are misunderstood.

"You're luckier than most. You're an Indian. I have taught you to listen to the trees and to the earth and to the sky above. You can tell by the call of a bird if there's rain comin' or there's trouble ahead. You can track an animal and find your way in the dark without the moon to light your way. So how, I want to know, can you look into your woman's eyes and not know without a doubt how she feels about you? That she loves you more than life itself?" Red Cloud refilled his pipe.

"I want you to smoke this pipe and think about what I've told you," the Indian continued. "Rest your head back against my hand. When you're through thinkin', you're gonna' go to sleep. And tomorrow you're gonna' try again."

Johnny, already quite drowsy, reached into his pocket and produced his newest project. He held it up for Red Cloud to see. It was a small Montana agate stone, newly set in a simple band of silver. "I made this for her," the young man murmured. "I was going to give it to her tonight."

Red Cloud took the ring and eyed it closely. The clear stone was imbued with touches of black. But when the Indian held it up to the light, there were visible hues of gold and blue coursing through it.

The old Indian smiled and handed it back to the young man. "I see your eyes and hers in this stone. It is a true gift of your love."

"Her friend Eric would buy her a diamond," Johnny's words were starting to slur. He was very tired.

Red Cloud tapped him smartly on the head. "Pay attention to the signs, boy! Pay attention to the signs! She will hold this ring closer to her heart than any other. Just because her *heart* belongs to *you*." He let the young man have one more puff on his pipe before he took it back from him. "Now, look deep into your soul and remember the signs you've been given. Think hard and then get some sleep."

CHAPTER 23

The bathroom upstairs in the cabin was not the biggest room in the house and when all three wolves crowded into the tiny room to wake up their mother, she awoke with a start amidst a sea of fur, scratching paws and wet tongues.

Jesse struggled under their weight to sit up. When she finally did, the wolves continued their play. "No, no, babies," Jesse stammered between the licks and the bodies closing in on her. "Let me get up." She used Shadow and Mesa's backs for support. Their combined weight in the small room could have crushed her if she wasn't careful. Finally standing, she eased her way out of the bathroom followed by the pack. Kitten was nonchalantly cleaning herself on Jesse's bed.

"Momma did a stupid thing last night," she said, giving Kitten a quick scratch on the top her head between the ears. The bobcat purred and rubbed against her fingers. "I don't know if he'll be back." Shadow cocked his head to the side and talked softly with little yips. Jesse smiled sadly and rubbed the ruff of his neck with her other hand. The tears were spent last night. Now she just had a throbbing headache and puffy eyes. She took a deep breath and went downstairs with the clan at her heels.

"Get up, boy," Red Cloud said, hovering over Johnny's sleeping form. He had crashed on the floor where he'd been sitting the night before.

Red Cloud had given him a blanket, but Johnny found it difficult to move—his bones were stiff and his head ached. "What time is it?" Johnny cringed at the sound of his voice coming out of his own head. He touched the back of it where he had been hit by the branch.

"Time to get up," Red Cloud said, pouring a cup of coffee for his young friend. "I cleaned that gash out and put some medicine on it. Make sure Jesse keeps an eye on it for you. I'll give you some of the salve I made to take with you."

Johnny groaned, remembering what had happened. He slowly got to his feet.

"Making things right is easy, remember," Red Cloud advised. "Summoning up the courage to do it is the hard part." He smiled at the young man. "Here is some courage. Drink up."

Johnny wretched at the first taste of the concoction but kept it down. "This isn't coffee," he snarled.

"A special blend," Red Cloud quipped. "It will make you strong and healthy again."

"Only Jesse can do that," Johnny sighed. "But what do I owe you, old man, before I go?"

"I got that pane of glass to fix the window in the other room," Red Cloud suggested. "Do you think you could put that up right quick?"

"No problem," Johnny responded, his face contorted by the nasty taste in his mouth.

"You're a good boy," Red Cloud smiled, making sure the younger man finished every drop of the homemade brew before he took the cup from him. "Get this done quick and be on your way. It's time we had some snow around here."

"My head hurts too much to ask why those two events could have anything to do with each other." Johnny combed his fingers through his blood-matted hair. Even that hurt. "So where's the new pane of glass?"

The wolves and the bobcat were outside early. Jesse had showered and washed her hair, hoping to scrub away the disastrous effects of the night before. Instead of her usual jeans and shirt, she decided to put on a dress. A long one that was comfortable and unrestricting. Eric had always hated that dress. He had called her a hippy and was sure she had been on some kind of drug when she bought it. Jesse sort of smiled, thinking about her old friend. He would have been able to cheer her up and offer sound and logical reasons why her night had turned to shit. She thought about calling him but did not pick up the phone. She grabbed a sweater and went outside instead.

The sun was shining and it was already quite warm for the end of August. Jesse looked up at the bright blue sky and wondered when all this predicted snow was supposed to arrive. According to Joseph and Charlie, there should have been over three feet of snow by now. She didn't think about it too long, for her thoughts kept returning to Johnny. Where was he? Was he ever coming back? She sat on the porch steps, and draped the skirt of the dress over her legs and hugged her arms tightly around her bent knees. She observed her owl, sleeping in the tree. Her eagle soared in a high circle above the cabin. The ravens were off with the wolves so the landscape was pretty quiet, except for the occasional call of a meadowlark or the magpies. A white-tailed deer passed by on its way to the lake, now used to the woman who lived in the cabin, and cognizant of the times the wolves and the bobcat were not at home.

Jesse heard the tapping of a woodpecker in the distance and then remembered her eagle feather. She got up and went inside where she retrieved it from the mantelpiece. She stepped back out onto the porch, twirling the feather between her fingers, and was about to sit back down when she heard the crack of a footfall on a twig to the north. Fully expecting the wolves to round the corner, she was surprised and stood very still when she saw Johnny coming back.

At first, she did not intend to react, but as he came closer, she could see that he was quite a mess. She stuffed the feather in her pocket, sprinted down the steps in her bare feet and ran to meet him. She did not care if he was still angry with her or not.

When he saw her coming, he quickened his steps. At the sight of her long hair and dress billowing out behind her as she approached him, he suddenly lost all his strength. He fell to his knees and reached his arms out wide to her. She was upon him in seconds and his arms encircled her legs. He locked on tightly to her, smothering his face into the folds of her dress. Jesse's hands fell to his head and caressed his matted hair.

"Oh, my God," she sobbed, "you're hurt!"

He looked up at her with tears in his vivid blue eyes. "I love you, Jess," he cried. "I didn't mean to hurt you."

Jesse's legs crumbled despite his firm grasp around them. She dropped to her knees and placed her hands along his jaw line. Scratches of dried blood dotted his face. She kissed him passionately and then kissed him again, her hands holding him tight. "My heart has been yours from the moment we met," she whispered into his ear. "Please tell me we are not making a mistake." She kissed him on the forehead and trailed her lips across his dirty face.

"Red Cloud said it's meant to be," Johnny murmured, reveling in her kisses and embrace. "As far as I'm concerned, that's as good as the Creator telling us himself."

They held each other a while longer, half hidden in the tall grasses that gently swayed in the breeze. The meadowlarks started chirping again and the eagle swooped down and caught a mouse. The woodpecker continued its labor on a nearby cottonwood tree.

Slowly, Jesse helped Johnny up. With her arm around his waist and his around her shoulder, she bore the brunt of his weight. She got him into the cabin and helped him upstairs, making him sit on the edge of the bed. She hurried into the bathroom and filled the tub with hot water and a healthy dose of bubble bath. She returned to his crumpled form and helped him undress. There was no time or need for modesty. She pulled off his boots and yanked him out of his pants. He had removed his shirt, but the sleeve was caught on his wrist. She unbuttoned it and slipped it off, adding it to the heap of his other dirty clothes. Again, she helped him off the bed and got him, somehow, into the tub. The hot water and suds climbed a good few inches, nearly to the rim of the claw foot tub, when he eased himself down into the water. It rose another inch when he lay back against the back of the porcelain tub. Soon he was covered by white foam up to his ears.

Jesse washed him gently, but firmly, with a soft washcloth—scrubbing off every speck of dirt. His eyes were closed when she washed his face and neck but he could not hide the smile upon his lips, enjoying her care.

"You like that?" she asked, smiling herself.

"The Creator is good and benevolent," he whispered back. "It is a good day to die."

"I don't think it's that bad, chief," she sassed back. She doused his head with handfuls of water and carefully shampooed his hair.

"Mmmmm," he murmured, smelling the scent of the shampoo. "That's what your hair smells like when I hold you close. Like wildflowers and lavender."

"So now that you have my secret you can just smell your own hair and you won't need mine," Jesse quipped. She was carefully washing around where his scalp had been cut.

Johnny's hand shot out of the water and grabbed her arm, surprising her. She looked into his beautiful eyes, now leveled upon her. "Do not tease me like that," he said with a hint of fear in his countenance. "Promise me, we will always be together. You cannot leave me, now that I've given you my heart."

Jesse returned his gaze thoughtfully. She bent over and kissed him again on the lips. "It will be a good day to die, the day we die together."

He cupped his wet hand on the side of her head and pulled her to him. He kissed her long and ardently. With her mouth still on his, she placed her hands where his head met his neck; then she dunked him under the water to rinse the shampoo from his hair. She changed her grip and pulled him back up to the surface just as quickly.

"There. You've been baptized as my one and only," she snickered at the startled look upon his face. She pulled her hands away and reached for a towel, placing it on the commode beside the tub. "Now it's time to soak," she smiled. "When you're ready, you can come out."

He lay back against the edge of the tub again and closed his eyes. "You'll be here to dry me off?"

"I think you better do that yourself." Jesse got up and dried off her hands and arms with another towel. "The wolves will be all over those dirty clothes if I don't get them washed."

"There's some salve in my pocket from Red Cloud," he mumbled, numbed by the hot water. "He said you should put it on my cut."

"I'll find it. Now rest," she said warmly, leaving the bathroom and closing the door quietly behind her.

Jesse searched Johnny's pockets and found the salve. She also found, upon further investigation, the ring that he'd been carrying in the pocket of his jeans. She sat on the edge of the bed and studied it carefully. The muted colors changed from gold to blue when she turned it with her fingers. Suddenly, she remembered the stone he had found and kept with him for all those days. She wondered if this was the same piece. She placed the ring next to Red Cloud's salve on the edge of the bed, next to the clean clothes she had picked out for him. She bundled up the dirty clothes and took them downstairs.

The bobcat had returned home and was pestering Jesse for some meat when Johnny finally appeared in the kitchen. Jesse had made him some French toast and a pot of very strong coffee. He pondered the scene before his eyes and smiled. He was tired but very happy to be home.

"You look much better," Jesse smiled, turning to him when she felt his presence. Kitten took the opportunity to grab the meat she was holding in her hand. The bobcat lay on the table and chewed on her prize.

"And you found my surprise," Johnny said, walking up to her with the ring in his hand. They stood, facing each other, a breath apart.

"It is the most beautiful ring I've ever seen," she murmured gazing down at it. "You made that, didn't you?"

"I found it one day when I was playing with the wolves," Johnny said lowly. "It shines with the colors of our eyes."

"And the black spots, like Shadow's fur, completes it." Jesse looked up at her young man, her love for him plainly evident.

He took her left hand into his and placed the ring on her ring finger. "I made it for you," he whispered. "Will you wear it for me?"

"Forever," she replied. They kissed, again. This time gently. "Now," she said, pulling a chair away from the table, "sit down and eat. No man of mine is going to starve to death after giving me such a beautiful present." She put the plate of food down in front of him and stuck out her hand. "And give me the salve, please."

Jesse rubbed the strange mixture onto his cut while Johnny wolfed down his food. Jesse stifled a giggle, watching the man and the bobcat—at opposite ends of the table—tackle their respective meals with ravenous abandon.

"Did you eat already?" Johnny asked when Jesse sat down beside him. Kitten finished her meal first and bounded off the table and out the front door.

"Yes," Jesse lied. "I had some eggs this morning."

"Well, I've got an idea," Johnny offered, before shoveling more food into his mouth. "I need to put the wood into the back room and then let's take a day off. How about if we just take a nice long walk and spend the day together?"

"That sounds wonderful to me," Jesse chimed. "The wolves showed me a new place yesterday. I'd love for you to see it."

When the dishes were done, and Johnny had unloaded the last of the wood from the truck, Jesse grabbed the picnic basket from the storage room. She put a bottle of wine and a couple of glasses in it, along with some bologna, cheese, and the remaining grapes from the fridge.

"Okay," Johnny announced, shutting the door to the backroom. "I'm all finished." He saw the picnic basket on the table and smiled. "It looks like we're ready to go." He grabbed the blanket from the back of the couch and wrapped it over his arm. "I don't think I've ever been on a picnic before."

"In case we get lost in the forest," Jesse laughed, picking up the basket and her sweater, "we'll need sustenance to keep up our strength!"

Kitten ran under the porch when they started off. Jesse cast a cursory glance for the wolves, but did not see them.

"They'll find us, I'm sure," Johnny said, noting her observance. "Which way to the new spot?"

Jesse took the lead and Johnny followed. "With that red sweater, I feel like I'm following Little Red Riding Hood. Thank God I'm friends with the big bad wolf," he joked. Jesse laughed and skipped on ahead.

With the sun shining down through the mass of cottonwoods and lodge pole pines, the waterfall and pond looked almost magical when the pair arrived. Johnny stood still and stared at the area in amazement. "I've never seen this place," he finally uttered to Jesse, who had gone on ahead and was setting her basket down on a rise in a small clearing just to the right of the waterfall. "You said the wolves brought you here?"

Jesse beckoned to him with a wave of her hand to join him. "Yes," she called out. "They were actually fishing in this little pond—much to Kitten's delight."

"The bobcat was here, too?" Johnny asked, trudging up the rise to meet her. "And here I thought I knew every inch of this property." He stood still again with his blanket over his arm and gazed out over the water. "It's pretty, isn't it?"

"Maybe Red Cloud would say *enchanted*, no?" Jesse giggled, eyeing the blanket. There was a thick layer of needles from the pine trees under their feet. She wasn't relishing the thought of sitting down in her cotton dress without a cover.

"I don't think he knows that word," Johnny laughed with her. "He'd say it was a gift from the Creator."

"Well, that's true," commented Jesse. "Because the Creator made everything, so everything is a gift." Jesse reached in her pocket and suddenly felt the feather she had put there earlier. "Oh, speaking of the Creator," she went on, "I have a present for you that I found here yesterday."

"Oh?" Johnny's eyes widened, turning to face her.

"Just a minute." Jesse turned away from him so he could not see her pull it out. Miraculously, the feather was still intact after all they had gone through that morning. She smoothed out the tip and turning around, presented it to him. "It's an eagle feather. I found it stuck in a log over there."

Johnny's eyes stared at the object and his mouth parted. His body stiffened and he did not move a muscle to take the gift Jesse was offering him.

"Don't you like it?" Jesse asked quietly. His dazed appearance gave her cause for concern. "Have I done something wrong?"

Johnny tore his eyes from the feather and they softened when they met Jesse's. "Hold on to it for a second," he told her. He stepped back, took the blanket from his arm and shook it out.

"Everything's okay, right?" Jesse was still apprehensive.

"Better than okay," the Native American smiled. "It's the best present I've ever received." He put the blanket out and laid it flat on the ground. "Now, go ahead and sit down, Jess," he commanded. "I'll be right back."

Jesse did as she was ordered to do and watched him with a puzzled look. He rummaged through the foliage for a little while. "Do you want me to keep holding the feather?" she queried. He was still making her a little nervous.

"You're doing just fine," Johnny called out, now looking in the bushes. Just when Jesse thought he had thoroughly lost his mind, he cried out, "Ah, here's some!" He wrestled with something in the tall weeds and finally stood up. He returned to Jesse and the blanket with a long length of Creeping Jenny vine in his hands. "This will have to do," he said breathlessly, plopping down on his knees in front of her. Jesse stared at him with skepticism in her eyes.

"Do you trust me?" he asked, meeting her gaze. He snickered when he saw the look of consternation upon her face.

"I guess I better," she answered warily, still holding the eagle feather in front of her.

"Sit on your knees here in front of me," he insisted, "so our knees touch."

Jesse maneuvered herself around and got closer. The sun filtered down upon them through the trees, warming their skin. Johnny spoke some words in his Native tongue. Words that Jesse could never hope to understand. As he spoke, he untwined the vine and straightened it. When his eyes fixed on Jesse's for a brief moment, his chanting voice soothed the young woman. He took the feather from her trembling hand and offered it to the sky while continuing his monologue. He placed the feather into his hair and then took the vine and offered it to the sky, still speaking in his language. He took the vine and wrapped it gently around Jesse's left wrist and then wrapped it around his own left wrist. With a few more words he took the rest of the vine and wrapped their right wrists until they were bound together. He then raised their bound hands toward the sky and prayed some more. "Canhinyan tohunhunniyan kin," he said, guiding their hands back down to the blanket. "Can you say that?" he inquired of Jesse quietly.

"Help me," she pleaded.

"Canhinyan," he said again slowly.

"Canhinyan," she repeated.

"Tohunhunniyan," he prompted.

"Tohun…"

"Tohunhunniyan." He smiled at her.

"Tohunhunniyan."

"Kin."

"Kin," she smiled, proud of her achievement.

He leaned in close and repeated the words one more time before he kissed her. Jesse kissed him back. They continued kissing, bound together, for long minutes before Johnny slowly sat back on his heels and began loosening the cord of vine. He smiled at her again as she watched him untie their hands.

"Was that an eagle feather ritual?" she finally found the courage to ask when Johnny took a deep breath and stretched his arms up and out to relax. "I mean, is that why you got kind of freaky when I tried to give it to you?"

"Yeah," Johnny smiled with mischievous eyes. "I'm sorry if I scared you." He moved off his knees and lay on his side close to her. "One doesn't get the gift of an eagle feather every day, you know."

Jesse slid off her knees and lay down facing him. "I'll remember that the next time I come across one," she vowed.

"We won't have to do that again," he said, his passion stirring. He ran his fingers through her hair and brought some locks of it up to his nose. He inhaled deeply. "Ah, lavender," he smiled, his eyes smoldering. He freed her hair and trailed his fingers down to her shoulder and along her arm.

"Are you hungry?" she asked, intoxicated by his touch. She inched her body closer to his and rested her head in the crook of his other arm. With the small wounds on his face, he reminded her of the warrior she imagined when reading her Indian history books.

"Very," he groaned, pressing up against her. He wrapped his leg over hers and coerced her to lie down on her back. Now straddling her, he bent down and kissed her deeply. She complied with his kiss, feeling his warmth and strength. She stirred beneath him, her own heat welling up inside her as his kisses traced across her cheek, to her ear where he nibbled for a brief moment. She could hear his breath becoming heavier. She relaxed and allowed him free reign over her body. His kisses followed down along her neck to her heaving chest. Her head swam with visions. Her brave warrior, newly returned and relatively unscathed from his battle, was now on top of her, loving her. Her mind regressed back to another time where she imagined what an Indian woman must have felt when her man returned. The present slipped away as her eyes transfixed on his dark brown hair, shimmering in the sun above her. The eagle feather blended with that beautiful, silken hair and became a part of it—like a facet in a diamond.

His hand caressed her breast and her body arched willingly toward him. He felt her heart beating, faster and faster, like a frightened rabbit. Jesse moaned when he sat up on his knees again and brought her with him. She unbuttoned his shirt and touched his tawny brown, hairless chest. The muscles rippled under her fingertips. They kissed, tongues exploring, lips wet with desire. He slipped the straps of her dress off her shoulders and the loose bodice drifted down gently around her waist. His fingers, like soft feathers, danced on her rounded breasts.

Helpless in this game, and quickly losing control of her senses, Jesse found the buttons of Johnny's jeans and ripped them open, freeing a taut, throbbing shaft of muscle. She touched it and Johnny's breath caught in his chest. Their senses now at a fevered pitch, Johnny pushed his woman's dress out of the way and with magnificent force entered Jesse's body. At that moment they both held their breath. With their eyes riveted upon each other, their bodies moved slowly together like they had performed this dance a thousand times before. Johnny held tightly onto Jesse's hips. Jesse's fingers clung like a vice to her lover's back.

"Canhinyan tohunhunniyan kin," Johnny gasped with labored breath.

"Lovers forever," Jesse breathed, not knowing she had mimicked his words.

They slipped to the point where there were no words to express and they became not two separate beings, but one. Soon Jesse shuddered as her body released to Johnny's tempestuous thrusts. Johnny followed her a moment later, his life producing essence spilling unreservedly into Jesse's womb.

Johnny collapsed, tenderly, on top of Jesse. She smiled and held him tightly in her arms. They lay together, still as one, for a few glorious moments while their passion receded and the sun warmed them from above. When Johnny lifted his head and looked at his beloved, her eyes were closed and there was a contented smile upon her lips. He kissed both of her eyelids and then her lips. She slowly opened her eyes and her smile grew wider at the sight of him so close.

"I love you," she whispered.

"I love you," Johnny replied.

In the distance they heard a howl. They listened quietly as the rest of the chorus joined in.

"They'll find us soon, you know," Jesse talked softly. "I'd hate for you to have to explain your way out of this one."

Johnny laughed and slowly rolled over. They both moaned when the separation became complete. Johnny helped Jesse put her dress back on before he put himself in order. He kissed her whenever he got the chance.

"I like picnics," he declared as Jesse opened the picnic basket and gave him the bottle of wine.

"Do you now?" Jesse replied with a smirk on her face. "Then, I guess we'll have to go on another one real soon."

"Can you go on a picnic at night?" Johnny asked devilishly, removing the cork of the bottle with the corkscrew. "How about when it's raining, can you go on a picnic in the cabin?"

"Traditionally, you go on a picnic in a park," Jesse laughed, handing him some food. "That's the way it's usually done."

"And, so…" Johnny feigned apprehension, "everybody on a picnic in a park is doing what we just did? Doesn't that get kind of messy?"

Jesse punched her lover in the arm. "Eat your food, chief," she demanded. "You've got about twenty seconds."

Johnny looked at her quizzically. Unfortunately, not heeding her words, Shadow was on top of him in an instant, narrowly missing the young man's fingers when he snatched the bologna and cheese out of Johnny's hand. The man was checking to make sure all his fingers were still intact when Cheyenne came for him next. Mesa headed straight for the picnic basket and Jesse got it closed just in the knick of time.

"Picnic's over," she observed, getting slobbered with licks and a few strange sniffs. Shadow started pawing at the blanket and Johnny, suddenly realizing what was afoot, agreed with a nod of his head. He put the cork back into the bottle and picked up the blanket as soon as Jesse stepped off it. Shadow was very interested in the new scents. He tried to grab a corner of it from Johnny's hands with his powerful teeth. Johnny shook the blanket off and hung it up around his neck. He took Jesse's hand and with the wolves at their heels, they headed for home.

That night, after everyone had been fed and the food and dishes were all put away, Jesse headed for the couch, where they usually ended up. She wrapped herself in a blanket and turned on the television. Johnny came in from playing with the wolves, shut the door and locked it. He came up behind her on the couch, nuzzled her neck and cleverly grabbed the remote from her lap. He turned the set off.

When Jesse looked at him curiously, he smiled that rakish smile of his and said, "I'm kind of tired. Let's go to bed." He took her hand and led her up the stairs.

Jesse prepared herself for bed anticipating what might be coming next. She slipped on her sleeping gown and stepped out of the bathroom where she was greeted by a magnificent sight.

Johnny had lit the candles in the fireplace and stood naked, straight and tall, in front of them. His long shiny hair was glistening in the candlelight. Jesse's heart skipped a beat. She inhaled deeply and exhaled slowly. She lifted the gown up over her head and let it fall to the floor as she slowly walked toward him.

There was no timidity, only love. When she reached him, he ran his fingers through her long hair and placed it so it fell luxuriously down her back. The passionate urgency of their first encounter now over, the couple would have all night to explore and experience each other, as neither had done before.

Jesse's golden eyes opened and saw the blue Montana sky in her lover's eyes as Johnny sat, propped up by his arm with his head leaning against his hand, watching her.

"Ayuco anpetuhankeyela," he expressed lovingly.

"Good morning," Jesse sighed.

"How do you know my language?" he asked, somewhat bewildered. He kissed the tip of her nose.

"I haven't the faintest idea what you're talking about," Jesse smiled, cuddling up next to him. "Why, what did you say?"

"Good morning," Johnny replied, holding her close and pulling up the blankets around them.

"Oh," Jesse said, bewildered. "I have not the slightest clue, my darling, from whence my intelligence originates," she feigned an English accent.

"I guess we just think alike," he surmised, shifting a bit and leaning over her. "You need to look outside." He reached over and pulled back the heavy curtain next to the bed.

"I like the view in here, just fine," she smiled, checking out his body as he inclined over her.

"Be a good girl," he said playfully, coercing her to roll over on her side with his hand on her shoulder. "You've got to see this."

Jesse sighed and did as she was told. Upon looking out the window, she had to blink a couple of times to focus on the sight laid out before her. "Oh my!" she gasped excitedly. The land and the cabin were covered with a soft blanket of newly fallen snow. "When did that happen?"

"You've got me," Johnny smiled. "Look," he pointed out to the field. "The kids are loving it."

Shadow, Cheyenne and Mesa were playing and prancing in the white stuff that came up high enough to cover an inch or two above their paws. Shadow's nose was white from nuzzling in it. Cheyenne was almost camouflaged as her fur blended perfectly with the white powder. Mesa good-naturedly charged Shadow and they fell over, rolling in a mass of legs and fur. Shadow stood up and shook himself off. Mesa went after him again and they repeated their mock battle. Jesse laughed at their cavorting.

"It's their first snowfall," Johnny mentioned, laughing with her. "And your first one in Montana. Do you want to go out and play?"

"You bet I do!" Jesse beamed. They bounded out of bed and scurried into some clothes. It took some time finding the required gloves and scarves that Jesse had tucked away into a closet. Johnny had his boots on first and opened the front door. He was greeted by a perturbed bobcat that ran into the cabin through the hole in the screen door.

"Maybe I'd better stoke the fire," Jesse suggested, seeing Kitten in her foul mood.

"I'll do it," Johnny offered. "You go on outside."

Jesse kissed him as they exchanged places and she hopped into her other boot just before reaching the door. She ran out onto the porch and down the stairs. The wolves looked up and stared at her for one brief moment before they ran to greet her. They had her down in the snow in seconds, talking at her with their yips and yowls.

Johnny joined the party soon afterward to try to even up the sides, but they had him down to his knees even quicker. The Indian howled with glee and Cheyenne, with her paws firmly set upon his chest, howled in reply.

Shadow tugged at Jesse's jacket sleeve and got her up. The black wolf, covered in snow, wanted to go for a walk and he wanted his whole pack to go with him. He yipped at Mesa and the smaller wolf fell in behind him. He nudged Jesse on ahead.

"I think we're expected to tag along," Jesse called out to Johnny, who was now being urged by Cheyenne to get a move on too. "Are you okay with that?"

"Well, I guess we can take one more day off," Johnny acquiesced, following Cheyenne as she hurried to catch up. "But tomorrow, these wolves and you, my woman, have got to let me do some work!"

"We promise!" Jesse's voice echoed in the quiet.

The wolves, as they fully expected, got their way. They all traipsed off into the woods to experience their first winter day.

CHAPTER 24

❀

It was another five weeks before the snow started falling in earnest. Had she been alone in the cabin on those days in October, Joseph's omen might have come to fruition. She would surely have gone stir crazy after the first week. Instead, she had Johnny's gentle touch and constant companionship, which saved her from going insane.

He worked tirelessly on his new creations, every piece embellished with his trademark wolf design. Jesse, at first, tried to help, much to Johnny's surprise and encouragement. But it was soon discovered that Jesse's talents lie elsewhere—very, very far from any piece of wood. So she filled her hours, while Johnny toiled on his labors of love, roaming the Internet and finally emailing her old friends on a regular basis.

As indoor activities took precedence over outdoor ones, she now had plenty of time to read her books. Johnny liked it best when she read aloud as he worked. He especially liked learning about the wolves, although several of the stories tended to end on a sad note. He learned that after centuries of vilification, the wolves were still not welcome to live side by side with man, and those that did, usually did not survive in the end. Jesse ordered all kinds of books off the Internet for their amusement, which they eagerly awaited from the Post Office. Johnny loved the mysteries and the occasional torrid romance story. He loved the soft timbre of Jesse's voice.

The Dodge Ram was made for the snow and as long as Johnny was at the wheel they had no trouble getting into town, which was a great relief to Jesse. They had plenty of supplies and food, and all Jesse's creatures were healthy and energetic. The wolves spent most of their time outdoors. They reveled in the lower temperatures, coming alive on the coldest days and nights. Arleen told them she could hear their howls now at night and she lived twenty miles, as the crow flies, away. She said their music was haunting, yet comforting. It gave her a kind of peace knowing there was life out there in the cold fall nights. Shadow had developed one curious habit on the rare occasions he was inside the cabin. He'd nudge at Jesse's stomach, and whether she was sitting down or standing, he'd nose his way under her sweater and give her a couple licks. It tickled the woman, but as with all her animals' not very normal behaviors, she consented to his curious routine.

Kitten, who loved her nights by the fire, was becoming a regular house cat, meowing and purring at Jesse or Johnny's touch. Sometimes, one of them would awaken to find her curled up at the foot of the bed.

There was also plenty of time for lovemaking, which made the humans' evenings that much more pleasurable. During the longer nights, when lying in each other's arms, Jesse loved to listen to Johnny's measured breaths and feel his heartbeat against her breast.

She had purchased an Old West cookbook and tried her hand at the culinary arts. Johnny said each dish was the best he'd ever tasted. Sometimes she doubted his honesty, but he always ate every bite of everything she cooked.

And so the nights and days passed, one into the next, and Jesse was so very happy until she caught some kind of nasty bug and started throwing up in the mornings, feeling sick as a dog. She kept the news from Johnny, hoping it would pass. She didn't have a clue where the nearest hospital or doctor was, and did not want to worry him by asking.

One morning, as they drove into town to Arleen's store with some more chairs, the secret came out. Jesse had to have Johnny stop on the side of the road, where she promptly threw up in the snow. Johnny was out of the truck and at her side in a heartbeat.

"What's wrong, Jess?" he asked, very concerned. He rubbed her back as she wretched and vomited some more.

"The flu, I think," she gasped, wiping her mouth. A new round welled up and she did it again. "I don't know what's up. It just isn't getting any better, though," she confessed, comforted by her lover's touch.

"We'll drop the stuff off at the store and I'll take you into Browning," Johnny stated, helping her up. "There's a clinic there."

"Maybe it's just a mega fur ball," Jesse tried to joke. Her stomach was roiling inside her.

"Yeah, right," Johnny was not laughing. "How long has this been going on?"

"Not long," she lied. "Just a couple of days."

He got back behind the wheel and hit the accelerator. They arrived at the store in record time. Arleen was just opening up.

"You guys are out early," she called to them when they entered the store. She was busy in the back. "Hey, I've got a present for you, John…" She was shocked when she looked up and saw the look of trepidation on Johnny's face and the green hue of Jesse's skin. Jesse put down one of the chairs just inside the store and ran to the bathroom.

"What's going on?" Arleen asked Johnny. "What's the matter?"

"She's got some kind of bug," Johnny's voice was nervous. "I gotta' get her to the clinic in Browning."

"I don't think she's going to make it to Browning in that condition," Arleen observed. "Let me give Doc Bainbridge a call." She grabbed the phone and dialed the number.

Johnny carried one of his new chairs to the back of the store. He was shocked to see that the space was empty. He set the chair down and went to get the one Jesse had set just inside the door.

"Hey, Doc," Arleen said into the phone. "It's Arleen Stewart. Can you see a patient this morning?" Johnny dallied by the counter, waiting for Arleen's next words. "It's Jesse Harless, the woman who moved into Joe Stillwater's old cabin. It looks like she's got some kind of stomach flu.…Yeah…Sure, that's no problem. Charlie Stillwater's son is with her.…Okay.…Thanks, Doc." She hung up the phone and smiled warmly at the Native American. "He can see her right now. He's just down 89 about eight miles, before you hit the turn to Pendroy. It's a brick house on the west side of the road with a white fence and it'll say Bainbridge on the mailbox—you can't miss it. He'll be waiting at the door."

Jesse came out of the bathroom slowly, holding her stomach. "Damn it," she cursed. "I feel lousy."

"Johnny's gonna' run you over to Doc Bainbridge. He's south of here about eight miles."

"That's okay," Jesse stammered. "It goes away…"

"Johnny, get her over there now," Arleen insisted, walking around the corner and taking Jesse by the arm. She handed her over to Johnny who was just as insistent on getting her out the door. "I'll put the chair in the back and see you guys when you get done."

Johnny refused to let Jesse wiggle herself away from his grasp. He put her into the truck and locked the passenger side door. He ran around and got behind the driver's seat, gunning the truck into motion. He peeled down the two-lane highway. The Doctor was waiting, as Arleen had promised. Jesse started to get out of the truck, but Johnny was there immediately to help her. He held her by the arm and walked her across the yard to the front steps of Dr. Bainbridge's house.

"Bring her on inside," the Doctor ordered, holding the door open for them. My office is the first door on the right.

"Really, Johnny," Jesse sighed as he helped her up onto the examining table. "I'll be all right. This is probably unnecessary."

"When the Doctor tells me that," Johnny scolded her, squeezing her hand, "I'll believe you."

"Thank you, young man," the Doctor said, entering the room. "I need to ask you to wait outside."

"Yeah, okay," Johnny acquiesced reluctantly. He looked seriously into Jesse's eyes. "I'll be right outside."

"Go back to the store, Johnny," Jesse declared. "You need to get the rest of that furniture unloaded."

Johnny looked at her dubiously. He then turned his gaze to the doctor for his advice.

"I'll call Arleen when we're done," he said. "It could take some time."

Johnny looked back at Jesse and wanted desperately to kiss her.

"It's all right," Jesse smiled, knowing his dilemma. "I'll see you in a little while, okay?"

"All right," Johnny sighed. He let go of her hand and walked slowly out of the room. The doctor shut the door between them, locking him out.

Johnny was consumed with fear. He looked around the main hallway and saw a couple of very uncomfortable looking chairs where he could wait. But he was too nervous to sit down, so he trusted his woman's suggestion and left the house. He got back into the truck and returned to the store. It was probably smart to stay occupied. Parked in front of the store, he grabbed another rocking chair from the bed of the pickup. Arleen was waiting with the door open.

"It'll be okay, Johnny," Arleen tried to soothe her friend. "The Doc's good. He'll figure out what's wrong with her."

"She told me she's been like this for a couple of days," Johnny retorted, lugging the chair toward the back of the store. "When I think back, I'm sure she's been having this problem longer than that."

"The Doc will take care of it, Johnny," Arleen couldn't think of anything else to say. The Indian was incredibly worried and obviously very much in love with Jesse. Arleen had not realized it until she saw the look of panic in his eyes.

He dropped the chair down next to the others and stormed out to get the rest of the furniture he had made. He shrugged off Arleen's offer to help, so she just stood at the door and facilitated his passage in and out.

His brow was furrowed and he worked in silence. Arleen let him think things out. When he set down the last piece, a very heavy table, his head finally seemed to clear. "Hey, Arleen," he called out, not realizing she was right behind him. "Oh, sorry. I didn't see you there."

"That's okay," Arleen smiled warmly. "This new stuff is better than the first." She was inspecting the new merchandise with wide, excited eyes. "Damn, Johnny. You're really good."

"If I'm so good," Johnny snapped, still occupied with thoughts of Jesse, "what did you do with the other pieces?"

"That's what I was going to tell you when you came in," the woman smirked. "I've got a little present for you." She reached into her pocket and pulled out a check. "Sorry it isn't cash, but I don't want to keep that much money here in the store. I'd be picked off in a New York second if I kept that kind of cash in the register."

Johnny looked at her with stormy eyes and grabbed the check from her hand. The check was made out to him for the sum of twenty five hundred dollars. He looked back at her, stunned.

"I sold every piece," she smiled. "Even the stuff you made for me. I took a cut naturally, but that's all yours."

"I can't believe this," Johnny stammered. "This is a shit load of money!"

"Clayton bought two rockers. Some tourists picked up the table and chairs. They actually rented a little U-Haul to take them away. A couple in Conrad bought the cabinet. Gave me fifteen hundred bucks and didn't blink an eyelash. Like I said, you're damn good." She moved the chairs a little to display them better. "The word's getting out, Johnny. Three of these are already spoken for and I want the stuff you made for me replaced. But you don't have to worry about mine until spring. I sure could use that help, though. I know you're going to be busy, but I'd really like to clean up this area and make it kind of like a showplace. You know, add some paneling and some lights. I've ordered the building supplies I want and it should be delivered in another week. Can you help me get it up?"

"Sure," Johnny said, his eyes still staring at the zeros on the check. "As soon as I'm sure Jesse's all right," he added, remembering where she was.

"No problem," Arleen understood. "I'm hoping she can help too." She headed to the back of the store, grabbed two cups and filled them with hot coffee. "I'm starting to get calls about orders. Your work is going to make you rich." She walked back and handed him one of the cups of coffee. "And, of course, it'll put my store on the map."

"I can't believe this," Johnny sighed. "Jesus, it's just a bunch of wood."

"It's the wolves carved into the pieces," Arleen noted. "We need to come up with a name. You know, like *the wolf line* or something. People also want to know if they can get them with other animals, like bears or a moose."

Johnny thought about it. "I guess so," he finally concurred. "It's easy with the wolves, 'cos I see 'em every day. I'll have to have Jesse get me some pictures of other animals so I can copy them."

Arleen sat down in one of the chairs and suggested with a tap of her fingers that Johnny should join her. He was a little fidgety, but he submitted to her request and plopped himself down, almost spilling the coffee onto his lap.

"Be careful, Johnny," Arleen warned. "The price of these items we're sitting in has just gone up."

"Well, young lady," Dr. Bainbridge observed after listening to Jesse's symptoms. "I'm going to step out on a limb here and say I don't think you've got a bug." He got off his stool and went to the cabinet over the sink. He reached in and grabbed a paper cup. "I need a urine sample and then we'll know for sure. Can you do that for me?"

"Sure," Jesse assented. "Where do I...?"

"Down the hall, second door on the right," he started scribbling down some notes. "Just leave it in the bathroom and then come back in here."

Jesse followed the doctor's orders. Her nausea, like the other days, was starting to subside. After she finished, the doctor was waiting in the hall. "When was your last period, Jesse?" he asked professionally, still writing down notes.

"Ah," Jesse had to think a bit about that, "a month ago, I think." She thought about it a little more. "You know, I haven't been paying attention. It might be a little longer than that."

"So, you're not on the pill, then?" he inquired, stepping into the bathroom to retrieve the cup.

The realization as to where he was going with this line of questioning suddenly hit her like a ton of bricks. "No," she said, her breath caught in her throat.

The doctor nodded his head. "Why don't you get undressed for me back in the room. There's a gown next to the examining table."

Oh, shit! Jesse thought to herself, walking slowly back to the examination room. She had never even thought about that. She had always been careful in Denver. She and Eric used to boast about their respective condom collections. "Jesus, God," she whispered out loud, after she was back in the room. She leaned back against the closed door. "I'm fucking thirty-seven years old! I'm too old to have a baby!"

Johnny rocked a little too hard in the rocking chair while Arleen spouted off about anything she could, trying to take Johnny's mind off of Jesse. It was too hard; she just could not do it. "Hey," she finally said, finishing her cup of coffee. "You and Jesse have gotten pretty close, I take it."

"Why do you say that?" Johnny's eyes met hers with a hint of annoyance. "We're friends, that's all."

"Johnny, Johnny, Johnny," Arleen sighed, getting up from her chair. She took his cup with hers to the back. "I may look it, but I wasn't born yesterday." She thought briefly about pouring a shot of whiskey into Johnny's glass to help calm him down, but decided against it. "You guys have to be living together. You're always there when I call or stop by. Your mother and father haven't seen you in over a month. You know they do come into the store once in a while." She returned with more coffee. "And, by the way, they think your stuff is good, too."

"Yeah, I bet," snarled Johnny, recognizing he and Jesse had been caught.

"Bringing that wolf up here was a pretty big issue. The ranchers are still not very happy about it. Luckily, those animals haven't gotten in anybody's way, yet. And now you're flirting with a bigger issue that's going to end up just fueling the fire. Damn it, John, people up here don't like folks who cross the line. You better be prepared when this news gets out."

"It won't get out," Johnny stated. "We're just minding our own business, like everybody else should."

"But they won't and you know it. This is juicy gossip, man. They'll ride you or Jesse out on a rail." Arleen did not return to her chair. She paced back and forth in front of the Native American, clearly troubled. "And if I find out you're doing this to get back at your father or for some other damned reason…"

"My father has nothing to do with it," Johnny spat, springing out of his chair. "I love her, Goddamn it! I didn't ask for it. I never expected it. I just love her and she loves me. We aren't hurting anybody. Why can't you all just leave us alone?" He glared at her and started to storm off.

Arleen grabbed him by his jacket and held him back. "I'm the only friend you two have around here, so don't lose it with me."

Johnny shuddered and stopped in his tracks. She handed him the cup of coffee. "Take it," she snapped when he tried to refuse. "I had to make sure you weren't up to any of your old tricks, John. I've been around here long enough to know you aren't as perfect as Jesse thinks you are." She forced Johnny to take the cup. "I just needed to hear you say it," her voice quieted. "I've seen how you two look at each other. I have to know it's real, for my own peace of mind, before I can try to help."

Johnny turned his blue eyes toward her. She met his gaze straight on. "This is going to get out, Johnny. Your people are going to be as pissed as mine. Joseph will probably evict you from his cabin."

"He can try," Johnny retorted. "If he does, I'll build her a better one. One up in the mountains where nobody can find us."

"Are you going to marry her, then?" she questioned him.

"We already did it," Johnny replied, a hint of anger still in his voice. "She doesn't know it, but I did the ceremony myself." He drank some of the coffee with a gulp. "She gave me an eagle feather. I happened to have the blanket at the time. Except for the horses, we're legal in my world and the eyes of the Creator."

"Oh, man," sighed Arleen. "Your father's going to have a stroke."

"Red Cloud is on our side," Johnny volunteered. "He said it was meant to be."

"Well," Arleen interjected, "you'd better make it legal in the white world if you don't want people calling her your *squaw*."

Johnny set the coffee cup down on one of the shelves and pressed his hands hard against his head. "I know," he moaned. "Goddamn it, I know." His eyes softened. "Just let me hear she's all right first, okay? This waiting is tearing me up inside."

Like a cue, the telephone rang on the counter. Arleen rushed to pick it up. "Hello?" she shouted into the receiver.

"The boy can pick her up now," the doctor's words were short.

"She's okay then?" Arleen asked hopefully.

"She's fine and ready to go."

"Thanks, Doc," Arleen said hurriedly. She indicated for Johnny to move with a nod of her head. He was out the door and starting the truck before she could hang up the receiver.

"Now, these should help with the morning sickness," the doctor told Jesse as she slipped into her jacket. He handed her a bottle of pills. "And I want to see you in two months. Here's my number. My wife can set up an appointment for you."

"Thanks, Doctor," Jesse murmured quietly. "I appreciate your help."

The Doctor wanted to dislike the young woman, for it was obvious who the father was. But she seemed so helpless and confused. He could not find it within himself to be harsh. He placed a hand on her shoulder as they passed into the hall. "It will be all right," he said warmly. "You're going to be fine."

"Yeah," Jesse muttered incoherently. She was still in a state of shock.

The Doctor opened the front door just as Johnny wheeled the truck into his driveway. "You get home and get some rest. You'll feel better once the pills take effect." He gave the Indian a disdainful look when Johnny ran up the walk to meet them. "Get her out of this cold. She needs to stay warm."

"Thanks, Doctor," Johnny's eyes were welled up with tears. "Is there anything I need to do for her?"

"I'd say you've done enough," the Doctor replied. "Just get her home."

Johnny looked at the man, stunned, but the doctor turned on his heel and went back inside his house without another word. "What the hell…"

"It's okay, Johnny," Jesse tried to smile. She was close to tears herself. "Can we please just go home?"

Johnny glared at the door to the doctor's house, but then gave up. Jesse held onto him so tightly, it almost hurt. He turned his concentration back to her and helped her into the truck.

Once she was safe in the truck, Jesse's tears flowed uncontrollably. She sobbed into her hands, unable to stop. Johnny pulled the truck off to the side of the road and stopped.

"Jesse, what is it?" he demanded, trying to pry her hands from her face. "I thought he said you were all right." Jesse's chest rose for a new bout of wailing. Johnny pulled her forcibly to him, holding her close. "You're scaring me, Jess," he murmured. "Tell me what's wrong?"

"I fucked up," Jesse cried, her face pressed to his chest. "I'm so sorry, Johnny. I just fucking fucked up!"

"All right," Johnny worried. "You've got to settle down. What did you *fuck* up?" He took her face into his hands and made her look at him. Her eyes were already puffy and turning red.

"I'm pregnant, Johnny!" she screamed. "I'm so sorry! I fucked up."

Johnny's eyes widened with surprise. He looked at her, baffled, but not upset. As a matter of fact, the more he thought about it, he couldn't help but smile. He kissed her, tasting the salty tears upon her lips.

"Did you not hear me?" She returned his stare, more bewildered than he was.

"Yeah!" Johnny's smile grew wider. "You're going to have my baby! How great is that!?"

"Johnny," Jesse rejoined him, "this wasn't supposed to happen!"

"Why not?" he asked, kissing her again. "And let me add that it takes two in this particular situation to *fuck* up. Which, we've been doing quite a lot of lately."

"Johnny," the young woman asked incredulously, "what are we going to do with a baby?"

"Love and raise it," he grinned, "just like all our other babies." Jesse stared at him blankly. "Although, I don't think we'll be able to throw him outside for the night when we want to be alone."

Jesse hiccupped. "You're not upset about this?"

"Do you love me?" he inquired, still smiling.

"Yes."

"And you know I love you, right?"

"Yes," she hiccupped again.

"And you swore to stay with me forever just...let me think," he pondered a quick second, "over a month ago, right?"

"Yes."

"Sooner or later, this was bound to happen," Johnny surmised. "And I'm pretty happy about it. God knows if it happened much later we'd be giving birth to our grandchildren. So it might as well be now rather than later."

The corners of Jesse's lips turned up even though she desperately tried not to smile. "This is serious!"

"And I am serious," Johnny countered. "I love you. We're having a baby. What are you going to do when the wolves start procreating, have a complete breakdown?"

Jesse socked him on his arm. "Damn you!" she muttered, her sorrow dissipating.

"No," he smirked, kissing her one more time, "this actually might save me, in the long run." He held her tight and she hiccupped one more time. "Now, rest your head on my shoulder and let me drive. Let's go home."

"So we're supposed to be happy about this?" Jesse questioned him as he drove the truck back onto the road and sped off.

"Well, in…how many months?" he asked.

"Approximately eight," she answered soberly.

"Well, in eight months you're probably going to have a few choice words to throw at me for a few hours, but then it should be good again. So yes. We're happy about this." He glanced at her briefly before returning his eyes to the road. "We're the happiest we've ever been!"

A little while later, Arleen was watching from the window when they sped by. "Shit!" she said aloud, shaking her head. She had thought about the symptoms and what the doctor had said. "Like we need this now." She put her coffee cup down and went back to work, grateful for the distraction.

CHAPTER 25

"You what?" Johnny demanded, throwing down his chisel. He looked up at Jesse with angry eyes.

"I called your mother and asked if they'd like to come for Thanksgiving Dinner." Looking at her lover's stare, she realized her grave mistake immediately. "Red Cloud suggested I do it."

"What in the hell does Red Cloud have to do with anything?" Johnny had been having trouble with one of his pieces all morning. The bear he had been carving looked more like a buffalo and, try as he might, he could not fix it. "And when in the hell did you talk to *him*? He doesn't have a phone!"

"He came over yesterday while you were at the store," Jesse answered quickly. "He brought us the turkey."

"What the f…" Johnny stopped short before he cursed. "You're telling me that Red Cloud walked all the way over here—with a turkey—and decided we should have Thanksgiving dinner?"

"He came by to see how I was doing and to congratulate us on the baby." Jesse suddenly didn't feel so good. She sat down on her chair in front of the computer. Johnny was very angry and she could not believe how much it upset her. She wanted to cut out her tongue for bringing it up at all.

"How did he know about the baby???" Johnny screeched. Cheyenne, who was lying next to him, decided it was time to get up and leave the room.

Jesse took a deep breath. She wanted him to stop berating her. "I don't know how he knew about the baby!" she snapped. "He just knew, okay? You'll just have to ask him yourself!" She got up, feeling sick, and headed out the door. "I'm sorry! If it's any consolation, your mother said they wouldn't be able to come."

"Does *she* know about the baby?" Johnny called after her, knocking his stool over when he stood up.

"How the hell should I know?" Jesse screamed back, heading for the bathroom. "If she does, I didn't tell her—if that's what you're thinking! I didn't tell Red Cloud either!" She slammed the bathroom door, lifted the toilet seat, promptly dropped to her knees and threw up. *So much for happily ever after,* she thought, vomiting again.

Johnny stormed into the bathroom and stopped in his tracks. He didn't realize how angry he could still get and he was suddenly horrified that he'd been angry with the one person who meant the world to him. He got down on his knees and pulled her hair back away from her face. "I'm sorry, babe," he said, rubbing her back. "You just caught me at a bad time. I'm having trouble with my work."

"I didn't plan any of this," Jesse coughed. "I'm not stupid, you know."

"No, babe," Johnny apologized. "You're not stupid, I know that."

"I've read and learned enough to know that the *last* holiday your people would celebrate would be Thanksgiving. Jesus! Thanks for shoving us off our land. Thanks for massacring our families. Thanks for killing us with typhoid tainted blankets. Thanks for poisoning the rest of us with booze and drugs and taking us down and keeping us there!" She sat back on her heels and felt his body next to hers. His heart was beating rapidly in his chest. "But Red Cloud said we should do it. He said he'd come and help cook. He gave me the turkey and he said to call your mother and invite them. And if I felt up to it, I was to call Arleen." She flushed the toilet and reached out for a washcloth, but couldn't manage it. Johnny got up and grabbed it for her. He washed some cold water over it and wrung it out before he gently tried to wash her face. She slapped his hand away and took the washcloth from him, determined to do it herself. "He also said I shouldn't tell you because it would be a nice surprise. Thank God I didn't listen to everything he said. You probably would have beat the crap out of me tomorrow."

"No, Jess, no," Johnny said hastily. He got back down on his knees and tried to take her into his arms. She swatted at him, trying to push him away. He would not take *no* for an answer and forced his arms around her, holding her tight. "I would never hit you!" he vowed. "That would be like hitting myself." He took her face into his hands and kissed her hard. "Don't ever say anything like that again. I'm sorry. Do you hear me? I'd didn't mean to get so mad." She looked at him distrustfully. "Oh God, Jesse," he shrieked. "Don't look at me like that. Don't ever look like that again." He held her close and refused to let go until she settled down. "We'll have your party," he whispered into her ear. "I'll call Arleen myself. Forgive me, Jess. I promise I'll never talk to you that way again."

Jesse finally started to calm down. "I'm sorry too," she mumbled into his shirt. "I guess we're both a little on edge." Johnny let her go just enough so that she could look at him. Her eyes were filled with tears. "It's this baby," she sighed. "That's the problem."

"There's no problem," Johnny warned her, in a serious tone. "The *baby* is our thanksgiving. We will celebrate like we won the war." He helped her up to her feet. "Come on, let's put you on the couch."

Cheyenne was scratching on the front door from the inside. Shadow was scratching and yipping on the outside. Johnny made Jesse sit down and he covered her shoulders with a blanket. He then went to the door and let Shadow and Mesa in. Shadow made a beeline for Jesse, resting his head in her lap. She smiled down at him and rubbed his nose. "There's my good boy," she tried to smile. "Where have you been all day?"

Johnny returned to the couch with some milk and cookies. "No, not for you," he gently scolded Shadow who was sniffing at the plate. "These are for your mother." He lifted the plate up over Shadow's head, which he realized was silly, because the wolf was now big enough to knock it out of his hand with no trouble at all, no matter how high it was. On his hind legs, Shadow was over six feet tall.

"There's some grapes in the refrigerator," Jesse suggested. "We should all have a treat."

Johnny got up and went to the kitchen. Shadow turned his attention back to Jesse and started nosing at her sweater. She lifted it up, so he could get in his licks. When Johnny returned and saw the wolf, it hit him.

"I'm sorry again, Jess," he sighed, sitting down. Shadow growled a low growl, deep in his throat. "Of course Red Cloud would know about the baby. Shadow knew about it before we did."

"Uh, huh," agreed Jesse, petting her wolf. "I'm as scared as you are of what's going to happen when everybody else finds out."

Johnny brushed her hair away from her face and dangled the grapes over Shadow's head. The animal grabbed them like a fish locking onto a baited hook. "None of that matters. We'll be fine and so will the baby." He turned her face to his with his hand. Her eyes looked lifeless, like a doll's eyes. "Nothing's changed, Jesse," he said desperately. "It's better. Remember the check I got yesterday? We've got money coming in and I've got more work to do. We're help-ing Arleen fix up the store, and who knows what will happen after that."

"I feel like I've put you in a trap," Jesse murmured, her tears welling up again in her eyes. "You need to open up an account at the bank and put that money in it…and the money in the jar. That's your money. You deserve it. I don't want you to be angry with me. I don't want you to feel that you owe me anything. If you want to go, I understand."

Johnny shook his head in disbelief. "Why are you talking like this?" he implored. "What's wrong?"

"The anger," Jesse sighed. "I saw it in your eyes. That was the anger I saw when I first met you. I've changed and now you have too."

The Indian sat back and took a deep breath, expelling it slowly. He had to think and he had to think fast. His anger had upset her and he did not have the slightest clue how to patch things up. He searched in his mind for Red Cloud's words; *pay attention to the signs. A woman is not so hard to figure out. You can track an animal. You can guide yourself in the night. Figure this out, man,* he thought to himself. *Figure this out!* What was different now? Nothing, as far as Johnny could determine. The baby, that was the key. Wait. There *were* changes. Big changes for the woman. Hormonal or something. She was feeling vulnera-ble. *She* was feeling trapped. There had to be words to sooth her troubled soul.

"You're right," he started slowly, taking her hand. "There are changes and I know you're upset. I am still angry with my father, Jess. And when you men-tioned you had called them, it came out. I don't want him to know yet. I'm afraid of what he'll do to try and mess this up." He stroked her hair and she responded, leaning her head against his hand. He smiled and her eyes softened. "This is our choice. Something within us made it happen. I do not regret it and I wish you wouldn't either. I'm not going anywhere. There is no place else I'd rather be than by your side. The money is *ours*. You helped inspire me to earn it. Please tell me what to say to you so you won't worry so much. You've got enough things going on in that beautiful body of yours and I don't want to make it any tougher for you, just because I don't fully understand."

Jesse touched his face with her hand. She leaned in close and kissed him with a gentle sweetness. "Just keep loving me," she whispered. "I don't ever want to make you angry. We've got enough things going against us—it would kill me if we turned against each other."

Johnny kissed her fervently. "I love you, Jesse," he smiled. She was returning to her own self, at last. He could feel it, see it and taste it in her kiss. "Please have my baby. Nothing can stop us from being together once that happens."

She fell into his arms with Shadow caught between them. He nudged in, licking them both as they kissed. When they came up for air, Johnny shifted, feeling suddenly aroused. The wolf took advantage of it and crowded his way onto the couch.

"Hey boy," Johnny growled playfully, "stop hogging my woman!"

Jesse laughed as the wolf enveloped her his paws and some more licks. "It's all right," she countered, breathless from the wolf's strength. "I've been neglecting him lately. He deserves his time, too."

Johnny got up, adjusting his jeans. "Well, they'll be sleeping outside tonight," he insisted. "I'm going to call Arleen." When he went over to the phone, the other wolves joined Shadow and Jesse around the couch. "The competition is fierce around here," Johnny quipped, dialing the number.

Arleen had plenty of other things to talk about after she accepted their dinner invitation. As Johnny listened patiently, Jesse took the opportunity to climb out from under her furry family and walk into the workroom. Johnny did not notice. When he finally hung up, he saw that the room was empty. "Hey," he called out with a perplexed look, "where did everybody go?"

"We're in here," Jesse answered. "We're looking at your work."

Johnny joined them. Cheyenne rubbed up against him and demanded some attention from her male human. He rubbed her neck briskly and let her lick his face.

"Johnny," Jesse observed, looking at his latest carving. "I don't see anything wrong here. It's a beautiful buffalo."

"Arrrgh," Johnny rumbled. "That's the problem. It was supposed to be a bear."

"Oh," Jesse said, embarrassed. She eyed the carving closer for a few more seconds and then got up off the stool. She fought her way through the cluster of wolves so she could hug her man again. "I'd stop fighting it," she advised. "The world needs a few good buffalo chairs, now and then." Johnny smiled and returned to his work—making a buffalo instead.

"Were you the only one to get the pigheadedness in your family? Or is it in your genes?" Winona snapped at Charlie, who had turned his back to her. "It's got to be the genes, because your sons are just as pigheaded as you are!" Winona slammed the frying pan onto the stove and threw in the meat she was going to cook for dinner. Charlie started to leave the kitchen. "If you want *any-thing* to eat tonight, you better not think this discussion is over."

"What discussion is there?" Charlie retorted. "It seems like it's your way or the highway, woman."

"You're going to have to accept this sooner or later," Winona reasoned. "Your son fell in love with a white woman and she's having his baby."

"Jesus!" Charlie spat. "Do you have to keep repeating it?" He yanked the chair from under the table and sat down with a thud. "What did I do to make that boy hate me so much?"

"He doesn't hate you," Winona said in an effort to make peace. "He's just always been different. Frankie and Joe always did what you told them to do. When Johnny asked why, you never gave him a reasonable answer. He could not understand 'because I say so'. He always saw an open window when you said the door was closed."

"He's never forgiven me for not killing those men," Charlie sighed. "He could never understand why I didn't seek revenge." He looked up at his wife with tired eyes.

"Now that he's in love," Winona offered, "maybe that will change." She turned the burner under the pan to low and joined her husband at the table. "He's in love with Jesse, Charlie," she sighed. "Is that such a bad thing? It took him forty years, but he's finally doing something with his life." She placed her hand over his where it rested on the table. "Indians marry white people, old man. It happens every day. I wouldn't be here if it didn't."

"One bad egg didn't spoil the whole bunch," Charlie rationalized. "You're more Indian than white."

"And I'd guess Jesse's got some Indian blood somewhere in her family," Winona suggested. "No pedigreed debutante would do what she's done to save that wolf."

Charlie gave his wife a weak smile, shifting his hand to hold on to hers tightly.

"You told me you liked her, once," Winona continued. "You said she had guts for changing her life. Well, it looks like she's changed our lives, too. And from what I can see, that's not such a bad thing. She respects our ways and she loves our boy. And whether you like it or not, she's giving us a grandchild, and I am thrilled about that. I doubt the little fellow will be blue-eyed and blond, so what's the big deal? As a grandfather, maybe you'll be able to get across to Johnny's son what you couldn't get through to Johnny—that you love him and only want him to be proud of who he is."

"I'm not going to be able to go over there tomorrow," Charlie said. "You know that, right?"

"I don't think you should...yet," Winona agreed. "They're going to be shocked enough, seeing me." The woman got back up and returned to her cooking. "You've said it yourself a hundred times. These kids, nowadays, have their own set of standards and ideas. We did our best to raise them right. Maybe we need to start trusting their choices."

That night when Jesse and Johnny lay tangled in each other's arms in bed, with the moon peeking through the window and casting shadows around them, Johnny posed a question to his woman. "It may be a little too late to ask, but would you marry me, Jess?"

"Why would it be too late to ask?" she queried, raising herself up to look at him.

"Will you?" he insisted.

Jesse rolled her eyes up skyward as if to ponder his question and then laughed at the troubled look that crossed his face. "Yes, Johnny Stillwater, I would."

"Good," he declared, rolling her onto her back and climbing gently on top of her, "because I need to confess something before we go any further with this discussion. Just so we're on the same battleground here."

"What?" Jesse asked nervously, looking questionably into his eyes.

"Remember the picnic?" he started, a little nervous himself. When she nodded with a dreamy smile upon her face, he ventured, "Well, remember that ritual I did when you gave me the eagle feather?"

"Yes." Jesse was listening.

"It was pretty much our family's traditional wedding ceremony," Johnny cringed when the words came out, yet he continued hastily. "I didn't expect to do it, but when you gave me the eagle feather...well, that's what the bride does and...I know I should have told you...but at the time it just felt right...and I'll buy you a horse someday and..."

Jesse put a finger to Johnny's lips to quiet him. "It was a beautiful ceremony," she hummed. "And you're the most beautiful man I've ever known—especially when you're nervous," she smiled lustily. "Just consider yourself lucky I said *yes*."

"Well, this time," he went on, "we can do it with a preacher or something. That way it'll be on the up and up."

"One's enough," she stated. "No preacher could *ever* do it as well as you did. And, as far as I'm concerned, a piece of notarized paper is just that; a piece of paper. It's the bond between two people that makes it official."

"There were no witnesses," he warned.

"Thank heaven," she quipped, remembering what happened next. "But, you're wrong. The most important witness was there in all His glory. And as far as I'm concerned, His presence made it more legal than any church wedding could ever do." She giggled at his befuddled look. "The Creator gave us his light that day. Don't you remember? You talked to Him for a good ten minutes."

"Oh, yeah…" he smiled, seeing her logic. "As always, wife, you are correct."

"Now kiss me, husband," she said, putting her arms around him and pulling him down on top of her. "I feel another picnic coming on."

"We can do that?" he asked eagerly, with his eyes wide in anticipation. He rubbed against her body with his own, settling in.

"According to the Internet, for as long as we want."

"You're a good wife," Johnny sighed, kissing her slowly. "Thanks for checking on the details." His next kiss and several after showed his appreciation—and his love.

CHAPTER 26

❁

Something told Jesse to be up and ready early the next day. She was dressed and coaxing Johnny into the shower when she heard Red Cloud's voice at the bottom of the stairs. "You people up?" he called out. "I'm here and ready to cook."

"Shit," Johnny had been trying his best to convince Jesse to take another shower when he heard the old man's voice. "Get downstairs," he kissed her quickly. "I'll be there in a minute."

Jesse hurried down the stairs and greeted the Indian. "You are true to your word, Red Cloud. And I'm ready to help."

The old Indian smiled at her and waited for her at the bottom of the stairs. "I brought Rex. I hope that won't be a problem."

"I'm afraid that's up to the wolves," Jesse warned, accepting Red Cloud's outstretched hand. "I'm not sure..." she stopped in mid-sentence when she reached the last riser and glanced into the living room. Red Cloud tightened his grip on her hand when she became distracted. Winona Stillwater was on her hands and knees stoking the fire in the fireplace. Jesse's gaze returned to Red Cloud, who brought her safely down the last step.

"Rex has already met them," the old man replied. "They've been very kind, as far as wolves are concerned." He squeezed Jesse's hand and directed her into the living room. "And Winona was good enough to bring us here in her truck, so us old ones did not have to walk so far in the snow."

Jesse looked at her mother-in-law with trepidation. Winona, pleased with the now roaring fire, stood up and dusted off her hands before turning to face the young woman. She returned her gaze, smiling.

"I was able to make it after all," Johnny's mother spoke softly. "I hope that will be all right."

"Of course it is," Jesse said eagerly. "I'm so happy you'll be with us."

"Where's the turkey?" Red Cloud asked. "You kept it cold but not frozen, right?"

"Aaaah," Jesse was momentarily confused. Seeing her mother-in-law had thrown her off track for a moment. "...Yes. It's in that room there," she pointed to the storage room. She saw Winona glance at the eagle feather that Johnny had hung on the wall along with the blanket and the now dried up string of vines. She suddenly knew why he had done that. She also saw that Winona recognized it, too. "And Charlie?" the younger woman asked.

Winona turned her eyes back to her daughter-in-law. She walked up to her and gave her a warm hug. "He had some tribal business to attend to," she said, holding Jesse close for a moment. "He couldn't come."

"That's too bad," Jesse exhaled. "But you're here and that's wonderful. Thank you for coming."

"I wouldn't have missed it," Winona said wisely. "We haven't seen our son or you for some time now. Your wolves are healthy and strong; and I've seen some of Johnny's work at the general store. This cabin is so warm and welcoming and I'm anxious to hear about everything you've been doing to make it so nice."

Red Cloud came out of the storage room with the turkey in its roasting pan. "Let me help you with that," Jesse offered, knowing how heavy it was.

"No, daughter," Red Cloud was adamant. "You talk with Winona. I said *I* was going to cook."

"This doesn't happen often in our world," Winona whispered into Jesse's ear. "We must welcome this present and let him be." She took Jesse's hand into her own. "Now come show me where my son does his work."

Jesse led her into the workroom and smiled when Winona's eyes grew wide with admiration. "He's been very busy," Jesse mentioned, allowing her time to look at every piece. "He's made three thousand dollars and Arleen says there's more to come."

"I've always known in my heart he was talented," Winona said. "I thank the Creator and you for letting that talent come out."

"He's a good man, Winona," Jesse boasted. "I love him..." she cut herself off, grasping what she almost said. "I mean, I love *his* work and what he's done."

Winona looked at the young woman and smiled. "I know you love him very much," she responded perceptively. "One would have to be blind not to see it. And I have to wonder if even blindness could conceal it."

"I don't want to get him in trouble for this," Jesse spewed out. "I know it's wrong for us to be together."

Winona's body stiffened. She walked resolutely among the newly constructed pieces of furniture and toward Jesse. She took both of Jesse's hands into hers and held them tightly. She looked deeply into her daughter-in-law's eyes. "This is not wrong," she said seriously. "It is the rest of the world that is not right. You love my son and he loves you. There is nothing wrong with that. To be apart would be the worst thing you could do. The Creator sees to it that races mix. Otherwise there would be no hope for tolerance or a good understanding of other heritages and histories.

"You are more Native American than you know—if not by blood, then by spirit. None of my people have tried to help the Creator's creatures like you have. You gave everything up to try and help one wolf. By choosing to do that, you have helped other animals who might not have seen the light of day or the stars by night if you hadn't been here to take them in. You have given your heart to a man who did not think he deserved love. He has become the man not even I could teach him how to be."

Still holding Jesse's hands, she placed them on her stomach. "There is a life inside you who will understand and respect both of our worlds. With the love you both give him, he could someday be the one to bridge some of the many gaps between our people. Don't fret about this child in your womb. Be strong and he will be strong. Be fretful and he will die."

"But the prejudices he will face," Jesse countered on the verge of tears. "How can we subject him to that?"

"He is already ahead in the game," Winona smiled. "He will learn from both white and red. Arleen and Clayton will care for him as much as Red Cloud and I do. He will grow up with strong values and not be afraid—I promise."

"But Charlie..." Jesse heaved with a catch in her throat.

"Charlie is my business and Johnny's," the older woman declared. "Your only duty to help us is to give us Johnny's son. A grandson, no matter where he comes from, is my husband's greatest wish."

"I get so sick," Jesse confessed. "And my emotions are so screwed up."

"Aaaah," Winona grinned, "I can take care of that. You've been to a doctor?"

"Yes. He gave me some pills."

"I have better medicine," Winona proposed. "I will relieve your pain and your doubts before I leave tonight." Johnny's footsteps thundered down the stairs, startling them both. "Your love gives my son strength," Winona added quickly. "Let me give you the strength to see you through this. It will be worth it." She kissed Jesse on the cheek and wiped away the tear that had fallen there.

Seeing no one in the living room, Johnny's gaze turned and found the two women just inside the door of the workroom. He was dumbstruck when he saw his mother holding Jesse's hands.

"I like the buffalo you're carving, son," Winona said, giving him a loving smile.

"Boy," Red Cloud called from the kitchen three hours later. "Come in here and peel these potatoes."

Arleen had been regaling the small party with tales of customers and their rave reviews over Johnny's furniture. Johnny was enjoying the testimonials on behalf of his work. But when Red Cloud spoke, he jumped to attention, leaving his wife's side with a kiss on her cheek.

"Hey, old man," Johnny retorted, joining his long time friend in the kitchen. "Didn't you hear? I'm about to be famous. I shouldn't have to be doing this kind of work."

"You're not famous yet, boy," Red Cloud corrected him. "So get in here and help me."

"Red Cloud," Arleen piped up from the living room, "let me know when I can get in there and make the salad."

"Yeah, yeah," the Native American answered. "One cook at a time, missus. I'll let you know."

There was a scratching at the door and now it was Jesse's turn to jump up. She opened the door for three wolves and a very tired old canine, who traipsed in like royalty. The aroma of the turkey caught the attention of all four noses and they headed straight for the kitchen.

"Sweet bejeezus, what's all this now?" the old man queried, stepping gingerly out of the way of the many paws and snouts that were suddenly crowding him.

"Johnny," Jesse tried to help out, "grab me the grapes, will you?"

Johnny, the closest to the refrigerator, shooed Cheyenne to the side and opened the door. He grabbed the bowl of grapes and handed them over the sea of fur to his wife with a wink.

"I can't believe how those animals have grown," remarked Winona. "They were just pups only a few months ago."

"I can't believe Rex fits in with them so well," Jesse noted, tempting the wolves to follow her with the sweet fruit they loved.

"Aw, Rex is an old wolf at heart," Red Cloud said, giving his old companion a piece of fry bread.

Shadow was still engrossed with the smell of the turkey. He was the last one to leave the kitchen, and that was only because it appeared Jesse might be handing out pieces of whatever was cooking. While Cheyenne and Mesa were content with their grapes, Shadow looked a bit perturbed at his mother's offering. Nonetheless, he ate them just the same. Jesse had fed the wolves extra portions the day before, hoping they might not be enticed by the holiday feast, but the new smells were too strong to ignore.

"Do you think we'll see a baby this spring?" Arleen asked, petting Mesa as he gobbled down his grapes.

Johnny glanced over at Jesse for a quick second to see if she was all right with the question, knowing what Arleen was really fishing for.

"Keep your mind on your work, boy," Red Cloud interjected as Jesse smiled at them both. "You'll slice a finger off if you're not careful."

"Not 'til next spring," Jesse smiled, playing dumb. "Wolves don't reproduce until their second year."

"Oh," Arleen pouted. "I'd love to hear the pitter patter of little feet...and little howls."

"End of May," Johnny announced from the kitchen, answering Arleen's real question. He had told her the news yesterday because she had already guessed. "Around the thirtieth is our guess."

Arleen smiled at Jesse who was retaking her seat, with Shadow in tow looking for more treats. "Are you okay?"

"Better now," replied Jesse, giving Winona a quick look. "Winona gave me this wonder medicine and my stomach's been good all day."

"So," Arleen went on, "what do you want? A boy or a girl?"

"She's got no say in the matter," Red Cloud declared, filling a pot with hot water. "Put those potatoes in there, boy, and get them cooking." He grabbed a dishtowel and wiped his hands. When he looked into the living room, every eye in the place was on him. "It's a boy," Red Cloud stated matter-of-factly. "No question in my mind."

"And how do you know that, Red?" Arleen asked doubtfully. "I'd say there's at least a fifty-fifty chance here for a girl."

"Nope," Red Cloud confirmed. "It's a boy and I already know his name, too."

"Oh no you don't," Johnny retorted, returning to the living room now that the potatoes were in the pot. "Don't be filling Jesse's head with any silly names. She gets to pick this one herself."

Winona shook her head slowly and sat up in her chair. Shadow had come to greet her and she happily gave him some attention.

"I haven't even thought about that yet," Jesse answered. "I wasn't really happy with the news until today."

"Can't help it," Red Cloud persisted. "Yes, the baby will come in May. Yes, it is a boy. And his name is…"

"Damn it, man, I'm warning you, don't say it." Johnny was adamant. He went over and sat on the back of the couch, leaning against Jesse. "My kid's not gonna' be called some silly name like Running Bear or Dancing Wolf. It's not…"

"I'm not talking about his Indian name," Red Cloud remarked. "I'm talking about the name Jesse's gonna' give him."

"I don't care!" Johnny was smiling, but he was growing frustrated with the whole conversation.

"Well, I'd like to make a bet on this and we'll have to figure out some way…" Arleen chirped. "…I've got it!" She reached down in her purse and dug for a piece of paper and a pen. Mesa looked with her, sniffing the contents of her bag. "Here," she announced proudly. "Red Cloud, you will write down all your predictions on this piece of paper. You'll seal it and we'll keep it some-place safe until it's all said and done. Would that be fair?"

"I suppose so," Johnny relented with a sly look.

Arleen handed the pen and paper to Red Cloud who took it into the kitchen and sat down at the table. He put the tip of the pen to his lips and looked upward, considering his predictions for a moment before he started to write them down.

"Hey, medicine man," Johnny quipped. "We can do without the drama."

"I can still put you over my knee," Red Cloud barked. "Be quiet while I think."

The room fell silent as they watched the old Indian write. "The baby will be born…" he wrote down the date. "The baby will be a…" he wrote down the gender. "The baby's name will be…" he scrunched up his face, taking his time spelling it out. "…Don't ask me, why." He finished his document and set down the pen. He looked up at his audience and grinned. "Now what do I do with it?"

"Fold it up," Arleen ordered. "Jesse, do you have an envelope?"

"...I think so, yes. Johnny, there should be one in the workroom in the drawer where the pens and paper are."

Johnny got up and retrieved the envelope while Red Cloud folded his piece of paper about five different times.

"Good," Arleen declared. She took the envelope from Johnny's hand and motioned for him to sit back down. "It's a money envelope; that's perfect. Nobody can see through it." She walked over and handed the envelope to Red Cloud who placed the small piece of paper into the envelope and sealed it.

"Thank you," Arleen said when she handed it to him. "Now, where should we put it?"

"Jesse and Johnny shouldn't know where it is," Winona joined in the game. "Why don't you two go into the bathroom for a minute and shut the door."

Jesse looked at her husband who raised an eyebrow at her and gave her a sly smirk. He took her hand, ushering her into the bathroom. He looked positively devilish when he closed the door.

Winona took the envelope from Arleen and whispered to her that she should go upstairs, in case they were listening at the door. Arleen nodded in agreement and placed herself at the bottom of the stairs. Winona took the envelope and searched the room. She went into the workroom. She returned with a pushpin from the desk and nudged Arleen to make some noise going up the stairs. Winona went over to the eagle feather and blanket hanging on the wall and attached it to the wall with the pushpin under one of the folds of the blanket. Red Cloud gave her the thumbs up sign, and Arleen wandered upstairs for a little while before returning noisily.

While this was going on, Johnny and Jesse heard nothing. They were kissing and petting like a couple of kids sneaking around on the porch after a date. Arleen caught on quickly when they did not come out upon being called. She tiptoed to the bathroom and listened at the door for a moment, a smile growing on her lips. Red Cloud sat down on the couch and Winona returned to her chair. Arleen opened the door quickly and stuck her head in, startling the pair when she discovered their little tryst.

"I said you can come out now," she laughed, yanking Johnny away from Jesse by grabbing his shirt. "Good Lord, you two, we can't leave you un-chaperoned for a minute."

"Hey," Red Cloud asked as they guiltily returned to the room. "How do you turn this television on?"

Winona and Jesse set the table while Arleen made the salad, allowing Johnny to show the old Indian the modern state-of-the art technology of the plasma screen T.V. Red Cloud was suitably impressed.

When the food was finally on the table, the small party took their seats. The wolves and Rex found places near those people who would most likely give them a treat. The humans held hands while Red Cloud said a prayer in his Native language.

Arleen was given the honor of saying a prayer in English. She said, "Lord, bless this our bounty on this day and the true joy of allowing us to celebrate it together. May both our worlds, some day, find this kind of peace."

Johnny leaned over and kissed Jesse gently. "Happy Thanksgiving, babe," he whispered.

"Happy Thanksgiving," she whispered back. And they all settled in to enjoy their feast.

CHAPTER 27

Jesse cast aside what was left of her *civilized* background when she visited Dr. Bainbridge's office for her second and final visit. The good doctor was not happy that Johnny insisted on being a part of the appointment, and even unhappier about Jesse's new medications. Disgusted with the doctor's *holier than thou* attitude, Jesse decided to put an end to the doctor's care and to trust her mother-in-law instead to carry her to term. She refused to subject Johnny or herself to the doctor's criticism and innuendo and certainly did not want the prejudiced man to have any more contact with her unborn child.

The winter was not as intolerable as Jesse had been told to expect. Actually, as time passed, she grew to love Montana even more. The wolves and the bobcat thrived in their environment. They were happy and healthy and Jesse was grateful that they stayed close to home. Johnny created new furniture and the cash was coming in. The newlyweds were quite comfortable and very happy.

Like Thanksgiving, Johnny never gave Christmas much thought. His family, who were not rich, had never made a very big deal about it. But, *paying attention to the signs,* he noticed Jesse's preoccupation one day as he finished a newly constructed chest of drawers. The customary Wolfsheim or Native American music she liked to play on the CD player had been replaced with the lilting sounds of harpsichords and choirs of angelic voices. Some of the songs sounded familiar.

Jesse passed by the door to the workroom several times, in and out of the storage room, usually with another box. When he heard the sound of a heavy box, which she was obviously dragging into the living room, his curiosity was finally piqued.

"Need some help?" he offered, craning his neck around the side of the chest of drawers to get a peek at what she was up to.

"No thanks!" Jesse answered cheerfully from the other room. "I've got it."

"Can I ask what you're up to?" he asked.

"Nope," she replied gently.

"Okay." Johnny shrugged his shoulders and returned to his work.

He heard her moving furniture around, and then the sound of something metal, like poles, clanking together. Her busy work, just out of his range of sight, took her about a half an hour. At one point, he noticed the living room seemed to take on some color. After that, he'd look up and see her, with arms crossed, taking a step back and looking critically at whatever it was she was making. Finally, she started going back into the storage room a lot, returning the boxes she had brought out earlier. She smiled at him innocently enough when she chanced to look into the workroom and saw that he was watching her. When she stepped to the front door and let the wolves in, Johnny was on his knees just finishing up the last of his work.

"Shadow," Jesse's voice rung out, "don't you even think about it! Come on, kids, let's get some grapes."

That was enough. He stood up, put his rag down and wiped off his hands on a clean one. With his chest of drawers completed, he decided it was time for a break. His eyes widened when he stepped into the living room and saw what she had done. There, in the corner of the living room was a Christmas tree, sparkling with purple and blue lights and decorated with all sorts of ornaments.

"Babe," he said so she could hear him in the kitchen, "there's a tree in the house."

Jesse was smiling when she came around the corner with the wolves behind her. "Do you like it?"

"Where did it come from?" he asked incredulously.

"That big box I lugged in. It's artificial."

"Wow!" he expressed, walking over to it to get a closer look. "That's pretty cool." He looked closely at the ornaments that were intricately painted with faces of wolves. He also saw other animals that were carved out of wood and painted. There were moose, deer, elk, bear and bison. He spied bird nests with little cardinals and blue jays and crystal eagles hanging by silver strings.

"Where did all this come from?" he asked, putting his arm around her waist when she joined him next to the tree.

"I found the tree and a lot of the ornaments at a Christmas store Arleen and I discovered when we were buying stuff for the cabin a long time ago. I ordered the wolf ornaments through the mail."

"I could have cut down a real tree," he said, still eyeing the decorations, "if you wanted it. Although this one looks real enough."

"I wouldn't think of killing a living tree for a human holiday."

Johnny squeezed his arm around her a little tighter. "It's very beautiful."

"You don't mind?"

"Of course not," he smiled.

Shadow and Mesa approached the tree skeptically, sniffing at it again. "If you boys even think of marking this tree, you'll be outside 'til spring," Jesse warned them, placing her hand on Shadow's neck. The wolves explored it a little more and then, satisfied it had no animal scent, lost interest and returned to the kitchen for some more food.

"This holiday is important to you?" Johnny asked his wife.

"For the first time since I was a little girl," she answered, "it suddenly seems right. I've got my beautiful husband, my wonderful animals and a baby on the way. Even though it's a white man's holiday, I figured it's as good a time as any to celebrate all Creation." She gazed at her husband lovingly. "For the first time in my life, I have a family of my own and I want to thank the Creator for his gifts. I know we angered your father and cousin when we fell in love, but if the Creator's on our side, maybe someday they'll learn to live with it and forgive us—or at least the baby." She kissed Johnny gently. "…Of course, it could just be the hormones, too," she added as an afterthought.

Johnny smiled and hugged her. "I like the first reason best."

The next day when Arleen came and took Jesse to Great Falls for some shopping, Johnny took advantage of his time alone. He had mulled over Jesse's words most of the previous night and now knew it was up to him to make things right. Accompanied by the wolves, he trudged the three-mile path through the forest to his parents' home.

Winona was shocked to see her son when he and the wolves crowded in through the front door. "Well, who's this coming to see us?" she smiled, rubbing Shadow and Mesa's necks when they weeded their way through the kitchen to greet her. "What are you guys doing here? Is Jesse all right?"

"She's fine, ma," Johnny declared, hanging his coat. "We were just out for a walk and thought we'd drop by."

"I'm very happy you did," Winona beamed as her son gave her a hug. She held him very tight for a brief moment. "Can I get you something to eat?"

"Actually," Johnny countered, "I was wondering if dad is home. I was hoping we could talk."

Winona looked at her son, surprised to say the least. "Of course he is," she stated. "He's out back working on the truck."

"Lights still going out?" Johnny asked, returning to the hook on the wall for his coat.

"He gave up on that a long time ago," his mother grinned. "I think he's changing the fuel filter or something like that."

"I'll be back," Johnny smiled, heading through the house and out the back door.

Winona grabbed some treats for the wolves to keep them in the house.

Outside, the sun was shining on the rusty old vehicle and Charlie was bent over the engine, tinkering with a wrench. Johnny watched him for a few minutes before making his presence known. His father looked older and more tired than the last time he had seen him.

"Maybe you should think about replacing that old thing," Johnny finally announced, walking up behind him.

Charlie was stunned to hear his son's voice, but caught himself and did not show it. "Yeah, but your mother's used to having me around," the old man joked, not looking up. "Or, did you mean the truck?"

Johnny snickered. "Yeah, the truck," he said. "You're irreplaceable."

"Damn straight." Charlie put down the wrench and painfully straightened up. He turned and faced his son. "I'm officially an antique."

"Do you need some help with what you're doing?" Johnny offered, unsure of what to say.

"I think I'm done," Charlie replied. "Why don't you get in and see if it starts up."

Johnny jumped into the cab of the pickup and turned the key. It grumbled a bit, but the engine eventually fired up.

"That's good," his father finally called out, slamming down the hood. "You can shut it off." Johnny followed his orders and shut the engine down. Charlie put the wrench in his pocket and wiped off his hands on his jeans, approaching his son who was climbing out of the vehicle. "She's got some good miles left in her. Maybe I'll trade her in next year, sometime."

"Trade it?" Johnny asked cynically.

"Don't be a smart ass," Charlie returned glibly. He eyed his son carefully a moment before speaking again. "What brings you to the reservation, son? Is everything all right?"

"Everything's fine," Johnny remarked. "I was hoping we could have a talk."

"Now, there's something we haven't done in a long time," his father sighed. "As a matter of fact, I can't remember the last time we *talked.*"

"Yeah, neither could I. That's why I figured I'd give it a shot."

"Your mother told me you were married," Charlie said, walking with his son toward the house. "Where'd you get the feather?"

"Jesse found it," Johnny replied. "It just sort of happened. Neither one of us planned it."

"And the baby?" Charlie asked, rubbing his eyes.

"Another surprise."

"It sure was."

"Hey," Johnny quipped. "I know you don't approve of this, but I love Jesse and she loves me. We're happy, man. I don't expect you to be. I'm just here because Jesse wishes you guys would understand. She doesn't know the *secret.* She sees past the *blood.* All she knows is that she loves me and wants to give me a child." Johnny stopped his father from going inside. He wanted to talk to him alone. "You know," he continued, "*I* don't even know the *secret* of why we're not supposed to be together. Nobody has ever explained it thoroughly enough for me. Whether you want to approve of it or not, I love my wife and child. He'll be red, as well as white, and he'll learn to respect both sides." Johnny sighed, refusing to let his anger rise. "I'm not an Elder, pop. I'm not a full-blooded Indian. There is no secret as far as I'm concerned. Let Joseph and Frankie carry it to their graves and put it on *their* sons' heads. Just let me be free to love my wife and child. And if it's not too much, maybe you could learn to love them too."

Charlie considered his sons words. "So you didn't do this to pay me back for being a horrible father?"

"There's a lot worse things I could have done to you if I'd thought that," Johnny retorted.

"You're making good money with this furniture you're making?" he asked, scraping the snow away from the back door with his booted foot.

"Yeah," Johnny answered. "More than I ever imagined I would."

"It's good stuff," Charlie said. "I've seen it at the store."

"Jesse inspired me, pop," Johnny reasoned. "She's helped me to be the man I never thought I would be."

"You should probably talk to Joe about buying the cabin," his father suggested. "That is, if you two plan to stay here in Montana."

"Jesse won't leave the wolves," Johnny stated. "She would like to stay here if you'll let us."

"I got no say in that," Charlie murmured. "You two need to do what's right for you."

"You've got a lot to say in it," Johnny countered. "If you don't want to recognize your grandchild, I'm not going to subject him to your hatred. It'll be hard enough on him when he has to face the rest of the world."

Charlie sighed. "Stay in Montana. You don't know half of what you'll need to teach him. You never paid attention to the stories I told you when you were growing up."

Johnny drew a deep breath and exhaled slowly. "Thanks, dad," he whispered.

"I love you, son," the old man muttered. "I'll love your kid, too."

Johnny opened the door for his father, who patted him on the back before going into the house. Johnny followed him inside. Winona and the wolves were waiting for the two men in the living room.

"Ah," Johnny went for broke and added, "Jesse would like you guys to come over for Christmas if you can make it."

"Of course *we* can," Winona spoke up quickly to keep Charlie from making up an excuse. She gazed lovingly at her son and husband. "We'd love to come."

Johnny did not tell Jesse about his talk with his father. But Jesse noticed that her husband seemed happier and more at ease as the holidays approached. On Christmas day, Clayton brought his boys and Arleen brought her husband, Richard, who was home for a rare visit. Red Cloud brought Rex. When Frank, Mary, Winona and Charlie showed up at the cabin door, Jesse was overcome with surprise and delight.

The wine flowed and the party was lively. Charlie was most pleased to see the eagle feather and blanket hanging with honor on the wall. He was also proud as a peacock that he was soon to be a grandfather; making sure Johnny did most of the host's work and insisting Jesse stay off her feet.

After a fine roast beef dinner, Jesse handed out a small present to each of her guests. Tim and Mike, their musical talents more accomplished with a few months practice, sang Christmas songs and soon everyone joined in. Outside, the wolves were frolicking in the falling snow. They howled along when the humans sang a rowdy version of Jingle Bells.

Richard filled Jesse in on the wolf recovery program at Yellowstone and, as usual, Clayton eventually fell asleep, but this time with Kitten curled up at his feet. Red Cloud told some Native American stories and before they left, Arleen pulled Johnny aside and gave him a very big check.

That night, alone together, Jesse and Johnny exchanged their presents by the light of the Christmas tree and a warming fire in the fireplace. Jesse gave Johnny some new shirts, a couple of pairs of black jeans and cowboy boots. Johnny gave Jesse a locket with his picture in it and a cradle he had constructed secretly for the baby. It was made of cherry wood with three wolf pups carved in the headboard. Jesse, still somewhat emotional, shed tears of joy and showered her man with kisses. The wolves got fresh new bones and Kitten got her favorite treat, a newly thawed, gigantic trout.

"Did you have a good Christmas?" Johnny finally asked, when he and Jesse sat snuggling together on the couch.

"The best ever," Jesse replied sweetly. "How about you?"

"Pretty darn good for my first," he smiled at her. "Now that I've got the hang of it, I'll do a little planning next year. Which present did you like the best?"

Jesse thought about it for a minute, fingering the locket around her neck. "The cradle and my locket are so very perfect," she said, "but I think the best present I got this year was the hug your father gave me before he left."

"I'm just full of miracles, aren't I?" Johnny murmured.

"Good men usually are," she smiled back, giving him a special Christmas kiss.

CHAPTER 28

❀

As the green grasses of spring finally poked through the melting snow, Jesse was bestowed with many new surprises. There were new baby owls and eaglets chirping for their meals in the trees. A delicate fawn passed through the Stillwater's front yard, cautiously close to its mother. The crocuses in the rock garden bloomed in shades of blue and purple. The sun seemed a little brighter and the days lingered a little longer. There was a renewed sense of hope and excitement as the world around Jesse and Johnny's cabin slowly came back to life. Jesse was now seven months pregnant and Johnny was enamored with her rounded belly. Shadow tolerated Johnny's affections but, otherwise, he was very protective of the soon-to-be mother.

Jesse still took walks with her animal *children*, but was tiring more easily and found it difficult to keep up. She had pined for a warmer day when she could spend more time with them outdoors and was thrilled when one finally arrived. She left Johnny to his work and struggled eagerly into her boots. She grabbed her jacket, kissed her husband good-bye and stepped sprightly onto the porch. The wolves were anxious to get started, roughhousing in the yard. They greeted her excitedly when she joined them.

Jesse's heart sank when she saw a truck pulling up. She did not want to be bothered by strangers that day, especially those who were probably lost and would be hard to get rid of once they saw the wolves. The driver slowed down as it approached the cabin. The wolves stopped playing and stood at attention, watching the intruders as keenly as Jesse.

When the truck came to a stop and the passenger side door opened, Jesse was awestruck. She recognized the woman from almost a year ago. Nancy Middlesex, the wolf refuge owner from Colorado, hopped out of the truck.

"Jesse?" Nancy asked dumbfounded, seeing Jesse's stomach. "I don't know if you remember me…"

"Nancy!" Jesse acknowledged her with a warm smile and walked over to meet her. "You're the last person I ever expected to see out here!"

"This is the last place I ever expected to be," Nancy said, extending her hand. "I hope you don't mind."

"Of course not," Jesse smiled, ignoring Nancy's hand and giving her a hug instead. "What's up?"

"Is this Shadow?" Nancy asked flabbergasted at the wolf who was now close enough to defend Jesse if she needed it. His ears pricked up when he heard the woman say his name.

"Yes, that's my baby," Jesse laughed. "Come here, boy," she coaxed him. "You don't remember this lady, do you?" Shadow approached the woman cautiously, sniffing the air around her. Jesse noticed a young man get out of the driver's seat of the truck.

"He's beautiful!" Nancy exclaimed, offering her hand so he could check her out.

"And that's Cheyenne and Mesa over there," Jesse added. "They're a *little less* trustful of new folks, thank God. Their parents were killed by hunters."

"This is one of my volunteers, Ted Andrews," Nancy introduced her driver. "We would have called you, but we didn't realize our cell phone wouldn't work. We left Denver in such a hurry to get up here and, unfortunately, we've got even less time to get back. You got my email, right?"

Jesse bit her lip. "Email? I'm sorry, I haven't checked them for a couple of days."

"Oh, shit!" Nancy sighed. "I knew we should have stopped and called from a payphone. We were just so rushed."

"That's okay," Jesse calmed her, taking her hand. "What happened?"

"We ran into a snag at the refuge," Nancy explained. "And you were the only person I could think of who might be able to help."

Johnny, hearing the strange voices, came out onto the porch. He eyed the strangers warily, unsure what was going on. "Jesse," he called out, "is everything all right?"

"Johnny," Jesse turned and beckoned him to join her. "This is Nancy Middlesex. She's the one who runs the wolf refuge outside of Denver where I took Shadow once." Johnny came up behind his wife and shook Nancy's hand when she offered it. "Nancy, this is my husband, Johnny Stillwater."

"It's nice to meet you," Nancy said.

"It's nice to meet you, too," Johnny said with a guarded smile. "I guess you're one of the people I should thank for sending Jesse up here."

"Well," Nancy quipped with a laugh, "I don't know about that, but thank you for letting us barge in on you like this." The volunteer walked up and shook both Jesse's hand and Johnny's. "Okay, I hate to do this," Nancy blurted out, "but I'm going to have to be blunt. It's a lot to ask, but I didn't know where else to go."

"You must have been pretty desperate to come all the way to Montana," Jesse said. "Please, fill us in on the details. Can we get you something to drink or eat?"

"Can you come with me back to the truck, first?" Nancy said as Ted ran on ahead and opened the back of the enclosed truck bed. "It'll be a little easier if you see what I've got."

Johnny took Jesse's hand and followed the two strangers. Shadow walked along with them, at Jesse's side.

"*Somebody* left us a *present* at the front gate three nights ago," Nancy told her story. "The vet took one look at 'em and decided they were purebred wolves."

Johnny and Jesse walked around and peered into the back of the truck. In a large cage were two wolf pups, scared and hungry. "Oh, my God," Jesse exclaimed in a whisper. She broke free from Johnny's grasp and crawled into the back of the truck to get a closer look. Johnny was unable to stop her.

"We have mostly hybrids at the center, Jesse," Nancy went on. "And we're at our limit. The state won't let me have *one* more. If I keep them, I'll lose my license and everything I've got. The vet, knowing I'm at my limit, was going to put them down." Johnny cast a glance at the woman with narrowed eyes. Nancy didn't notice. "Is there any way you could take them? I didn't know where else to turn."

"Aaaah," Johnny started to speak, but Jesse interrupted him.

"Of course we can," Jesse replied. Shadow had gotten a whiff of the newborns' scent. He, too, was anxious to get into the truck.

"Ah, Jesse," Johnny smiled forcibly, "can I talk to you about this for a minute?"

"Sure, sweetie," Jesse said, not really paying attention. She asked Ted, "Can you get them out of here? We'll put the cage in the house."

"Jesse," Johnny's tone was a little stronger, "babe, I really think we need to…"

Jesse backed out of the truck and held onto the ruff of Shadow's neck. "When's the last time they ate?"

"We gave them some formula about an hour ago," Nancy said. "They were too nervous to eat much of it."

The volunteer looked at Jesse, who pointed toward the house; then at Johnny who was not in the least bit happy; and finally to Nancy. His eyes were filled with indecision.

"Jesse…" Johnny stated clearly, taking her by the arm this time.

"Hey, Ted," Nancy interjected, hoping to alleviate the tense situation, "come to the front of the truck with me for a second. I need you to help me find something." She indicated with a sharp nod of her head to get the hell away from the couple for a few minutes. Ted happily obliged.

"They need to get those animals out now," Jesse said, annoyed. Shadow was desperately trying to get into the truck and he was proving to be a handful for her. Johnny's grip tightened on her arm, forcing her to look at him. "Honey, that hurts…" she complained.

Johnny pulled his wife out of the way, grabbed Shadow and shut the back of the truck. Shadow stood up on his hind legs and put his front paws up on the window glass, trying to scratch his way in. "We need to talk about this, Jess," Johnny said firmly. "And you're going to talk to me right now." He led her away from Nancy and Ted, who had gotten the hint. They had shut themselves into the cab of the truck. Johnny appreciated their discretion.

"Honey," Jesse almost whined, trying to escape his grasp. "I've got to get those babies out of the truck. Why isn't that guy doing what I told him?" She looked frantically back at the truck.

"Because he saw the look on my face." The tone of Johnny's voice finally hooked Jesse's attention. She turned slowly and looked him dubiously in the eyes.

"Oh no you don't," Johnny warned quietly. "I have been trying to get you to listen to me for the last five minutes. You've been deaf and dumb ever since you saw those pups."

"That's the way *they* are right now, Johnny," Jesse pleaded, "deaf and dumb!"

"How old are they?" Johnny remained calm but firm.

"Probably two weeks, if that," Jesse sighed, still trying to wriggle out of his grasp. "Their eyes haven't been open very long."

"Jesse, baby," Johnny implored, "you're seven months pregnant. Can you honestly tell me you have the strength to take care of two newborn pups?" She started to answer, but he shushed her with a finger to her lips. "I've got a full load on my plate right now. Jess, I don't have time to help you with this."

"You don't have..."

Johnny shushed her again in a hurry to finish. "Hourly feedings? Up all night? What's that going to do to our baby? What's that going to do to you?" Johnny loosened his grip on her arm, but placed his hands firmly on her shoulders. "Those pups are adorable, I can see that. And they could use our help. But damn it, Jess. You are my main priority. Please think clearly about this for just one minute. That's all I'm asking here. Can you give me that?"

Jesse saw the look of worry on her husband's face and she loved him for it. She could not be mad at him because she knew he was right. She took a deep breath, exhaled and tried to relax. She smiled at Johnny and gave him a quick kiss. She then looked back at the truck, which was now surrounded by wolves. Cheyenne and Mesa were interested in the contents of the vehicle. They were having trouble seeing through the tinted side windows, but they sensed something and they were very intrigued. Shadow was talking to them in that language they used. Cheyenne and Mesa were talking back.

Jesse knew Johnny did not have the time to help. She also knew that this project could tax her health. Her husband was right—this was not a smart idea. But then Cheyenne howled—not the happy howl Jesse heard in the evenings when she was calling to Mesa and Shadow, but a wrenching cry that touched the woman's soul. She slowly turned back to Johnny, who had heard the howl, too.

"I know it's probably the stupidest thing I could ever do," she said calmly. "But I want them."

Johnny nodded his head, not surprised by her answer. "What happens if we can't take care of them?"

Jesse sighed. "Then at least we'll be able to say that we tried. I don't think they'll have much of a chance if we don't." She put her arms around Johnny and hugged him tight. "I promise I won't do anything to jeopardize our baby," she whispered. "I'll let you know if I can't do it."

"Trust me," Johnny murmured back, nuzzling her neck with a kiss. "I'll know before you do. So, what you need to promise me is this: if I say it's over, it's over. If you don't, I promise I *will* get angry and it won't be pleasant. I love you too much. I will not let anything happen to you or our baby."

"I promise," Jesse acquiesced. She gave him a squeeze and headed back for the truck. "Hey, where'd they go?"

"They're inside the truck," Johnny informed her, taking hold of Shadow's ruff.

"Did you give them your angry Indian look?" Jesse smiled wryly as she popped open the back of the truck.

"You bet I did," Johnny answered back. "I can scare *them* all I want. I don't live with them." He held Shadow and grabbed Mesa when he came around to the tailgate. "Okay, guys," he shouted, "we'll take 'em." Cheyenne moved behind Johnny and watched the proceedings from there.

Nancy and Ted were out of the cab of the truck in an instant. Nancy was beaming. "I've got plenty of formula here," she rattled off.

"It's the cage I'm going to need," Jesse said, starting to climb back up on the tailgate.

"Let the young man take care of them, Jesse," Johnny stated. "Come here and help me hold these guys."

Jesse obeyed her husband and stepped away from the truck. Ted Andrews climbed in and pulled the cage to the edge. The pups were almost frightened to death. They huddled together in the farthest corner of the cage, away from all the activity.

"Nancy," Jesse ordered, "please run into the cabin and grab the blanket that's on the back of the couch. Ted, don't move them any more just yet."

Nancy ran to the cabin and Shadow decided to go with her. He strained against Johnny and Jesse's holds. They almost lost him, but Jesse got down on her knees and held him with her arms around his chest.

"It's okay, boy," she murmured. "This will be over in a second."

"Jesse," Johnny was sharp. "Be careful there."

"I got him," Jesse replied. "It's okay." Nancy was back in a few breathless seconds. "Put that blanket over the cage please. Good. That'll help. Now, let's catch our breath, okay? This is going to be traumatic enough for these pups. We need a nice smooth ride." Jesse looked up at Johnny and gave him a quick smile. He pouted and met her gaze with narrowed eyes.

"Okay, guys," said Jesse, returning to the task at hand. "If you could both carry that cage, I'd appreciate it. Go ahead and move them to the porch."

Nancy and Ted slid the cage carefully over the tailgate and picked it up. They walked calmly to the porch, followed by Jesse and Johnny. Cheyenne cautiously brought up the rear of the little procession.

"Johnny," Jesse said, "I think Mesa will be okay. I've got Shadow, so could you please sneak on ahead and get the door for them?"

"Sneak?" Johnny questioned, slowly letting Mesa go.

"Quietly, then," Jesse corrected herself with a roll of her eyes, "and have them put the cage on the kitchen table, please. Those wolves are wallowing in their own vomit and shit."

"Maybe we'll eat out tonight," Johnny commented, thinking of what was about to be placed in his kitchen. He quietly walked around Nancy and up the stairs.

"Thank God Kitten's upstairs," Jesse mentioned. "At least I hope she is. And please shut the door when they get inside, Johnny."

When everyone else had entered, Jesse stooped down and rubbed Shadows neck before letting him go. "I'll let you in later, okay?" The wolf was up the stairs and at the door like a shot as soon as she let him loose. "So much for communication around here," she observed, following him up the stairs.

Johnny came from around the back of the cabin. "I'll get him," he announced. "I do hope you know what you're doing, woman," he sighed, grabbing Shadow again so Jesse could get inside.

"So do I, babe," she answered before closing the door. "So do I." Ted and Nancy were standing away from the table, waiting for her. "May I ask you guys to go out the back, too?" she asked her guests. "These guys need some quiet and as little commotion as possible."

Nancy smiled. "It looks like you've learned a lot about these animals since the last time I saw you." She ushered Ted ahead of her to the back of the house.

"I read a lot," Jesse answered quietly, waiting for the sound of the back door to close. She sat down on one of the chairs and tried to relax. The animals were mewling and the cage was shaking from their fright. "It's okay, babies," Jesse murmured in her lilting voice. "I promise everything's going to be all right." She made sure the cage was centered on the table and sat back to give the pups a chance to calm down.

"Jesse," Johnny poked his head in the front door and called to her quietly, "they're going to leave right away. They say they've got to get back."

"Tell them to hold on for a second. We should give them some food," Jesse suggested. "I think there's some fried chicken left in the fridge. And tell them they can come in the back and use the bathroom before they go."

"I've got the formula and stuff," he added. "Do you want it?"

"Yeah," she said. "Bring it on in. The pups have quieted down a bit."

Johnny put the box of food on the floor next to Jesse and tiptoed in silence behind the cage to the refrigerator. He grabbed the chicken and a couple of cans of pop. Jesse smiled, watching him be so careful. He threw her a wink and headed back outdoors.

Jesse sat with the pups for a few more minutes. When she heard the back door open quietly and someone go into the bathroom, she got up. She went outside, careful not to let the big wolves through the door. Johnny had been trying to coerce them out into the yard, but it wasn't working. He helped Ted load the food into the truck.

"If I'd known about your condition," Nancy's voice sounded tired as she came around the side of the cabin, "I wouldn't have brought them."

"I would have been very angry if you hadn't," Jesse replied with a smile. "We'll do our best, Nancy. Please try not to worry. I owe you this favor." She took the woman's hand into her own. "Are you sure you can't stay for a little while? I could warm up that chicken." Ted hightailed it back around the house to use the facilities.

"Ted's my best volunteer," Nancy sighed. "On the rare occasions I leave the refuge, it's only because he's there to keep an eye on things. That vet's going to be snooping around looking for those pups and I've got to be there when he does." She gave Jesse a big hug. "I'm in your debt," she murmured into Jesse's ear. "Whatever happens, I can rest easy knowing you'll do what you can to save them. That knowledge alone will give me the strength to get back."

"Call me when you get back to the refuge so I know you got there safe," Jesse demanded. "Leave a message if we don't pick up."

"You've got a great place up here, Jess," Nancy observed. "And your husband's very good looking." Johnny was crouched down on his knees, holding Cheyenne and talking soothingly into her ear. The wolf would not take her eyes off the cabin.

"Thanks," Jesse accepted her compliment with a smile. "You should come back sometime when you can spare a few days."

"I wish I could," Nancy smiled back. "Are you ready, Ted?" she asked her helper who had returned to the truck.

"Let's go!" Ted shook Johnny's hand before getting into the driver's seat. Johnny shut the cab door, locking him in.

"Good luck," Nancy said, giving Jesse one more hug. "Let me know what happens—good or bad."

"You've got my word on it," Jesse said. "Drive safely."

Nancy ran to the truck and climbed in. Ted started the engine and turned the truck around, speeding off as fast as they had arrived.

As Jesse watched the trail of dust diminish, she leaned against her husband as he came up to her and put his arm around her waist.

"What's next?" he asked, brushing a lock of hair from her face.

"I've got to get them fed," Jesse said. She smiled at Johnny and headed back into the house. Minutes later, sitting back in her chair at the kitchen table, Jesse breathed deep and exhaled slowly. She lifted the edge of the blanket and opened the door as non-invasively as she could.

Johnny stayed outside to give his wife an hour by herself with the pups. He still could not believe those people had the balls to just bring those pups all the way up here and drop them off like a side of beef, which he realized he was probably going to need to keep this new lot fed. The wolves had stopped scratching at the cabin door but had not strayed far from it. Cheyenne sat next to Johnny on the porch with her eyes glued to the entrance. Shadow and Mesa finally gave up their watch and retreated into the woods for a short run. Kitten came back shortly after the strangers had left. Johnny had let her out the back door before he'd gone out front to see what the fuss was all about. Now the bobcat was in her usual spot under the porch, keeping guard over the land while the big boys were gone on their ramble.

Johnny's mind returned to all the work he absolutely had to get done and wondered how he was going to make up the two hours this little event had cost him. He absentmindedly brushed his hand through Cheyenne's long, white hair as he considered his options. When she shifted her weight from one paw to the other, it broke Johnny's trance and his thoughts came back to the present situation. "Okay, girl," he said to the wolf. Her golden eyes, so much like Jesse's, looked up at him with anticipation. She started to pant and got up. Her tail, close to her body, waved slowly down at the tip. "Let's see how your mother's doing in there." He opened the screen door, which he was going to have to replace pretty soon, thanks to constant abuse from wolf and bobcat claws. Next he opened the big wooden door and peeked in. Cheyenne took the opportunity and eased herself in between the small crack. "Cheyenne," Johnny said, a little frightened. "I don't think you were supposed to go in there."

"It's all right, Johnny, she can come in," Jesse called from within. "I'm glad you're back. I could use a little help."

Johnny didn't bother to tell her that he had been just outside the door the whole time. He looked at her and smiled. She was standing in front of the fireplace, gently holding the two wolf pups wrapped together in a towel against her breast. Their little heads were tucked up under her hair that hung loosely over her shoulder.

"Are they sleeping?" he whispered. Cheyenne was now at Jesse's side, sniffing at the two babies.

"Yes," she murmured. "Could you do me a big favor and clean out that cage? Just throw everything in it out in the trash, including the tablecloth underneath. We don't need any of it." She smiled at the disgusted look he tried to hide as he headed for the kitchen. "And if you could wash it out with some soap and hot water, and then dry it, I'd love you all the more."

"You'd better," Johnny sulked, confronting the filthy cage. It took a good twenty minutes to complete the unpleasant task. When he was finally finished, the pups were awake and mewling for more food. Cheyenne sat on her hindquarters watching them and waiting to see what Jesse was going to do next.

"Now, one more favor and then you can go back to work," Jesse said politely.

"You're so generous," Johnny smiled sardonically, holding the cage up for her inspection.

"Could you move that chair and put the cage down there in the corner, not too close to the fireplace, but close enough that they'll get some heat?"

"Just tell me the spot," Johnny huffed as he pushed the chair to the side. "Is this good?"

"That'll be perfect," she commented, before heading back to the kitchen with her prizes.

"And I'm sure you'll want a blanket in there," Johnny second-guessed her.

"Actually, those towels that are sitting in front of the fireplace on the table will do nicely. And the blanket can go back over it like it was."

"Yes, your Highness," Johnny complied. He turned to see the pups' little heads competing for the bottle. He shook his head with wonder and followed Jesse into the kitchen. The pups were clean and, miraculously, a little less afraid. "Can I help feed them?"

"If you'd like," Jesse smiled. "There's another bottle on the stove. Grab another towel and join us."

There was a bit of confusion as Jesse maneuvered the little beasts so Johnny could take one into his blanket. One little animal protested with his tiny paws until he got his very own baby bottle to suck on. Johnny watched the little paws try to hold on as it sucked ravenously at the nipple.

"I suppose you've named them already," Johnny asked quietly as the puppy settled down in his arms. He half sat on the kitchen table for some stability because the little guy was quite a handful.

"Actually, no," Jesse admitted. "I haven't."

"Speaking of names," Johnny went on. "Have you come up with any ideas for our little guy in that tummy of yours, yet?"

"I have thought about it…" she said methodically. "…I was meaning to ask you, do you have any suggestions?"

"As long as it *isn't* Charlie, Joseph, Frank, Eric, or Johnny junior, I'm pretty open."

"Aw, those were the ones I was thinking about," Jesse laughed. The pup in her arms squeaked. "Only kidding." She leaned back against the table next to her husband. "There is a name that I like, but it's not very ordinary."

"I wouldn't expect our son's name to be ordinary," Johnny retorted. "After all, he'll be one of a kind."

"Well, it's an old Gaelic name," Jesse said. "It's Phelan."

"Fey lan?" Johnny inquired. "You're right. That's not ordinary at all. I don't think I've ever heard it. How is it spelled?"

"P-H-E-L-A-N. It means *little wolf*." Jesse's eyes met Johnny's.

"Guess that's pretty perfect," Johnny noted, with a grin crossing his lips. "And the best part is—if I've never heard it, I'm sure Red Cloud hasn't either. Good girl," he leaned over and gave her a kiss on the cheek. "It's about time I finally get one up on that old Indian. I like it. Phelan it is."

Johnny turned off his work light and rubbed his eyes. It had been a very long day and he was exhausted. He looked at the clock on the wall in the work-room. It was shortly after midnight. He did not like working so late but with the arrival of the pups he had been forced to, to make up some time. He rose from his stool and stretched, then rubbed his hands on his lower back. The lights were low in the living room. He hoped Jesse had gone to bed. He was disconcerted to hear her voice when he entered the room.

"Johnny," Jesse whispered. "Come in here, babe. You've got to see this."

"What I don't like seeing is that you're still up," he answered her, still trying to work the kinks out of his back as he walked.

"Quiet," she hushed him. "Look at this."

Johnny came up behind her and put his arms around her expanding belly. He nuzzled her neck and looked over her shoulder. The last thing he wanted to see was that cage again, but when he looked this time he was struck dumb with bewilderment. "Is that Cheyenne?" he finally asked, after focusing hard on what he thought at first was a trick of the light.

"I took the babies out to feed them," she whispered, rubbing his hands on her tummy, "and, when I came back, Cheyenne had opened the cage door and was curled up inside."

"Isn't that cage too small for her?"

"I think it's just right," Jesse remarked. "I took a big chance, but I was pretty tired. So I put the babies in with her and they've been like that ever since." Jesse smiled. "She washed them with her tongue and cuddled with them a bit. And now they're sound asleep."

"Should we let the boys in?" Johnny asked, bending over and peering in a little closer. Cheyenne opened one eye and saw it was Johnny. Her eyelid closed and she went back to sleep.

"No," Jesse suggested. "I think we'll wait until tomorrow. Let's give our new mother a little time alone with them."

"Sounds good to me," Johnny sighed. "Do you want to sleep down here, just in case?"

"You know what," Jesse smiled, taking Johnny's hand, "let's throw caution to the wind and sleep upstairs. What will be will be." She started up the stairs and Johnny put his hands on her hips to give her a lift up. "Pretty soon you're going to have to use ropes and pulleys and hike me up like a piano."

"I can still carry you if I have to," Johnny smirked. "Get upstairs, woman, and rock me to sleep like you did with those pups."

CHAPTER 29

In late April, Jesse sat out on her porch swing, amazed at how perfect her life had become. The wolves had accepted the two pups as their own, and except for a little playtime and some snacks, Jesse or Johnny were not allowed any say in their care and upbringing. Cheyenne had taken over as surrogate mother that very first night. She even began producing milk for the pups. Daddy Shadow was a fierce protector. He sent Kitten running for her life the first time the bobcat seemed to consider the pups a tasty treat. The feline learned Shadow's lesson well. She gave the babies a wide berth and after a few more days, she learned the pups were there to stay and not to be harmed. She spent a lot of time under the porch, but the pups eventually found her and accepted her as part of their family. Uncle Mesa was the perfect babysitter. He played with them for hours and had begun to teach them how to hunt. They were growing like weeds and stumbling all over the place.

The cabin was a wreck. The pups had chewed on just about every piece of furniture they could sink their baby teeth into. Nothing was sacred as Cheyenne weaned them from their milk, and the males were now regurgitating their own food for the constantly hungry pups. Johnny kept the door to the workroom locked up tight, even when he was inside working. The little terrors were into everything. At just over nine weeks old, they were the pride and joy of the family and the little princes knew it—anything not bolted down was theirs to play with and recently they were allowed a new honor. They could strut their stuff on small trips with Cheyenne, Mesa and Shadow, just like big wolves to the edge of the woods and back. Shadow and Cheyenne were strict disciplinarians, but never harsh or abusive.

Jesse named the pups, both males, Midnight and Lakota. Although they were both born black as most wolves are, their fur was turning into hues of brown and gray, like Mesa's, as they grew older. Midnight was aptly named, for his favorite time to try howling was at the witching hour. He didn't necessarily care to sing when the others did. He preferred the hour when most everyone else was asleep, and expected everyone to join in with him when he was in the mood to sing his little heart out. Johnny just called him *Nightly*, because that's usually when the little beast caused some kind of commotion. Lakota was named for the tribe of the same name and was not as wild as his brother. Jesse hoped to christen a wolf in honor of every Native American tribe one day.

Under Winona's knowledgeable care, little Phelan was doing very well inside Jesse's womb. Active and kicking, especially when Jesse was around the wolves, it seemed the little guy was anxious to get out on his own. Jesse, too, was more than ready for that to happen. She felt big as a horse and every day was a little more uncomfortable. But she was looking forward to the end result—holding her own baby in her arms.

Johnny spoiled her rotten and doted on her hand and foot. He did most of the cooking and he *tried* to clean up after the wolves. He washed the clothes and made the bed. At night, he'd rub Jesse's tummy and tell his unborn son old Indian stories while they lay in bed. He was a couple of days from finishing up his largest order of furniture to date, and he had told Arleen, after this order was done, he would be on hiatus until sometime after the baby was born. Arleen was content with that news because Johnny and Jesse had worked hard to renovate the store for her. By February, the store was looking shiny and new and just like the old time general store Arleen had envisioned.

There was plenty of money in the bank, thanks to Johnny's talent. He had refused to open his own bank account, so Jesse cleverly got a signature card signed and put his name on hers. She had caused quite a stir when the bank teller asked Jesse if she was *sure* she wanted to do that, *with him being, well, you know.* Jesse threatened to close all her accounts and take her money elsewhere. The bank manager spent a good hour calming her down, and eventually kept the accounts in place. Jesse was actually glad the man had apologized profusely and groveled enough, because banks were few and far between in the country and she really did not want their money any farther away than it already was.

On this particular day, Jesse swung gently on the porch swing with her feet bare, loving the warmth of the spring sun as it rose up and covered the little cabin with light. Cheyenne, needing a break from motherhood, had entrusted

Jesse with the care and handling of the pups and joined Mesa and Shadow on their daily run. Kitten had gone with them. For it was spring and the woods teemed with new life and adventures.

Her loving husband had made her a scrumptious breakfast and a very quick lunch. He was presently in the workroom staining the last of the *buffalo* chairs and Jesse and the pups were forbidden in the house while the toxic substance was in use. She sat lazily on her swing and watched the pups, who were deep in the tall grass, just in front of the cabin, trying desperately to catch their first mouse without Mesa's help. The billowing white clouds formed a series of different pictures as they lazed across the bright blue Montana sky. Jesse picked out a bucking bronco, an eagle, and a lion as they wafted by. The pups squeaked and squealed, jumping on various items of interest and each other as they played. The young woman giggled every time a little head popped up out of the weeds. The book she had brought out to read lay untouched next to her on the seat. Her eyelids were growing heavy as the warmth and peace of the day lulled her to sleep. Not intending to shirk her duties, she did her best to fight the drowsiness that had befallen her, but there was a moment when her will was lost to her desire and her eyes drooped shut.

She thought the shot and the yelp she heard was in a dream, but when her eyes darted back open, the pups' attentive ears told her it was not. She listened carefully and heard a howl next. The pups' interest was piqued. They started to head toward the woods as Johnny came out the front door and onto the porch.

"What's going on?" he asked, concerned. "Is that Cheyenne I heard howling?"

"Help me get the pups," Jesse said, laboring to get up from the swing. "Something's not right."

The Indian bounded down the porch steps and picked up the pups with little effort. They were still small and not sure enough on their feet to elude a quick capture. He ran with them back into the house and locked them into their cage. Jesse could hear their whines and whelps as she started down the porch steps, with a hand pressed for support against her back. She could hear two howls now—the voices were distressed.

Johnny was back outside and ahead of her quickly. "Stay here, babe," he demanded, heading for the woods. "I'll find them."

Jesse trotted along behind him the best she could. She grabbed hold of her expanded belly, and her baby, and held him tight so she could run a little faster. Johnny was hell bent on finding the wolves. He had no idea she was trying to keep up with him and that's the way Jesse wanted it. She panicked a little when she heard the next howl—it was Shadow. She knew all her baby's voices. They were getting closer. Either the humans to the wolves, or, Jesse hoped to God, the wolves to the humans. Johnny was now a blur up ahead of her. At the sound of Shadow's howl, her Indian picked up some more speed. Jesse was losing ground quickly. Her heart was racing and her breath labored. Her legs were giving out. She had to slow down or she was going to fall down and risk losing the baby.

She came to a halt and rested against the trunk of a tree. She was not far from the truck path that led to the lake. She had traveled about a mile before she was forced to take a break. The wolves were howling again. *Was that Mesa?* she frantically asked herself. *No, No. That was Cheyenne.* She leaned hard against the tree and tried to calm down. As her breathing quieted and heart stopped pounding in her chest, she heard Shadow howl again. So there was Shadow and she had also heard Cheyenne. *Oh, my God*, she screamed inside her head. *Where's Mesa? I haven't heard him!* She pushed herself off the tree and continued on, trying her best to follow Johnny's trail. He was way ahead of her now and she had no way of knowing which way he'd gone. She walked into the truck path clearing and looked toward the lake. There was no sign of anything wrong. The lake was as calm and blue as the sky. There were ducks swimming lazily near the shore.

Jesse took a deep breath and gathered her thoughts. Calmer, she realized that there would be no trouble here because she was still on her own land. Those wolves were off the property. She'd heard the shot. Shadow called out one more howl somewhere over her head. She turned and tried to discern where it came from. As the howl faded she surprised herself and grasped the direction. It came from the east—from the northeast to be more exact.

She took another deep breath and started back for the cabin. She needed to stop; she was taking chances running through the woods like an idiot. She needed to do what she could to help rather than hinder this situation. She went to get the truck.

Johnny's native sense, his sense of tracking, clicked into high gear the moment he hit the woods. He used his ears to pick up the direction he must travel. He used his eyes to pick up paw prints and clumps of newly shed winter coats on the budding branches of bushes and snapped twigs. He used his nose to find the wolves' territorial boundary markers. He used his hands to leave his own set of clues on where he had been. He knew exactly where he was heading. The wolves had traveled off their property and across the main road. They were somewhere on the ranch that bordered Clayton Phillips' property. Johnny didn't know the name of the rancher who lived there. He'd seen a couple of cows once in a while, but not a whole helluva lot else. He'd wondered, on the many times he'd passed the place in the last couple of months, if anybody was even living there anymore. If they'd just turned left, rather than right after they had crossed the road, the wolves would have been safe.

The Native American's search was close to the end. Just off the crest of the first hill he spotted Cheyenne. She was confused and hiding under the broken limbs of a dead tree. When the wolf spied Johnny, and then heard his call, she made a beeline for him. She was at his side in a few seconds.

Johnny checked her over quickly. There was blood on her nose, but she wasn't hurt. It was somebody else's blood. He quickened his pace, urging Cheyenne to show him where to go. Another couple hundred yards further he saw the black form of Shadow silhouetted against the sun. Shadow was sitting up straight and when he saw Johnny, he tipped his head back and howled into the sky. Johnny's heart was pounding against his chest. He ran as fast as he could because Shadow did not come to meet him like Cheyenne had done. He knew he had found both Shadow and Mesa. But he couldn't see Mesa from his advancing vantage point. That meant Mesa was down.

Shadow finally broke his watch and slowly came toward Johnny, who could now hear Mesa's pants and quick breaths. At the moment the wolf was still alive. He thanked the Creator when he got to the spot and Mesa tried to get up to greet him. His left front flank was covered in blood, but everything else seemed intact.

"No, boy," Johnny tried to smile. "I gotcha." He swooped down and picked the ninety-pound animal up like it was a sack of potatoes and placed him gingerly around his neck. It was the best place to carry him as quickly and as smoothly as he could back to the cabin.

When Jesse emerged from the woods, she smiled, seeing Kitten at the front door on the porch. "I'm coming, baby," she called out, gathering her strength for one more sprint. She was on the porch in two minutes and Kitten rubbed up against her legs as Jesse opened the front door.

"I need you to watch over the pups," Jesse said, grabbing a trout from the refrigerator and handing it to the bobcat, who had followed her into the kitchen. The feline continued to rub against Jesse even with the fish in her mouth. Jesse placed one hand on the table for support and leaned over, stroking the bobcat's fur. "It's going to be all right, Kitten. You'll be safe in the house until we get back." The bobcat purred and rubbed a little more. "Now, eat your dinner," Jesse ordered, pulling herself back up. "I've got to go help daddy." She grabbed the blanket from the back of the couch and some towels. She didn't have the time to waddle upstairs and get a pillow, so she grabbed a couch pillow instead. She took the spare truck keys from the hook on the wall and headed out the door after making sure the pups' cage was securely locked and the little tykes were still inside. They were crying piteously, but Jesse had no time to console them. She threw the blankets, towels and pillow into the back of the truck and then hiked up the stairs and went inside once more. She grabbed some dog food, a bowl and filled a gallon jug with water. She also took the money-filled Mason jar out from the cupboard, trying to cover every scenario she could think of.

Finally, she got into the truck with the rest of her supplies and started it up. She drove slowly at first, scanning the woods for any sign of a familiar body—human or animal. She veered right at the truck path and headed for the main road. At the edge of their property she looked left to the dam and then to the right. She decided to turn right. Slowly, she drove along the dirt road. About a mile down, she saw Cheyenne crossing the road in front of her. She hit the brakes and threw the truck into park.

"Hey, Cheyenne," Jesse called out, opening up the cab door. With great difficulty, because of the baby, she got out. Cheyenne started to run, but then recognized the vehicle and Jesse's voice.

"Now, that's my woman!" Johnny yelled, from off to Jesse's left.

Jesse looked up and saw Johnny and Shadow with Mesa hanging over Johnny's shoulders. "Good God, man!" Jesse yelled back, "that's a ninety pound wolf you're carrying, do you know that?" Jesse ran to the back of the truck and threw down the tailgate.

"Maybe I will, once the adrenaline wears off," he smiled, running to the truck. "Thanks, babe," he huffed, meeting her at the back of the truck. "Can you help get this bad boy on the truck?"

Jesse had already climbed laboriously onto the truck bed and was throwing out the blanket to cover the floor of the bed. She dropped to her knees and took hold of Mesa's neck, easing him down as Johnny moved out from under him. "I don't think I could have made it back to the cabin," her husband puffed. Shadow and Cheyenne were now upon him. "That guy's heavy."

Jesse looked Mesa over as the wolf tried to lick her face. "I don't see any blood spurting out," she observed.

"I think he was just grazed," Johnny reported, jumping up onto the bed and sliding Mesa to the front of the vehicle, just under the cab window. "It already looked like the blood was drying when I found him. But I don't want to take any chances. Are you up for taking a ride to Browning?"

"Browning?" Jesse questioned his choice. "Isn't there a vet in town?"

"After Bainsbridge, I'd rather take my chances in Browning. I don't think a vet in town is going to believe that this is a dog—or treat an injured wolf."

"I'll stay with him back here," Jesse offered, covering Mesa up with the rest of the blanket. The animal kept trying to get up, but his left leg was giving him no end of trouble.

"You'll be okay back here?" Johnny questioned Jesse's choice.

"I'll just lay down with him," she stated, shifting her legs around to do so. "We'll be fine. Oh…" Johnny was already off the truck and putting up the back of the tailgate, "could you grab me that bottle of water out of the cab?"

Johnny ran over to the passenger side and yanked open the door. He came back with the food and the water. "Were you a girl scout or something?" he smiled, putting her supplies within her reach into the bed of the truck.

"Yeah," she smirked. "Like you were a boy scout, I'm sure."

He threw her a wink and stooped down slapping his knees. "Come on, Cheyenne, Shadow. Let's get in the truck." Shadow jumped in readily, but Cheyenne shied away from the door at first. She returned to sniff at the door-jamb and Johnny grabbed the opportunity. "Sorry," the Indian groaned, pushing the wolf up into the cab. "We don't have time to discuss this, Chy." He slammed the truck door closed with the animals safe inside.

He ran around and sprinted onto the driver's seat. "You're sure you'll be okay?" he asked again, sliding open the back window. Knowing how Jesse felt about her animals, he was relieved to see her so calm and in control.

"Hit it," Jesse called out. She had propped herself up against the back of the cab and Mesa rested his head on her thighs. She was grateful for the pillow between her back and the metal of the bed of the truck. When Johnny threw the truck into gear and pulled out onto the road, there were some nasty bumps.

Shadow stuck his head out the back window and Jesse smiled up at him. "Hey, boy. Everything's all right. We're right here." She took one of the towels and soaked it with some of the water she had brought along. She wrung it out slowly, first over Mesa's mouth. He accepted it. She then took the towel and wiped down Mesa's wound. It was still bleeding, so she pressed down over the open gash with the towel and her hand. She could feel Mesa's pulse coursing through his leg as the blood continued to pump.

Johnny took a deep breath and exhaled slowly when he finally got the vehicle on the road. Now, he just had to get everybody to the veterinary hospital in one piece. Turning left onto 89, he hit pavement and a much smoother ride followed. His foot hit the gas pedal and the truck accelerated. Cheyenne sat next to him, staring in wonder at the sights spinning by. Shadow sat shotgun, used to rides in the truck, and stuck his head out the window to catch the wind as they sped through it. His tongue lolled out and flapped in the wind. The big wolf was enjoying the ride. Cheyenne leaned closer to Johnny until most of her body was pressed against her master's side.

Newly appointed Veterinary Medical Resident, Joshua Kennedy, was a little bit bored that afternoon at the Animal Care and Emergency Clinic. There was very little business save for a cat whose tail got caught in a door, causing her to lose the tip of it; and a dog with a touch of arthritis. Dr. Kennedy could not understand why someone spent good money to put up the small, but efficient, emergency clinic here in Browning. The residents could barely afford medical attention for themselves, let alone for their pets. But the animals trickled in and, when they did, he was happy he was there to help.

He had now been fully employed at the clinic for a grand total of three weeks. He cringed at the thought of having to serve there for another two years. He would surely forget all his education at the rate he wasn't using it. He sat back in the rolling office chair at the receptionist's desk and put his feet up. "At least they could hire a receptionist," Josh pointed out to the empty room. "It would be nice to have *somebody* to talk to." He looked over at the computer screen that had *gone to sleep* two hours ago, and hadn't been touched since. He considered maybe bringing in a computer game or something that might help make the days go a little faster.

The young doctor, with sandy blond hair and pale blue eyes, saw the dark blue truck as it slid into the parking lot off the road, but he had learned not to get excited by every vehicle that pulled in. He assumed this truck was going to make a u-turn like everybody else. When the driver threw the truck into park and shut off the engine, Josh's interest was snagged. *Damn,* he thought to himself as he sat up and stretched his neck to get a better view of the occupants. *He's got some really big dogs in that truck.* He saw the Indian get out and rush to the back of the truck. That got the doctor off his feet. The tailgate clanged down and the Indian was reaching for something in the back.

Kennedy got up and went to the door. He opened it and stepped out into the mid-afternoon sun. "What'cha got there?" he asked, walking toward the vehicle. Shadow popped his head through the driver's side window. The Doctor jumped back a full foot.

"We've got a…" Johnny wasn't sure what to say. He looked at Jesse whose hand was still pressing against Mesa's wound as her husband pulled the blanket toward the edge of the truck.

"Our dog's been shot," Jesse snapped, sliding across the bed of the truck to the tailgate. "We need some help."

Josh Kennedy rushed to the back of the truck to help. Johnny reached in and started to pick up the wounded wolf. "No," the doctor ordered. "Leave him in the blanket; we can both carry him that way." Jesse was forced to let her hand go as the two men grabbed hold of the blanket and swung Mesa out of the truck. She crawled to the tailgate, clumsily climbed off and found her footing on the gravel parking lot. She put her hands around the baby in her womb and held him as still as she could against herself, while she hurried to the door. She got there just as the doctor and Johnny arrived and opened the door wide to help them in.

Johnny followed the doctor into an examining room and they placed Mesa onto a metal examination table. He was just a bit bigger than the table and his feet dangled off the edge.

"Okay," Kennedy said, giving the animal a close look. "In case you didn't know it, this is not a dog."

"I know," Johnny admitted awkwardly. "The wife thought you might turn us away if you knew he was a wolf."

"And a pretty big one, too," the doctor noted, pulling a lamp over the table so he could see the wound better. He poked a bit with a sterile swab and cleaned up some of the blood. "I'm also gonna' take a stab in the dark here and say this wolf is a pet."

"Part of the family's more like it," Johnny muttered, watching the doctor work. "Why?"

"Because I don't think a wild wolf would be trying to lick my arm, like this one's doing right now."

Johnny looked from the wound to Mesa's head. The wolf was licking the doctor's coat quite steadfastly, so he started to move toward the other end of the table.

"It's okay," the doctor assured the Indian, sitting back and giving Mesa a pat on the head. "He's just nervous, that's all. He's a good boy. And a lucky one too."

"Can you fix him up?" Johnny asked hopefully. He faced the doctor from the other side of the table.

"I need to clean this wound and he's going to need quite a few stitches, inside and out. But, for the most part, the bullet just grazed him. Now, don't get me wrong, it took out a pretty big chunk of flesh, but, yeah, I can fix him up. There's no bullet to dig out."

Johnny sighed with relief. "Thanks, Doc. We appreciate you helping us."

The doctor rolled his stool back to the cabinet. "No problem." He opened the cabinet doors and took out what he needed for his work. "Why don't you go and talk to your wife," he suggested. "I'll be okay with…what's his name?"

"Mesa," Johnny told him. "If you're nervous around him, I'll be happy to stay here and keep an eye on him for you."

"Believe it or not, I've studied some on these guys. I've got a soft spot for them, myself. We'll be fine. Go give the wife the good news. By the looks of her condition, I'm sure she could use it right about now. When's the baby due?"

"In a month," Johnny said, opening the door. He smiled at the young doctor before he left him to do his work. "Thanks again for your help…" he paused, just before closing the door, "…and your acceptance."

Jesse was at the payphone when Johnny came out. "Thanks, Clayton," she said and hung up. She looked at Johnny with wide, inquiring eyes.

"He's going to be fine," Johnny smiled, walking over to his wife and taking her into his arms. "The Doc's stitching him up right now. The bullet just grazed him. But it made a pretty big hole. That's why all the blood."

"Can I see him?" she asked. "Is the doctor all right with him alone?"

"Yeah," Johnny chuckled. "We found ourselves a sympathizer."

"*You* found him," Jesse hugged him close. "*You* saved our wolf."

Johnny could tell that Jesse was close to collapsing. He held her closer. "Why don't you sit down a minute," he suggested. "I should go check on the other two in the truck."

"I should go with you," she said. "They'll be pretty confused."

"You *should* sit down," Johnny reiterated. "I can…"

"I'll sit down when we get back in the truck," Jesse avowed, digging deep into her energy reserves to pull Johnny toward the door. "Do you think we should let the kids out one at a time so we can keep an eye on them better?"

"We'll leave it up to them to decide," Johnny sighed, following his wife. She was stubborn and pregnant. But he could tell she was emotionally and physically drained. Johnny would let her go outside with him now, but when they got home he'd start calling the shots. If he got his way, she wasn't going farther than from the couch to the kitchen for the next month.

Outside at the truck, Cheyenne and Shadow perked up when they saw their masters coming toward them. Johnny unlocked the door and opened it a crack. Shadow pushed it open the rest of the way, almost throwing Johnny aside with his force. He was out of the cab and at Jesse's side in a heartbeat. Cheyenne opted to stay in the truck. She didn't know where she was and didn't want to take the risk of finding out. Johnny got into the cab of the truck with her. The white wolf placed her two front paws on Johnny's thigh and licked his face.

"Okay," Johnny grimaced. "That hurts." The wolf's weight on his leg was excruciatingly painful, so he gently, but firmly, tried to move her paws back down on the seat. "You don't want to get out a minute, girl?" he asked, successful at lifting up one paw. Now she took those paws and stretched out across his lap. "Oh, I don't know if that's any better, pup," he sighed, looking to Jesse for help.

Jesse had received her greeting of licks from Shadow and was now watching him as he inspected the immediate area. He marked the boundaries of the parking area quickly and then checked out the door where Mesa had disappeared.

"Babe," Johnny called out. "Could you give me a hand here?"

Jesse walked over to the truck, smiling. "Trapped, huh?" she asked. "Come on girl," she coaxed Cheyenne. "I know you've got to go too." Shadow terminated his door exploration and ran to Jesse when he heard her speak. When Cheyenne saw that Shadow seemed to be all right, she stood up, this time on Johnny's other thigh, and after a brief moment of hesitation, bounded out onto the gravel. Shadow stayed with her while she quickly searched for a place to relieve herself.

"Ouch," Johnny commented, rubbing his thighs.

"Did the big bad wolf hurt you?" Jesse smiled, helping him out of the truck.

"She's as heavy as Mesa and catching up to Shadow," Johnny noted, taking Jesse's helping hand.

The door to the clinic opened, startling everybody. Shadow and Cheyenne froze when the Doctor came out. "Hey, Mesa's ready," he remarked with his eyes riveted on the healthy wolves. "Would you look at these two, then,"

Kennedy smiled, stooping down to one knee. "Can you guys come see me?" he beckoned with his hands out and palms up to welcome their perusal.

Jesse walked over to the doctor. "Come on Shadow, Cheyenne," she called to her wolves. "Come meet the man who saved your brother." As always, Shadow moved first. He walked slowly to Jesse, sniffing the air around them.

Johnny limped over to the doctor, trying to get the circulation back in his legs. Cheyenne followed the human she loved almost as much as Shadow.

"They look good," the doctor announced, as Shadow sniffed him. He was most intrigued with the scents on the doctor's hands. "I'd love to give them a physical if I could."

"Do you make house calls?" Jesse inquired, knowing it would be impossible to get Cheyenne inside the clinic. The white wolf refused to come close enough for the doctor to touch her. She paced back and forth behind Johnny, not even daring to approach Shadow because he was just too close to the strange human.

"For them I would," the doctor replied. "Just give me your address."

"There's two more at home," Johnny threw in. "And a bobcat, if you can catch her."

"Jesus!" Kennedy breathed. "And I thought I'd be bored around here."

Johnny took hold of Shadow and, with a little more effort, grabbed Cheyenne and herded them back into the truck. Jesse followed the doctor back inside the building. While Dr. Kennedy entered the pertinent patient information into the computer, Jesse drew him a map to the cabin and then pried the mason jar out of her sweater pocket. "How much for today, Doc?" she asked.

"Don't worry about it," the young doctor smiled. "It was a pleasure to help out."

Jesse put three hundred dollars on the counter. "Then consider this a donation to the clinic." Jesse looked kindly at the doctor, who was baffled at the amount of money she gave him. When he looked back at her, she smiled. "Taking care of wolves is a risky business in this part of the country," Jesse said. "We can't thank you enough for helping us out."

"Hey, doc," Johnny said, coming in the door, "are we going to take him out the way we brought him in?"

"Ah," Joshua Kennedy was momentarily at a loss for words. He put the money in the drawer and saved the computer work sheet. "Yeah. We'll just carry him out on the blanket. If you'd like to keep an eye on him, you can come with us, Mrs. Stillwater. He's going to sleep for a while. I gave him a sedative." He led Jesse and Johnny back to the examination room. "When he wakes up he'll try to walk, but I think it'll be a little too painful for a couple of days at least. Just keep an eye on him. He's in great shape, so he should heal up pretty quickly."

The doctor opened the examination room door and Jesse went in first. She walked quietly to the table where Mesa was asleep. His breathing was deep and regular. Johnny checked his wife's eyes. There were no tears. She was still holding up, albeit precariously.

"Okay, are you ready?" the doctor asked Johnny as they both grabbed hold of the blanket. "Let's get you guys on your way." Johnny nodded his assent and they carried the wolf carefully outside.

With Mesa and Jesse loaded up in the back of the pickup, Johnny shook the young doctor's hand heartily. "Thanks again, Doc. We really appreciate what you've done for us today. And you're welcome to come out whenever you like."

"I'll come by in a couple of days," Kennedy answered. "Just to make sure Mesa's all right. If I can get a closer look at the other two, that'll be great."

"You won't be able to shake 'em loose with a stick once they're at home."

"I'm sure it's been rough on everybody today," the doctor reasoned. "Mrs. Stillwater..." He started.

"It's Jesse," Jesse corrected him. "Please—and that's Johnny."

"Are you going to be warm enough back there, Jesse?" the doctor finished his question. "I could get another blanket from the clinic..."

"We're good," Jesse said. She smiled at the doctor before returning her gaze to the sleeping wolf beside her. "I'm going to lie right down next to Mesa here and I'll be fine. Thanks again, Doc."

"It's Josh," Dr. Kennedy insisted. "And thank you. I'll see you in a couple of days." Johnny waved as he pulled the truck back. Shadow's head was outside the window waiting for the next rush of wind. "And watch the bumps!" the doctor reminded him.

The stars were out when Johnny finally felt relieved enough to take a little break. He leaned against the porch railing and took a deep, long breath, reveling in the cool night air. Mesa was sound asleep in a make shift bed of blankets on the living room floor, not far from the pups' metal den. Johnny was still amazed that he had actually been able to carry the ninety pounds of *dead weight* into the house. Cheyenne was with the pups and Shadow was prowling in and out of the lodge pole pines checking to make sure his boundaries were still intact.

Johnny went into the house and warmed himself some soup on the stove in the kitchen. Hopefully, Jesse was finished with her hot bath and safely tucked into bed. He was about to go up and check on her when he saw the headlights coming up the dirt road that led to the house.

"Good God," Johnny sighed. "Now what?" He dragged himself back outside and waited for the vehicle to pull up. It was Clayton Phillips. Johnny's heart rate went up a couple notches when Phillips descended from the driver's side of the cab.

"Evening, Johnny," Clayton announced, walking up to the steps.

"Evening, Clayton," Johnny muttered back.

"You've had quite a day, I hear," Clayton said with a weak smile. "You must be pretty tired."

"Wish you'd been here a while ago," Johnny expressed. "It wasn't easy getting that wolf into the house."

"Jesse's all right?" Clayton questioned the young man.

"I think so," Johnny murmured. "I was just on my way to check."

"I went over to the McGill ranch," the Town Marshal said. Johnny raised his head and looked at Clayton with narrow eyes. "I went there after Jesse called and told me what happened."

"I suppose you better tell me," Johnny moaned, stepping aside to let Clayton come up on the porch. "Did Mesa kill something?"

Clayton sat down in the rocker on the porch and sighed heavily. "I don't know how to tell you this, 'cos I don't want you to get upset."

"Clayton," Johnny said, distressed. He leaned back against the porch support and crossed his arms over his chest. "I'm already upset. What the hell happened? Are we going to have to put that wolf down?"

"Oh, no!" Clayton replied rapidly. "That's not it at all." The man could not tell if Johnny was more worried about Jesse's reaction or the wolf itself. Suddenly, it was apparent to the marshal that Johnny cared about the animals as much as Jesse did.

"Okay," Johnny breathed. "Then just tell me. I can take it. And I'll make it good. Whatever it costs."

"Johnny," Clayton rocked back in the rocker and held it there. "McGill's in bankruptcy. The drought pretty much cleaned him out. The wife left him six months ago and he's down to nothing. I'm buying the few cows he's got left before the bank gets a hold of them and he's moving out. The only thing he's got left in this world is his damn horse and I don't think he's going to be able to keep him, either."

Johnny watched the rancher and said nothing. He indicated with a nod of his head to continue.

"He said the wolf attacked his horse," Clayton blurted out. "When I checked the animal, I couldn't find a mark on him. When I questioned him further, he ranted and raved about how the wolf was staring at him from the ridge over his house." Clayton rocked the chair forward, braced his arms across the top of his legs and bowed his head. "McGill's gone over the edge, Johnny. It's like he took all his anger and frustration and put it into that one bullet, as if Mesa represented everything that was wrong in his world. Like he needed one last trace of control. I left the man crying, Johnny. He's been beaten so far down, I don't think he'll ever get up. I couldn't do anything to him. I just hope you and Jesse can understand."

"I do," Johnny finally said after a few seconds of silence. "I'm sorry for the man and his troubles. I know what it's like to have nothing, especially now when I have it all." Johnny pushed himself away from the porch and touched Clayton's drooping shoulder. "I'll explain it to Jesse," he murmured. "I'll do my best to make her understand." Clayton looked up and started to get out of the rocker. "No, stay there," Johnny insisted. "Let me get you a drink. I think we could both use one right about now. It's been a hard day for all of us."

CHAPTER 30

❦

"I don't think this is a good idea," Johnny stated, reluctantly putting his arms in the coat that Jesse was holding open for him. "This rain's not going to let up and if the road's washed out by the dam, I won't be able to get back home."

"Arleen said the road was fine," Jesse comforted her husband. "And you know this is important."

"Meeting a bunch of people who like my furniture is not as important as you and our baby," Johnny insisted. "There will be plenty of time for *whatever* you call it..."

"Networking," Jesse smiled, handing him the keys to the truck.

"*Networking*—after the baby is born." Johnny looked out the window again. The thunderstorm was getting stronger. A bolt of lightening flashed and the lights flickered. The thunder cracked just over the cabin immediately after, startling them both. Johnny walked over to the front door and opened it. The rain was coming down in sheets.

"According to Red Cloud," Jesse negotiated, "the baby's not due for at least three weeks. So there's no reason why you can't run over to the store tonight, meet some new friends and make some money."

"Make friends, yeah," Johnny replied sarcastically. "I do that real easy."

"Josh said he'd be there," Jesse countered. "And Arleen will be at your side all night."

"I'm not going to be there all night," Johnny insisted. "I'll stop by and check things out—then I'm coming home." He shut the door to keep the driving rain from entering through the screen door.

"Josh can come back with you if this doesn't let up," Jesse suggested. "I can open up the futon in the work room now that it's cleaned up."

"I doubt anybody's going to show up in this storm," Johnny reasoned. "I'm going to call Arleen and check." Johnny stepped away from his wife, went to the phone and dialed the number to the store. Arleen was there and they conversed for a short while.

Jesse took the opportunity to check the fire in the fireplace. There were three sleeping wolves stretched out in front of it. The babies were cuddled up under Cheyenne's soft white coat. Kitten was sleeping on the chair close by. Jesse was looking forward to relaxing on the couch with the new book that had come in the mail.

It was the fourth of May and Mesa was limping about, but feeling much better. The pups had grown a bit and Jesse felt as big as a boat. Johnny had taken care of everything for her, and he deserved a little break. She would take it easy and go to bed early, even though she wasn't feeling any differently than she had for the past nine months. Red Cloud's calculations were probably right. She figured little Phelan would probably wait another three weeks, at least.

"There's people already there," Johnny told his wife, hanging up the phone. "Arleen says they're very anxious to *meet the artist*."

"They can have the *artist* for a couple hours," Jesse smiled, pulling up the collar of his jacket close around his neck. "But be home by midnight, Cinderella, just in case."

Johnny hugged his wife close, kissing her good-bye. "I'll be back soon. Do not go anywhere!"

"I have no intention to move from this room," Jesse smiled, hugging Johnny back. "I'll read for awhile and then probably go to sleep, as it's all I seem to be able to do lately."

"Okay," Johnny took a deep breath. "I'll be back soon. You know the number at the store. Call it if anything happens while I'm gone."

"See you in a couple hours," Jesse shooed her man out the door. "Drive carefully!"

Johnny darted out the door and down the porch steps. The rain was pouring down heavily. His jacket was drenched by the time he got into the truck. When he drove away, Jesse started to shut the door but felt some fur against her leg. "Mesa," she cooed to the wolf, who was gazing intently out the door. "Do you want to go out for a minute?" The wolf's eyes scanned the downpour and then gazed up at Jesse. "Yeah, it's pretty miserable out there, boy."

The wolf turned around and limped across the room to the back door. There he stopped and looked back at Jesse.

"My clever boy," she smiled. "Okay, I'm coming." She waddled across the room behind him and let the wolf out. The rain, coming from the east, was buffered by the cabin and was not as intense on the back patio. Mesa hobbled out the door to do his business. Jesse stood in the doorway and casually kept an eye on him—with his injury and her condition, the two had become constant companions in the last two weeks. She was relieved to see he was on the mend. Josh Kennedy, who had lately become good friends with Johnny, Jesse and all the animals, warned her that there may be a scar but otherwise Mesa would fully recover.

When Johnny told her about McGill and the incident that had led to the shooting, she swallowed her anger quickly and accepted the fact that nothing would be done. She had her wolf and that was all that was important. McGill moved out two days later and nobody had heard a word from him since. Clayton had taken in the man's cows and the horse and slipped him some money when he left. Jesse could not help but feel sorry for the man. She hoped that he would find a better life somewhere else.

Jesse rubbed her hands energetically up and down her arms to warm them. It was getting colder and the dampness was settling into her bones. She looked up the stairs and sighed. Her sweater was up on the bed where she'd left it earlier. A quick glance back outside told her Mesa wasn't quite finished nosing around the yard. She left the back door open a bit so he'd be able to get back inside without having to wait for her and decided to go upstairs to retrieve the article of clothing.

Jesse climbed the stairs slowly, using the banister for support. Upon reaching the top floor, she was honestly surprised when she felt a little tug inside her, not unlike a tiny cramp. She shook it off and toddled over to the bed where she grabbed her sweater and a pillow. She chose to get a few more items so she would not have to come back up again. Heading back for the stairs with her load of goodies, she felt another twinge as she stepped on the first riser going down.

She was about halfway down the stairs when Mesa nudged his nose through the crack in the door and let himself in. The rain was coming in with him. He scooted in the door and saw Jesse on the stairs. He put a front paw on the step as if he was going to come up.

"No, boy," Jesse warned him. "I'm coming down, it's all right." She quickly took another step to let him know what direction she was going. Mesa stood on the step a couple of seconds longer until Jesse took another step down.

Finally convinced she was on the right course, Mesa stepped off the riser and shambled over to the fireplace to lie back down.

Jesse took one more step and then another and was almost to the bottom when her socked foot slipped on the wet wood and she lost her balance. The pillow, sweater and other stuff flew up into the air and she saved herself at the last second by grabbing onto the banister with her left hand. "Whew!" she exclaimed, using the strength in her hand and arm to pull herself back up. It was not easy but she did it. Jesse stood on the last stair and caught her breath, placing both of her hands on the banister to steady herself the rest of the way.

The heads of the wolves raised and perused the situation when they heard her stumble. Shadow, seeing everything was all right, put his head back down on his front paws, but he did not go back to sleep. His golden eyes followed Jesse as she stepped down onto the floor and tried to bend over to reclaim her things. She could pick up the pillow because it was standing on end against the door, but the sweater was another story. She could not bend over far enough to grab it, so she'd have to come up with another strategy.

The clever woman opted to step on the sweater and sweep it over to the couch with her foot. Then when she sat down, she could finally pick it up. She had just kicked it when the next cramp hit. This one nearly brought her to her knees.

"Oh, shit!" she panted, expelling little breaths. She felt the liquid running down her legs and then saw it on the hardwood floor beneath her. Her water had broken.

Shadow was up now and sniffing at her feet. "Go away, Shadow," she said, panicky. "Come on, boy. I gotta' get to the phone." She drew another couple of deep breaths and the cramping eased up. She waddled over to the telephone and picked up the receiver. "Well, I shouldn't be surprised," she said out loud as Shadow watched her. She depressed the switch hook a couple of times in a futile effort to get a dial tone, but the line was dead. Jesse looked around the room and wondered what to do next. Shadow was trying to lick her legs in an effort to clean her up. "Really, pup," Jesse said, embarrassed. "Go lay down, okay? Momma's got a little problem here and you're not helping to fix it."

It was only seven o'clock and Johnny probably wasn't even at the store yet. Jesse came to the conclusion quickly that this wasn't going to be an easy night. She went to the kitchen and got a glass of water and then worked her way back to the couch. The next cramp hit her like a truck and she collapsed onto the piece of furniture overcome by the pain. She took her short breaths and tried to calm herself again. With a shaky hand she spilled some of the water out of the glass onto her face. Suddenly she was very, very warm and she was breaking out into a sweat. She held onto the glass tightly and when the next cramp subsided, she took a very small sip. Shadow pressed against her and licked her face. With an eye on the clock, Jesse counted the minutes. Five minutes later she shrieked when the next spasm hit. Shadow tried to put a paw on her leg but she brushed it away. She was consumed with a cramp that coursed through her whole body. She felt like she would surely die if this condition continued much longer. When it finally subsided Jesse lay back on the couch. The baby was coming and there was nothing she could do about it. She was scared to death and had no idea what to do next.

Shadow ran around the couch a couple of times trying to figure out what was wrong. Now Jesse was crying and she wouldn't let him lick her face or bulging stomach. The animal, frustrated, suddenly realized the back door was open. He ran out of the cabin, followed closely by Cheyenne, who had been watching the proceedings with Mesa. Mesa picked up the pups by the scruffs of their necks, put them unceremoniously into their metal den and lay down in front of the open door. His job, apparently, was to keep the pups in place.

When Jesse cried out with another spasm, Shadow took off into the woods and Cheyenne started to howl.

"Come on to bed, Winona," Charlie whined for the seventh time. "There's nothing out there." He sighed and threw his hands into the air, giving up. Winona was not listening to him.

"Just a minute," she finally answered him sharply. "I know I can hear the wolves howling."

"It's just the wind," Charlie reasoned. "For God's sake, not even the wolves are going to go out tonight. And even if they are howling, what's so odd about that?"

Winona shook her head and went to the front door of their small house. She opened it wide and stuck her head out into the rain.

"Now, you're going to catch your death," Charlie snapped. "Get inside here woman. You're losing your mind."

Winona turned her ear to the direction of the sound she was trying to detect. She listened again and a slow smile came to her lips because she realized she was right. She was about to tell her husband *I told you so,* but she turned to the south and froze. "Come here," she said, in a serious tone. She waved her husband to the door.

"I'm not going out…" he was forced to shut his mouth. This time he heard the howl—as plain as day. "That doesn't sound right, does it?" he whispered, coming up to the door behind his wife.

"It's Shadow," Winona murmured back. "He's right there at the edge of the woods."

Charlie craned his neck around his wife and looked out. It was difficult to see because the heavy rain created a veil of water, obscuring everything. The wolf howled again. Charlie put his hands on his wife's shoulders and forced her gently out of his way. He stepped out into the rain and peered into the area where the sound had come from. Out of the blackness of the trees, Shadow took a step toward him. "Where's Johnny and Jesse tonight?" he demanded of his wife.

"I think Johnny was going to that show or whatever Arleen was doing at the store," Winona said quickly. "I'm sure Jesse didn't go. She hasn't left the house for a couple of weeks."

Shadow howled again—a long, mournful cry. It made the hairs on the back of Charlie's neck stand on end. "Something's wrong," he surmised, turning to make sure his gun was right where it was supposed to be.

The words hit Winona like a sledgehammer and the light switched on in her brain. "The baby!" she cried. "Jesse's gone into labor!" She rushed into the house and grabbed her bag. She did not have time to rag on Charlie who had just chastised her for packing it so far ahead of time. She grabbed her coat from the hook on the wall. "Charlie, I've got to go to the cabin, right now."

"I'll drive," Charlie said, grabbing his coat too.

"There's no time for that," Winona commanded. "You call the store and try to get Johnny. I'm going with Shadow, now."

Before Charlie could stop her, Winona was gone. "You'll get lost out there!" he screamed into the rain. "The stream is probably flooded!"

"Shadow will get me there," Winona's voice was like a whisper, even though she was screaming back at him. The downpour was intensifying. "Get Johnny home as fast as you can!" She traipsed off after the wolf, who met her halfway and greeted her before he led her back into the trees.

Charlie stood at the door for a moment, not quite sure what to do. Now he could hear the call of another wolf far off in the distance. He hoped Winona was right about the baby. His body quivered slightly, dispelling the thought that it might be something worse. He ran back into the house and grabbed the receiver off the telephone. The line, unfortunately, was dead. He stared at the telephone for a few seconds, wondering what to do next. The Native American slammed down the receiver, grabbed the keys off the table and headed out of the house to his truck.

Arleen cast a glance at Johnny across the room and smiled. The young man was clearly astonished at the attention being lauded upon him. He was also very nervous. She excused herself from the gentleman she was talking to and milled cheerily through the crowd of potential clients and eager buyers, toward the artist. His eyes were pleading with her to join him.

She felt a little guilty having the show so close to Jesse's due date, but the sales rep from Neiman Marcus insisted, saying it was tonight or never. It worked out in the end, because everybody was happy and the orders were pouring in. Johnny would be all right, she concluded to herself. And next time Jesse would be there to wheel and deal and get him through it with a minimum of hassles.

"How ya' holding up?" she whispered into his ear, approaching him from the side.

"I'd give my left nut for a drink right now," Johnny replied through clenched teeth, smiling at another well-wisher who wanted to shake his hand.

"I can get you one, if you want," Arleen offered. She gave the high sign to Josh who was across the room.

"No thanks," Johnny smiled. "I've got to get going soon. It'll be hard enough driving sober in this rain."

"How was the dam water when you came through?" Arleen inquired.

"Rising," Johnny said.

"It'll be okay," Arleen said soothingly to her friend. "The people are starting to thin out. It won't be long now."

"Did we make any money?" Johnny asked out of the side of his mouth.

"Oodles," Arleen smiled. "We'll be cleared out by weeks end."

Josh grabbed a glass of wine and picked his way gingerly through the assembly of people. He cut left, walked around the front counter and chanced a look outside to check the weather. A truck was pulling up. He couldn't believe that more people were arriving, especially on a night like this. He casually studied the person as he approached the front door. The man who got out of the truck was not a customer. This man, an Indian, was haggard and soaking wet. He stumbled when he stepped onto the boardwalk in front of the store. This man was burdened with a mission.

Josh opened the front door and held it for the aged Native American. Charlie thanked the young man with a nod of his head and the trace of a smile.

"I'm looking for Johnny Stillwater," the newcomer said, wiping the rain off his coat and stamping his shoes, which were soaked through the soles. "He's here?"

"Right over there," Josh pointed to the younger Indian. It was evident the man had no time for trivialities.

Charlie followed the direction of Josh's pointed finger and saw what looked like his son. The only problem was that this young man was smiling and being friendly—not the sullen, angry boy his father knew so well. Charlie shook the cobwebs from his head and started to pick his way through the crowd toward him.

Josh caught Johnny's eye above the sea of heads and pointed out the stranger to him. When Johnny saw his father, his first reaction was a tempered surprise. But as the older man moved slowly and apologetically through the crowd, trying desperately to reach him, Johnny's mood changed. He saw the look of fear in his father's eyes. He realized the man had not come to check out his work. Suddenly, Johnny feared something was very wrong. Johnny touched Arleen's arm, which gave her the clue to look up and see Johnny's father, too. She gently urged her friend forward to meet his father halfway.

"Johnny," the Native American sighed with relief, when they were finally close enough to touch, "you gotta' go, boy; you gotta' go home now."

"Dad?" Johnny asked, baffled.

Charlie grabbed his son's arm and pulled him to the side. Josh was right behind him. "There's some kind of trouble," Charlie muttered quietly. "Shadow came to the house. The wolves were howlin' louder than the storm." A look of panic crossed Johnny's face. He looked to his father for comfort, but saw none in his dark brown eyes. "I'm worried about your mother. She followed Shadow into those damned woods. She thinks the baby's comin'. I hope to God she's right." Johnny started for the door.

"Wait, man," Josh said, bracing his hand against the wall to stop Johnny from going any farther. "I'm going with you. Let me get the keys to my truck."

Arleen was way ahead of them. She appeared almost magically with their coats and keys in hand. "Go. And be careful," she commanded. "I'll take care of things here."

"Thanks," Johnny said gratefully. The three men hurried outside.

"The roads are mud, John," Charlie yelled out over the deluge. "I don't know what kind of shape the dam's gonna' be in."

"We're taking my truck," Johnny called back, getting in behind the wheel of the Dodge. "Get in."

Josh got his bag out of his car before he and Charlie piled into the vehicle. He barely got the passenger door closed before Johnny took off in a spray of mud and water.

"Watch it son," Charlie warned. "The streets are slick as a trout."

For the first time since she had started to follow Shadow, Winona realized she wasn't quite sure where they were. She had blindly fallen in behind the beast, certain that he knew the way back to the cabin. But suddenly, deep in the forest that lay between the two houses, she did not recognize a single sight. She stopped in her tracks and tried to determine where she was. Shadow returned to her side and yipped at her.

"Where are we boy?" she asked, feeling a little awkward talking to the wolf. "Aren't we going too far west?" The wolf hurried off and the woman was forced to trust him. A few minutes later everything became clear. She could hear the rushing water, but she had not seen it as they hurried along. Shadow had cleverly directed her upstream where she could still get across. The wolf jumped over the water. Winona got wet up to her knees. But she crossed and now Shadow was heading back southeast. Winona stopped a moment and combed her fingers through her sopping wet hair to get it out of her face. In the distance, she could hear Cheyenne. She would never doubt that wolf again, she thought, falling in behind him once more. They were almost to the cabin.

Johnny turned onto the dam road and headed west. The road was slick and muddy but Johnny managed to keep the truck on the road. There was little conversation during the eighteen-mile trek as the three men kept their eyes trained on the road ahead.

"Shit!" they said in unison when they saw the water up ahead.

Johnny threw the truck into park and got out. He ran up to the water's edge.

"How's it look?" Charlie called out from behind him.

"Can't tell," Johnny yelled back. "Can't see where it ends!"

Charlie walked up beside his son and took a look for himself.

"What if we go left and see if we can get across further down?" Johnny suggested, the panic rising in his voice.

"No, son," Charlie disagreed. "Too much mud. We'd sink that truck to the running boards before we got fifty feet."

Johnny turned and looked at his father, clearly distressed. "What do we do, then?" he screamed, losing control. "We've got to get across—now!"

Charlie wiped the water off his face and took his son's arm, leading him back to the truck. "The rock bed's on the right. There'll be more traction there and less chance of getting stuck. We stay to the right and I think we'll be able to get through."

Johnny took a deep breath and attempted to relax. His father was right. That was probably the way to go.

"It's okay, son," Charlie said. "We'll get there—I promise."

Jesse had no choice. Her baby was coming whether she wanted it to or not. Mesa sat at her side, licking the sweat from her face—the water glass had been emptied a long time ago. The contractions were now only two minutes apart. She could actually feel the baby moving down the birth canal, on its way out. She took a breath and pushed, screaming in agony. "God, get us through this!" She dug the fingers of her right hand into Mesa's fur. He stood still, lending her support.

She stopped pushing and rested her head back against the arm of the couch. She was a strong woman, she told herself. She had to do this. She had no choice. She braced herself for another push but eased up a bit instead. She couldn't believe it. Did she hear a voice? It had to be Cheyenne, she resolved. The wolf had been howling—just outside for sometime now. "Great," she sighed to Mesa. "Now, I'm hearing voices." Mesa looked up at her with compassionate eyes.

"Jesse!" a voice rang out. "I'm coming."

Jesse held her breath. She heard the voice clearly that time. There was a scuffle of paws and feet at the back door. Jesse lifted her head up and tears flowed freely from her eyes when the door opened wide and she saw Winona stepping inside the threshold. Shadow and Cheyenne were with her.

"I'm here, Jesse," Winona called out, rushing to her side. "It's going to be all right."

"Winona!" Jesse screeched. "It's coming!" The young woman was forced to bear down. This contraction was the worst one yet.

Winona shoved the coffee table aside and surveyed the situation in an instant. The baby was definitely on its way. She ran to the kitchen and turned on the water in the sink. She grabbed a dishrag and soaked it and dashed back to the couch. "Mesa," she said gently, "you're going to have to get out of the way." She placed the rag on Jesse's head and dabbed at the sweat.

"He's okay," Jesse panted. "He's helping me out."

Winona saw the young woman's hand firmly imbedded in the animal's fur. "Okay, but we've got to make room, honey. We've got to spread those legs, I can see the head."

Jesse placed her right leg on the floor while Winona helped her get her left leg up on the couch. She groaned in agony, forced again to push.

"That's a girl," Winona urged. "Come on, it's time to get this baby out." She positioned herself on the floor between Jesse's legs and readied herself. The forehead of the baby slipped out. "Push, Jesse!" Winona cried. "Come on, honey, just a few more times." Jesse screamed as she pushed again. Finally, Winona had something to grab onto. She rested the baby's head in her hands and held gently onto it. "One more time, honey. Give it all you've got."

Jesse screamed the loudest as her flesh ripped open when the shoulders of the baby came out. Winona was now on the couch. With the baby's head now on her legs, she held the baby by the shoulders as the rest of his body eased out. Jesse panted to grab her breath, almost passing out. "No you don't," Winona ordered her. "Hang in there with me, Jess. We've got a baby boy here." She took the rag and wiped the baby's face off, pulling out the mucous from his nose and mouth. The little guy did not cry. With wide blue eyes he looked about and yawned at his grandmother.

"The contractions are still there," Jesse screamed. "I thought he was out!"

"Afterbirth, honey," Winona soothed. "It's all gotta' come out. I need you to push again. It'll be easier this time, I promise."

A few moments later, the delivery was complete. Jesse's grip lessened on Mesa's fur as she closed her eyes to rest. Winona cut the umbilical cord and was gently cleaning the baby up when the front door slammed open and Johnny ran inside. "Jesus!" he exclaimed with tears running down his face.

"It's over, Johnny," Winona smiled up at her boy. "Everybody's okay."

"There's blood all over!" Johnny screamed. "Jesse…"

"Ssssh," Jesse whispered, raising her left hand feebly toward her husband. "We need a little quiet for a second, okay? I've put the wolves through enough, already."

"This was the last time you'll *ever* talk me into doing something against my better judgment," Johnny spoke softly, taking her hand into his. He scooted around the couch to be by his wife's side.

"Yes, sir," Jesse sighed, giving him a weary smile. "You're in charge from now on."

"God, babe," Johnny uttered, casting a sidelong glance down the rest of Jesse's now limp body. "There's so much blood."

"Sorry about the couch," she murmured, obviously still in pain.

"I never liked it anyway," Johnny exclaimed. "I'll buy you a big, comfy new one as soon as that baby turns eighteen."

"Why eighteen?" Jesse asked incredulously.

"That's probably the next time I'll ever let one of you out of my sight—long enough to go buy one."

Charlie and Josh came in the door quietly. Winona looked up and smiled at her husband as Johnny collapsed to his knees at Jesse's side. "Charlie, could you get Jesse some water please? And I need some very warm, clean water for the baby."

Joshua quietly approached the couch. "I'm Dr. Joshua Kennedy," he introduced himself to Winona. "I'm a Veterinarian, but is there anything I can do to help?"

"I think we're going to need some stitches," Winona smiled up at the young man, holding her grandson close to her breast to keep him warm.

"Jesse?" Josh inquired quietly.

"You fixed up Mesa, Doc," she sighed, exhausted. "Right now, I'll take any help I can get."

While Josh tended to Jesse, Winona cleaned up the baby and Charlie worked on cleaning up the mess. Johnny clutched tightly to his wife. Jesse lay peacefully in his arms.

"Mothers first," Winona finally said, bringing the baby to Jesse. The new mother held out her hands and took the baby into her arms. Johnny cried softly, as he held both Jesse and their child.

Shadow nosed his way through the close huddle and sniffed out the newest member of the family. "Hey, Shadow," Jesse murmured, smiling at her wolf, "this is Phelan." Shadow sniffed a bit more and then licked the baby's tiny chest. The baby felt the big, black animal and grasped the fur on the side of Shadow's neck into his tiny little hand. "Phelan," Jesse whispered into her newborn's ear, "this is Shadow, your new best friend."

CHAPTER 31

"Are you going to sit there and tell me," Arleen retorted, holding the top of the jack-o-lantern Jesse had just finished carving, "that it's been almost six months and you have not checked that envelope?"

"I'm not kidding," Jesse laughed, eyeing her artwork. "We've been a little busy around here, you know. I guess we forgot." Jesse took the tea light off the table and stuck it inside the hollowed out gourd.

Arleen stood up from the table, placed the top on the pumpkin and headed for the front door. When she got there she hollered out through the screen, "Johnny! Get in here!"

Johnny was out in the yard with the *critters*, lounging with the baby, a bevy of wolves and a very fat bobcat on a nice big blanket in the afternoon sun. Phelan, on all fours, was crawling around with the mindset to leave the comfort of the blanket and seek out the tall grasses that surrounded them. Every time he ventured close to the edge of the down-filled coverlet, Shadow, who was right by his side, would pick the baby up by the seat of his little blue overhauls with his mouth and carry him back to Johnny, dropping him gently on his father's chest. The baby giggled, loving every ride. Johnny couldn't help but chuckle along with his son, too. "What do you want?" he yelled back as a query.

Arleen opened the screen door and held it for Jesse, who brought the finished jack-o-lantern out and put it on the porch. "Jesse says you guys haven't checked Red Cloud's prediction envelope. I can't believe it! *You* checked it, didn't you?"

Johnny knitted his brow, considering her question. "Heck, I forgot all about that," he finally announced. "Heck, I don't even know where you guys put it." The screen door slammed shut behind Arleen when she disappeared back into the cabin. Johnny smiled at his wife and gave her a come hither look. She returned his smile seductively, slowly walking down the porch steps and out into the grass toward him.

Jesse had lost the baby weight and she cut a stunning figure with her long hair and dress flowing in the breeze that surrounded her. Johnny stared rakishly at her as she approached him. With his hand pressed to his heart, he pretended to swoon and lay down on the blanket—just in time for Shadow to drop the baby onto his stomach again. "Ugh," Johnny groaned. Phelan giggled and rolled off him, back to the blanket. "You're getting heavy, boy!"

Jesse laughed and ran the rest of the way, scooping up Phelan into her arms and spinning him around. Phelan giggled more and babbled incoherently, grabbing hold of his mother's long, brown hair. Shadow lay down with a thud onto the blanket—welcoming the break.

The screen door slammed again and Arleen ran down the steps, waving the envelope in her hands. "You guys," she scolded. "I can't believe this hasn't been opened yet." She hurried to the blanket and plopped herself down next to Shadow. Mesa and the pups, now pretty big themselves, came over to her.

Arleen ripped it open and pulled out the carefully folded piece of paper. She scanned it quickly and her jaw dropped.

"What does it say?" Johnny turned over, hoisting himself up on one arm. With his free hand he tried casually to snatch it out of Arleen's grasp.

Arleen saw his hand coming and adroitly kept it from him. "Well," she announced proudly, "it says it will be a boy..."

"We already knew that," Jesse commented, holding her baby out with her hands and kissing his tummy. The baby giggled again and squirmed in her delicate hold. She bent over and put him on the blanket, sitting down next to Johnny. Shadow appeared to sigh, seeing the infant on the blanket again. He started to get up, but didn't have to. Phelan went after the pups, who were more than happy to play with him. Now it was Mesa's turn to stand guard.

"And," Arleen went on, "he was to be born on..."

Johnny grabbed at the piece of paper again, but Arleen refused to give it up.

"...May 5th," she finished the sentence.

"12:05 a.m. to be exact," Jesse moaned, remembering the night.

"Well, that's wrong," Johnny quipped. "He said the end of May, right? That's why I went out that night. We thought we had at least three weeks. Mom thought so, too."

"I think Mesa's accident and the truck ride had something to do with that," Jesse interjected.

"But he still got the date right," Johnny said. "Why didn't he tell *us*?" Johnny furrowed his brow, mulling over the dates in his head.

"This," Arleen was positively bubbling over with excitement, "you're not going to believe."

"Oh, for gosh sake," Jesse sighed. "Tell us already."

"This baby boy's name was going to be..." she held the suspense a little longer. "Apparently, Red Cloud isn't the best speller in the world, is he?"

"Arleen!" This time Jesse grabbed for the piece of paper and surprised herself when she actually got it. She looked at the piece of paper and smiled. "No, I guess he can't." Red Cloud had spelled out on the paper with a shaky hand F-A-Y-E-L-A-N-D. "Okay, now that's spooky," she commented, handing the piece of paper to Johnny.

"The whole thing's spooky," countered Johnny. "But that's Red Cloud. Never could pull anything over on that old man."

"We didn't bet money or anything like that, did we?" Arleen asked, crinkling her nose up.

"Well, if we did," Johnny sighed, "he'll remember that, too. You can count on it." His attention was immediately distracted by an unfamiliar sound. Shadow was on his feet too. "Car's coming," he proclaimed. "I don't recognize it."

Jesse got off the blanket and watched for the dust cloud that appeared shortly thereafter. "I'm not sure either..." she said slowly, staring at the vehicle as it approached. She walked toward it with Shadow at her side. "Oh, oh," she declared. "Johnny, we've got company."

Johnny sat up and followed Jesse's line of sight. "Oh, shit!" he said, almost under his breath.

"Isn't that Joseph's SUV?" asked Arleen innocently. "What the heck's he doing up here at this time of year?"

"Stay there," Jesse warned her companions. "Let me handle this."

"So, they're finally getting around to seeing the baby?" Arleen was confused. She looked at Johnny and saw the secret in his eyes. "You didn't tell him, did you? You guys haven't told him anything!" Arleen got up too. "Oh *shit* is right, boys and girls. We're all in for it now."

"Aw," Johnny declared, resting back on his bent arms as the SUV pulled up to a stop, "maybe he won't notice."

Arleen shot him a glare as Joseph and Bianca both got out of their vehicle, followed by Max.

"Well, at least you're alive," Bianca admonished, walking toward her friend. "Jesse, we've been worried sick. We haven't heard from you in months."

"So worried that she talked me into driving all the way up here," Joseph added. His eyes scanned over Jesse and Arleen before they rested, not too happily—upon Johnny. "I told you she was all right." Joseph's tone was cold. Johnny met his stare with one of his own.

"Where did all these wolves come from?" Bianca asked, giving Jesse a hug. "Oh, my God!" she screamed into Jesse's ear. "That one just picked up a baby!" She pushed her friend to the side and started to make a dash for the blanket. But the baby was cooing and obviously enjoying the ride. The wolf plopped the baby down on...who was that...Joseph's cousin's lap? Bianca stopped in her tracks. Slowly, she turned and looked at Jesse, who walked up and slid her arm around Bianca's waist. "What's up, Jess?"

"It's been a busy year," Jesse sighed, smiling at her friend. "And there have been a few changes."

"A *few* changes?" Bianca mimicked Jesse's words.

Arleen walked briskly to Joseph and stood directly in his face, breaking the staring match with Johnny. "Aren't you taking a chance coming up here this late? It could snow any day now, you realize that."

"I didn't have a choice," Joseph sneered, leveling a quick glare at Bianca. "*She* was too worried to wait until spring."

"Well, I know you recognize Shadow and you should remember Mesa and Cheyenne," Jesse remarked brashly as both women ignored Joseph's retort. "The pups are Nightly and Lakota. They came from the refuge near Denver early last spring. And, of course, Kitten is still here—under the porch, as usual."

"Uh, huh," Bianca was listening while Max and Shadow were busy sniffing each other.

"I don't remember if you were ever properly introduced to my husband," Jesse continued calmly.

"I don't believe so," Bianca answered hesitantly.

"Johnny, come meet Bianca and bring Phelan with you." Jesse kept an eye on Arleen who was making small talk with Joseph. Joseph's dark eyes met Jesse's head on when she glanced his way. The tension was increasing rapidly, but Jesse refused to acknowledge it.

Johnny got up and grabbed the baby while Jesse brought Bianca closer to them. "This is Johnny Stillwater," Jesse went on to her friend. Johnny gave the baby to Jesse and shook Bianca's hand.

"Mrs. Stillwater, I presume," Johnny's eyes flashed with mischief.

"Ah, no," Bianca was quick to point out. "Joseph and I are just friends, that's all."

"Yeah, right," Johnny snapped. He cast a glance back at his cousin who was walking brusquely toward them. Behind Joseph, Arleen threw up her hands in defeat, mouthing the words *I tried.* Johnny gave Arleen a wink to let her know he'd take over. "And this is our son, Phelan."

Bianca cleared her throat. "It's nice to meet you both." Her eyes were drawn to the baby boy with dark hair and golden eyes. "Aren't you the cutest thing," she murmured, touching Phelan's hand. The baby's eyes were wide and inquisitive. He reached out from his perch in his mother's arms and grabbed fast onto Bianca's necklace, pulling her closer. "With quite a grip, I might add," laughed Bianca nervously.

"How old is he?" Joseph asked, joining them.

"He'll be six months next week," Johnny said proudly.

"He's got his mother's eyes," Bianca smiled, when Jesse let her hold him.

"We thought he was going to have blue eyes like Johnny's, but they turned gold in a week—almost like the pups," Jesse noted. She cast a surreptitious glance at her husband.

Johnny leaned over, in front of Joseph, and gave his wife a kiss. "Come on, cousin," he added with a laugh, for as he expected, Joseph had tensed up. "Let me get you a beer and show you some of my work. I've got quite a little business going, thanks to Arleen and the store."

Arleen smiled cautiously at the men when they passed her on the way to the house. She ran over to Jesse and Bianca, once Johnny closed the door.

Johnny reached into the refrigerator and grabbed a couple of beers. He smiled at his cousin mockingly when he returned to the living room and handed him one. "So, cuz," he quipped, taking a swig of his beer, "who throws the first punch?"

"Are you out of your fucking mind, John?" Joseph growled, glaring at his cousin. "What the fuck have you done here?"

"Let's see..." Johnny snapped back. "I grew up, started my own business, fell in love with a white woman, married her in a *Native American* ceremony and we made a baby. What's new with you?"

"I told you to stay away from her!" Joseph seethed. "This is not our way! Now there's one more half-breed in the world and our race is that much thinner."

"My son…" Johnny said slowly, checking his temper, "is already more Indian than you'll ever be. *Never* insult him or my wife again. If you do, I will kick you out of this house."

"My house!" Joseph warned. "I'm the one that'll do the kicking if it comes to that."

"If that's the problem," Johnny said defiantly, "we can be out of here tomorrow."

"You disobeyed my orders," Joseph sighed, exasperated. "You blatantly disregarded the wishes of your people and those who came before you. How can we ever protect our race as long as people like you keep corrupting it?"

"I have corrupted nothing! You're the one who refuses to see the light." Johnny faced his cousin. "It's people like you who can't see the future because you won't let go of the past. Jesse didn't kill our people—and if her ancestors did, she has made it right by loving me and giving me a son. She believes in me, and feeds my spirit. She has helped me become the proud Native American man I am today. You fed my anger and resentment, constantly reminding me of everything that was owed to me, but I could not have—because I was a poor, abused Indian, and the white man wanted nothing more than to keep me in that rotten state.

"Well, more and more of those white people treat me pretty good, now. They buy my work, pay me money and shake my red hand. And my white wife holds me to my traditions and makes sure I stay proud of who I am." He drank some more of his beer. "Tell me Joe, how can you say it's *me* corrupting everything when it's *you* running behind everybody's back? You love a white woman but you will not honor her by acknowledging that love in either of your worlds. You corrupt her by making her feel unworthy of your respect in front of others, and you corrupt yourself by pretending you are someone you're not. So you're in love with a white woman. I, on the other hand, think that's pretty great, because that's the kind of love that will eventually bring us all together." Johnny turned away from his cousin and looked outside through the window. He smiled, seeing the women busy chatting and playing with the baby—his beautiful child. "If there's ever to be peace between our races," he reasoned, quietly, "it will not be because of what the white man or the red man says. It will be because of people like my son who learn to love and respect them both." He finished his beer and went into the kitchen for another.

"You have grown up," Joseph observed hesitantly. "I just hope you know it's hard for us old dogs to learn new tricks." He chugged what was left of his beer. "Why don't you get me another one of those too? Maybe it will help all of this go down a little easier." Johnny was way ahead of him. He handed him the beer as the last of his words left his mouth. "You have your convictions, Johnny, and I will respect them. I only ask that you realize I have my own convictions and like you, I must follow the path I have chosen."

"Agreed," Johnny smiled, clinking his beer bottle against Joseph's in a toast. "I'm not asking you to change. Just stop trying to change me. So, do you want to see my work?"

"Yeah," Joseph smiled. "Let's see the *rest* of what you've done—then I'll check out that boy of yours when we're finished."

The wolves surrounded Charlie and Winona's truck when it pulled up next to Joseph's and parked. Red Cloud ambled to his feet from his lawn chair in the truck bed and leaned over the side of the vehicle, giving each of the bigger ones a pat on the head. The pups, excited with all the company, stood wiggling their tails as Winona climbed down from the passenger seat. "Look at these good babies," she clucked, picking up Nightly and giving him a kiss.

"Lord, woman," Charlie said, coming around from the driver's side. "Don't spoil those things." Lakota raced over to greet the Indian and tried unsuccessfully to climb up on his pants. Charlie relented, awkwardly, and picked *him* up. Lakota covered his face with licks and kisses.

"Lord, Lakota," Winona couldn't resist, "stop spoiling that old man." She grinned smugly at her husband before turning her attention to Jesse, Arleen and their guest. Charlie took Lakota with him to open the tailgate and help Red Cloud get off the truck. Winona put Nightly down and he nipped at her heels as she walked over to the women.

"It's a fine day for a powwow, don't you think?" Jesse welcomed Winona and handed her son over to his grandmother.

"I *knew* it would be," smiled Winona, unable to take her eyes off the woman she hadn't met yet. "It was Charlie who said we'd be under a foot of snow."

"Winona, I'd like you to meet a friend of mine. This is Bianca Wheland, from Colorado."

"You're the one who sent our Jesse to us?" Winona asked, shifting Phelan into the crook of her arm and extending her hand to shake Bianca's.

"Well, actually that would have been Joseph. But I'm a friend of his," Bianca smiled, noticing Winona's vivid blue eyes.

"According to Jesse," Winona gracefully corrected the young woman, "she would have never met Joseph or Shadow if it hadn't been for you. So, in our book, you're the one who sent her to us."

"I hope that's okay," Bianca said, nonplussed. "I have to say I never expected all this."

"It was meant to be, young woman," Red Cloud announced, coming up behind Winona. "Everyone had to play their part to make it happen." The old Indian perused Bianca carefully. "I'm Red Cloud and I'm happy to finally meet you." He grabbed her hand and shook it purposefully. "It has been too long."

"Too long?" Bianca questioned, looking to Jesse for some help. Jesse just smiled and shrugged her shoulders.

"You should have been here a year ago," Red Cloud claimed. "I will speak to Joseph."

"I *was* here just over a year ago," Bianca remembered. "We came for a visit."

"I know," Red Cloud said, but his thoughts appeared to be elsewhere. "I *must* speak with Joseph."

"You're scaring the young woman," Winona cut in, handing the baby back to his mother. "Save your mind games for another day."

"You spoil all my fun," replied Red Cloud with a grin. "Are you women ready?"

"We just need to pick up the blanket," Jesse confirmed. "The truck's packed and ready to go." She smiled at Bianca. "I hope you're up for a powwow, 'cos you're going whether you want to or not." She turned and headed toward the cabin. "Johnny! Joseph! Let's get going! Everybody's here and ready to go!"

"That voice could wake the dead," Johnny joked with his cousin as they walked out the front door. Joseph stopped in his tracks when he realized who was in the front yard. He threw a panicked look at Bianca, who appeared paralyzed herself.

"I'd say your cat's about to climb out of the bag, cousin," Johnny murmured under his breath. "Red Cloud looks pissed." Johnny bounded down the stairs and trotted over to his parents. "We've got visitors!" He smiled, giving his mother a hug and his father a pat on the back. "Hope they're welcome to come along."

"Of course they are," Winona exclaimed. "Joseph, come give me a hug!"

"Good Lord, woman," Charlie said, taking the blanket from Jesse. "Stop with the greetings all ready. We've got to get on the road. Gourd dancing starts in an hour."

Joseph walked slowly down the steps to his aunt. She hugged him and gave him a kiss on the cheek. "Stop looking like a buck caught in the headlights," she whispered into his ear. "We're glad you're here. Today, Phelan gets his Indian name and you should be there to witness it."

"I'm sorry," Joseph whispered back. "I cannot."

Winona smiled at him sadly and pushed a lock of his hair away from his face. "All our lives changed in May and we have accepted that—even your uncle. Your lady is very beautiful and there is no need to hide."

"She is my friend," Joseph murmured. "And that is how it will be."

"Woman!" Charlie declared. "Stop whispering secrets and get in the truck. Everybody into the trucks, now!"

"Charlie," Joseph called out, "we're pretty tired from the ride. I think we'll just hang out here. We'll see you when you get back."

Red Cloud suddenly appeared at Joseph's side. "Boy, we need to talk for a minute. The others will wait." Charlie threw his hands up into the air and moaned, seeing there would be another delay. Red Cloud guided Joseph away from the bustle of preparations.

"Any wolves coming on this trip?" Johnny called out to the animals as Winona and Jesse climbed up into the bed of the truck with Phelan. Shadow was the first in line, with Mesa and Nightly right behind him. Their butts wiggled and the tips of their tails wagged as they waited their turn to jump up into the truck with Jesse. Johnny had to pick up Nightly, who was still too small to make the leap. Mesa and Shadow made the jump with no problems and settled down next to Jesse and Phelan.

Johnny secured the tailgate and ran over to Cheyenne and Lakota while Arleen climbed into the front seat of the cab. Johnny gave the remaining wolves hugs and whispered something to them. Cheyenne gave him a lick and herded Lakota toward the cabin. Kitten peered out from her safe spot underneath the porch.

"Keep an eye on Cheyenne and Lakota, then," Johnny ordered Bianca as he hopped into the driver's seat. "Kitten can take care of herself. Just don't go crawling under the porch." She gave him the thumbs up and headed for the SUV to start unloading their suitcases.

When Joseph and Red Cloud were a safe distance away from everyone else, Red Cloud took the younger man's arm and pulled him close. "So, you hide this woman from me and your family," Red Cloud retorted. "What is it with you kids, today?"

"I am not a kid," Joseph struck back. "I'm damned near fifty years old. And what else was I supposed to do? I was brought up being told to be a good Indian. Stick with your own kind. Don't corrupt the blood. Don't reveal our secrets. Jesus, Red Cloud, now I come here and find my cousin's married a white girl and everything's all love and acceptance. My mind's pretty messed up at the moment. This is like some kind of bad dream. So don't start getting on my case."

Red Cloud nodded his head and took a deep breath. "It is a difficult road we all travel," he finally said. "I am sorry for your pain."

"I have no pain. I'm just doing what I was told to do. I wish somebody would write down the rules, so I could stop screwing up when they change."

"Of all my boys, you are the wisest," the older Indian said. "You don't screw up."

"Oh, don't I?" Joseph queried. "I left the reservation and made my living in the white man's world. I've stayed away. Here's Johnny—until today the family's most *unlikely* to succeed—a part of the family, happily married with a good business and a baby."

"*He's* off the reservation," Red Cloud noted. "He's living in *your* house. Never measure *your* happiness by someone else's. Johnny has his life and you have yours. Deal with your own, boy."

"What should I do?" the Native American asked. "Sell everything I own and move back here?"

"Good God, man," Red Cloud barked. "Don't do that. You have done good for the tribes back home. You remind them of their purpose. Just don't hide from us. That is all we ask. We all love you no matter who you are or whom you love. This woman, Bianca; she is a good woman, I can tell. Give her a chance, boy. If you let her, I think she would make you proud."

"It's hard back in Colorado, you know that."

"Then bring her here when you can, and show her the respect she deserves. A few short days can last a lifetime to a woman when you treat her right. Its all in the signs."

Joseph laughed. "Ah, yes. Pay attention to the signs. I remember you telling me that years ago!"

"Try not to forget. I won't be around forever to keep reminding you."

Charlie revved the engine of his old pickup, letting Red Cloud know it was time to go.

"You and Bianca rest now," Red Cloud said to Joseph. "You have driven a long way to be faced with some pretty big changes. Remember, your world does not have to change because of them."

The makeshift parking lot was packed. Charlie started a new row, away from everybody else, so he and Johnny could park side by side. The wolves were excited and romped between and around their humans as they unloaded the trucks. Red Cloud carried the lawn chairs. Winona and Arleen carried the cooler and the diaper pack. Charlie carried his grandson, who was babbling incoherently, mesmerized by all the activity around him. Johnny and Jesse corralled the wolves and kept them close. But Shadow insisted on leading the party, so they walked ahead of the others. Jesse noticed that only a few people stopped and stared at the animals as they passed by. For the most part, it seemed like everybody else was pretty used to them. Many of the people knew the wolves by name and would stop and pet them, chatting casually to both Johnny *and* Jesse.

The group found a shady spot, about twenty feet from the main circle where gourd dancers were already stepping to the beat of the drums. Johnny spread out the blanket and set up Red Cloud's chairs. The women doled out cold water and sandwiches. Frankie and Mary joined them a while later and the family circle was complete.

After a quick lunch, Charlie took his sons to the sacred circle and participated in the dance, proudly holding his grandson in one arm and his rattle in his free hand. Winona, Mary and Jesse, with their shawls wrapped over their shoulders, joined their men a short time later and danced behind them, completing the tradition of the gourd dance ritual.

Red Cloud held court in his lawn chair with the three wolves lying at his feet, chewing on their *powwow* bones. He proudly pointed out his family to those tribesmen who came by to chat. Shadow kept a sharp eye on Phelan and his grandfather.

The Master of Ceremonies called an end to the dance in preparation for the Grand Entry. Red Cloud visited briefly with the emcee at the head table during a small break.

The Grand Entry was spectacular, with vivid colors and elaborate costumes. Phelan, eternally inquisitive, wanted a closer look. He started crawling toward the circle, but ever-faithful Shadow was there to bring him back.

Following the Grand Entry, the emcee made a few announcements. After the routine messages were relayed to the audience, he added, "There is much to do today and we will begin with our regular program shortly. But first we are going to do something a little out of the ordinary. According to our Medicine Man, Red Cloud, we may break with tradition, just as the Creator did by giving us this unusually beautiful October day here in Montana. And if Red Cloud says it's okay, I'm not going to be the man to argue with him." Laughter filtered through the crowd.

"So," the Master of Ceremonies continued, "I am asking Charlie and Johnny Stillwater to come to the center of our sacred circle today, and Red Cloud, if you would be so kind to join them."

Johnny rolled his eyes heavenward and gave his wife a kiss before getting up. Charlie grabbed his arm and pulled him to his feet. Red Cloud pushed them both along and into the circle. The emcee stepped off the podium and handed the microphone to Red Cloud in the center of the circle. Phelan, of course, started crawling toward his father and grandfather the minute Jesse let him go.

"Traditionally, it is the way of our people to earn their Indian name as they grow older," Red Cloud stated loud and clear. "But I believe this child earned his Indian name the night he was born and has lived up to it every day since. The wolves who have been brought back to this land keep watch over this child and are teaching him many things that we have long forgotten. *Walks with the Wolves*, would you get your son, please."

Phelan was doing his best, crawling on all fours, to get to his father, but he still had a distance to go. Johnny called out, "Shadow, bring Phelan. Here, boy!"

Jesse let the wolf go. He covered Phelan's ground in about ten strides, picked the boy up by his overalls and carried him gently to his father in the center of the circle. There were gasps and smatterings of *oohs* and *ahs* throughout the attentive crowd.

Johnny stooped down and received his son into his hands from Shadow's toothy grip. Phelan was excited and in a fit of giggles. That was his longest ride yet. Shadow sat on his haunches next to Johnny and looked up at Red Cloud. Johnny held his son up by his little hands, making him stand on his own two feet.

"Phelan Stillwater," Red Cloud announced. Phelan smiled at the Medicine Man, recognizing his godfather's voice. "Your father and grandfather give to you your tribal name. You will now be known by your people as *Sun of the Wolf* from this day forward. Live by that name and be proud of it." Red Cloud said a prayer in their Native tongue to the Creator. Johnny and Charlie repeated the words. He called to the four directions and asked that they accept and protect their newest son. Shadow got up and nudged the baby boy. Phelan giggled and tried to wriggle from his father's grip. Johnny let go of one of his son's hands and Phelan grabbed onto the wolf's fur, still standing up. When the baby let go, he plopped down on his rear end into the dirt. Again, he started crawling, this time toward Red Cloud. Shadow walked slowly behind him for a few seconds, before Jesse called him back to her. The wolf picked the baby up and trotted out of the circle to his mother. A thunderous round of applause filled the air when Shadow placed his prize into Jesse's lap.

With the ceremony over, Red Cloud gave the microphone back to the emcee and left the circle with Johnny and Charlie.

"Hey, Red," Johnny asked, placing an arm around his old friend's shoulders as they walked back to the family, "I've got a question for you."

"And I have the answer as always," the wise Indian answered. "What is on your mind?"

"We checked your predictions this morning," Johnny said. "I thought you told us Phelan was going to be born at the end of May."

"I never said the *end* of May," the wise man spoke clearly. "I said May. You heard that from your white doctor, not from me."

"So why didn't you tell us?" Johnny asked, bewildered. "And how did you know?"

"Your white doctor didn't know Mesa was going to be hurt and Jesse would be riding to Browning in the back of a truck. And I never told you, because you didn't ask. Remember, you didn't want to know."

"You spelled his name wrong," Johnny smiled, trying to catch him on a technicality.

"Damn fool white people," Red Cloud grinned. "Never could understand their alphabet."

"This is a special day indeed," the Master of Ceremonies announced as the dancers started to fill the circle. "It was a good day when these animals were returned to our land and our people. A piece of our history has been restored—the history of our reverence and kinship to the wolf. May our children learn to respect and love them as our ancestors once did. Let us dedicate the first dance to *Sun of the Wolf*, Shadow, Mesa and Cheyenne."

Back at the cabin that evening, Bianca and Joseph were finally able to catch up on all the news of the past year, as they sat comfortably on the porch with Johnny and Jesse, after the others had left. Bianca held Jesse's sleeping baby in her arms, rocking slowly back and forth in one of Johnny's rocking chairs. "He's so advanced for his age," she commented to her friend as she gazed down at Phelan. "Crawling around like some kind of monkey."

"More like some kind of wolf," Jesse smiled. "He spends most of his waking hours with the wolves. They've been very good teachers."

"Most of the time," Johnny countered, giving his wife a wink.

"Well," Jesse confessed, "we did have a bit of a problem in the beginning when they were regurgitating food for him. And the first time Shadow picked Phelan up, I almost fainted. It took us a little while to realize that as far as the wolves are concerned, he's just one of their pups."

"But that could be dangerous, couldn't it?" Bianca asked in a serious tone.

"One of us is always there," Jesse answered quickly. "It doesn't give us a lot of time to get anything else done."

"What amazes me is that it appears you've been accepted on the reservation," Joseph remarked to Jesse. "I never thought I'd see *that* day."

"I'm *tolerated* on the reservation," Jesse said, snuggling a little closer to Johnny on the porch swing. "I know my place and if I should happen to forget, there's always someone to remind me. I tend to stick close to Red Cloud at those events. He helps immensely—after all, it was his conniving that brought Johnny and me together in the first place."

"And your father," Joseph added, "you've settled your differences?"

"We talked it out. Of course my opinion really changed when he was the only one who could think clearly enough to get us home during a blinding rainstorm, on a flooded road, the night our baby was born." Johnny looked at his cousin and smiled. "The older I get, the smarter he gets—that's what's amazing. And he loves Phelan. Can't deny an old man his right to love his grandson, can I?"

"No, you can't," Bianca chimed in. "I think it's wonderful. I know this has not been easy for you two, because Joe and I have had our own issues to deal with. Thank God you're here, rather than in Colorado. Here you've had a chance to do what you feel is right." She looked back down at the baby in her arms. "*Sun of the wolf*, you're a lucky little boy."

"So I take it," Joseph stated, leaning back in his rocker, "you're going to be staying in Montana, eh, Jess?"

Jesse smiled at him warmly. "Yeah, I guess you could say that." She squeezed Johnny's hand. "There's no place else on earth I'd rather be."

"Well, then. I guess we should be thinking about giving you two a wedding present."

"You already have," Johnny chuckled. "Bianca gave me the check, and I've already loaded your new rocking chairs into the SUV."

"And don't forget the table and chairs, Joseph," Bianca warned the Native American. "We'll come for those in the spring."

"Yes, dear," Joseph chortled. "If you keep this up, we'll end up being his Colorado distributor."

"I've got no problem with that," Johnny laughed.

"Actually," Joseph continued, "I've got something else in mind for your present."

"Really, Joe," Jesse said, "you and Bianca have done more than enough already."

"Not quite." Joseph glanced at Bianca, who smiled knowingly at him. "I've thought about this for a while now, and after today, I'm convinced it's the right decision. I'm giving you the cabin."

"What?" Johnny exclaimed. "That's not..."

"You don't have a say in this," Joseph silenced his cousin. "You two have made this a home and I believe Jesse. There's no other place on earth you two should be than right here. After all, you did most of the work building it."

Johnny looked at Jesse with wide eyes before turning his gaze back to Joseph. "How about if we buy it, Joe? We've got the money."

"How about you promise to take care of it and build on some more rooms for all Phelan's brothers and sisters, and a guest room for us?"

"Jesus, man," replied Johnny, "I don't know what to say."

"*Thanks* will do just fine."

Jesse jumped up from the porch swing and startled Joseph, bending over and giving him a big hug. "It's outrageous, but thank you. We'll build you a guest wing!" She went over and gave Bianca a hug, too.

Somewhere just in the trees, Shadow decided to howl. The conversation stopped when Cheyenne and Mesa chimed in. The pups on the porch woke up and scurried down the steps. Phelan awoke in Bianca's arms. The pups started yipping and joined the chorus. Bianca, as well as Joseph, were both floored when Phelan emitted a little howl himself.

"Oh, this is too much," Bianca beamed, repositioning the baby in her arms so he could keep singing.

Johnny got up and went over to Bianca, taking his son and leaving the porch. "We've given up thinking the child is going to be normal," he quipped. "I pretend these howls, in wolf language, mean *daddy*. 'Cos, I'm sure his first actual word won't be that. It'll probably be *wolf* or *Shadow*. Jesse excused herself, following her husband and baby. In the yard they also started howling, bringing the wolves home. Joseph and Bianca laughed and sat back to enjoy the music and the rest of their evening at the Stillwater cabin in the wild country of Montana.

CHAPTER 32

It was in March of the next year when Phelan took his first steps. As was his custom, he was standing in the kitchen, holding tightly onto Shadow's fur, as Jesse was doling out food to her eclectic brood. Kitten was on the table with her trout, above the melee of paws and feet. Cheyenne seemed to be eating more than her share lately. After the female wolf finished with her own meat, she tried, much to Mesa's chagrin, to eat his. The pups were almost full-grown, and their voracious appetites added to the activities.

Johnny was gulping down his sandwich, keeping a watchful eye on the proceedings when he said, "Maybe I should be making a bigger kitchen instead of working on that extra bedroom. There's way too much fur in this room." He gave his son a quick wink and Phelan started babbling at him.

"I need to start feeding these guys outside," Jesse sighed. "I didn't expect them all to be home this morning." She put Shadow's dish on the floor away from the others. The wolf walked over to the bowl, but Phelan had been looking at his father and did not move when Shadow did. Left without his *security fur*, he looked away from his father to find where Shadow had gone. He turned and waddled after him.

"You did just see that, right?" Johnny proclaimed with a mouthful of food.

"What?" Jesse asked, not paying attention. She was trying to get Mesa out of the way so she could open the refrigerator door.

"Look at your son," Johnny remarked. "Phelan, come here boy. Come here to me."

Jesse knitted her brow, wondering what her husband was up to. Phelan looked at his father. "Woof eat," the child answered.

"Yes, I know," replied Johnny. "But you need some food too. Come here and have some of my sandwich with me."

Phelan hesitantly removed his tiny fingers from his new grip on Shadow's fur and walked, with tiny steps, over to his father.

"Oh, my God!" Jesse whispered excitedly. "He's walking!"

"*Thank* God," Johnny remarked with a grin. He picked his son up and put him on his lap. "I thought our boy was going to spend the rest of his life running on all fours."

"Mama, food," Phelan said, happy to be on his father's lap. Jesse untangled herself from the mass of wolves and went to her son, giving him a big kiss on his forehead.

"You are my big boy," she beamed. "But you already ate! Do you want more?"

"Woof. Eat."

"Here," Johnny laughed. "Finish mine." He handed a piece of his sandwich to his son, who took it into his tiny hands and started munching on it sloppily.

Jesse sat down next to them. "You're going to get chubby, little one," she laughed.

"Like Cheyenne," Johnny quipped. "She seems to be eating quite a bit lately, have you noticed?"

"She's been doing a lot of digging out behind the house, just a few hundred feet into the forest, for a week or so now. She's made a very functional den," Jesse smiled. "I think we're going to have some new members in this pack, very shortly."

Still holding his son, Johnny leaned his elbow on the table and rubbed his forehead with his fingers. He looked up at his wife and shook his head. "More woofs?" he sighed.

"More woofs," Jesse smirked. "I'm sorry."

"Shadow?"

"A proud papa."

"Good Lord."

"Goo lawd," Phelan mimicked his old man.

It didn't take Jesse long to realize that a walking child was usually a missing child. He got out of the house, using the hole in the screen door, every chance he could get and tried to *run* with the pack. His legs still wobbly at first, he spent most of his time on the ground where he would revert to crawling, which he had mastered. The wolves did their best to keep an eye on him while they were around the house, but he was not quick enough to keep up with them on their daily journeys.

Johnny was busy with the addition and did not have the time to baby-sit, so the job fell to Jesse and the little guy kept her hopping. At least Charlie was lending a hand with the construction, so Johnny did not have to do all the work on the house by himself. Jesse's best days were when Winona came along with her husband.

Phelan's vocabulary was growing, but it was a jumble of English and Indian. He babbled constantly to his mother, his father and the wolves, and mimicked all of them. Jesse figured the only ones who truly understood him were the animals.

The most challenging part of the day was putting the little tyke down for his nap. He preferred to sleep when the wolves slept. But their schedule rarely agreed with Jesse's. She needed those precious hours to get the housework done and tend to other chores.

While reading to him as they shared the hammock one sunny afternoon, she was thrilled when Phelan unexpectedly fell asleep. She eased gently out of the hammock and was happier still when he did not wake. She took this break and went to check on Johnny and Charlie, who were just about done with the new room.

"Where's the little monster?" Charlie asked when she brought them some lemonade.

"Sleeping in the hammock," Jesse said, taking a seat on the sawhorse. "He's been up since dawn."

"Howlin' time," Johnny added. "I can't wait until he becomes a teenager. They always sleep, right?'

"You did your fair share," Charlie declared, sitting down next to Jesse. "Don't worry, daughter. Winona's cooking fried chicken and bringing it over for dinner tonight."

"There is a Goddess," Jesse sighed.

"And if you'd get off your duff," Johnny chided his father, "we could get this room finished tonight."

Jesse left the men to their work and did a few things around the cabin. She got the bed made, washed the dishes and spent a few rare moments with Kitten who purred, happy with the attention. The wolves had been gone most of the day. It was just under an hour when she tiptoed back onto the patio to check on her little prince.

The horror struck her like a lightening bolt. Phelan was not on the hammock. She could not think clearly for a second. Her mind raced. *How could he have gotten off that hammock,* she asked herself, searching the terrain. Where in the hell could he have gone? She would have heard him at the door. Johnny would have called her if he had toddled off to see him. She ran around the house, but he was not there. She looked in the house and under the porch, just to make sure. Quite panicked, Jesse took a deep breath and gathered her senses. Where would her son go?

One place finally came to mind. She headed into the woods behind the house. With determined, hurried steps she traipsed through the firs and the cottonwoods, up the first hill, until she found it. There in front of Cheyenne's den were Shadow, Mesa, Nightly and Lakota—and also a pair of little human legs wriggling deeper into the hole.

"Phelan!" Jesse commanded quietly. She rushed to the den and grabbed hold of his feet. "Come out of there right now!"

Shadow got up and gave Jesse a nudge. She reached in a little further and grabbed the seat of her child's overalls. With a gentle, but firm tug, she pulled the child out.

"Babies!" Phelan announced, covered in dirt. "Shy got caksi!"

Jesse wrapped her arms around her son and held him close. "That's wonderful, Phelan," she sighed. "But we mustn't disturb them."

"Shadow, goo. Shy, goo."

"Oh, I'm sure they don't mind, but Cheyenne has to take care of them, okay?" she reasoned. Cheyenne poked her head out of the den and climbed out. "Hi, momma!" She whispered to Cheyenne, freeing one of her hands from her grasp on her son and stroking the wolf's fur. "Congratulations!"

Shadow nudged Jesse again. Cheyenne stepped wearily to the side of the den and lay down.

"See caksi, mama," Phelan squealed. "Shadow, see caksi."

Jesse realized the wolves were going to let her take a peek into the den. "You stay right here!" she ordered her son. "And I'll take a quick look. Okay?"

"Caksi, mama," Phelan crawled off his mother's knees and sat down next to Cheyenne. The wolf licked some dirt off the little boy's face.

Very carefully, Jesse flattened herself out and eased into the hole. She was not particularly fond of small places and this hole was just big enough for her to squeeze into. She crawled in just far enough until she could hear the mewling of the newborns. There were definitely more than two, but it was too dark to see how many. She pushed herself back with her hands and inched her way out. Due to the close quarters of the small den, she would wait until Cheyenne felt her pups were ready to come out before she would check on them again. Phelan was petting Cheyenne when Jesse's head cleared the hole.

"Papa see," Phelan announced. "Tunka see."

"Yes," Jesse sighed, her heart rate finally returning to normal. "Let's go tell papa and tunkašila." She got to her feet and brushed off some of the dirt. She looked at her son, smiled and took a deep breath, her nerves finally settling down. Mother kept a firm grasp on her son's hand while they walked slowly to the cabin. Phelan babbled on and on about the wolves all the way back.

With the birth of Cheyenne's three pups, Jesse noticed a subtle difference in her wolves. Shadow, a father and alpha male to a pack of eight, had his own responsibilities now. As leader, it was his responsibility to take care of his lot and keep them safe.

Unlike Lakota and Nightly, the new pups were raised in their den and Cheyenne was in complete charge of their care and upbringing. They were wilder than the others—this generation of lupines were returning to their roots. Lakota and Nightly were busy uncles, babysitting, while Cheyenne, Shadow and Mesa went off to hunt. They still knew there was food waiting for them at the cabin, but they preferred to catch their dinner themselves. Only when the hunting was scarce, did they come home to chow down, their food now on the cabin porch.

As spring turned to summer, Shadow, Mesa, Lakota and Nightly returned home regularly to play with Phelan and they still liked to lounge in the backyard on sunny afternoons when it was too hot to do much of anything else. On rare occasions, one or two of them would stay the night.

The pups, two females and a male, were introduced to their human family in stages. It was always exciting for Phelan and Jesse whenever Cheyenne brought them to the cabin for a visit. Jesse liked to spoil them with grapes and scraps of meat. The male that Phelan called Sápa, was the spitting image of his father with a shiny black coat of fur. Jesse named the females Léga for her shiny gold coat that glimmered in the sun, and Shoshone, a beige-colored beauty with a black stripe of fur down the center of her back.

Johnny and Jesse finally got the opportunity to *humanize* their child, now that the wolves had their own to take care of and were not always underfoot. Phelan was a remarkably smart and clever boy. Jesse attributed his surefootedness and early vocalizations to his four-legged teachers. The rest of his abilities—his intelligence, compassion and love for all living things—came from the hard work and infinite patience of those humans who adored and cared for him. Red Cloud taught him the old ways of his people and their language. Charlie and Winona spoiled him with their grandparental love. Johnny let him watch as he carved and constructed the furniture that had now turned into a lucrative business. Clayton had him in the saddle with him at the tender age of one. Arleen spoiled him with candy and kisses, every time he came into the store. Jesse read book after book aloud to him and he loved the sounds of Johnny's flute and the Native American drums. She encouraged him to play with his own drum and rattles, and made sure, at every opportunity, he had time with the wolves.

Every night, when he heard their howls, he would insist on going outside to join them in their songs. By the time he was two, he was more coordinated and far more intelligent than other children his own age.

His father had already started teaching him the secrets of the wilderness. His tracking skills, while crude, were advancing and he was learning to trust his intuition, although he had no idea what that was all about. He could tell when the animals were troubled or if a storm was on the way. Johnny wanted to take credit for his son's inherent abilities, but he knew in his heart, Phelan had been endowed with special gifts.

The child knew, for instance, the day that Uncle Cay (as he called Clayton) came to visit, that there was something terribly wrong. He could tell by the way his mother held so tightly onto his tiny hand while they were standing on the porch together. He could also tell by the sound of her voice and the look of concern in her eyes. He could not understand a lot of the conversation, but it upset the little boy because Clayton's words upset his mother.

"Jess," Clayton tried to keep his voice upbeat, but he knew his news was distressing, "it's an open meeting. We'll all go and try to talk some sense into them. They'll have to listen."

"They won't," Jesse snapped, looking at the flyer Clayton had given her. They were posted all over town.

A special town council meeting had been scheduled for the following week—to address the *wolf* problem that would likely occur if these animals were allowed to continue to run free. The well being of local cattle, sheep and humans was at risk. All ranchers and business owners were invited and urged to attend. "They've already condemned them—the flyer's pretty succinct," Jesse retorted.

"Look," Clayton reasoned, "I've talked to Red Cloud and he'll be coming. Arleen will be there and even Josh Kennedy is bringing some information to pass out." He gazed at Jesse, who was standing rigid on the porch clutching her son's hand, and knew that she wasn't really listening to his words of encouragement. He hated having to tell her this, but he had insisted on being the one to do it. "We'll be there to help, Jess. They'll listen to reason, I promise." Jesse's eyes were on Clayton but her focus was someplace else. Her mind was racing and she was scared. "Hey, is Johnny home?" the lawman asked, frustrated. "He should know this too."

Jesse blinked and recovered her voice at least. "Yes," she said. "He's inside working."

Clayton took a few hesitant steps toward the porch. When Jesse finally stepped out of his way, he knew he was welcome to go inside. Behind him he could hear the little boy trying, with limited language, to ask his mother what was wrong. She murmured something back as they followed him into the house. Clayton found Johnny working in the back. He knocked before he entered.

"Clayton!" Johnny called out, smiling. "Come to give Phelan another riding lesson?"

"I wish," Clayton responded sadly. He walked into the room and gave Johnny another one of the flyers. "I'm afraid I've got some bad news."

Johnny's expression darkened as he read the flyer. When he raised his eyes he searched out Jesse's, before he spoke. "We'll just go and explain our side," he articulated slowly, making sure Jesse was paying attention to him. "I'll call dad right now. I'm sure mom will baby-sit for us." He got up from his stool, still smiling at Clayton, although not as happily as when he first saw him coming in the door.

"That's what I told Jesse," Clayton said with a hint of hope in his voice. Thank God, Johnny was thinking with a level head. "Red Cloud and Arleen are going to be there. And Doc Kennedy is coming as well."

"That'll be good," Johnny answered back. "Maybe we can get some more people from the reservation." He walked over to Jesse and placed his hands upon her shoulders, making her look at him. "We'll handle this, Jess. We'll do it together, okay?"

Phelan started to whimper. He did not like his mother in this strange mood. Johnny looked down at him and smiled. The sound of his tiny sobs snapped Jesse out of her stupor. She looked at her husband, clearly this time, and smiled back. She stooped down and picked her child up into her arms. "I'm sorry, baby," she soothed, brushing his dark hair away from his eyes. "Daddy's right. Everything's okay." She wiped a tear away from his cheek and held him close. Johnny peered around Jesse and gave his son a wink. The little boy started to cheer up. "So, you'll be there with us, Clayton?" she asked, rubbing her baby's back as she held him.

"I'll be there with my souvenir bear paw and my boys," Clayton smiled, grateful to see the clarity in Jesse's eyes return. "Whether they've heard my story or not, they're going to hear it again."

Jesse kissed Phelan on the forehead and passed him over to Johnny. "Maybe we should take Shadow with us?" she asked her husband, who was busy cheering up his son.

"It couldn't hurt," Johnny advised. "He does have a way of soothing even the most savage of human hearts."

"Okay," Jesse decided. "We'll do that, then." With her senses back she whipped herself into action. "I'll have to do a little research and talk to Josh about what information he'll be bringing. I'll also get some pictures together."

Clayton sighed, relieved. He cast a glance at Johnny, who returned it warmly. "Let's let mommy do her work," Johnny suggested to his little boy while Jesse headed for the computer. "Clayton, how about a pony ride for our boy here? I could certainly use a break."

"Let's go," said Clayton, happy to get out of the house and confident they would solve their problem. Despite his early trepidation, he had grown accustomed to Jesse's wolves. Surely, once these men—some of whom had actually listened to his accounts of their harmlessness as well as helpfulness—got a chance to talk with Jesse and meet Shadow, they would eventually come to a peaceable accord.

That evening Jesse left Johnny with the baby and took a walk with her wolves. There were so many now, she could barely keep track. Sápa was so much like his father, it was difficult for Jesse to tell them apart in the shadows. The young wolf carried his father's temperance and loyalty to the family. When Shadow was off herding the girls back into line, Sápa stayed close to Jesse's side as she trudged along the well-worn path to the lake.

Cheyenne had blossomed into one of the most beautiful wolves she had ever laid eyes upon. Her pure white fur glistened like a beacon in the low light. That frightened the young woman, for if Cheyenne was so easy to see, surely she could be the first one to catch a bullet. Luckily, Cheyenne had never fully given her trust to any human, except for the crush she carried for Johnny. Still,

Johnny knew even he had boundaries he could not cross with her, which Jesse hoped would keep her safe.

Mesa ran back to Jesse as she walked along, and splayed his front paws out, looking for a game of chase. Jesse sprinted after him for a while, but eventually tired. Mesa ran in circles around her. With no sign of his old wound to hinder him, he was the most rambunctious of the lot, full of energy and life. He, like Shadow, was far too trusting of humans. The scar on his shoulder was proof of that.

Jesse could not cry for her children because their future had not yet been written. Perhaps they would live for years—perhaps not. All she could do was continue to love them and pray to the Creator to keep them safe, because she would never put them in pens or restrain them behind fences. If they could not be free as they had the right to be—like every other wild animal that took their chances in these woods—they were better off dead.

The autumn wind was crisp and rustling the gold, red and brown leaves on the trees when Clayton stood on the town hall steps and fidgeted with the change in his pants pocket. He greeted the townsfolk and area residents as they arrived. It was going to be a packed house, he surmised, seeing how many had already gone inside, and the line of trucks and cars still looking for parking places along the street. He saw the Pendergast truck and Jannings' vehicle parking a couple blocks away. It was Pendergast who would be their toughest customer tonight—he owned the most land and the most cattle and sheep. The crotchety old man didn't like any change—good or bad. And Jannings was the hot shot who had moved up from Texas after he sold his oil wells, which shortly afterward ran dry. He had a fancy ranch about thirty miles south of Jesse and Johnny's place. He wanted everything dead, and a trophy wall in his garish house displayed his devotion to that end, proudly.

Clayton exhaled a sigh of relief. There, coming around the corner, was the Stillwater clan, complete with Red Cloud and Shadow. Josh Kennedy was bringing up the rear, carefully balancing a stack of handouts. Jesse looked beautiful in a well-tailored black dress and her Indian beaded suede coat. Johnny looked dapper in his black jeans and a leather jacket. Red Cloud looked like Red Cloud in dirty jeans, a plaid shirt and torn jean jacket. Charlie had a white collared shirt on and dark slacks.

"Well, don't you all look great in your Sunday best," Clayton called out to them as they came up the street. Pendergast and Jannings were crossing the street just ahead of them.

"What the fuck is that animal doing here?" Jannings asked Pendergast, loud enough so the others could hear. "What's this going to be? Some kind of three ring circus? See the Indians! See the fierce wild wolf! Hey, maybe Clayton will do his Buffalo Bill impersonation."

Pendergast, a heavy brute of a fellow with rosy cheeks and a total of ten hairs on his otherwise bald head, chuckled half-heartedly, although embarrassed by his friend's obnoxious, yet normal behavior.

"We don't need your half-ass comments, Jannings," Clayton spoke up. "This is a serious meeting and both sides will have their say."

"You goddamn wolf lover," Jannings spat at the Town Marshal. He was short and skinny with tight lips and beady eyes. "You don't have any control over this meeting, so get out of my way." He leaned over to Pendergast who was now trying to subtly distance himself from his loud-mouthed friend. "While we're at it, why don't we pick a new Marshal tonight, too," Jannings concluded.

"Why don't we put this to rest," Red Cloud suggested, urging his own group closer to the door. "There's a lady present." Jesse held tightly onto Shadow's leash and kept him close beside her.

"I don't see any *lady*," Jannings sneered. "Just some liberal, white squaw with a craving for mangy dogs and lazy ass Indians."

Johnny's eyes flashed and he started for the rancher. Clayton put his arm out and blocked him from getting any closer to the man.

"You're a damn Indian lover too," Jannings declared, stepping away and around the Native American, careful not to get too close. "Jesus, Phillips," Jannings smirked, "if your kid wasn't so toe-headed, I'd think he had an Indian for a mother."

"Pendergast," Clayton seethed, "I suggest if you want to be a part of this meeting, you'd better get inside. Jannings, you're out!"

"You can't keep me from going in there!" Jannings screamed, heading for the stairs.

"No, but I can," the County Sheriff stepped out of the shadows and took Jannings by the arm, stopping him. "How much have you had to drink, Jannings?" he asked, smelling his breath.

"Obviously, not enough," Jannings spat at him, trying to break free of his grasp. Pendergast took the hint and went inside the hall. Charlie grabbed hold of Jesse and Red Cloud, and ushered them inside.

"Well, you've got five minutes to get yourself out of here," the Sheriff warned Jannings, "and sober yourself up. This is no place for a showdown, man. I'll take you in so fast your head will spin, without the benefit of liquor."

Jannings spat on the ground at the Sheriff's feet. "There's only one way to take care of this problem, Sheriff. And if you don't do it, I will. I promise you that."

"Get your ass moving," the Sheriff replied. "And keep a sharp eye out in your rearview mirror for the State Patrol, because you can be guaranteed I'll be giving them a call." The lawman shoved the rancher back toward his car. Jannings stumbled, but walked away.

"You better keep your wolves off my fucking land, Indian," he yelled back at Johnny who was pressing hard against Clayton's hold. "I can't wait to have that black one's head stuck on my wall."

"Settle down, Johnny," Clayton murmured to his friend. "He won't get inside."

"I want that fucker dead," Johnny muttered, half under his breath.

"We'll handle it, John. Now settle down. Jesse doesn't need to see you riled. She's going to have a tough enough time in there without that scum. He's the one whose been firing everybody up."

Inside the town hall, Charlie found a place for them to sit. Shadow's eyes scanned the unfriendly faces and Jesse felt a low growl deep in his chest.

"It's okay, boy," she soothed, scratching his neck. "Be a good boy and lie down here beside me." She trailed her hand down his back and pressed him to lie down. He preferred to sit instead.

"He'll be okay," Red Cloud offered, sitting down on the other side of Jesse. "You need to be okay too."

"We made a mistake," Jesse muttered. "This isn't going to work." Every eye in the place was on her or the wolf. The townspeople sat as far away as possible from the Stillwater clan, their lack of trust for the animal acute.

The door opened and more strangers came into the room. Jesse was finding it difficult to breathe. But after that group, she saw Arleen's brave face, along with Clayton, Tim, Mike and her beloved Johnny. They came over quickly and sat down around her. Johnny took the seat next to her, keeping Shadow between them. Then, he touched her hand, which was wound so tightly around Shadow's leash, her knuckles were white. He pried it open and took the leash himself, cupping his free hand over hers.

The Sheriff gave them a tight smile as he passed on his way to the podium. The town council members sat at a long table to the side of the podium. They too, were watching the wolf. "Okay people, let's take our seats. I'm here to keep order and this *will* be a civilized meeting. Anybody who wants to speak their mind on this issue will be allowed a fair amount of time. There will be no heckling or outbursts. I am under orders by this council to keep the peace." He turned and faced the head council member, who thanked him and stood up. The Sheriff took a seat at the back of the room by the door.

The head councilman went to the podium and glanced over the room. "This meeting was called for by…one of our citizens, whom I don't seem to see here, at the moment. Mr. Jannings has told me that there are some serious issues due to the fact that wolves have been reintroduced to our land."

"Ah," Clayton Phillips piped up, "Mr. Jannings wasn't able to make it this evening."

"I had to send him home to sober up," the Sheriff added. There was a muted chuckle from a few people in the room.

"I see," the councilman said. "Well, then. Is there anyone who would care to speak on Mr. Jannings behalf?"

Pendergast raised his hand and was recognized by the council. He lumbered up to the podium and cleared his throat. "As you all know, we are a ranching community and it is difficult, to say the least, to keep food on our tables, with the way things are right now. We've had to deal with a drought, which, thanks to God, has seemed to ease up the last couple of years. Other predators such as bears, mountain lions, coyotes, foxes and wild dogs are dangers to our livestock. Mad Cow disease has turned folks away from beef consumption. Now we're expected to put up with these wolves, who according to Mr. Jannings, could be a real threat to our livestock as well as all of us." Jesse and Josh shook their heads. The rest of the audience listened carefully to what the man had to say. "Every cow or sheep we lose to these animals costs us money—money that we don't have to replace them. There's no fence that can keep them out. You've heard the stories. Christ, we grew up with them. They can rip a human's throat out with one bite…"

"And they can huff and puff and blow your house down," Mike mumbled, causing Tim to laugh. Clayton gave them a stern glance.

"One pack can decimate a herd of elk and moose. What does that do to hunting season and the dollars it brings to town? There's no good that can come from this. Mr. Jannings knows. He had a problem with Mexican wolves down in Texas. Thanks to people like him, those beasts are almost extinct. You've heard the stories passed down from your ancestors. It took a lot of years to get the old wolves out of here. And now this little lady thinks she can come in here and start the carnage all over. Mr. Jannings says we've got to say *no!*"

Another person stood up. Pendergast let him speak. "Jannings says they can go through a herd of sheep in one night. I can't survive if that happens. As Pendergast says, I have barely enough money to keep them fed."

"Sheep eat grass," Josh spoke up. "This year, I've noticed, they all look pretty healthy to me. The drought is what you needed to worry about and like Pendergast says, the water's coming back."

"Sir," Pendergast stated flatly, "I'm not sure we've been introduced."

"My name is Doctor Joshua Kennedy. I run the vet clinic up in Browning. I'm here to help clarify the difference between bedtime stories, hearsay and what a wolf is really all about."

"Well, you'll have to wait your turn," Pendergast said haughtily. "A veterinarian has no idea what a rancher goes through."

"Oh, believe me, I do," Kennedy interjected. "I grew up on a ranch in Wyoming. I was up at the crack of dawn every morning, milking cows and getting them out to pasture. I rode the range and went to school at night after my chores were done. It took me three times the length of time it would take your child to get through school, 'cos my father and I ran that ranch. I lost my mother to a pack of wild dogs."

All eyes turned to the doctor. He suddenly had the floor. "The dogs were abandoned by people and ranchers who didn't want them anymore and they were left to fend for themselves."

"Just like wolves," Pendergast declared. "That's what we're talking about."

"It's a funny thing about dogs," Josh continued with a sad smile. "Their distant cousin *is* the wolf. But because they're also *man's best friends*, they've been forced by humans to inhibit their wolf behavior, and breeders have done their best to extinguish those traits altogether. Their heads are screwed up from birth. As puppies, they're cute and cuddly and so very innocent, but if they exhibit any traits that are distasteful, such as biting, chewing, barking, or protecting their family, they're suddenly considered a nuisance and the cuteness wears off pretty quickly. We live in a world where it's easier to discard things rather than fix them. If we don't like something, we get rid of it. When our appliances break, we throw them away. When we don't like our spouse, we get a divorce. Why care if we dump a dog on the side of the road or drown a bunch of unwanted kittens. Our *superior* intelligence tells us they can't think or have feelings like human beings. They're just *stupid* animals. *Stupid* animals who can wake a family up if their house is on fire or fight to the death to protect their masters when they're in trouble. *Stupid* animals who can waste away themselves when their beloved master dies.

"When these *stupid* dogs are abandoned and they find others of their own kind, they eventually revert back to their ancestral roots. But because they're not wolves and they don't understand the rules of a wolf pack, they run wild and kill anything that gets in their way. They have no trouble attacking cows, pigs and sheep. Their dog food was made out of it. There's no order, no alpha male and female to set the rules—they become monsters and, as you say Mr. Pendergast, rip out the throats of anything that gets in their way.

"Wolves don't attack man, Mr. Pendergast, unless they're in fear of their own lives or the lives of their pack. They have collective memories. They know that man has done his best to eradicate them through the centuries. They know their enemy all too well. Do you know that a wolf pack has distinctive human traits? There is an alpha male and an alpha female. They pretty much run the pack. When they mate, they mate for life. Depending on the food sources, they will produce, in the spring, from one to five pups. Those pups are born deaf and blind. Their only defense in the first few weeks of life is the pack. The packs' sole purpose is the care, feeding and upbringing of the pups. Each member of the pack has an active role in the pups' lives. They provide the food, they play with them, they teach them to respect each other and the skills they'll need when they grow up.

"The pack is a collective unit—they cannot survive without each other. One wolf cannot kill a moose or an elk or a cow. The hooves of herbivores can kill or maim a wolf in seconds. The pack thrives on communication. They go hungry for days, finding just what they need to eat. They cannot bring down a healthy, full-grown animal, so they wait and search for the sickest, the weakest or the oldest of the herd. In nature, that's called *survival of the fittest*. It benefits the herd when the weak or old are taken from their midst. The wolves keep the populations of ungulates at controllable levels. They don't decimate whole herds. They can't possibly do it.

"When they do get a kill, they leave no part of it to waste. Wolves do not kill for sport. If there are pups waiting at the den, they eat only what they need to survive and lavish the rest on the little ones. The survival of the pack is of utmost importance. Just like humans should practice, right? Tell me, do the children in your lives come first? Do you take the time to play with them and give them the attention they deserve?

"Those wild dogs did not get that kind of upbringing. Most of them were abused and starved and ignored. So when they revert to their wild state—that's what they become—wild and dangerous, for their human protectors neglected to teach them right from wrong and most importantly, respect. Where there is no respect, there is only carnage and destruction.

"If you want to learn about the nature of wolves, stop listening to stories passed down through the centuries by men who hated and feared them for what they represented. Read a book. Watch something other than a football game on T.V. Stop believing we're the wisest creatures on this planet. We're the *stupid* ones when you think about it—we had to invent tools to do our killing because we were too lazy to do it with our bare hands. Once we had these weapons, we took control and became the *strongest* force on earth. In the end, that arrogance will destroy everything—including ourselves and the planet."

"But what about McGill?" a voice said from somewhere in the crowd. "He had to shoot one because it attacked his horse."

"That wolf did not attack anything," Clayton responded. "McGill was afraid of it, like I was when I first saw them." Clayton took a deep breath and began his story. "I can tell you first hand, it's a scary sight when you first look up and see one staring at you. Now when I look back on it, I think I was scared because it looked like it was wiser than me. And I've come to find out they are. This wolf here, his name is Shadow, by the way. He and his mates risked their own lives to save mine. That bear was wounded and wanted blood. I would have had no chance if those wolves had not distracted it. I've learned since then, that bears and mountain lions can kill wolves, so they took a very big chance when they helped me.

"They come to my ranch. They play with my son and my ranch hand. Shit, they even play with my dog. I keep the chickens out of their reach—that's not too hard to do—and did you know they love grapes? This *man-eater*, sitting here, is a pushover for a bunch of grapes. Jesse says they like the sugar. I also know what they depend on most to keep from starving—rabbits and mice. As far as I'm concerned, they can have every one of those critters on my land."

"Young lady," the head councilman interposed, "it's Jesse Harless, right?"

"Jesse Stillwater, sir," she corrected him. "This is my husband John Stillwater."

"Mrs. Stillwater, then. What can you tell us about your wolves?"

Jesse's hands were shaking and her mouth felt terribly dry. She looked at her husband and noticed that sometime during the proceedings, about twenty Native Americans had come into the hall, and were standing quietly against the back wall. Some nodded and others smiled at her when she saw them, showing their support.

"Well, sir," she finally said, "I'm a city girl from Denver who was given an eight week old wolf pup a couple of years back. He was definitely not welcome in the city and I just couldn't let him spend the rest of his life behind a chain link fence in a refuge. A good friend, who grew up on the Blackfeet Reservation, thought I was pretty crazy, but let me rent his cabin just a mile off the dam road. I sold everything I had and came up here with this boy right here," she looked down at Shadow and he licked her hand, "to try to give him a chance at a normal life." Jesse sighed and continued. "I figured he might not be welcome, so I cheated and made sure he was well fed and cared for. But I also knew that someday it would probably come to this.

"We both grew up. I fell in love with a wonderful man who loves and respects these animals as much as I do. Our son, who just turned two and a half, is just as smitten as we are. And Shadow became what he is today, an alpha male with his very own pack. His alpha female, Cheyenne, and her brother Mesa, were the only survivors of a hunting spree, just before I moved up here. The hunters killed the parents and three other pups. I have done my best to keep them on our property, but they are wolves and they make their own boundaries.

"I accept full responsibility for my actions and can only blame myself and my naïveté for whatever fear, loathing and pain I have caused you. I assumed those people who lived in the wild knew which species were their true enemies and understood the nature of those beasts who lived near them. And if it's any consolation to you, I am well aware that my actions will be the end of my wolves, because I gave them false hope and led them to believe that humans would not harm them. That, unfortunately, is what I'm most sorry about, because humans understand deceit—animals do not." A tear fell from Jesse's eye to her cheek. She bent down to Shadow, who stood up and licked her face. She buried her face in his fur and wept.

"I would like to offer that these wolves have been roaming the area for over two years now, and there have been no reported problems," Clayton offered to the now silent group. "I like to think we're sensible and responsible landowners. We've shared this land with the bear and the mountain lion for as long as people have settled here. I would think that the wolf could also find a place here, too."

"My people accept this gift and the responsibility," Red Cloud announced, standing up. "We have known the wolf for centuries and have been a lesser people because of their absence. These animals are welcome on our reservation. If there is trouble, we will gladly give them a home away from your cattle and your sheep."

A woman, sitting closer to the Stillwaters than the others, got up from her chair and cautiously approached Jesse. She held her hand out and Shadow sniffed it. She ran her fingers through the fur along his neck. When she bent over, Shadow sniffed again and licked her cheek. She laughed nervously and allowed him to do it again.

"You know me," Arleen spoke up. "I've known Jesse and Shadow since the first night they got here. I've played with these wolves and I've held them on my lap. They take care of Jesse and Johnny's son like he's one of their own. The little guy was walking before he was a year old. He crawled like a pro just before six months. Those wolves taught him how to do that. I can tell you, they're a pleasure to know and to watch. When you do that, you'll realize there's a lot they can teach you."

"If you'd like to meet Shadow," Charlie joined in, "please come and say hello. He's as gentle as a lamb, but he will protect those he loves from harm."

One by one the assembly of people came up and spent a few moments with the wolf. Jesse sat back in her chair and tried to smile. Some people shook her hand; others shook Johnny's. The few that didn't, at least left with a little more knowledge than they had come with. The council members never did make a decision. They joined the group that wanted to touch the animal and feel a real live wolf. Red Cloud and Clayton talked with the Sheriff. He told them that everything would be all right and he'd make sure of it.

When they left the town hall, Jesse was exhausted but hopeful. She held on to her wolf with one hand on his leash and her arm wrapped tightly around her husband.

"I think we should celebrate," Arleen announced, clearly elated. "I've got a bottle of scotch over at the store. Let's have a drink before we go home."

"The truck's parked over there, anyway," Johnny reasoned when Jesse indicated that she'd rather not. "We can go over there for a minute."

"Sure," Jesse acquiesced. "That's fine. I'm just kind of tired, that's all."

"I know, babe," Johnny murmured. "A drink will help you relax so you can go to sleep."

The group trudged the couple of blocks to Arleen's general store, feeling good about the way the night had turned out. Josh was glad that quite a few people actually asked for his handouts. Charlie was impressed that his son held his tongue and avoided a full-scale riot.

No one noticed Jannings when he staggered out of the saloon down the street. They were laughing and congratulating themselves on their job well done. When the man spoke, no one was sure where the voice came from.

"So, did you get your way?" The drunken man could barely stand up. "I was afraid of that. I knew I'd have to solve this problem myself. Those people are so stupid, they'd believe the devil if he came down and promised them a sunny day in hell."

Clayton moved first. He started walking toward Jannings after motioning the others to get into the store. "Hey, it wasn't a victory for either side," Clayton tried to rationalize. "We'll just have to see how things go."

Red Cloud and Charlie held onto Johnny and started pulling him away. Arleen, now panicked, was still fumbling with her keys. Joshua tried to help her. Clayton stood in front and to the side of Jesse and Shadow. It was the wolf who first saw the gun in Jannings' hand. Shadow growled and prepared to pounce. Jesse bent down to try to calm him. As she did, the words Jannings spat out behind her back turned her blood to ice.

"One way or another, that animal's going down!" He fired the gun twice. Clayton was on top of him the moment after the second shot rang out and took Jannings down.

Jesse felt the sting of the bullet in her back, but did not falter at first. Shadow, who had started to leap over her to get to Jannings, slumped and fell over her shoulder, pulling her down to the ground. She grabbed onto Shadow and held tight. "Shadow," she whimpered, "Shadow, baby, are you all right?"

Johnny tore away from his father's and Red Cloud's grasps. "Jesse!" he screamed, running to her side.

Jesse was on the ground holding Shadow in her arms. He was still breathing, but his breaths were labored. She, herself, was suddenly feeling very cold. She hugged Shadow closer for warmth. Johnny took both of them into his arms. There was rage and fear in his eyes when Jesse opened hers and looked at him.

"Jesse," she heard him say to her. "Are you hurt?"

"It's okay, baby," she whispered, finding it hard to catch her breath. She coughed and spat up blood. "I've got him. He'll be all right."

"Josh!" Johnny screamed. "She's been shot!"

Jesse felt the commotion above her, but she couldn't really see it. It all seemed like a strange dream. "I love you, Johnny," she tried to smile. "But I gotta' go with Shadow. I don't want him to do this alone."

"Jesse!" Johnny screamed. "Stay with me! Jesus God, get me some help!"

"I'll help you, babe," Jesse coughed, trying to focus on her husband's eyes. "Just let Shadow and me get a little sleep." Her golden eyes closed and her body went limp in Johnny's arms.

CHAPTER 33

✿

Charlie insisted on driving Johnny's truck as they chased the ambulance the twenty-five miles to the Medical Center in Conrad. He was sorry that Johnny, sitting between him and Red Cloud in the cab of the truck, could see the paramedics, as they did everything they could to keep Jesse alive. They were pounding on her fragile chest and using a machine that supplied some kind of electric shock. Charlie's attempts to back off a bit, so that it was not as easy to see the activity, were met with curses and screams from his frantic son.

Josh had promised to do what he could to save Shadow, whisking the flaccid animal off to his clinic in his truck, once they pried him loose from Jesse's deathlike grip.

When the shocks stopped and the paramedic continued only with CPR, Red Cloud dug into the pocket of his tattered jean jacket and pulled out a little rattle. He propped himself in the corner of the cab, close to the door and at the edge of the seat, and started to chant. Charlie, recognizing Red Cloud's confined version of the Ghost Dance, ceased his words of encouragement to his son and let him weep in peace.

At the emergency room, Charlie took his son into the waiting room, leaving Red Cloud, who was deep in his trance, in the truck. Johnny's father took care of the details, giving what information he could to the attendants for their records. No longer able to see his wife, Johnny paced back and forth in the waiting area, his hair matted and his clothes covered in Jesse's and Shadow's blood.

When Charlie found him some time later, he held back his own tears in an effort to give his son a last bit of strength. "They'll let us know," he murmured to him. "They've got her down in surgery right now." Johnny looked at his father with red, pleading eyes. "They think the bullet punctured a lung. They're not sure, Johnny. They don't know if they can save her."

Johnny collapsed into a chair and covered his face with his bloody hands. "Please don't take her," he whispered to his God. "Please let me see her one more time."

Charlie sat down next to his boy and put his arm around his hunched shoulders. He sighed and said a prayer himself. When the front door opened and Red Cloud slowly entered with measured dance steps, shaking the rattle, Charlie knew where the old man really was. Red Cloud, in a trance now, danced subtly and tirelessly for the next four hours.

Jesse woke up like almost every other day, with Shadow licking her face. She fully expected to feel some pain in her back, but miraculously, when she stretched, she felt limber and quite well. She snuggled with her wolf and kissed him on his nose and their tongues brushed. Shadow was magnificent. His coat was black and shimmering in the light. She eased him aside and sat up, wiping the sleep from her eyes. They were in a beautiful green meadow, dotted with wild flowers of every color in the rainbow. Shadow got up on his paws and tugged at her dress.

"Okay, boy," she smiled at him. "Just a minute." As her eyes focused, she did not recognize where they were. The cabin was nowhere in sight and they were surrounded by trees and mountains and the bluest sky she'd ever seen. All the colors were so vividly clear and bright. She got up slowly and looked around some more. Shadow was romping around her, wanting to play. "Shadow," she said slowly, "you better know where we are, 'cos I sure don't." She spied a river running through the grass just off to their left and as her eyes followed its course, she saw a crystal clear waterfall, cresting over the blackest of rocks. At the base of the waterfall was a deep blue pond and there she saw so many wolves, she could not hope to count them all. "Look, boy," she said in wonderment. "Look at all those wolves!"

Shadow leapt through the tall green grass and ran toward them, stopping every few feet to see if Jesse was keeping up. "Go on," she laughed, seeing how eager he was to join them. "I'll be there in a second." Shadow ran on ahead and mingled. The wolves talked in their special language and Shadow answered them back. They played and danced with each other. Shadow was acting like he did when he was a pup.

She walked to the edge of the pond and cupped some of the cool water into her hands, drinking what she caught. It was the freshest water she'd ever tasted.

Shadow ran back to her and drank some of the water himself. Then he jumped in with a splash and dog paddled around a bit before he climbed back out. Another wolf, with beautiful gray and brown fur, topped with white tipped guard hairs, came close to her and sniffed her up and down. She lay back on the ground and let him check her out. After a few more sniffs, he cocked his head to the side and gazed at her with huge copper eyes. She raised her hand and touched the fur on his neck. The wolf sat back on his haunches, threw his head back and howled. She could feel the reverberation of the music in his throat. Shadow shook off the water from his coat and playfully attacked the other wolf. They sparred and nipped at each other, becoming fast friends. Jesse sat up and leaned back with her arms braced behind her in the soft, silky grass. She studied all the wolves and each one seemed more beautiful than the next. Eventually, Shadow interacted with each of them and they accepted her beautiful black wolf with easy grace and a sense of joy.

"There you are." Jesse heard the voice coming from behind her. She expected to see Johnny, but was just as happy to see Red Cloud coming toward her through the grass. "I reckoned you would be here."

"I'm glad to see you," she smiled with her long hair dancing around her face in the gentle breeze. "I was afraid we might be lost and never get back."

"Would that be so bad?" Red Cloud asked, sitting down cross-legged beside her and taking in the sights.

"No," Jesse replied. "It is so very beautiful. Johnny would love it here."

"Speaking of Johnny," Red Cloud announced, "he wants you to come home."

"Can't he come here?" Jesse suggested. "He could build us a beautiful cabin right over there in that clearing. Phelan would love all the wolves."

Shadow loped over to the Native American and almost bowled him over with his paws. Red Cloud put his hands on the wolf's neck as the animal licked his face. "This place is better left as it is," he sputtered between Shadow's slobbering kisses of affection. Shadow bounded back to the other wolves and got to know them better. "The Creator has given this land to the wolves. Only a few of us are allowed to visit it."

Jesse returned her gaze to the pond and the animals. "They seem so at peace."

"They are," Red Cloud remarked. "And they're safe here. No human can harm them."

Jesse knitted her brow trying to remember her recent past. "Is Johnny all right?"

"He will be as soon as we go back," Red Cloud said. He slowly stood up and reached out for Jesse's hand. "Come on, daughter. We need to go home."

Jesse looked at the older man quizzically. Then her eyes turned to find Shadow. "Come on, boy," she called. "Red Cloud says we have to go home."

Red Cloud took hold of Jesse's hand and gently pulled her to her feet. Shadow looked up at the sound of her voice and their eyes met. He ran back to her and stood up on his hind legs, throwing his front paws over her shoulders. He stood a good six inches taller than Jesse at his extended height. He licked her face and Jesse kissed him back, rubbing her hands along his strong flanks. Then like a shot, he ran back to the other wolves.

"I think he wants to stay," Jesse said with a hint of sadness.

"I think it's best he does," Red Cloud whispered into her ear. "Like I said, here he will be safe. And someday, I promise, you will see him again."

He held tightly onto Jesse's hand and guided her away from the pond, the wolves and Shadow. She was confused because the path in front of them was growing dark. They walked into the blackness, hand in hand, and Jesse smiled when she heard Shadow howl. It was the happiest of his howls and it touched Jesse's heart. Her wolf was free and out of harm's way.

"Wake up, Jess." Jesse heard another voice and her eyes slowly fluttered open. "Come on, babe. Come back to me." It took her a few seconds to focus. She was in a white room with fluorescent lights and a white curtain hanging down beside her. But there next to her, just inches away from her face, was Johnny, leaning in close. "Hey, babe," he smiled. Someone was stirring in a chair behind him. Out of the corner of her eye she could see Red Cloud stretching as though he had just awakened himself.

"You're dirty," Jesse noted, returning her gaze to her husband. "Where the heck have you been?"

Johnny laughed quietly and kissed her lips tenderly. "To hell and back, babe," he sighed. "To hell and back." She tried to get up, but realized quickly that wasn't going to happen without a great deal of pain. "Whoa," Johnny exclaimed. "Just lie back. You're not going anywhere for a while."

"I'm going to remember what happened, right?" she asked drowsily, squeezing Johnny's hand. She saw Charlie standing at the foot of her hospital bed and returned his smile. He squeezed her foot, which was buried under the covers. Red Cloud materialized beside him.

"You don't have to if you don't want to," Johnny advised her. "Let's just say it was *not* a good day to die."

Jesse's eyes met Red Cloud's. He gave her a wink and a shake of his rattle. Her eyelids were growing heavy again. "At least Shadow's safe," she whispered with a smile. "For him it was." Jesse fell back into a deep, healing sleep.

Johnny wept again, grateful that his wife had returned to him. Charlie stepped quietly over to his son and put his arm around the young man's shoulders.

"Come on, John," Charlie murmured, "you need to get some rest. Jesse will be all right, now. I promise." He led his son away from Jesse's bed.

"Dad," Johnny uttered, wiping the tears from his face. "I understand something now that I never thought I would."

"What's that, son?" Charlie asked, smiling at his boy.

"When mom got hurt, you were more worried about her than you were about those guys who attacked her."

"I hated those men, Johnny," his father sighed. "But I realized my love for her, you and your brother, was stronger than that hate or any need for revenge. If I'd killed them, like I wanted to, I would have spent the rest of my life in jail. I wouldn't have been there to keep you safe."

"Yeah," Johnny agreed, facing his own emotions. "I'm sorry, dad. I didn't know."

"It's all right," Charlie whispered, giving his son a hug. "I love you, boy."

"I love you, too," Johnny murmured, hugging him back.

A few weeks later, Johnny brought his wife back home. She held her son, who seemed so much older and wiser than when they were parted. Phelan stuck to his mother's side like glue, never letting her out of his sight for the first few days she was back. When she was able, Johnny and Phelan took Jesse to their secret place, by the waterfall, and showed her where they had buried Shadow. There was a wooden marker, carved with his likeness to mark his grave.

Jesse comforted Cheyenne and tried to tell her that Shadow was okay. The white wolf was nervous and seemed disoriented. She hardly ate and Jesse was afraid she would lose her, too. Cheyenne's howls, as well as the others', were mournful for some time afterward, but Mesa took charge of the pack, as the beta wolf always does, and life eventually returned back to normal. The pack raised their pups and two years later, Mesa was the proud papa of a brood of his own with his mate Léga. Cheyenne was the pups' favorite aunt.

The townspeople, headed by Mr. Pendergast, took up a collection to help with the Stillwater's medical bills. They testified against Jannings, and with the help of a crack shot lawyer from Billings, Clayton Phillips made sure Jannings was locked up for a good, long time. With no one to work his ranch, it eventually fell into bankruptcy and Jannings lost it all.

The ranchers eventually learned to accept their new neighbors; educated by Josh Kennedy about the precautions they should take. Pendergast's heart melted when Nightly and Lakota came to visit one day and gobbled up bunches of grapes, picked from his arbor, straight from his hand. He fortified his chicken coop, nonetheless, and bought himself a very big dog that the wolves learned to respect. But he learned to love the sound of the wolves' howls at night as everyone else did in the county.

On a fine afternoon, some years later, Jesse and Phelan—now six years old—lay stretched out in the tall grasses on the crag that overlooked the valley, which marked the southernmost border of the Blackfeet Reservation. Cheyenne and Sápa slumbered beside them while Mesa and the rest of the wolves searched for mice and rabbits. Phelan and Jesse watched the rolling, cumulus clouds, picking out the different images that formed as they drifted across the deep blue sky. Jesse rubbed her fingers into Sápa's deep, rich black fur.

"There's Clayton on his horse," Phelan announced excitedly, pointing to one of the clouds. "See! The horse is up on his hind legs!"

"Ah, yes," his mother agreed. "And look over there—see the elephant?"

"Wow," the young boy smiled, "that's pretty neat." He fell silent for a few moments, searching out the next formation. "Look, mama," he finally called out, "over where the buffalo was. There's a wolf!"

Jesse turned her head and followed where her son's finger pointed. "You're right, Phelan," she agreed. "It is a magnificent wolf."

"And the cloud is darker than the rest. It's Shadow!"

Jesse smiled, watching the picture in the sky. "Looks like him to me."

Phelan turned to his side and braced himself on his bent arm. "Momma, tell me again about the place where Shadow lives now."

"It's a beautiful place," Jesse sighed, whimsically. Phelan never tired of hearing the story and she never minded telling it to him. "The grass is tall and there are beautiful flowers made up of every color in the rainbow. There's a waterfall that empties into a deep blue pond where the wolves like to gather and play. The water is the freshest water I've ever tasted. And Shadow has many friends who love and keep him company."

"Are our wolves as safe as Shadow?" he asked with wide eyes. Jesse loved how his long dark hair, like his father's, framed his face and made his eyes shine like gold.

"Not as safe," Jesse murmured. "But someday they will be, because people like you will stand and fight for them and teach others that our wolves deserve to have their rightful place on this earth."

"That'll be a big job, won't it?" Phelan observed, his mind racing with a myriad of different thoughts.

"You're a brave warrior like your father," Jesse mused. "No job will ever be too big for you. You will win this battle and many others."

"Look," Phelan said again, pointing toward the horizon. "Is that a new wolf?"

Jesse sat up and studied the area where Phelan pointed. It was a solitary, dark cloud that definitely had a form, strangely like a wolf. Suddenly the wind picked up as the cloud moved toward them. She stood up and gazed intently into the distance. Phelan got up too, and slipped his hand into his mother's. "It does look like a wolf, doesn't it?" she admitted. Cheyenne and Sápa stood up also, sniffing at the wind. Then Jesse heard a howl—a howl that she remembered from a dream long ago. The other wolves ceased their activities and looked into the wind too. Cheyenne was the first to howl back.

"The wolf is running to us, momma," Phelan said, awestruck. "Can you see it coming across the sky?"

Jesse smiled as the rest of the wolves joined in Cheyenne's song. The dark cloud of dust roiled toward them. Jesse and Phelan closed their eyes and let the wind whip by them. It tugged at their hair and Jesse's dress, whipping it out behind their backs. In the hub of the tempest, Jesse felt Shadow's spirit pass through her like a bolt of lightening. It almost knocked her off her feet. She held her ground and kept her son close by her side. Shadow's ethereal presence, for that one brief moment, filled her heart with joy.

"I felt him, momma," Phelan said, when the wind was gone as quickly as it had come. "Did you feel him?"

"He honors us because we honor him," Jesse smiled, kneeling down and hugging her boy close. "We've just been given a very special gift."

"I'll do my best, momma," Phelan vowed. "I'll keep our wolves safe."

"Hey, you two," Johnny called out, walking up from behind them. Mesa and Léga romped over to greet him as he approached. "It's time to come home. Eric, Bianca and Joseph just arrived."

Jesse got up and Phelan ran to his father. Johnny scooped him up into his arms and the boy wrapped his legs around his father's waist, holding on tight. "You'll never believe it," he continued when he reached his wife and gave her a kiss. "Eric brought a girlfriend. She seems very nice."

"Fashionably dressed, I assume," Jesse laughed, taking Johnny's hand as they walked back toward the cabin.

"She's gorgeous, of course," Johnny noted. "But believe it or not she seems pretty down to earth. Not at all what you'd expect. She's crazy about Kitten and can't wait to meet the wolves."

Jesse smiled at the thought of how they'd all grown up. Even her best friend, the hotshot lawyer, was coming into the fold. Somehow, with the small gift of a furry, black wolf pup, Jesse had found everything she had not even known she'd been searching for—her purpose for living, her knowledge of her place upon this earth and the responsibility she owed to protect it, the companionship of good friends, both human and animal, the peace that the wide open spaces of Montana bestowed upon her, and the love of her life—her brave, young warrior who loved her with all his heart, believed in her and had given her a beautiful son. A son who would, hopefully, help to bridge the gap between white and red as well as fur and skin. She realized how grateful she was for having the courage to take a chance that no one favored, and for never learning the *secret* that might have kept her and Johnny apart.

She looked forward to introducing this new human, Eric's girlfriend, to her lupine and Native American family. Slowly, but surely, maybe everyone Jesse touched would some day see the light and become a part of Shadow's dream.

The End

List of References and Further Reading

W.O.L.F. (Wolves Offered Life & Friendship)
P.O. Box 1544
LaPorte, Colorado 80535
Http://www.wolfsanctuary.net

Rocky Mountain Wildlife Foundation
P.O. Box 215
Guffey, Colorado 80820
Http://www.visionswest-art.com

Askins, Renée. *Shadow Mountain*. New York: First Anchor Books. 2004

Crisler, Louis. *Artic Wild*. New York: First Lyons Press. 1999

Dutcher, Jim and Jamie. *Wolves at Our Door*. New York: Simon & Schuster—Touchstone Edition. 2002

Landau, Diana (Editor). *WOLF Spirit of the Wild*. New York: Sterling Publishing, Co. Inc. 2000

Lopez, Barry Holstun. *Of Wolves and Men*. New York: Simon & Schuster—Touchstone Edition. 1995

Matthiessen, Peter. *In the Spirit of Crazy Horse*. New York: Viking Press. 1983

Mech, L. David. *The Way of the Wolf*. Stillwater, MN: Voyageur Press. 1991

Mowat, Farley. *Never Cry Wolf.* Boston: Bay Back Books—Little, Brown and Company. 1963

Riley, Patricia (Editor). *Growing up Native American.* New York: Avon Books, Inc. 1993

DVD—*Wolves at Our Door.* Produced by Dutcher Film Productions for the Discovery Channel. FHE—Artisan Home Entertainment. 1997

DVD—*Wolves.* Produced by the Enterprise. National Wildlife Federation. Primesco Communications. Wolfco Productions. 2001

0-595-33287-0

Printed in the United States
23049LVS00002B/1-36